IN THE CANNON'S MOUTH

In April 1917, aged nineteen, P. J. Campbell was posted to the Western Front as a subaltern. From May until November the 18-pounder battery of Field Artillery in which he served was in action almost continuously. He was taking part in the third battle of Ypres, generally called Passchendaele today. As the author says: 'To all of us it was just THE BATTLE—the battle which had begun on July 31st, 1917 and was still being fought throughout the whole of August, September, October and even into November. We feared it might go on for ever.'

Miraculously, he survived, and in January 1918, after sick leave, he rejoined that battery about three miles behind the line. Here there was green grass, men were playing football, and there was relief from the mud and destruction of the front line. But a massive German attack (before the Americans were ready to take part in the fighting) was expected. Here are the fears, the horror, the uncertainties, the comradeship and the occasional laughter of battle, seen with the extraordinary clarity of youth and written down by a now elderly author as freshly as though the events he describes had happened six months, not over sixty years ago.

P. J. Campbell was a mathematical scholar of Winchester and Brasenose College, Oxford. After the war he became a schoolmaster. He retired in 1962 and lives in Devon with his wife. He was interviewed about his First World War experiences in two of the episodes of the television series *Soldiers* broadcast in 1985.

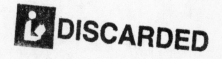

HAMISH HAMILTON PAPERBACKS

In preparation

Harold Acton
MORE MEMOIRS OF AN AESTHETE

Monica Baldwin
I LEAP OVER THE WALL

Kenneth Clark
**THE OTHER HALF:
A SELF PORTRAIT**

J. Christopher Herold
**MISTRESS TO AN AGE:
THE LIFE OF MADAME DE STAËL**

Diana Holman-Hunt
MY GRANDMOTHERS AND I

Hesketh Pearson
A LIFE OF SHAKESPEARE

Hesketh Pearson
WALTER SCOTT

Cecil Woodham-Smith
**THE GREAT HUNGER:
IRELAND 1845–9**

*For a complete list of available
titles see the end of this book*

In the Cannon's Mouth

P. J. CAMPBELL

A HAMISH HAMILTON PAPERBACK
London

First published in Great Britain 1977 and 1979
by Hamish Hamilton Ltd
Garden House, 57–59 Long Acre, London WC2E 9JZ
First published in this edition 1986

ISBN 0-241-11879-4

Printed and bound in Finland
by Werner Söderström Oy

*To the men with whom I served
in the Army-Brigade, Royal Field Artillery,
of this story: and to today's young men
who have equally great difficulties
to overcome*

ILLUSTRATIONS

MAP

FOREWORD

I was nineteen and young for my years.

Today's more sophisticated young men may find it hard to believe that anyone could have been so immature as I was. But there were many like myself, products of a public school education and a middle class home. In fact, we were not altogether unlike themselves.

We had the same needs, physical and spiritual. We were in need of love and hope, laughter, occasional pleasure, affectionate comradeship always. This was what we needed, and what we were given.

May the young men of today be equally fortunate!

P.J.C.

FOREWORD

1

The Sound of the Guns

The day came when I saw my name on the notice board by the Orderly Room of the Base Camp at Havre. A list was put up each day of the officers next to go. The typewritten sheet simply informed me of the number of the division to which I had been posted, the time of the train's departure, and the names of three other officers going with me. Redman and Trotford had been at Edinburgh with me and on the troopship that brought us from Southampton ten days earlier; and Manley I had got to know by sight in the camp.

Dick Adams also had been with me at Edinburgh and on the ship, and being young and full of hope we had considered the possibility of our going up to the line together. Dick was not only my greatest friend, he was unlike any friend I had ever had before. The short crossing to Havre had taken two days and three nights, owing to a report of mines, and we had carried our valises up to the top deck and unrolled them as close as we could put them. The wind was cold on deck, but our affection kept us warm and neither of us would have wished to be anywhere else. We were setting out together, knights in shining armour, on the Great Adventure. Lying under the stars, watching the lights of England slip away behind us I had no thought of fear in my heart in spite of the unknown that lay ahead.

I had ceased to pray, but the prayer I might have uttered was that Dick and I should be sent to the same division. That was my great hope.

But it was not to be. Dick had gone up before me and to a different division, I was going up with Manley instead. Redman, Trotford and I were newcomers to the War, but

1

Manley had been up before, he had been wounded in the fighting on the Somme last year and awarded the Military Cross. Now he was returning to the line.

Impressed by his experience and the ribbon on his tunic we three looked up to Manley, but his face was very different from Dick's and I did not like it.

Only a very little time was needed to show me that the face, not the ribbon, was the right criterion. He told us in the train on the following day that we should be sent to the Divisional Ammunition Column, not to one of the batteries. Newcomers always were, he said. Colonel Owen was the Column Commander and he was a holy terror to young officers. 'Especially to those,' he added, looking in my direction, 'who thought they knew everything because they had been to a Public School.' I had unwisely said something about what we did at Winchester. He told us anecdotes about the Colonel, what he had said to this subaltern, how he had threatened to court martial that one for some minor offence. Manley thought it very funny. 'Of course he wouldn't dare speak to me in that way,' he said, 'he knows I know more about the War than he does. He's never served in a battery.'

When he grew tired of trying to frighten us he started to tell stories of another kind. 'Heard the one about the tart who got up in the middle of the night to use her pot?' he began. I had heard it half a dozen times, but I had to listen to it again, and from one story he went on to another until he fell asleep. The train dragged its way through the night and I also fell asleep at last in spite of Manley's snoring and the ugliness of his open-mouthed face on the opposite seat. By this time the great adventure had lost its capital letters and my armour its lustre.

I woke with a jerk when the train stopped and saw that the others were already moving about in the carriage, collecting their kit. I heard a noise outside, but was so overcome with sleepiness that at first I did not realise what it was. Then I realised.

It was The Guns!

The sound was terrifying, more sinister than anything I had ever imagined.

I had to hurry, fearing that I should be left behind. We all jumped down from the train. I saw that we were standing among the ruins of what had once been a village or small town. Hardly anything of it was left, just mounds of rubble, and one red brick wall ten or twelve feet high on which the name of the place—MIRAUMONT—had been painted in large black letters against a white background. A small clear stream was flowing beside the railway line, there were hills on each side, and it was from behind the hill across the railway that the terrible noise was coming.

The Sound of The Guns! It was a long way off, a continuous muttering. It seemed to have nothing to do with us. Here was a railway train and an engine letting off steam, here were soldiers, very many of them, washing in the stream, smoking, talking, standing about; over there was this terrible noise. No one seemed to be taking any notice of it, but that noise was the reason for our being here; we were going to the place where it came from.

If the noise had been nearer I might have been less frightened, or if we had been in any danger, or if any of the others had shown that they were listening to it. But I seemed to be the only one. I was afraid, my heart had failed, my courage had turned to water, but nobody else was paying any attention to the noise. I could hear nothing else, could think of nothing else. There seemed to be nothing else in the world, only that growling thunder, sometimes increasing in intensity, then falling away to a mere muttering until a sudden and louder crash reawoke the echoes to roll along the horizon.

The morning was bright, the sun was about to come up, but that sound took all beauty out of the light. It was a long way off, but it seemed the more menacing on that account. It was doing no harm to any of us, but its power to inflict evil seemed all the greater because it had not yet begun to inflict any.

We washed in the stream, bought cups of hot tea at the YMCA canteen, and breakfasted on buns and chocolate. Manley had found out where we were to go, and leaving our valises to be collected later we set out to walk the rest of the way, Manley, the two other officers and myself. The sun was well up in the sky by this time and the sound of the guns was less. One of the others commented on the comparative silence.

3

'Oh, that was the Morning Hate we heard,' Manley said. 'It's always like that at dawn.'

He was pleased to be back. He had been wounded not far from where we now were, but all the country over which we were walking had been behind the enemy lines at that time. Now the Germans had been driven back, Manley was elated and full of enthusiasm at the achievement. 'My God! It's wonderful,' he kept on saying. 'We've got the Hun on the run.'

All the villages had been destroyed, they were as flat as the little town we had first seen, and on both sides of the road the country was covered by shell holes. 'What a wonderful sight!' Manley said. 'I wish I could have seen it six months ago with the bodies of all the Huns. I bet our chaps enjoyed sticking bayonets into the filthy swine.'

There was a great deal to see as we walked along, but I could not take it in, my mind was stunned, my body was already tired, I saw nothing. We walked all day. First one way, then the other. Manley or the Railway Transport Officer had made a mistake. We went to the wrong place and had to return to Miraumont.

We rode in a wagon for the last hour or two, but it was late when at last we arrived at the headquarters of the divisional artillery. Manley went on to his old battery and I never saw him again. I was told to report to one of the sections of the ammunition column, as he had foretold.

I found my way to the officer's mess. They were having dinner when I reported, they had nearly finished, I was not made welcome. The dinner had been eaten, there was nothing left, it would be a trouble for the servants to start cooking again. Something was found for me to eat. Then where was I to sleep? There was another tent, but it would be a trouble to pitch it at this time of night. Someone suggested I should sleep in 'The Church' and the others agreed that this would be the best place. I wondered what 'The Church' was, but I did not mind where I slept. All I wanted was two yards of ground on which to unroll my valise which had come with us on the wagon. The church turned out to be some kind of tent, open at both ends and covered with a tarpaulin sheet.

When I had finished eating I listened to the others talking

4

and answered some questions about myself. I was not asked many, they were not interested in who I was or what I had done. I was glad when they said it was time to turn in and I could go to the church. I unrolled my valise on the ground, took off some of my clothes, and got inside the warm friendliness of my blankets. In spite of all my discouragement I fell asleep almost at once, but woke again after a few hours. It was raining. There were holes in the roof of the church and water was pouring down on to me. I moved my valise to another part and managed to find a place that was nearly dry, but I was cold and could not go to sleep again.

I dozed at last, but was roused into consciousness again by the sound I had heard in the early morning. The sound of The Guns! They had never been altogether silent, I had been aware of the noise ever since leaving the train, but for much of the day it had been spasmodic rather than continuous. It had seemed less evil and I had decided I might be able to learn to endure it. But the noise burst out again in all its fury and terrible power. It was nearer to me now. Through the open end of the tent I could see a red glare in the sky and red flashes stabbing the darkness.

Again my heart failed me, the noise was utterly terrifying. It was more than I could bear. I was still far away from danger. This was the sound of our own guns firing, but if I could not endure this what hope was there for me when I was in the middle of the fighting, and what would happen if I failed?

The year was 1917 and the month was May.

2

The Column

I became acquainted with Colonel Owen the first time I was Orderly Officer. He came to Number Two Section looking for trouble and found it. He saw a muddy horse rug lying in the lines. I heard a great shouting and the words "Orderly Officer", so I ran towards the noise and saluted the colonel. He took a dislike to my appearance at once. Had I seen that bloody rug? Had I found out whose it was? Had I put the man under arrest? I should find myself under arrest if I went on like this. If I thought he was going to allow his command, as fine a unit as any in France, to lose its smartness, to be messed about by a useless boy who looked as though he ought to be at a girls' school—and would probably be no more use there—I was bloody well mistaken. By God, he wasn't the man to tolerate that sort of thing! He would make my life bloody hell.

He succeeded in doing so at first. Every day he came to inspect us and find fault. I was not always his victim, but often I was. I knew very little about an officer's duties and never learnt them while I was with the Column. Not one of the other officers tried to help me, either with advice or with a friendly word. They thought I was a prig, they may have been right, but it was not from choice, I would not have been one if I had known how not to be.

The morning was spent in the lines, the men at work, cleaning something, harness, the mules, the camp, the officers watching them and telling them to work harder. At some time during the morning Captain Westerman, our Section Commander, came to inspect what they had done. He always said it was not good enough and would have to be done again in the afternoon. He was, I believe, a kindly man and left to himself would have treated us with consideration, but he was old, he had been brought out of retirement at the beginning of the War, he realised he was unfitted to hold any command, he was as frightened of the Colonel as we were and suffered from him more.

I was made to think that harness was what mattered most, having clean harness was going to win the war, but ours was never considered clean, however long the men were kept at work.

After tea, the Colonel found other occupations for his young officers. He made us attend what he called his riding school, or he or one of his staff gave us a lecture on the role of artillery in war. I heard one of the others say that the Colonel knew very little about any kind of war and nothing at all about this one, indeed that he had never been in action in his life.

While we were attending lectures, the men were set to work on making gardens. Gardens! This did astonish me. Nothing was ever planted in them, but the ground was dug and flower beds marked out with stones which then had to be painted. The gardens were outside the Colonel's headquarters and in full view of that part of the camp occupied by the General commanding the divisional artillery and his staff.

At the day's end the Colonel would sometimes come into our mess and laugh and make jokes, calling each of us his laddie and asking some pointless questions. We disliked him even more when he was pretending to be friendly than when he was abusive.

I heard the others talking about a probable move to a different part of the line. They said it would soon be time for us to start attacking again. They were right. After a week in this camp we moved up to Flanders. By ill chance it was my turn to be orderly officer on the day we left camp and marched to the entraining station. I was ignorant of most of the duties of an orderly officer and many of them were not carried out. The Colonel was beside himself with rage. One of our wagons overturned before we were out of the camp, and though this was not the fault of the orderly officer it was he who received

7

the blast of the Colonel's anger. Not only had he witnessed the mishap, but the General himself happened to be riding past at the time.

The General was waiting at a short distance from the camp to take the salute as we marched past him. Even I could see how ragged our marching was. I learnt afterwards that divisional ammunition columns were notoriously bad. Any battery commander having an officer, N.C.O. or man who he thought was no good sent him to the D.A.C. to get rid of him. This was what had happened in our division and I saw the result on this long day's march. Another wagon overturned soon after we had passed the General and the wheel of a third fell off. The Colonel and poor Captain Westerman rode up and down, cursing the officers, we cursed our men, the men kicked their mules, and the mules lay down whenever they got the chance.

Then the rain began. We were all wet through by the time we halted for the midday meal. The mules were watered and fed, the men were given their dinner, and then the officers went to get theirs on the lee side of the mess cart. I went with them, but was told at once of the things that the orderly officer had to attend to. There were so many that I got no dinner at all. One of the servants brought me a mug of rain and tea and I had some damp chocolate in my pocket. Then we went on.

The country through which we were marching was more desolate than anything I had ever imagined. It was last year's battlefield, the Somme battlefield. The war had passed over it and left it behind; there was nothing left but destruction. I saw no living thing off the road, and on it only our wet dispirited selves. The villages we passed through were so utterly destroyed that I should not have known we were in the middle of one if there had not been a board with the name of the place set up by the roadside. All the earth was shell holes, there was hardly a bit of ground that was not part of one, and because of the rain the holes were half full of water. There were no trees or flowers, only a little coarse grass in some places, and splintered stumps where woods had once been. Refuse was the only thing that grew there:

8

Cartridge cases and unexploded shells
Barbed wire
Empty tins
Vests and shirts and scraps of uniform
Picks and shovels
Rusty rifles
Broken and abandoned wagons
and
Wooden crosses.

Very many wooden crosses. Sometimes a man's name and his regiment were on the cross. Often just the words Unknown British Soldier, or unknown German one. Sometimes his helmet had been put on top of the cross, or his rifle had been stuck into the ground, muzzle downwards, above his feet.

Mile after mile was like this.

But the rain had one good result. The General rode away to get out of it, and when he had gone the Colonel and all his staff followed his example, and then poor Captain Westerman stopped nagging us and we left our men alone. In the late afternoon the rain stopped, the sun came out from behind the clouds, and in the same moment I realised that we had crossed over the battlefield and come through to the other side. I saw trees again, silver birches beside a lake, the sun shone on their wet trunks, and the young green leaves were shaking off their wetness. I saw children too, for we came to a village that was alive, not just a name on a board. Sunshine, trees, children. I was no longer afraid of going mad.

But the Colonel had not yet finished with us for that day. He sent for us in the middle of our evening meal. We were ordered to go to him at once. All the subalterns in the column were there, standing at attention in front of him. He shouted and stormed at us. He had never seen such march discipline. He was going to give us bloody hell. If we thought we could sit about on our arses all day . . . and go out whoring at night . . . by God we were mistaken! By God! . . . he was going to make us work for our pay. By God! . . . he would break some of us if anything like that happened again. We were to learn 'Field Artillery Training' off by heart. Every word of it. That was our bloody bible, not a snivelling lot of Sunday School fairy tales.

He was drunk. Even I could guess what had happened. The General had sent for him before he sent for us, the General had told him what he thought about our marching, he had probably said a good deal about the Column and none of it complimentary. And the Colonel had come back to his own mess and had first tried to console himself with the whisky bottle, and then sent for us and was trying to forget his own smarts by making us suffer.

'Some of you lazy bastards will be wishing you'd never been born before I've done with you,' he said.

I could not help feeling a little frightened by his threats, he might be able to make our lives even more unpleasant than they already were, but the thought of what the General must have said to him gave me some satisfaction. I hated him as much as ever, but after that night I feared him less, I despised him.

Night Work

We saw much less of the Colonel in Flanders than before; our lives became easier instead of harder. There was real work for us to do, not just harness cleaning. Nearly every night I had to take ammunition up to one or other of the batteries in our division. It turned out to be less dangerous than I had expected. I had supposed that one was always under fire in the gun line, but night after night I went up and returned without having gained the experience for which I was fearfully waiting. I heard enemy shells bursting in the distance, and by this time I could distinguish the sound they made from the sound of our guns firing, but none ever fell near me. 'You're lucky,' someone at the battery would say to me perhaps, 'he was knocking hell out of the place half an hour ago, you've come just at the right time.'

Lucky? I supposed I was, but I wanted to find out what it was like, I could not enjoy being lucky until I knew what it was that I had escaped.

One thing that surprised me was the friendliness of all the officers I met in the batteries. I thought at first it must be that I had come across some exceptionally nice ones, but they were all the same. Then I learnt that it was the unfriendliness of the officers in the Column that was exceptional. In the fighting line everyone was friendly, but men in the Column lived a long way back, and where there was no danger there was no comradeship either.

All ammunition had to be taken up by night in Flanders. The enemy held the high ground and would have seen us by day. It might be all right for a single horseman, or two or three together, to ride along those roads, but not for half a dozen wagons of ammunition. I was always frightened of losing my way in the darkness, even though I had ridden along the same roads in daylight. Everything looked different at night and I had to make up my mind so quickly when I came to a turning, it might be the right one, but it might be only a track that led nowhere.

Once I got lost—in the middle of the village of Kemmel, hardly more than a mile behind the front line, underneath the long roof of the church, which looked all right in the darkness, but I had seen all the holes in it by day. I thought I was on a road, but it came to an end. We could not go on and we could not turn back, teams of six mules needed a lot of space in which to turn round. And I found there was only one wagon behind me, I had lost the other five. I was nearly in despair, I could see no way of extricating ourselves.

Then I heard voices in front of me and half a dozen soldiers came out of the darkness. I asked for their help. Between us we were able to turn the wagon round and I led it back to the road, where the other five were waiting for me. I never saw the faces of the men who had helped me, but I heard their Irish voices; they were like the voices of angels.

On another occasion I was too late when I arrived at the battery position. I had been up once already; this was our second journey that night, but we had been delayed and the officer at the battery told me that all the rest of their ammunition had been put away and camouflaged, tracks had been covered over, the men had gone to sleep. If he got them out and they had to do it all over again it would be daylight before they were finished.

So there was no help for it. I should have to take all my wagons back to the ammunition dump where they had been loaded up an hour or two earlier. One of them overturned in a ditch at the side of the road as we came away from the battery position.

The sergeant who was with me wanted to leave it there. He said it would be light before we got away, but I insisted on unloading the boxes of ammunition in the upset wagon. I sent the other five away, but the sergeant and I stayed. We took all the boxes out. Then when the wagon was empty, the mules

12

were able to pull it back on to the road, and we put the boxes in again. This was not courage on my part, the sergeant was probably right. All the ammunition at the dump would not have been worth the life of one driver, but I had not yet learnt what was important, I had been given a job to do and it never occurred to me that it might be better not to do it.

Then we galloped along the road until we caught up the other five wagons. If the Colonel had seen us galloping I should certainly have been threatened with a court-martial, it was against all regulations, but I was slowly learning and one thing I had already learnt—that there was no chance whatever of my meeting the Colonel or the General or anyone who cared about my march discipline so near to the line when day was breaking. It was a very strong reason for preferring the vicinity of the line.

I was beginning almost to enjoy myself. I was lonely and had no friends; I was inexperienced and ignorant of an officer's duties; I never knew what mistake I should make next or who would have to pay for it, whether it would be myself or the men under me, yet youth was strong and happiness began to find a way through. If the night had gone well for us, if I had found all the right turnings, if none of our wagons had over-turned, or not more than one, if I had exchanged some friendly words with the officer at the battery taking my ammunition, if the night was fine, then as we were on our way back to camp I could not resist a feeling of satisfaction that was very close to happiness. Day was breaking, it would be quite light before we were back, I should find a meal waiting in my tent, there would almost certainly be letters for me including one from home. And then sleep. I should sleep for six or seven hours, hearing nothing, free of all anxiety.

That was on the way back from the line, but even on the way up, before difficulties or danger had begun, I was buoyed up by a feeling of expectancy, every sense was alert, the night stimulated me. I had seen the drab ugliness of war on our long

13

march in the rain, now for a few short weeks I lived in its Terrible Beauty.

There *was* beauty.

Even in Flanders, even so close to the line, there was early summer, there was the great vault of the sky over our heads, there were the stars. There were other stars, the German star shells, fired from their front line, shooting in an arch, and falling a mile or more from where we were, but burning with such a fierce bright intensity that all the countryside was lit up in silver—I saw the flat plain, the low willows bordering the dykes, the taller poplars, I saw their leaves shaking in the night breeze. Then the beautiful light went out, and it was so dark for a moment that I could not see the ears of the horse I was riding.

I made friends with the stars overhead, I had no other friends. They encouraged me, they seemed to talk to me. There was a ringing noise in the night, the Music of the Spheres. I had never heard it before and have never heard it since. The Milky Way lay above me and we were marching on another Milky Way. That was the name of the track leading towards most of the battery positions. I did not know why, probably because there was a tiny hamlet marked on the map as Millekruisse. It couldn't be chance, I thought; there must be a reason why two Milky Ways were so much bound up with my life, but whatever the reason I felt less lonely because of them, I felt a personal affection for the track along which we marched and for the galaxy of countless invisible stars over my head.

But I was still waiting to receive my baptism of fire. The others said they came under fire every night when they went up to the line. Either I was very unlucky, or they did not mean what I meant by coming under fire.

Then one night it happened. I had left camp at six o'clock with ten wagons, which were to be filled with stones at the railway station. Stones, not ammunition. I must have misunderstood my orders, for I thought I was to bring the stones back with me and that I should be back in camp in two or three hours. It was not until I arrived at the station that I learnt I was to take them up to the line, not up to the Kemmel area,

14

where the batteries were, but to a place on the other side of the village of Neuve Eglise. They were to be used for making a road across no-man's-land after our attack. I did not know Neuve Eglise, I had never been up to this area, but there was a guide to take me to the place.

We had a long march, but while the light lasted it was easy, and I had never been given a guide before, it made me feel free of all responsibility. But I was hungry. Thinking I should be back so soon I had brought no food with me. The guide said we were going too fast. We could not go beyond Neuve Eglise, he told me, until after dark because the road was under enemy observation. So we slowed down. I was in the habit of going as fast as I could, three miles an hour if possible. We were generally trying to make up for lost time because of some delay, but to-night the roads were emptier than usual.

We came to the first houses in the village. We passed the church. Now we were through the village and on the other side. It was not quite dark, I could see a little way in front of me and on either side of the road, but the guide said it was dark enough. This was the time I was so glad to have him with me, I needn't be straining my eyes all the time to see the road ahead. He was a soft-spoken countryman. His home was in Wiltshire, he told me; I found it easier to talk to him than to the men in the Column.

Now it was quite dark. The road was much worse. It was made of planks. I passed word back over my shoulder, warning the drivers to be careful their mules did not catch their feet between them and to beware of holes. I did not want to have an upset here. There was a smell of dead mules, I could see their bodies lying at the side of the road. Our mules were frightened and tried to shy away from the bodies. I could hear the drivers behind me cursing them, trying to hold them in.

Suddenly there was a noise in front of us, not very loud. It was like a train rushing towards us, or like the quick tearing of a huge sheet of linen. Then there was a red flash and an explosion. It was on our right, just off the road. Another and another. Then three more in quick succession.

So that was all. It hadn't been very frightening, the noise was not so loud as I had been expecting. It happened, and it

15

was all over. My heart was thumping a little, but I was conscious of a feeling of elation—I had come under fire, and it was all right, I could take it. We just went on, I wasn't going to admit to anyone that that was the first time I had been under fire. 'Nearly there now, Sir,' the guide said. Now I should have to take charge again and I alerted all my senses.

A man came towards us out of the darkness, peering at us. I told him I had ten wagons of stones. He led the first one away to the place where it was to be unloaded, I waited to count the others coming up. Two, three, four, five. Then no more. I could neither see nor hear anything.

'Where are the others?' I said to the drivers of the fifth team.

'Don't know, Sir,' was the reply I got. 'Lost touch with them after that shelling.'

What a fool I had been. Of course I ought to have ridden back immediately after the shelling to make sure that everything was all right at the rear of the column, instead of just marching on as though nothing had happened. I called for the guide; I would send him back to bring up the other wagons while I stayed to attend to the unloading of these. But there was no answer, the guide had gone. No one waited about when his job was done. Well, I should have to go myself. And I should have to be quick. I couldn't leave these wagons up here longer than was necessary.

I galloped back along the way we had come. Past the place where the shells had fallen, past the dead mules. I didn't think about holes between the planks or in the road. Nearly to Neuve Eglise. There was no sign of my wagons and I had seen no one to ask.

Then I heard someone riding slowly towards me and I drew up. We peered at each other. It was my sergeant. He had been riding at the rear of the convoy, and he told me that one of the shells had fallen on the road and wounded two drivers and all the mules in that team. But by the time he had come up the wagons in front were out of sight and he had to attend to the wounded men. He couldn't follow me with the other wagons, he didn't know the way; he had left the damaged one at the side of the road and taken the other four and the

16

wounded men back to a place of safety on the far side of the village.

I told him to go back to them and wait there for me. I suppose I might have told him to bring them up to where we were, but I didn't think of it in time. Then I galloped back to where I had left the wagons unloading. I had ridden so fast that I arrived just as the last one had been emptied. I turned round, I took them back along the plank road. It was the fourth time that night I had ridden along it.

I had ridden fast, but half the night was over by the time we were all together again. Now what should I do? I could send my sergeant back with the five empty wagons while I took the four full ones up to the place where the others had been unloaded, but would there be time? Could I be sure of getting back here before daylight came? I looked at my watch again.

'What shall we do?' I said to the sergeant.

'It's up to you, Sir,' he replied. 'If you say to go up we'll go, we can leave the empty wagons to wait for us here.'

I thought I saw him looking in the direction of the eastern sky, I looked there myself. It was still dark, but I thought it was less dark than it had been, less dark there than in other parts of the sky, and the light came so quickly once it began to flow. I had noticed that on other mornings when we were returning from the line.

'We'd better go back to camp,' I said.

I was bitterly disappointed. The night had begun so well, but it had ended in failure. It seemed so difficult to carry out even a simple job like taking up ten wagon loads of stones to the line. But it was fully light, the sun had risen long before we were back in camp. I heard the larks singing and saw the Flemish farmers going out to begin their day's work. That was the strange thing about the war in Flanders, so short a distance separated peace from war. You could go up from the world of ordinary men and women, cattle and green fields, up into the very mouth of destruction, and back again to the same clean sights and smells and quiet noises, all in the space of a short summer night.

Perhaps I hadn't done so badly. Two of my drivers and

several mules had been wounded, but none seriously; I had lost a wagon, I didn't see how we could ever get that back; and I was returning with four wagons full of stones which ought to have been left up in the line, ready for road-making. But five loads had been taken there, and I had come under fire, and not been frightened by the experience.

'What's this I hear about your losing one of my wagons, laddie?' the Colonel said to me when he saw me in the camp later in the day. He was in his playful mood and he did not wait for an answer, nor say anything about the four that had come back full. I did not believe that even he could think it was worth going all the way to Neuve Eglise to bring back a damaged wagon.

A few nights later I had to go to the same place again with more stones. This time I was told to go a different way, a little further, but with more concealment from the enemy. It was one of the best nights I'd had. There was a full moon, I had no difficulty in finding my way, no shells fell near us, I took up my ten full wagons and brought them back empty. And I had eaten my supper and was in bed before three o'clock. But on the following night a man called Isaacs, an officer in one of the other sections of the Column, took up the stones. I knew he was going because I saw him in the camp not long before he set off and he asked me about the way. I told him what a good night we'd had, no difficulty, no shells at all, and he said he hoped he would be equally fortunate.

I was orderly officer the next day and had to get up for early morning parade. I was sharing a tent with Redman and when I returned to it I found him sitting up in bed, sipping the tea which our servant had just brought in.

'Heard about poor old Izzy?' he said.

'What about him?' I asked. There was a note of sympathy in his voice, which surprised me, for Isaacs was a Jew and was as friendless in the Column as I was myself.

'Gone west,' Redman said. 'Fini, napoo. Poor old Izzy!'

That was the way we talked in the Column, in order to show our familiarity with the expressions of front line soldiers, though afterwards when I was with front line soldiers I never heard one speak so unfeelingly about the death of a comrade.

18

Redman had just been told. They'd had a terrible trip, he said. Coal Boxes and Jack Johnsons all the way up. Izzy had been hit before they got there, and the wagons had turned round and come back. 'It's about time they stopped sending us out on that blasted stone fatigue,' Redman said. 'Poor old Izzy! He wasn't really a bad chap. There was really no harm in him, I mean.'

I sat down on my bed. This was our first death since I had been in the Column, and it was so unexpected. I had told him there was no danger, and he himself had said to me once that the only good thing about being in the Column was that it was less dangerous than in a battery. Did death always come when it was least expected? Redman said they'd had these big shells all the way up. I had experienced nothing of that sort, those shells on the plank road had sounded as though they could not kill anyone. Perhaps they had not been such big ones, perhaps I had not yet come under fire after all, not really. I should have to go through it again.

And I was sorry about Isaacs. He was not a friend of mine, but he had smiled at me once or twice. He had been smiling when I last saw him, as he said he hoped he would be equally fortunate.

4

C Battery

Then suddenly everything became different.

I had gone to our tent early on the previous evening. For once there had been no ammunition to take up and I knew our attack was being launched the next morning, the attack for which we had been brought up to Flanders, for which so much ammunition had been needed and the stones for road-making. The Column was under orders to move and the Colonel, to make sure that everyone had a tiring day, had ordered reveille to be at three o'clock. But I was awakened before then, long before daylight, by someone slapping the outside of the tent. A man came in and handed some orders to me. I rubbed myself awake enough to read them. I was to report at once to an Army Field Artillery Brigade and was given the map co-ordinates of its position. Would it be stones or ammunition I wondered, pulling my legs out of my sleeping bag. Nothing out of the ordinary anyway, I supposed. But Redman, who had taken the order from me, now explained. 'You're going away from the Column,' he said. 'You've been posted to this Army Brigade, whatever that means.' For a moment I was dismayed; I should be thankful to leave the Column, but it would mean another fresh start. There had been so many since I became a soldier and they had all been hard at first. I dressed and went out of the tent; I went to the latrine and I was there, sitting on the pole at Zero Hour, the moment when the artillery bombardment started and the infantry got ready for the assault. Books have said it was the greatest noise of the whole war, for a number of mines had been dug under the enemy front line and all were set off at the same moment. But I was so engrossed in my own concerns that I was hardly aware of the noise.

Then I set off just as day was breaking. An orderly was riding with me, he would take my horse back when I had arrived at my destination, I should have to make my own arrangements for collecting my kit at some later time. Everyone in the camp was up and about before I left, getting ready for the move, and I was aware of a feeling of great satisfaction that I should not be moving with them. The Colonel would have no difficulty in finding someone to curse, but it wouldn't be myself.

I said goodbye to Redman, but did not see any of the other officers. The Colonel and all his staff would be asleep still. He had an adjutant, an assistant adjutant, a medical officer, a padre and one or two others. The MO had once spoken a kind word to me, I had been badly bitten by a farm dog, he had cauterised the wound because of the risk of rabies, and had complimented me for not flinching. One kind word. None of the others, all living in comparative comfort and total safety behind the line, had ever noticed my existence. They had and have no share in the Brotherhood of fighting men, the fellowship of danger.

The place at which I had been told to report was four or five miles away, nearer to the front line, but still some way behind it. I noticed the beauty of wild roses growing in the Belgian hedgeside as I rode along and thought this was a good omen. They were the first wild flowers I had seen.

I found the place I had been told to come to, but could not report myself because no one was awake yet. This astonished me. In the Column there were always men awake and at work before six o'clock. I sat down on the ground to wait.

Presently I was joined by another officer who had come to report himself. His name was Vernon he told me, and his home was in South Africa. But he had been at school in England, he considered himself English and had therefore come back to join the British Army instead of enlisting in South Africa. I liked him, he was tall, fair-haired, nice-looking, he smiled a lot. There had been no-one like this in the Column.

I could talk to him. For the first time since leaving Havre I had a friend to talk to.

We spent all day together for Colonel Richardson, the commander of the army brigade, was in the line we were told. We should go there in the evening when the rations were taken up.

Vernon told me what an army brigade was. 'Like any other artillery brigade it consists of four batteries,' he said, 'but instead of staying always with the same division it is sent from one to another, wherever additional gun power is needed.'

He had been serving in a battery and was disappointed at being sent away from it. 'I hope to God they're not going to send us to an ammunition column,' he said, 'they're awful sinks.'

I told him I had been serving in one.

'Oh, bad luck!' he said. 'Was it awful?' 'Yes, it was. What's it like in a battery?' I asked. 'Oh, it's all right in a good battery. My battery was a good one. Most of them are.'

He was sorry to have been sent away, but the battery commander had been told to send one of his subalterns and he was the last to join. 'So it was only fair that I should go,' he said.

We spent the day at the wagon lines of the army brigade, where the horses stayed when the batteries were in action.

At last it was time for us to be driven up to Colonel Richardson. We were taken to a part of the line that was new to me, a few miles north of Kemmel, where most of my ammunition-carrying had been done.

We were directed to the Colonel's headquarters, a dark sandbagged dug-out. He looked different in every way from Colonel Owen. The first thing that struck me was the quietness of his voice. Colonel Owen had always been shouting. He was sitting at a table, looking at some papers, but he glanced up as we came in, and a captain sitting beside him smiled pleasantly. We saluted, told him our names, and said we had been sent to report to him.

'You've chosen a good time to report,' said the smiling captain, 'all our batteries are coming out of action tonight.'

The Colonel asked us a few questions, how old were we, how long had we been out. He made no comment, but said that I should go to C Battery, Vernon to B. Then he said that Captain Cecil, who was temporarily in command of C Battery, happened to be outside and would take me back with him.

Captain Cecil was a man of about thirty. He also asked me questions. 'First time out, is it?' he said. 'You'll have a great deal to learn, but I suppose you can learn.' He told me that the show, as he called it, had been a complete success, the infantry had gained all their objectives. The guns had been only two thousand yards from the line when the attack started, now they were out of range. 'But we've had the hell of a time in the last week,' he said, 'and a lot of casualties. Lieutenant Godwin was killed three days ago, I suppose you've been sent to take his place.'

Before we reached the battery he decided that there was no point in taking me with him because the guns were coming out of action that night. 'You may as well go back to the wagon lines, where you've come from,' he said, 'and report to Major Eric. He's the battery commander, I'm his second-in-command, I've come up because he's suffering from shell-shock.'

He asked me if I could find my way back, I was sure that I could, and this time I asked for C Battery lines and reported to an officer whom I found there. He was sitting without a coat, with the sleeves of his silk shirt rolled up, so I could not tell what his rank was. There was another officer with him, but I saluted the one without a coat and he acknowledged my salute. Again it was dinner time, as it had been when I arrived at the Column; again, the others had just finished their meal, but this time the coatless officer immediately called one of the servants and told him to bring me some dinner. 'What will you have to drink?' he asked. I was astonished, no-one had ever offered me a drink in the Column. If we wanted a drink in the Column we had to buy a bottle of our own and write our name on it.

He asked me where I had been at school and where my home was. He had been at Charterhouse, he told me. 'Damned good school,' he said. 'Brainy place too, though you might not think so from myself.' He talked about schools and univer-

23

sities while I was eating my dinner. He had been at Cambridge, he said, but they could only stick him for a year. Oxford was a good place too. Captain Cecil had been there and he had somehow managed to stay the course. He said nothing about the war or our attack or about the work I should have to do. He did not want to know about my experience or lack of it, but I put all this down to the fact that he was suffering from shell-shock, and therefore could take no interest in practical things. My valise and the rest of my kit had been left at the Column, but after dinner the Major ordered the battery mess-cart to be got ready and sent me back with it to collect all my things. I was away for three hours, but the guns had not yet arrived when I returned. They came soon afterwards. Everyone was tired, too tired to talk.

'Who's going to be Orderly Officer tomorrow?' Captain Cecil said. 'Who's had the easiest day? What time did you get up this morning?' he asked me.

'Half past one,' I told him.

'Whatever for?'

I could see he did not believe me and I did not want him to think me unwilling. 'But I had some sleep this afternoon,' I said.

'All right then,' he said, 'you'd better get up.'

Being Orderly Officer seemed not to make so much difference in a battery. I got up before the others and took the early parade before breakfast, and watched the horses being watered and fed, but after that there was nothing extra for me to do, and no-one found fault with me for what I had done or not done during the day.

Captain Cecil told me I should be in charge of the Left Section, the one Lieutenant Godwin had commanded. I had two guns and fifty horses and about the same number of men, gunners and drivers, under me. After breakfast he took me out with him and called up my two sergeants. Sergeant Denmark of F Sub-Section looked gruff, I thought; his look seemed to say that he was better fitted to command me than I to command him. But I liked Sergeant Feuerbach of E. Later in the day he gave me a Field Service Notebook in which he had written out the names of all the men in the battery, those in the Right and Centre Sections as well as those in my own, and he told me something about every man in the Left. He told me that I had a good section, the worst he had to say of anyone in it was that he was a bit of a lead-swinger and needed watching.

I found afterwards that he was not popular in the battery. His German name had prevented his being sent home for a commission, and the men disliked his sarcastic tongue. I heard him using it sometimes, it was like a whip lash. But he was an extremely capable non-commissioned officer, and though his own good qualities were not always appreciated he was quick to see the good in others.

I asked him about harness cleaning. In the Column this had been the most important thing, and I thought that Captain Cecil or the Major or even Colonel Richardson himself might soon be coming to inspect it. But Sergeant Feuerbach told me there were no inspections of that sort in C Battery. 'If I see one of my drivers with dirty harness,' he said, 'then I let him feel the rough side of my tongue, unless I know he's been up to the line and has had no time to clean it. But when he cleans it, that's his affair, I leave it to him, that's the way we do things in C Battery.'

He told me that I had nothing to worry about in the Left Section. 'But all the battery is good, Sir,' he said. 'I don't believe there's a better one in France. Officers and men have always worked together, they trust one another, you'll never be let down by anyone in C Battery.'

I did not pay much attention to what he said about the goodness of the battery, supposing that everyone talked in that way about his own, as at school we had always said that our House was the best in the School and our School the best in the country. It would have been considered disloyal to say anything else. But I had never heard anyone in the Column speak like that, and looking at the smiling faces of my men, hearing their laughter as they worked, I thought that it might be a good battery and that there was a better chance of happiness for me now than there had been in the Column. Here I saw no sullen faces, heard no sound of angry shouting in the camp.

My horses also looked well cared for and contented. Those in my section were all bay coloured, reddish-brown with black manes and tails; the Centre were mostly chestnuts, the Right were blacks. I thought mine were much the most handsome, and my own charger, a big mare called Theodora, was the most beautiful of all. No officer in the Column had ever been given a horse like this.

The sunshine under the trees, the glossy coats of my horses, the happy-looking young men, many of them no older than myself, all these things combined to make me feel that my loneliness and unhappiness were over.

There were three other young subalterns in the battery, I was sharing a tent with two of them. They both went to sleep after lunch, and when I saw that there was nothing the Orderly Officer had to do I also lay down on my bed. When they woke up they began to talk and ask me questions. Frank was spectacled and intelligent-looking. He had already told me that he had been up at Oxford for two years and that the girl he was engaged to was at Cambridge reading Maths, and very clever. The fact that my home was in Oxford counted in my favour with him, he knew a number of people who were known to myself, we had already talked about them, he seemed very friendly. Jack was friendly too, he appeared to follow Frank's lead in everything. If I asked him a question he would suck at his pipe and watch the smoke coming out and then say 'What do you think, Frankie?'

Frank told me that I was lucky to have come to C Battery. It was the best battery in France, he said. It was a Yorkshire Territorial battery, Territorials were better than Kitchener-Army men and Yorkshiremen were better than any others, he said. The other three batteries in the brigade were not Territorials and they came from Lancashire, they were inferior in every way, although Colonel Richardson, himself a Lancashireman, and Captain Cherry, his adjutant, always favoured them. Yorkshiremen were better at everything, he said, fighting, cricket, making money, anything you like to mention. Frank was a Yorkshireman, Jack was not, but he agreed that there was nothing wrong with the battery. I learnt that the other officers also came from Yorkshire, and the fact that my

26

grandparents had lived just inside the county and that I had walked on the moors, was a small point in my favour.

I said that I had been very impressed by what I had seen of the battery so far.

'So you should have been,' Frank said.

I said that Sergeant Feuerbach seemed very good.

'Sergeant Denmark is better,' Frank said.

I said that Captain Cecil seemed a very good officer.

'He's no good at all,'' Frank said.

I was silent for a moment. 'He told me what a bad time you'd been having,' I said.

'No worse than any other time,' Frank said. 'He thinks it was bad because it was his first time in the line during a battle, he doesn't know the first thing about battles.'

'It was quite bad,' Jack said. Don't forget about poor old Geoff.'

'I'm not forgetting. The fact that we had one officer killed doesn't make it the worst time we've ever had. Anyway, Cecil wasn't with us when Geoff was killed, the Major was still up in the line.'

I asked how the Major had been shell-shocked and they both laughed. 'You can call it that if you like,' Frank said, 'but other people might say it was too much whisky bottle.'

I told them about his generosity in offering me a drink, but Frank said I should find I was paying for it myself. The Major drank all the whisky, we paid for it in our mess bills, he said.

'I drink some of it,' Jack said, 'I'm not exactly a teetotaller.'

'He drinks more than all the rest of us put together, and then you've got to take into account what all his guests drink.'

Frank was annoyed at the mess bills being so big because he was saving up to get married. 'Not next leave, but perhaps the one after,' he had told me. He admitted that the Major was a good battery commander when he was sober. 'He has a good eye for a position and he chooses good N.C.O.'s' he said. 'The men like him and he leaves us alone, and you can trust him to find a good dug-out if there's one within a mile of us.'

He hoped the Major would be all right before we had to go back into the line. 'We've all had more than enough of

Captain Cecil,' he said. 'He's as much use as a sick headache in the line, he doesn't know the first thing about war. He's a proper wagon line hero. He's like you,' he said to me, 'he had spent all his life in an ammunition column until he came to us a few months ago.'

'I only spent a month in one,' I said.

'Did you ever hear the sound of a shell while you were there?'

I was foolish enough to tell them about the night at Neuve Eglise. Frank laughed in an unkind way. 'Wait till you've lived in the line for a month on end,' he said, 'and been shelled all day and all night all the time. Then you can talk about shellfire.'

Presently I asked about Edward, the third subaltern in the battery. Though I had seen him briefly, I had not yet spoken to him.

'He's all right,' said Frank shortly.

'He looks nice,' I said. In fact I had seldom seen anyone who had attracted me more at first sight. He had won the Military Cross. I had noticed the purple and white ribbon on the Major's tunic also when I saw him wearing it in the morning, but on Edward's ribbon there was a little rosette in the centre, which showed that he had won it twice. And he looked as young as or even younger than myself.

'He is nice,' said Frank, 'he's probably the best junior officer in the brigade, he's not afraid of anybody or anything, but if you want my advice I shouldn't take any liberties with him, not unless you want to get your head bitten off.'

'What sort of liberties?' I asked.

'Well, calling him by his Christian name for one thing, he keeps that for his friends.'

I had not intended calling him by his Christian name, but I did want his friendship.

We only stayed for a few days in the wood by the little stream, but instead of returning to the line we moved further away from it. I must have been the only person in the brigade

28

who was disappointed at the direction in which we were going, everyone else was pleased at the prospect of spending another week or two out of action. There were inter-battery sports and football matches and parties in the evening, but I did not enjoy any of them. I wanted to go up to the line. I should not be accepted by the others until I had been in action with them.

Another officer joined us while we were out at rest. Pearson was his name, but all the others were calling him Josh before the end of his first day. He was as much of a newcomer as I was, he had not even been under shellfire once, he confessed to feeling afraid, and said he wasn't going to do anything more than he had to or put his nose outside a dug-out if he could help it. 'I'm not one of your heroes,' he said. But he was married and this seemed to be the reason for his quick acceptance. All the others were sure he would have something to tell them.

'What's it like, being married, Josh?' Jack asked.

'I expect you've had as much experience as I have,' was the reply.

'But marriage is different,' Jack said. 'Did you feel embarrassed on the first night? Do you undress her? How many times a night do you have it?'

Frank said he was disgusted by the questions. If anyone spoke to him like that when he was married he would punch them in the face.

But Josh did not mind, he said the young had got to find out these things, at school they were not taught any of the things that mattered.

The Major wanted to know how he had managed to avoid having children. Was it quite simple to arrange these things nowadays?

Josh said that he and Mary knew a thing or two.

Edward asked at what age he had begun.

'Not at your age,' Josh said. 'It's always the young that get into trouble.' Edward said he was older than he looked.

Frank said the conversation made him feel sick. None of us

seemed to know what love was. Jack said it was the only thing he did know.

Whatever they talked about, whether it was war or love-making I was left out. All the others were on Christian name terms with one another, but no one asked my Christian name. Frank snubbed me whenever I opened my mouth. Jack did not make unkind remarks, but he always agreed with Frank. Captain Cecil sometimes took my side in an argument because I was always willing to go and do a job in the horse lines, which the others were not; but his support did me no good with the others. He had served so long in a D.A.C. that he was considered almost as much of a newcomer to the war as I was. The others disregarded what he said, even his orders. Josh did not get up for early morning parade when it was his turn to be orderly officer and when I, thinking he had overslept, got up to waken him he was not at all grateful.

The Major talked to me; he would talk to anyone who would listen, officer or N.C.O. or man, all the officers in the brigade knew they could get a free drink by walking across to C Battery mess. It was no wonder that Frank worried about his mess bills. Edward, the one I most wanted for a friend, just ignored me. He may have had a particular reason for resentment against me. Geoffrey Godwin had been his friend, I had usurped the place that Geoffrey had once had, I was riding his horse, the beautiful Theodora, sleeping on his bed, sitting in his place in the mess. Frank scornful, Edward resentful, Josh mocking, I felt very much out on my own.

But I was beginning to understand. I was hardly more than a schoolboy in my thoughts and outlook. Colonel Owen had said I looked as though I ought to be at a girls' school and should not know what to do if I was there. It was true. I did not know. I knew as little about life as I still knew about the War. Josh knew about life, the others all knew about the War, they were men.

'It will be easier for us,' I said to Josh one day, 'when we've been up there and know what it's like.'

'Speak for yourself young fellow,' he answered sharply, 'I know when I'm well off and if you want to live to grow up take my advice and cut out all this silly schoolboy stuff about

30

wanting to see the War. I can see it very nicely where I am, thank you.'

I did not want to see the War, but I did want to have friends, not to feel outside the battery ring. But I could not make Josh understand, he was already inside.

I should have to go through danger before I got there.

5

Preparing a Position

We left the pretty Belgian village with its hop-poles at last.
Before the end of June the brigade was on its way back to
the war. But we did not go into action at once. We were to
prepare a battery position.

Now there was a lot of battle talk in the mess. I sat listening
and did not interrupt. Never having taken part in one I could
not imagine what battles were like and wanted to learn as
much as I could before finding myself in the middle of one.
Josh listened too; I could tell he did not like what he was
hearing.

The Battle of Messines, the attack that had taken place on
the day I came to the Battery, had been a complete success.
But that had only been a beginning. The main battle was still
to come. The enemy had been driven off the ridges from which
he would have observed our preparations for the main battle,
but that was all that had been achieved so far. It was going
to be one of the biggest battles of the War. Most of the British
Army seemed to have come up north, we were to break through
the German line, liberate all western Flanders and clear the
Belgian coast which harboured the U-boats.

'It will be a great thing if it comes off,' said Edward.

'If!' said Jack.

'It can't be a bigger fiasco than the Somme,' the Major
said.

'I thought the Somme was a victory,' said Josh.

I also had thought so, but the others all laughed.

'You believed the newspapers,' Frank told him. 'You
should never believe anything they say about the war.'

'It was a bloody awful defeat,' said Jack.

Edward would not agree that it was a defeat, we had achieved something, he said. But he admitted that our casualties had been appalling, he had been up at the Observation Post on the first day and had seen the slaughter.

'Whole battalions of the New Army wiped out without gaining a yard,' Frank said.

Josh was upset by so much talk about casualties, and when the others saw his apprehension they did their best to increase it.

'It will be worse this year,' Frank told him. 'They say the Boche has invented some new armour-piercing shell that goes through any dug-out.'

'There are no dug-outs up here,' Edward said, 'you come to water as soon as you start digging.'

'Cheer up, Josh!' said the Major. 'You may be one of the lucky ones, you may only lose an arm or a leg or some other interesting part.'

'I would rather be killed than have my matrimonial prospects blighted,' Jack said.

'I can't think why you ever came out,' said Edward. 'A married man of your age ought to have been able to work things.'

'Not so much about my age.' said Josh. 'How old do you think I am?'

'I don't suppose you'll see forty again,' Edward guessed.

'I'm thirty-two.'

'Well, that's quite a lot for out here, it's much worse for the elderly.'

'I could have wangled a job at home,' Josh said. 'I suppose I was a fool, but I thought it was nearly over, I had no idea it would be as bad as this.'

Again they all laughed. 'As bad as this!' said Frank. 'Why, you haven't been up to the line yet, you don't know what it's like.'

'Don't take any notice of them, Josh,' the Major said. They're all envious of you, they're such skinny things, they're much more likely than you are to get a bit of jagged steel in a vital part.'

33

But Josh clearly disliked the thought of getting a jagged bit of steel in any part of his body.

Jack went up to Potijze with a working party to prepare the new position. Sandbag shelters were to be made for officers and men, pits for the guns to give them some protection, and space found for all the ammunition to be taken up in advance and stored safely away.

A few days later Captain Cecil went to see how the work was progressing and he took me with him. I was very pleased to go, and to go with him rather than one of the others. Frank might say that Cecil did not know the first thing about war, but he knew a great deal more than I did and he enjoyed imparting information. We rode for two or three miles, then sent our horses back and walked the rest of the way. He asked me if I had ever been under fire. 'Only once,' I told him, 'and then it was only a few shells and only little ones.'

'Well, there won't be only a few today,' he said, 'and they won't be little ones either.'

He told me how to distinguish shells by the sound they made, and how to tell whether they were going to burst at a safe distance or not. 'When you hear a slow rather tired noise,' he said, 'you've got no need to worry, that one's not going to hurt you. But if it's a rumbling noise like this,' and he imitated the noise that a child makes, playing at trains by himself, 'then you run to the nearest dug-out. And if you hear a sudden whistling scream getting louder and louder and coming straight at you, then you fall flat on the ground and pray, you've no time for anything else.' And he told me always to keep an eye open for the nearest dug-out, so that I should know where to run to. 'Nobody minds your dropping in on them in such circumstances,' he said. 'They know it may be their turn to drop in on you next time.'

We were walking across a flat plain. In the distance, rather more than a mile away on our right, German shells were falling with steady regularity. Sometimes the black smoke of the bursting shell was mixed with red brick dust, showing that a house had been hit. 'That's Ypres,' Captain Cecil said briefly. I was excited at the thought that I was seeing Ypres. It was the most famous name of the War, and here I was within sight of it! My brother had been killed in the first battle to which the town had given its name. Ypres! Now I really was at the front, I had seen Ypres, I had seen it being shelled. I could see some grey pinnacles rising out of the pall of smoke, like rocks out of the sea. Those must be the famous ruins, the Cloth Hall and the Cathedral. I should like to have stopped to watch, but Captain Cecil was hurrying on.

'That's a place to give a wide berth to,' he said. 'They never stop shelling it, they know that all our roads go through the town. Now we must walk quickly,' he presently added. We had been walking fast all the time and the morning was hot, I was sweating, I could hardly keep up with him. We came to a canal and crossed over it on a pontoon bridge. There was very little water in the canal, the bodies of horses and mules were sticking out of it above the surface, one could tell they had been dead for some time, but we stopped on the far side. 'There are good dug-outs on the canal bank,' Captain Cecil said. 'We can stop for a minute or two and get our second wind.'

A young and pleasant-looking gunner officer invited us in for a drink. I should like to have accepted; I was thirsty and hot, but Captain Cecil said we must go on. 'You don't want to stop even for a drink when it happens to be quiet,' he said after we had left him, 'because you never know when the Boche will start again, and we can get a drink from Jack when we're there unless he's finished it all.'

We were walking faster than ever and we seemed to be alone now. There had been men everywhere during the first part of our walk, men digging, filling sandbags, laying telephone lines, carrying heavy shells. But now there was hardly anyone to see. We were circling round the town, Ypres had been on our right at first, now it was behind us. We were crossing a maze of trenches, I could not have told where we were going, the shattered houses and sandbagged shelters all looked alike to me, but Captain Cecil never hesitated, though I knew he had only been up here once before. 'Come on!' he said, when I stumbled over some wire and stopped for an instant to push my helmet back away from my eyes. 'This isn't a place to loiter in,' he said.

We arrived. I wasn't sure whether to feel pleased or sorry that our journey had been so uneventful, we hadn't been under fire yet. We went round a wall of sandbags and into what had been a house, but instead of a roof there were more sandbags on top and bricks and broken rubble. It was so dark inside that for a moment I could not see anything. Then I saw Jack. He was only just awake, and was still lying on a bunk of wire netting. I knew that all work on the position had to be done by night.

'Got any whisky left?' was Cecil's first question.

Jack got up and lit a candle and poured some whisky into a mug for each of us, and filled it up with water.

'What's it been like?' Cecil asked when he had drunk about half of his.

'Not too bad,' Jack said.

I was looking at the dug-out. It looked rather comfortable, I thought. There were two bunks in it, one above the other, a small table and a chair, and some shelves had been cut into the walls. It was just high enough to stand up in, the ceiling was an arch of corrugated iron, strong enough to bear the weight of the stones and earth and sandbags on the top.

When we had finished our drinks we went outside, crossing over a road to reach the place where the work was being done. Jack showed Captain Cecil what they were doing and they discussed how much longer it would take. While we were standing there I heard a shell coming towards us, the others dropped to the ground, crouching behind a low wall, part of one of the unfinished shelters, and I followed their example. There was a loud explosion not very far from us, I saw the greyish-black smoke drifting away, smelled the bitter fumes of cordite, and heard the whine of bits of shell rushing through the air.

'That was a near one,' I heard a man say, and I felt grateful to him for making me feel I had got to the war at last. More shells followed, half a dozen in quick succession, but we were protected by the wall. Then we ran to a better place, but no one had been hurt. I was pleased to find that shells could fall quite near and yet cause no casualties.

Jack asked if we wanted to see the rest of the work that had been done, but Captain Cecil said we had seen enough, and the Major had told him to go and look at another position on the outskirts of the town, which we might have to occupy instead of this one. He wanted Jack to come with us.

We all three walked back along the road towards Ypres, but after a few hundred yards we left the road, crossing an area of rubble-strewn ground like that we had passed on our way up. But there were more houses here, or what had once been houses. None of them had roofs, there were holes in all the walls. Sometimes we were walking through a derelict garden, I saw flowers and over-grown bushes struggling against nettles and other coarse weeds. And in front of us, much nearer than before, I could see the famous ruins again, it looked as though my desire to enter Ypres was about to be gratified.

But the shelling began again, heavier than before, and louder, while we were still in the outskirts. We all ran. I saw the others dive through an entrance and followed them into almost total darkness.

'Come in, come in!' cried a cheerful voice. 'But shut the door behind you, don't let any of those big black bastards come in with you.'

Captain Cecil was apologising for the manner of our entry to an officer I could hardly see yet.

'Oh, don't mention it,' he said. 'We're accustomed to it, we keep open house here, we've still got some whisky left. Have some.'

We had some. When the noise outside seemed to have lessened I went slowly back to the doorway and looked out. No shells were falling close, the enemy had turned his attention to the canal bank, the place where we had been an hour or two earlier. From where I stood I could see all the bursts, some on this side of the canal, some on the other, one or two in the water. It was a spectacular sight, and since no one appeared to be in danger, at any rate there was no one in sight where the shells were falling and Captain Cecil had told me about the strength of the dug-outs on the near bank. I could give myself up to the enjoyment of it, as though I had paid for my ticket and was watching a military display. The shells were coming over at the rate of one a minute, I timed them with my watch. It was the ones that hit the water that were so spectacular. When this happened a great fountain of water leapt up into the air; I could see it splashing down on the bridges and the soft earth at the side. I wondered if one of the bridges would be hit, presumably this was what the enemy was trying to achieve; there were some near misses, but none was hit, and after about twenty minutes the shelling stopped and I rejoined the others, trying to give an impression that I had been with them all the time, for my newness to the war would certainly be shown up if it was known that I had gone outside to watch some shells falling.

'Well, we'd better be off while the going's good,' Captain Cecil said. Jack returned to where his men were, and we walked quickly down to the canal. 'What a place!' said Cecil. 'God help us if we have to take our guns to Dead End.' That was the name of the part of the town where we had been, because one branch of the canal came to a dead end there. He explained to me that you should always try to get out of the line in which enemy shells were falling because some might fall short, but if you moved to a flank you would be all right. 'The Boche never switches from side to side,' he said.

We recrossed the canal on the same bridge. Only a few yards from it on the far side there was a deep hole, which had not been there when we came up, in the middle of the track, and the lumps of darker earth lying round the edges of the crater had not yet been trodden into the ground. We walked very fast. It was not until we had left the canal about a mile behind us that Captain Cecil stopped and took off his steel helmet for a moment to wipe his forehead. He said we could relax now, we need not walk quite so fast. 'Well, how did you like your introduction to the war?' he asked.

I liked Captain Cecil. The others said he was no good, that he fussed about things which did not matter and knew nothing about those that did, but he was kind to me, looking after me like an elder brother, warning me how to take care of myself. And it was not only about the danger from shells that he warned me. As we left Ypres and the canal further behind us he began to talk on other matters. He advised me to change the bit on my mare's bridle. She had run away with me more than once and I had fallen off. A snaffle was not strong enough to hold her, he said. And he told me what a good time I should have when I went up to Oxford after the War. He had belonged to the Bullingdon, he said, and had ridden in quite a few point-to-points. 'I didn't do any work,' he said. 'Nobody does, only a few swots.' 'Frank told me that he used to work quite hard,' I said. 'Oh, he would!' said Captain Cecil.

That night, we all went to have dinner at the famous restaurant in Poperinghe, ten miles behind the line. The little town was full of shops and civilians, and soldiers briefly escaping from the war. I could enjoy it now. The glittering lights in the restaurant, the laughter and noise all round me, the good food and the wine, the pretty Belgian girl waiting at our table and smiling on us. I was elated, but it wasn't the champagne that had gone to my head. I had been under fire, it was all right, I hadn't been afraid, Captain Cecil had told the others that I never turned a hair, I was as cool as a cucumber, he had said, even when that heavy stuff was falling at Dead End. And though they might not pay much attention to all that he said, yet they would have to pay some. I had learnt that I could take it, and sooner or later the others would have to accept me.

Two days later I went up to Potijze again, and this time I stayed there, now in charge of the working party. Jack remained with me for one night, to show me how the work was done and give me the benefit of his experience. 'The men know what to do,' he said, 'they know much better than we do. If there's anything you want to know, ask one of the N.C.O.'s, he'll tell you. Stop work and get the men under cover at once when Jerry starts shelling, and get the wagons and teams away quick when they bring up ammunition. That's about all there is to it. Whatever you do, don't bugger the men about, that's the only unforgivable thing. That, and having unnecessary casualties.'

'Think you'll be all right then?' he asked the next morning

39

before he went away, using my Christian name for the first time.

'I think so,' I said. I was feeling a little nervous, but very excited.

He stood in the doorway, sucking at his pipe.

'There's half a bottle of whisky left,' he said, 'that ought to last you for a day or two.'

'Oh, I shan't want more than that,' I told him.

Still he did not go away. He blew a cloud of smoke out of his mouth.

'How are you off for cigarettes?' he asked.

I thought I had enough. Anyway, someone had told me there was a canteen a little up the road.

'I shouldn't go outside,' he advised. 'It's always a mistake to go out of a safe place into one that isn't. Look! I've got a packet and I hardly ever smoke them. Take these.'

He insisted on giving me a slightly crumpled packet of Gold Flake out of his pocket.

'Thank you, Jack,' I said. 'I shall be all right.'

'I'll be off then,' he said at last. 'Cheerio! Take care of yourself.'

We had been sleeping since daybreak, now it was the middle of the day, and as soon as Jack had gone I went across the road to see whether the men were getting their dinner. I had twenty men with me, they were on one side of the road, the same side as the position we were preparing, I was on the other. Each of the other batteries in the brigade had a similar working party in the line. A Battery were by themselves, but the officers of B and D were sharing with us the building known as Gibraltar Farm. That was its name on the map, and probably it had been a farm once. Each of us had a little place of his own to sleep in, but we ate most of our meals together in a larger place that was not so strong. We only ate there when it was comparatively quiet outside, for it had no protection on one side. We could look out to the garden, where flowers were still growing, and also some fruit bushes. We had red currants or rhubarb for dinner every day. It was nice to look at the flowers, but we went away at once if shells started to fall.

40

Work started as soon as it was dark, and went on through the night. We were making pits for the guns, and additional shelters. Every night, ammunition was brought up and had to be unloaded and put away, and then all our work had to be camouflaged and tracks covered before it was light enough for German aeroplanes to see what we had been doing.

I always stayed with the men while work was in progress. They knew what to do, as Jack had said, I didn't have to tell them, I shouldn't have known. I was astonished by their skill. Some of them had been miners, of course they knew how to dig and rivet the sides of shelters, how to place the arches on top and how much weight they could safely take, but even the others were far more proficient than I should have been. I tried to learn from them, watching them as they worked. I listened to their conversation, laughing at their humour, seldom making a remark myself. They talked freely to one another as though I was not there, sometimes I could not understand what they said and often I regretted the differences that separated me from them. I felt shy in their company, shy because I knew nothing about their home lives, only that they were very different from my own. I felt uncomfortable because of my privileged position. But they showed no resentment, and never took advantage of my inexperience. They grumbled a lot, meaning what they said, but saying it to make the others laugh, and because of the quick wit of these townsmen we all did laugh. Sometimes they made remarks about the officers, the Major and Captain Cecil and Josh were their chief butts. Their mimicry was so good that I would almost have believed Josh was there beside us. Because there was no malice in their remarks I laughed as freely as the others, knowing that I should be their next target.

For the first time in my life I, a boy from a Public School, was doing manual work beside men who were manual workers. In a flash of revelation, caused perhaps by the flash of a bursting shell outside, I saw that instead of my being superior to them they were superior to me. But I saw something else, that it did not matter which of us was better, what mattered was that we were working together against a common enemy, the shells that were bumping and banging in the darkness on

41

the other side of our sandbag wall, together we were making the place stronger, so that they should not hurt us.

We were shelled every night. Watching the men I learnt when I ought to feel afraid and when fear was unnecessary. Of a single whizz-bang they would take no notice, but a dozen at the same time could be frightening. Whizz-bangs were the smallest German shells, corresponding to the eighteen-pounders that we ourselves fired. Next in size were the four-twos. They were more disagreeable, but unless one burst within twenty or thirty yards it was unlikely to hurt you, and a good shelter was proof even against a direct hit by a four-two. But only the strongest kept out a five-nine falling even a hundred yards away. Four-twos and five-nines were the commonest shells used against us in forward artillery positions, but there were bigger ones, eight-inch and eleven-inch. These were terrifying, but fortunately we did not often suffer from them, they were used against the heavy guns behind us and the deep dug-outs in Ypres.

I was enjoying myself, but the happiest moment in the twenty four hours was when we stopped work. Then the men went to get their breakfast or supper, whichever they liked to call it, I saw them start it and then went across the road for my own. Day was just breaking. To the west, I could dimly see the ruins of Ypres, and the tall poplars, splintered and mostly dead, but still standing along the canal bank. On the other side, to the east, there was only the grey emptiness of the front line area. There was nothing to be seen there. I could not see the trenches or the infantry in them.

At some time during the night our rations had come up with the ammunition, and with the rations our mail. There were always letters for me, I found them by my plate where my servant had put them when he laid the table for me in my little room. He brought in my breakfast as soon as he saw me coming, and I read my letters while I was eating.

I was as happy as I had ever been. I could not help it. Happy to be where I was and with the night's work safely behind me, and happy because of my home, which letters brought so clearly before me. They took me away from Ypres, I was back in England as I read. My father wrote to me from my own Public School where he had gone to teach for the last part of the summer term, because they were so short of masters. He gave me news of masters I had known, and of boys who had once been my friends only a year ago, but who no longer seemed to have any part in my life. My mother wrote about the Oxford canteen in which she was serving, or about the wounded soldiers who had been up to our house for tea; she was so tired at the end of the day that she hardly knew what to do with herself, she said. My fourteen-year-old sister told me all her cricket scores, and whether they had won their last school match, and about a bicycle ride to Islip. Islip! I could smell the reeds at the side of the river, and see the forget-me-nots and purple loosestrife on the banks.

I could picture them, my father, my mother and my sister. But they could not picture me on the Potijze road, I could not make them understand what it was like. I might tell them I was happy, but that would not make them worry less. German shells could not differentiate between one kind of British soldier and another.

In addition to my letters there was usually a scribbled note for me from one of the others at the wagon lines. How was I? Was there anything I wanted? Josh and the Major had gone into Poperinghe again. The Major had told them to send me another half bottle of whisky. But I hadn't finished the last one yet. I drank the stuff when I was with the others to show them that I liked it, but in fact I did not like it, I had drunk very little since Jack left me.

Then sleep. The noise outside went on, it never stopped, day or night, but I did not hear it. When I woke I went to see how the men were. Then it was time for lunch. And still there was all the long afternoon to look forward to before work started again. Talking to the officers in the other batteries or to strangers who dropped in, reading my book when I had nothing else to do.

We read in the open room, our balcony we called it. Sometimes we took our chairs or substitute empty ammunition boxes outside and sat in the garden, enjoying the afternoon sunshine. Though so much had been destroyed, yet much was left still, some of the willows and poplars still had life in them, and

43

roses were as beautiful and smelled as sweetly here as in an Oxford garden. My servant picked a bunch for me and put them in a jar in my room, and when he saw that I was pleased he found other flowers for me as well. I had almost more than I wanted. Sometimes the concussion of a near shell outside, or my own clumsiness, knocked over one of the jars and water was spilled over my letters or books.

My servant took me to see where a pair of swallows had made their nest on a rafter of one of the shelters. No one disturbed them, everyone used the other entrance. The five young birds had just hatched and we watched the parents feeding them. There seemed as many birds here as there were at home.

I had not expected the war to be like this, and I never found it like this again. At Ypres, even in the summer of 1917, before the great battle began, there was still something of the old world left, something at variance with the war, a sense of homes that had once been lived in and gardens where children had played. At the wagon lines, which were in some fields by a farm, life still went on more or less as usual for the Flemish farmer and his family, and they all smiled when they saw us. In Poperinghe, at one of the souvenir shops, I had bought some pre-war picture postcards of Ypres, one of the Cloth Hall, another of the Cathedral, one of the children in the road by the Menin Gate, and one of sheep grazing in Les Plaines d'Amour outside the town, which was where Captain Cecil had made me walk so fast on the day he took me up to the line. There is no romance in modern war, but youth is romantic and in war, as in love, he looks for beauty and glamour even when it is not there.

I had not yet seen the other side, the fear and demoralisation, the faces of the dead, the horror of the places where men had killed one another, I had not heard the cries of the dying. All that was to come. At Gibraltar Farm I happened to be lucky, we had no casualties during the five or six days that I was there by myself.

Josh was less fortunate when it was his turn to be up there. The shelling was worse, our farm was hit more than once, the balcony was destroyed, one of our men was killed, and an

44

officer in one of the other batteries, and hundreds of rounds of our ammunition, were blown up. Jack said that the loss of the ammunition was our responsibility, his and mine, we ought not to have left it in the houses at the side of the road, we ought to have carried it further away, we should get hauled over the coals, he said. But no one seemed to mind about the ammunition. Everyone was sorry about poor Packer, and poor fat Morrice, the officer in D Battery who had been laughing and joking with me only a few days before. But there was plenty of ammunition in the dump.

And poor Josh was very sorry for himself. He resented my having had such a quiet time. 'It was a blasted picnic all the time you were up there,' he said. I had told him about our red currant pies and how we sat outside in the sunshine. He was angry with me for telling him such a cock-and-bull story, though fortunately I had kept most of my thoughts to myself. They had flattened the place out, he said, I shouldn't be able to recognise it.

During a whole morning I did not once hear his laughter, but in the evening he went into Poperinghe with the Major and Captain Cecil, and he was himself again when they returned. It was his turn to be Orderly Officer on the following day, and I heard him telling Cecil not to lie awake all night so as to see that he got up early. 'Something tells me I'm going to oversleep,' he said, 'and it would be a pity for you to lose your beauty sleep.'

6

In Action at Last

Now that my loneliness had passed away I could see I had
been lucky in being brought so gradually into the war. If
everything had happened at once, if I had gone straight into
action in the middle of a battle, my ignorance and the mistakes
I should have made might have damaged my relationship with
the others far more seriously; and the shock of battle and
sudden death, before I was prepared for them, would probably
have prevented my finding the calm happiness I was now
enjoying. Now I could fairly claim to have been under fire,
not just once for a minute or two, but day after day for a
week on end. I had been in charge of a working party in the
line, I had learnt the names of all the men in the battery
(and a few of the horses), and the other officers were
beginning to accept me. Jack was friendly, and Frank had
dropped his tone of sarcasm when he spoke to me, the Major
looked at me with amused tolerance, and Captain Cecil
defended me against Josh's mocking remarks.

Now I only had to wait for the beginning of the great attack,
then my experience would be complete, I thought. But the
attack was a long time coming. No more work was done at
the position on the Potijze Road and the working party was
brought back to the wagon lines. We were transferred to a
different division, from the Scottish Thistle Division to the
Lancashire Red Rose one, I was sent up to hand over the place
we had made to another battery, we were to go instead to a
position a few hundred yards in front of the canal.

But still we waited.

'What are we waiting for? Isn't there going to be a battle?'
Jack said hopefully.

'They're waiting for the weather to break,' the Major told him. 'They don't want to make things too easy for us. Everything went like clockwork last time and they're afraid that if it happens again we may lose our initiative. But if the ground gets churned up a bit first then we shall be properly tested.'

I did not mind waiting now, we were all content to be at the wagon lines. There were expeditions into Poperinghe and rides in the afternoon. I fell off my horse twice in one day. Captain Cecil said he would have to give me instruction, I could see for myself, he said, the importance of having a good seat. Falling off my horse was not the only danger, German long-range guns were active, hardly a night passed without shells coming over and some fell in our camp, we had casualties to men as well as horses.

What were we waiting for?

July was more than half over before we went into action at a place called "The Summer House", in front of the canal. Only three officers went up to the gun line at first. The Major took Edward with him, and I, to my great satisfaction, was the third.

So I was with the battery in action at last. Most of our firing was done by night. We were given an area to shoot at, but we chose our own targets, tracks leading up to the line, trench intersections, places where movement had been observed or from which machine-gun fire had been reported. We fired about two hundred and fifty rounds every night. I watched Edward working out the shoots. He calculated angles and ranges on our large-scale map-board, and then gave the orders and times of firing to the Number Ones of each gun. It looked straight-forward, I was sure I could do it, and on the third night I asked the Major to let me. He was amused by my enthusiasm and agreed at once, but he told Edward to check my figures. 'Chuck the things where you like,' he said. 'You're just as likely to hit Fritzes in one place as in another. But don't take any risks with the range, you must never shoot short, that's the only thing for which there's no forgiveness.'

But he told me in the morning that I had disturbed his rest. 'You were running in and out of the place all night long,' he said, 'no one could get any sleep. Fire all the stuff at one go and be done with it.'

'But it's called harassing fire,' I said.

'You've got it wrong,' he said, 'It's the Fritzes who are to be harassed, not us. Get it over by a Christian hour, nothing after two o'clock.'

'But if the Germans get to know that we don't fire after two o'clock,' I protested, 'they'll do all their work then.'

'Well, good luck to them!' he said. 'That's what brains are for.'

I was disappointed, I wanted to go on all through the night. Four rounds rapid fire from each gun ten times a night, that was the way to inflict the greatest number of casualties on the enemy, and in the end grudgingly he allowed me one or two bursts of firing during dinner. The concussion brought down bits of the walls and ceiling of our dug-out. I had quite spoilt his soup one night, he said.

We ourselves were under fire for a considerable part of the day and night, but we had good dug-outs and we seemed luckier than the other batteries. It was the beginning of the good fortune which we enjoyed all through the battle. D Battery had a direct hit on their officers' mess, one officer was killed, one wounded, and the third badly shell-shocked. A Battery position was so heavily shelled that more than once it had to be abandoned, and their officers came to spend the rest of the day with us, much to the Major's satisfaction.

He loved company, he must have someone to talk to, his own subalterns were no use to him, he said. Frank was always writing a letter to his girl, he complained; I was always reading; Jack would sit and listen to him, but he always agreed with everything he said and that was dull; Edward disagreed with everything and that was worse. Josh was the only one of us who had anything to say for himself, and then only at the wagon lines; at the guns he was always listening for the sound of the next shell and could pay no attention to anything that was said to him.

We had a lot of visitors in our mess. Every officer in the brigade knew there would be a drink for him if he cared to go over to C Battery and sit and talk with the Major, and passing strangers were often invited in. When there was no one in the mess for him to talk to he went outside and talked to the men, with whom he was very popular. He had the gift of being able to talk with everyone, but he did not want to do all the talking, they must talk back to him. Edward also had the gift of being able to talk easily to the men, he was not shy with them, as I was, he seemed to know something about the home life of every one of them.

I was enjoying myself. After the long uncertainty it was very satisfying to find that I was not unduly afraid of shell-fire and that I could carry out the tasks that were given me. As yet I had been given nothing difficult to do, but I hardly realised this. Each day was an end in itself, one thought about to-morrow, but not about the day after. It seemed after a few days that I had always been with the battery in action and that it would go on like this for ever. I liked and admired both Edward and the Major, I did not talk much to either of them, I listened to their talking, either to each other or to one of our visitors. When there was nothing else to do, I read. There was a ledge on the top of our dug-out where I could lie and read in the sunshine, able to dive inside within a second or two if I heard a shell coming close.

In the evening from the same place I used to watch the aeroplane fights through my field glasses. Often they were flying at such a height that I could not see the markings on the machines, the red blue and white rings of one of ours, or the black Maltese Cross of an enemy, and when one fell I could not always tell who had been victorious. Sometimes the plane fell like a stone, but more often it turned over and over, fluttering to the ground like a leaf in autumn. I was still unfamiliar with death, and was distressed to think of the man inside, even if he was a German. There was no baling out from aeroplanes in those days.

'Is there any chance of the man being alive still?' I once asked the Major when together we had been watching one flutter down.

'Not a cat in hell's chance,' he replied, and went on whistling.

I paid my first visit to an Observation Post. Edward was going up to register the guns and he took me with him. He was a little more friendly now, but was still rather inaccessible, his attitude of aloofness to me was almost the only thing I could have wished to be different.

The O.P. was in one of our support trenches, only a few hundred yards behind the front line, I had not been so close to the line before. Each gun at the battery fired in turn, and after the bursting shell had been observed Edward spoke over the telephone, changing its range or angle and fired it again until it was accurately on the target. I stood beside him in the trench, watching the shell bursts. He told me to keep my head down, and I tilted my helmet over my forehead, as he had done, so that only my eyes were exposed over the top of the trench. There was not much to see. Only trenches in the foreground, I could not tell where ours ended and the enemy's began. Nothing was to be seen in any of them, just a succession of trenches. But in the distance, about a mile away, country began again, and colour. I could see grass and trees on the top of a low ridge, red-brick houses and the tower of a church looking almost undamaged. It was a pleasure as well as a surprise to see these ordinary things: the low green hill, the houses, a church. They contrasted so happily with the trench scars immediately in front of us. The village was Passchendaele, Edward told me, but the name meant nothing to either of us. It was just one of the villages on their side of the line. Zonnebeke and St Julien, Langemarck and Polekappelle were others whose names I had noticed on our map board.

Edward addressed an occasional remark to me about the shooting. So many guns were firing that it was not easy to pick out our own shells, and if I took my eyes off the target, a grey block of concrete nearly a mile away, one of many, I was afraid of losing it. German guns were firing back at our side of the line and two or three times we had to duck our heads when a shell fell close to us. He was satisfied at last with the guns' shooting and told the signallers to pack up their equipment. Then we walked back the way we had come, along trenches at first, over the open when we came nearer to the battery.

A day or two later we received our orders for the great attack, though neither the time nor the day was yet given to us. We were to move forward from the Summer House two hours after Zero, the time of the launching of the attack, and go into action again in a position not far behind our present front line. But we were only to stay there for a few hours. We were to go forward again, over no-man's-land, nearly to St. Julien, at present more than a mile inside the German line. The orders were worked out in great detail: all our targets for the first part of the attack, the exact moment when we were to cease fire, and when we were to start again from the second position. And we were to send out a forward observing officer who would go up with the infantry and send back information about the progress of the attack. Jack was detailed to go.

But before the attack started there were changes in the battery. Major John, the commander of B Battery was wounded for the second or third time and Captain Cecil was promoted to the command in his place. Edward was given the captaincy in our battery and went down to the wagon lines, which was the place for the captain and second-in-command. We were none of us sorry that Cecil was leaving us. I ought to have been, for he had been friendly to me from the beginning, but I had less need of his friendship now and therefore accepted what the others said about him, and we were all pleased to have Edward for our captain.

I went down to the wagon lines for a few nights before the battle started, but I returned on the last afternoon, the afternoon of Y-Day, as it was called. Jack and I went up together. Poor Jack was in very low spirits. 'I wonder what's the chance of my being alive at this time tomorrow,' he said. I told him not to take any unnecessary risks. 'I shan't,' he replied. 'I'm not that sort of person, you can set your mind at rest about that.'

But we did take an unnecessary risk that very afternoon. Jack was going to see Colonel Richardson for his final instructions. The Colonel's headquarters were in a deep dug-out in the ramparts of Ypres and we walked through the middle of the town instead of going round on the outside, which would have been a little further. It seemed quiet when we came to the outskirts, and I was pleased at the thought of walking through the famous town. But almost at once we heard the familiar sound of big shells coming over and started to run. I did not know the way, I followed Jack. We crouched behind a great mound of rubble and stones, a shell burst on the other side of it not far away, I covered the back of my neck with both my hands. Then we ran again. We ran under a high archway, over more piles of stones, bending down whenever we heard a shell coming. Jack told me afterwards that we had run through the Cathedral. Then we were running down the middle of a road, the sound of the shells was behind us now, but we did not stop running. We came out into an open space, with water in front of us. This was the moat of the old city, there was a line of deep dug-outs by the water, and one of these was the Colonel's headquarters.

We went down a lot of steps. It was very dark inside, the walls were dripping with water, there was no air, it was a relief to be safe from the shells, but I was glad we did not have to live in a place like this; I thought the Summer House was much preferable. We were given a friendly welcome by Colonel Richardson and Captain Cherry, his smiling adjutant.

'What's it like outside?' Cherry asked us.

Jack told him that we'd had to run, we were still panting.

'Well, if it's any comfort to you,' Cherry said, 'for every shell we get, the Boche has been getting four or five.'

The Colonel began talking to Jack. It would all be perfectly straightforward, he said. The Boche had been given such a hammering that he would not know whether it was last night or to-morrow morning, when the attack started. It would be just like the last show over again. Jack would simply have to follow the infantry, unrolling telephone wire as he went, and stopping every now and then to let them know at headquarters how far the advance had gone.

'Just like going for a country walk,' Cherry said.

Jack was nodding his head at everything they said to him, but I knew him well enough to be sure that he was thinking

52

it would not be at all like a country walk. The Colonel told him there was no need for him to go putting his head into danger, his job was to send back information, and all the information in the world would be no use unless he was alive to send it.

'A living dog is better than a dead lion,' Cherry said. He added that if the show was a success, and everything pointed in that direction, then it might mean the end of the war and that we should all be home before Christmas.

They were very encouraging and I was greatly cheered by what they said about our prospects of success, but Jack said, after we had left them and were walking along the canal bank on our way to the battery, that he had not been impressed. 'I could be optimistic,' he said, 'if I lived at the bottom of a place like that. Bloody optimistic,' he added.

The Major also thought Jack was in need of encouragement when we arrived, and he gave him some and poured out some for himself. Then they took their mugs to one of the beds at the back of the dug-out while Frank sat in the doorway, where the light was better, working out our barrage fire for the next morning. 'Don't speak to him,' the Major had warned us, 'he's always like a bear with a sore head when he gets on to this job.' I thought he was hoping to provoke him, but Frank took no notice, he went quietly on, saying figures to himself, writing them down, working with entire concentration. Jack had told me he was the only person in the battery who knew how to work out the barrage for an attack, it was impossible for an ordinary person to understand, he said. I sat down beside him without speaking, I wanted to learn how to work out a barrage and I knew that he would let me ask him questions when he had finished.

I had a worry of my own to think about, for I was to lead the guns forward to the second position at $Z+120$, that is to say two hours after the battle started. I had been up to this position twice. It was terrible, nothing but shell-holes. And a ditch called the Bellewaardebeke in the middle of them. I could not imagine how guns would be able to move at all· over such ground, and at present it was within sight of the enemy lines. I had gone for the first time with Colonel Richardson and an officer from each battery, we had just looked at the place, made unfavourable comments about it, and come away. We had gone very early in the morning, it was misty and therefore comparatively safe, we were not under enemy observation. But when I went for the second time, with the Major, to show him the place and to reconnoitre the way there for our guns, the sun came out while we were standing on the position and we saw the German line staring down at us, not more than half a mile away and looking much nearer, a low bare hostile ridge curving round us. But we hardly stopped to look at it, we came away quickly without staying to think about the best way of getting the guns up.

This was the reason for my worrying now. The orders stated explicitly that field batteries were to keep off the roads. They were to be left for heavier transport. I was to take our guns along a track that went through the grounds of a château, past some ornamental waters fed by the same stream, the Bellewaardebeke, and then to follow along the stream until we came to our position. But the track in the château grounds had been heavily shelled and the water had escaped into the shell-holes, the place was not much better than a swamp. I was afraid the guns would be stuck if I took them past the château.

'You go by the road,' the Major said. 'Go whichever way you think is best, don't take any notice of the orders.'

I couldn't decide. If I went by the road I might find our way blocked by other transport, and it was just possible that I might meet a staff officer acting as a military policeman, who would order me to turn round and go back, and that would certainly make us late. But if I went the château way I might find the ground too soft for our horses, I might not get up to the position at all.

I wondered if I ought to go and have another look at the track, and see how many new shell holes had appeared since I had last been there and how much water was in them. But the thought of going up there again daunted me. Even the Major had disliked the place and had said you wouldn't catch him going there for a swim before breakfast. And Jack had told me that he made it a rule never to go anywhere unless he was ordered to. 'You'll have plenty of chances of getting killed,' he had said, 'without going out of your way to look for others.' If visibility had been poor I might have gone, but the evening was clear, I did not go. I couldn't help worrying about it, and wondering which way I ought to go. 'The important thing is to get off quick,' Frank said, when I had a chance of consulting him, 'before the place is blocked by everyone else.'

I went outside with him when he had the orders ready to give to the Number Ones of each gun. He explained them to each one, making sure that they understood them and that they had everything in readiness for the morning. Then we went back into the dug-out. Time passed very slowly. Jack had already gone. 'The longer I stay here, the harder I shall find it to go away,' he had said. Frank was continually getting up to look at the orders again or to verify something on the map. I was still wondering which way to go. Sometimes I decided in favour of the track. But then I thought of the soft black earth and the deep holes in the middle of the way, and all the water in them. It seemed madness to think of going off the road, and I changed my mind again. The Major was in a bad temper, he snapped at everything we said and was continually finding fault with the servants. We hardly spoke during dinner. But their obvious anxiety was a help to me. If they had been quite unperturbed I should have been more than ever distrustful of my own powers. But they were both worrying, so it was right that I should worry also, and I made up my mind that I would leave the decision about the way until I had actually started. I would be guided by my feeling when the moment for decision came.

Time dragged by. I couldn't go to my bed of wire netting because the Major was sitting on it, and Frank was still working. At about midnight there was a sudden fierce burst of shellfire outside. The concussion blew out all our candles. We were left in darkness, I heard cries of pain, about a dozen men came falling into our little dug-out, it was so full that no one could move, and no one could find matches to relight the candles. 'He's hit,' someone was saying. 'Who's hit?' shouted the Major angrily. 'For God's sake, get outside and stay out, and bring in whoever it is.'

55

It was Sergeant Appleby, the senior N.C.O., in the gun-line, our youngest sergeant, and one of the best-liked men in the battery. Our guns had just finished firing, the men were returning to their dug-outs when they were caught by the German shells, and they had rushed into the nearest shelter, but Sergeant Appleby had been hit by a fragment of shell. I thought he was dying, I was not accustomed to seeing so much blood and pain, but in fact he was not very badly wounded. They took him away to the dressing station on a stretcher, and he was back with us before the end of the summer.

Then at last it was quiet and I could go to sleep. But the Major was still talking in an angry voice to someone who had come in. 'Just a lot of bloody wind,' I heard him saying. 'Anyone would think this was the first battle there had ever been.' But I passed away into unconsciousness, of the battle and everything else.

Zero Hour and Z-Day

Zero Hour was 3.50. Frank had told one of the signallers to call us at a quarter past three. We got up at once, and after putting on the few clothes we had taken off we went outside, leaving the Major still asleep. It was very quiet, hardly a gun was firing, as though all the world knew what was going to happen and was waiting in silent expectancy.

'Do you think the Germans know?' I asked Frank.

'Oh yes,' he said, 'we always tell them. They may not know whether it's today or tomorrow, but all the firing we've done in the last week can mean only one thing.'

The morning was cold, there was a feeling of wetness in the air, but whether it was just the mist before dawn or a sign that rain was coming I could not tell. All the men were up; I could see them moving about behind the guns. Some of them were carrying shells from the pit where ammunition was kept and putting them down beside the guns in readiness. I heard the clink of the brass cases, one against another, as the shells were put down. We went to speak to the Number Ones. Frank had the big battery watch in his hand and he gave the correct time to each of them. We were going to fire a creeping barrage, that is to say we had to increase the range of our guns by a hundred yards every four minutes, so that our attacking infantry could follow closely behind the curtain of fire, and each N.C.O. was responsible for firing the correct number of rounds in every minute and adding to the range at the right time. There was very little talking. Everyone was alert, each man had his work to do and he was doing it; he did not want to be distracted.

Then we took up our position in the centre of the battery and about fifteen yards behind the guns. My eyes had grown accustomed to the darkness by this time. I could see the line of poplars on the canal bank behind us; by daylight you could see they were all dead, there was not a green leaf among them, but some were still standing at their full height or nearly, others had been split in half, a few had completely gone, there was just a gap in the line to show where one had been. And on the other side in the east, over the German trenches, the sky already looked lighter.

'Five minutes to go,' Frank shouted, looking at the big watch, and each of the Number Ones raised an arm in acknowledgment to show that he had heard. He told me that he had ordered his breakfast for half past four, and when he had finished he would come outside and take over from me so that I could have mine. 'And by the time you've finished the limbers ought to be up here,' he said.

It was still very quiet, the quietness gave a sense of unreality to the morning. How could so great an occasion be unheralded! But I could feel the palpitation of my heart.

One gun behind us on the other side of the canal fired a second too soon. Then Frank blew a loud blast on his whistle, but I only heard the first note, the bombardment began as he was blowing, all the guns in the Ypres Salient opened fire and the roar of artillery drowned every other sound. All the guns in the Salient! It sounded like all the guns in the world. It sounded as though the sky was falling, as though the thunder of the guns had cracked it, as though the world itself was breaking into pieces. Our shells were breaking it. Low down, all along the eastern horizon, I saw their red flashes as they burst, spurts of fire in the darkness. And now the German rockets were going up, their S.O.S. signals, the call for artillery support: red, green and yellow lights, and showers of beautiful golden rain. Frank shouted something at me, waving his arm in the direction of the rockets, but I could not hear what he was saying. A few German shells came back at us, one here, one there, a big one a little way in front of us, a salvo on the canal bank, but for the most part they were falling a long way in front, on the infantry, on the trenches from which the

58

attack was now being made. We should get it later probably, I thought; but we had no casualties at this time.

Daylight came. I had been wondering what I should see. I was expecting it to look altogether different, but it was the same, the same as any other day—the same flat landscape, the broken trees and shattered farms. Some lines of infantry were slowly moving forward, one man behind the other, a long line, going up towards the front. That was the only difference.

After half an hour our rate of fire dropped from four to three rounds a minute for each gun, then to two. Frank went to get his breakfast, I was left alone, I wondered whether I should know what to do if anything unexpected happened. But nothing happened, everything was working automatically, our guns firing, German shells throwing up fountains of earth on the left and on the right, but not in the middle of us.

Then it was my turn to go inside. The Major was just getting up; he was sitting on his bed, yawning. 'Anything happening outside?' he asked, but I could tell that his nonchalance was put on, for when his servant brought in his plate of eggs and bacon he swore at him for clumsiness and did not answer when I spoke to him. I hurried through my breakfast, I wanted to go outside again, and I had decided what to do about the guns. I would start off along the track, I would use the track for more than half the way, but when I came to the road that curved round the grounds of the château, if it was not blocked. I would turn right instead of going straight across into the gardens. This would bring me to the main Potijze Road in a few hundred yards, and then I had to turn left along the main road and I should come to the Bellewaardebeke in less than half a mile, and once there no one would know that I had not come through the château gardens.

I went outside again. Almost at the same moment the limbers arrived. Josh was leading them, they drove up behind the guns at a gallop. Josh's face was very stern, like myself he had evidently been expecting that everything would be different on the morning of the Great Battle and he had not yet realised that it was like any other day. Josh was not a light weight, and now with all his equipment on his back, haversack and water bottle, cape rolled up, field glasses, gas mask at

59

the alert position, steel helmet very straight on his head, he certainly looked prepared for war.

'What's this?' Frank shouted out to him. 'The Charge of the Heavy Brigade? or the Iron Duke at Waterloo?'

Josh did not smile. This was no time for smiling; and besides, though he could make jokes against himself he was not pleased when other people made them. He got off his horse and came over to us. 'What's happening?' he said. 'Who's winning?' But there was no news yet.

Now it was time for me to start. The battery had ceased firing, the guns had been limbered up, they were ready for me. I was going with them by myself, the others were to follow later with the wagons which Edward had brought up, and all the rest of the ammunition. The servants were busy packing up our things. I gave an order to the first team behind me and began to walk, I could hear the guns following me. It was as though some other person had pressed a button to set us all in motion, the machine was working automatically. Now I had come to the beginning of the track, I was walking along it, all our six-horse gun teams were stepping along behind me. I was conscious of a feeling of anxiety. This was the first time the Major had given me a job to do on my own, I was determined not to fail him. In fact there was no difficulty. We were hardly delayed at all, we had made a good start, no other batteries were on the track yet, we did not fall into any of the holes, we were not shelled. When we came to the road, I looked along it, saw that it was clear, and turned to the right. The die was cast. Some infantry transport was moving along the road; I got in behind it, nobody blocked our way, we blocked nobody else's. I saw a tank on the road, two others were stuck in the mud at a little distance from it, or perhaps they had been hit. I saw some German prisoners, no one was guarding them, they were coming back by themselves. I saw some of our wounded walking back. In little more than an hour, soon after seven o'clock, the guns were behind the Bellewaardebeke, ready to open fire again for the second phase of the attack.

Out of curiosity, while waiting for the others, I went to look inside the château gardens. There were a lot of new holes, the ground looked very soft, there was more confusion than I had found on the road; a gun, not one of ours, one belonging to another brigade, had fallen into a shell-hole, the gunners had fixed lanyards to the wheels and were all pulling on them, while the horses strained to extricate it. I was thankful we had gone by the road.

The rest of the battery arrived, and the other batteries of the brigade. We were next to the road, on the right hand side of it, B Battery was on our right, A and D were on the other side of the road in the grounds of the château. We asked one another for news. Someone said we had captured our first objectives, but nothing was certain yet. It was no good asking the walking wounded, they always said the attack was going well, they were so pleased to be out of it.

'I saw a lot of prisoners as we were coming up,' Josh said.

'Not many,' Frank said. 'Nothing like so many as last time.'

Cherry rang up to ask if we were in position. Everything was going well so far, he said, we had gained all our first objectives.

The time had now come to launch the second attack. All the guns opened fire again, the noise was even louder than before, for the other batteries were closer to us than they had been, there were field guns in a long line for as far as I could see. Edward went back to his advanced wagon lines, taking the teams and all the limbers and wagons with him. They would be wanted again for our second advance, but they could not stay up here; we were too close to the enemy. It was too early yet to feel sure that he had been defeated.

The Major and Frank went up to reconnoitre the way for our second advance. They went with Colonel Richardson and the other battery commanders. Josh and I were left alone. In front of us, across the Bellewaardebeke, the ground rose gently for five or six hundred yards to a low ridge. That ridge had been our front line in the morning. We could not see over it in front of us, but we could see other ridges on the right. All those had been German-held in the morning. Whose were they now? We did not know.

Cherry rang up again. He did not sound so optimistic this time. Some enemy strong points were still holding out, our advance had been held up for the moment, we were to reduce range, we were to repeat the last part of our firing programme, in support of another attack which was just going in.

'Look at the road!' Josh said to me.

It was packed with guns and wagons and other transport. All the way up to the top of the ridge in front of us, and for some way behind. But it was not moving, nothing was going over the crest. What was wrong? 'I can put two and two together as well as anyone else,' Josh said. 'They're not going on because they can't, because the Boche is still there and would see them if they went over the crest.'

I waited. Surely the line would start moving soon. Cherry had said it was only in one or two places that we had been held up. Surely the next attack would be successful. But the long line on the road did not move.

'I don't know about you, young fellow,' Josh said after a time, 'but I could do with a drop of Scotch and a bite of something.' I said that everything was packed up and the Major had said that nothing was to be unpacked on this position.

'Oh, that's all my eye,' Josh said. 'I can tell you I don't exactly enjoy fighting a battle at the best of times, but if the Major or anyone else thinks I'm going to fight one on an empty stomach—well, he can think again, that's all.'

I could not think of this as a battle, it was altogether different from any pictures of battles I had seen, it was like an ordinary day. And yet it was different. For one thing there was that long line of stationary wagons and guns on the road. Why didn't the Boche start shelling it? It would be terrible if he did, they were so close together they could hardly turn round. And in myself I felt a difference, a sense of expectancy that I had never felt on an ordinary day. Something was going to happen, but I had no idea what it would be. When the Major returned we should go forward again, over no-man's-land, into the very middle of the battlefield. That, at any rate, was what we had been told. Josh said it didn't look like another move, not yet anyway. But if the German guns were still in their original positions, why weren't they shelling us? The situation was obscure, Cherry said. We were to go on firing at a slower rate, and at a range not much greater than we had started at.

Josh had gone away, now he called me over to join him. He had poured out two mugs of whisky and he was sitting on the top of a shallow trench with his legs dangling inside and a plate of thick bully beef sandwiches beside him. The whisky was a good deal stronger than anything I was accustomed to pour out for myself.

'What did Medley say?' I asked. Medley was our cook, I had heard the Major telling him that on no account was anything to be unpacked except on his orders.

'He didn't say anything,' Josh answered shortly. 'Medley and I have a very good understanding together if you really want to know.'

He startled me by suddenly bawling out something in German, and he got up and went quickly over to the road. I saw that some German prisoners had stopped and were helping themselves to a drink out of our water cart. I followed him, he was talking at a great rate, I had not realised that he could speak German so well.

'Just like their blasted impudence,' he said, when he had driven them away.

I was rather sorry for them, they looked very wretched, 'I expect they felt they could do with a drop of something,' I said.

'Don't talk so damned soft,' he said. 'That cart may have to last us for a couple of days. Anyway, why should we give them anything? They're responsible for all this. If it wasn't for them we should be at home, I should be sitting down to steak and onions instead of eating bully beef and sweating my guts out in this god-forsaken country.'

He put a guard on the water cart and told him that no one was to drink out of it except men in our own battery. Hewlett was the man he told to guard it. Hewlett was one of our battery rogues. He had been the Major's servant once until he was sacked for some act of dishonesty, which he denied, but he and the Major had continued to be on very good terms, and within a few days the Major had recommended him for the Military Medal, for putting out a dump of burning ammunition which was likely to blow up at any moment. But even I should have known better than to choose Hewlett for a guard if I wanted to be obeyed. During the course of the day I saw him pouring out water for two other prisoners. He was speaking to them in his Yorkshire dialect, they were replying in German, but they seemed to understand one another very well.

It was not until midday that the transport on the road began to move. Then all the guns and wagons turned round and came back. So the battle had not gone according to plan. Cherry admitted that we had not gained all our objectives, and that it seemed unlikely now we should have to move before the next day. When the guns had all gone back the enemy began shelling the road, it was deserted by this time, but we suffered some casualties, our first during the day.

Some time later Frank and the Major returned. They were nearly exhausted and very discouraged. Frank said he had never known a worse day, they had been chased by shells wherever they went, not to mention aeroplanes and machine-gun fire, he didn't know how they were still alive. 'Talk about casualties,' he said. 'There were dead men all over the place, ours and theirs, sometimes two or three on top of one another, you had to look where you were going so as not to tread on them.' Some of them had been there for weeks, he said, but most of them had been killed that morning. 'And the wounded,' he said. 'Crying for help, and no one taking the least notice of them.'

'Why not?' Josh said.

'Everyone too exhausted. And besides, it wasn't possible to walk about in all that shellfire. And the doctors already had their hands full.'

I sat in silence, listening to all that he said. I had not seen the dead yet, not like this, I dreaded seeing them. Even Josh was silent. He had poured out a drink for both of them, and one for himself too. I did not want another one, I was too dejected. In spite of all appearances to the contrary I had been expecting them to bring back good news.

'It's utter lunacy,' the Major was saying. 'We shell the place for a month till there isn't a yard of ground left that isn't a shell-hole, and then they expect the infantry to be able to advance and they tell us to move our guns up there.'

There was no road, he said, there was nothing at all, it would have been utterly impossible to take guns up there even if the German positions had been captured. 'Why don't they go and look at the place and see it for themselves?' he said.

We had our tea. Edward had come up from the wagon lines to find out the latest news and when the limbers would be wanted for the advance. 'There won't be any advance,' the Major said. 'I'm telling you, it was as much as a man could do to walk about there. Guns! Why, you couldn't push a bicycle up there, or a ruddy pram.' Frank told him about the dead men and about the aeroplanes that had shot at them.

'Looks as though we can call it a day then,' Edward said.

'You can call it whatever you bloody well like,' said the Major, 'but there's not going to be another advance.' He had been drinking ever since they came back.

Edward went away again and the rain began. At first it was only a drizzle, but it turned into a heavy rain as daylight faded. Now it was our rockets that went up from the infantry in front of us, two or three times during the evening we had to fire on our S.O.S. lines, which were constantly being changed as fresh orders came in from Brigade Headquarters. No one seemed to know where our front line was, or the enemy's, or whether he was making an attack.

'Of course he isn't,' the Major said, 'he's got more sense. It's just a lot of wind, no one in his senses is going to make an attack on a night like this.'

I hoped he was right. If the Germans recaptured the ground they had lost in the morning we should find ourselves almost in the front line. Gradually the firing on both sides died down, now we had only the rain to contend with. The Major was playing hell with the servants, calling them a lot of lazy bastards, threatening to return them all to duty.

'Go easy, Major,' Josh said. 'They haven't done so badly, it's not exactly been an easy day for them either.'

'How the hell do you know whether a day's been easy or

not? I suppose they've been making meals for you all day and that's why you think it's been difficult for them.'

Frank advised us to keep out of his way. 'He's always like this after a battle,' he said. 'I know how to deal with him.' I was anxious about Jack, we had heard nothing from him since early in the day, but Frank told me not to worry, Jack knew how to look after himself, he said, he had probably found a better place for himself for the night than we had.

Our place was certainly nothing to boast about, it was very different from the safety and comfort of the Summer House. There was a shallow trench, barely three feet deep, and on one side of it two small excavations had been dug, a little below the level of the trench. Frank and the Major were in the larger hole, Josh and I in the other, there was just room for our two valises side by side on the ground. I told Josh I was sorry that the Major had been so beastly to him when he was sticking up for the servants, but he only laughed and said he did not mind what anyone said to him. Hard words didn't cut your flesh, he said; what was much more serious was the thinness of earth on our shelter. 'It may keep out the rain,' he said, 'but I'm damned sure it won't keep out anything else.'

Even the rain was not kept out. I woke up early, soon after it was light, and saw that water was trickling down into our hole from the trench outside. It was still raining. I woke up Josh, who was between myself and the wall. If we stayed where we were the water would soon be over our clothes, I said. He went to wake up the servants and told them to make tea for us all and then to get on with breakfast. Frank and the Major we found, were in a much worse plight than ourselves, they had not woken up in time, the water in their hole was deeper than ours, all their clothes were soaked. I thought the Major's temper would be worse than ever and tried to keep out of his way, but he had completely recovered.

'You were all pretty glum last night,' he said while we were eating our breakfast. 'Couldn't get a cheep out of any of you. What was the matter?'

'It must have been the rain,' Josh said, 'and if it goes on much longer we shall all need lifebelts.'

The Major went away to see how the men were. 'Who's

winning the war this morning?' I heard him calling out. It was his usual morning greeting to them and I heard a great answering shout from every man on the position—'They are!' 'Not so loud,' the Major told them, laughing, 'the fellows on the Staff will hear you. They think we are!' He was in very high spirits when he came back to us. 'You can just see the muzzles of the guns sticking out of the water,' he said. 'So that's all right, we can still fire them. But I wonder if they've got any boats. We could take the guns up by boat if they still want us to advance.' He said he could hardly wait for *The Times* to come, he was so eager to read about our victory.

Jack turned up during the morning, tired and dirty, but otherwise all right. I thought he was more cheerful than usual. 'Of course it was a bloody awful failure,' he said, 'but I'd been expecting that, so I wasn't particularly depressed.' He went down to the wagon lines, and in the afternoon Edward came up with the rations and full wagons of ammunition, and when he saw how wet Frank and the Major were he suggested that they also should go down and that he should stay up in their place. The Major thought this was a very good idea. He had already rendered us one great service, he had found an empty dug-out about a hundred yards behind the water-logged trenches where we had spent the previous night. I had heard Frank say that the Major could smell a good dug-out if there was one within a mile of us, and certainly he had found a very good one. 'Of course it was the first thing I saw yesterday,' he said, 'but there were other people in it then. But it's always worth keeping your eye on a good place and when I saw the other fellows going away I was into it before you could say "knife".' It was strong and clean and comfortable, and so large that there was room in it not only for ourselves and our servants but for all the signallers as well. It was marked on the map as "Lancer Farm" and was our home for the next five or six weeks.

It was not a dug-out in the ordinary sense of the word, in Flanders you could not dig down to a depth of more than one or two feet because you came to water. But you could strengthen houses or farm buildings of any kind by reinforcing walls and the roof with rubble-filled sandbags or blocks of concrete. The Germans were better at this than we were, probably because they could employ forced Belgian labour. and every building behind their line was converted into a small fort, with slits through which machine-guns could be fired. These were the pill-boxes, as they came to be called later. Almost indestructible by shellfire, they were extremely difficult to capture, and time after time during the fighting of 1917 our attacking infantry overran a line of pill-boxes and advanced to the top of the ridge behind them, only to be shot at from behind and forced to retire by unwounded enemy soldiers, unaffected by our barrage fire, who had come out of the forts. There were fewer of these forts behind our line, we had to wait until we captured the German ones. Then they afforded us invaluable protection in spite of facing the wrong way.

But the place the Major had found for us was British-made. Before going away he told Edward that he would take as many men as possible with him. 'I'll leave you enough to fire the guns,' he said, 'but no more. You've seen for yourself what happened to Frank and me last night and we were lucky not to be shelled as well. There's nothing by the guns fit for a Christian even for one night, nothing that would keep out an orange, and if he starts chucking five-nines about there'll be hell to pay. We can't do anything about it until the weather improves, but that's why I don't intend to leave more men up here than I have to.'

Then he and Frank went off to the wagon lines, Josh and I took our valises into Lancer Farm, and Edward stayed with us, in command of the battery for the time being.

In the late afternoon, when enemy shelling had died down, I went outside to do what I had felt no inclination for while shellfire on the position was so intense. I found a shell-hole on the other side of the Bellewaardebeke dry enough to squat down in and lowered my breeches, listening anxiously for the sound of a shell coming behind me. But I had chosen a lucky moment, I did what I had come out to do, pulled up my breeches, and returned to the security of our home as quickly as possible. By the next day there was a latrine, and even a strip of sacking at my back made me feel less vulnerable to the enemy.

Some of my experiences at the front proved easier than expected, but I had not anticipated how disagreeable others would be.

A few day later the Major returned with either Jack or Frank, and then it was our turn to go down and find dry clothes and enjoy an evening in Poperinghe. Now I felt a real soldier, I had taken part in a battle, I was as excited as a schoolboy going home for the holidays. A friendly Heavy Gunner with a car saw us walking and stopped to pick us up. We drove past the Menin Gate, through Ypres and all the way to Vlamertinghe, where the wagon lines were.

Inside Lancer Farm

The rain went on for two or three days, effectively putting an end to any possibility of further infantry action for the present. The Major wanted another spell at the wagon lines, and Edward, Josh and I went up to Lancer Farm again.

The infantry could not attack, but the artillery firing never stopped, day and night on both sides it continued. We were getting through our ammunition at a great rate and in constant need of fresh supplies. Often the wagons came up twice in one day.

I was out by the guns one morning at a time when half a dozen wagons on the road were being unloaded. The road passed between our guns and the grounds of the château, going on to Zonnebeke and into the German lines. Shells began to fall on or near the road and one horse was wounded. To be shelled at a time when wagons and teams were up was almost the worst thing that could befall a battery; horses became frightened and drivers could not dismount, they had to stay where they were, in a very vulnerable position. All one could do was to get the wagons unloaded as quickly as possible and then send them away.

Sergeant Denmark, the senior N.C.O. on the position, was directing the unloading, showing the gunners where to put the shells as they brought them across from the road. The task was nearly finished, a few more minutes and the wagons would be off. But at this unlucky moment shells began to fall on the gun side of the road, and close to where I was standing. Wherever I looked, spouts of earth or mud were leaping up. A man standing near to me was scratched by a fragment of shell, and the teams were on the road still. It was a nightmare situation and I thought Ramsden's wound, slight as it was, needed a dressing. 'Sergeant Denmark,' I called, 'come here quickly!' He turned round, with a face of thunder. 'Who's taking charge here, are you Sir, or am I?' he said. It was a terrible moment. I, an officer, had given an order to one of my men and he had not obeyed me. It seemed to me that I should never again be able to hold up my head in the battery.

In fact, the situation was under control. Ramsden had licked and sucked the back of his hand which was no longer bleeding, the shellfire stopped, the last round of ammunition was carried across and safely put away, and I saw the wagons being driven away as I walked back to Lancer Farm.

But I was utterly miserable, I had failed in a crisis, I had not known what to do, I should never again be able to give an order. I was wretched all day. It was particularly disappointing because I had thought I was getting on more successfully with Sergeant Denmark since being in action with the battery. If Edward had been more friendly I think I should have told him the whole story and asked his advice. But I was afraid this would only lower me still further in Edward's opinion. What could I do?

Then I made up my mind. I knew that another load of ammunition would be coming up later in the day, and when it came I would go outside, go on to the road where the wagons were. Sergeant Denmark was sure to be there, he was always there whenever there was a job to be done. I would show him that I was not afraid for myself, that I did care about the battery and wanted to share in whatever danger there might be.

I had to wait a long time It was not until we had finished our dinner that the wagons came. Then, without a word to either of the others, as though I was only going to relieve myself, I went outside, out of the dug-out, round the nearer shell-holes, and jumped down on to the road. The night was comparatively quiet. Some shells landed in the château garden, but none on the road while I was outside. The wagons were about a hundred yards away and I walked up to them. The drivers all seemed in good spirits. 'Get a bloody move on,' I heard one say to the gunner who was unloading his wagon,

'Ah don't fancy bein' stuck in this place all t'flickin' night.' I had not seen Sergeant Denmark yet. Then I saw him, and he saw me.

'What are you doing here, Sir?' he said.

'I just wanted to make sure everything was all right.'

'Don't be so daft. Officers have got their own responsibilities. But there's nowt in unloading wagons and putting ammunition away. Anyone can see to that.'

I was still lingering. 'Now that the rain has stopped,' I said, 'we'll be able to strengthen those shelters a bit.' I knew it was the first thing Edward wanted to do, to sandbag the roofs and walls of the flimsy shelters where the men were sleeping.

'Don't be so daft,' Denmark said again. 'How do you think it's going to help us or anyone else if you go asking to be hit?' His voice was still gruff, but there was no anger in it now, and I understood that he had been nearly as worried and anxious as myself in the morning. Then I went back to the dug-out and slept well, far better than I expected to. It was all right.

We did not always sleep all through the night. I woke one night at about two o'clock, the hour when courage may be at its lowest, and heard heavy shells falling very close. Eight-inch, I thought they were. They were coming over one at a time at intervals of about a minute, and the dug-out shook at each explosion. Strong as it was I knew that it could not protect us from a direct hit from one of these, and I lay in silent fear as I heard each shell rushing towards us through the night. A terrifying explosion followed and I pressed myself against the wall. But it had missed us, it had fallen on the other side of the road, where A and D Batteries were, they were having a worse time than ourselves. After each explosion I started to count. If I could get to two hundred it would probably mean that the enemy battery had finished for the night and no more would be coming. But I never got beyond one hundred and fifty before I heard the scream of the next on its way. This screaming sound was more frightening than the explosion, there was a fiendish malevolence in it, and it seemed to be coming straight at me.

I thought I was the only one awake and envied the others. Then I heard Josh's voice. 'For God's sake!' he said, 'give us a light someone, and put on the gramophone. Let's see if we can drown the sound of those sods outside.'

There was a candle beside my bed, stuck into an empty bottle. I lit it and got up, and wound up the gramophone. I put on our Gilbert and Sullivan record, the others would not let me play it on ordinary occasions, they said it was too loud and that they did not like that classical stuff, but its loudness was an advantage now. I realised that everyone was awake, servants and signallers too, each of us had been envying the others for being asleep, now we were all talking at once.

Then I put on Solveig's Song, another favourite of mine, but that was too much for Josh. 'Oh, for Christ's sake, take her off!' he cried when she was on her top notes. 'She sounds just like one of them herself.'

We were all talking, but Josh talked most. 'Does anyone want to hear my candid opinion of the War?' he asked. He told us without waiting for an answer. Then he told us his candid opinion of Staff Officers and of all the people at the Base or on the Lines of Communications. 'They're the real bastards,' he said. 'Pinching all our grub and not knowing what sound a shell makes! And wouldn't I just like to be one of them! Inland Water Transport! That's the thing for me in the next war.' By exaggerating his own fear of shells he turned them into objects for laughter, we were all laughing before he had finished and before the shells stopped.

I did not know when they stopped. I fell asleep again. When I woke up my candle was burnt out, the gramophone had run down, one or the servants was making tea, and a signaller was folding up the gas curtain over the entrance, letting in the daylight and comparatively fresh air.

'Morning, Josh,' Edward said, as soon as he saw he was awake. 'Had a good night? Sweet sleep and happy dreams?'

'Blast you and your happy dreams,' Josh said. 'I'll tell you how I'm going to spend today. There's a lot of rubble outside and we've got plenty of sandbags. I'm going to put so much stuff on top of this place that it will keep out even one of those seventeen-inch brutes that Frank says are always following him about. I shall need a lot of men to help me. Just see to that, will you, as soon as you've had your breakfast.'

9

Outside Bank Farm

The shellfire never stopped. Day and night it went on. But no further infantry attacks were made for more than a fortnight. The rain had drowned the battle.

At last the weather improved. The Great Offensive was to be resumed, the infantry would attack again, the artillery would go forward. We received our orders, all the minute details, the same creeping barrage, the exact times, the position to which we should advance. And each battery was to supply a Forward Observing Officer to go up with the infantry. 'Whose turn is it?' the Major asked. It seemed to be mine. He sent me down to the wagon lines for two days.

I was aware of a feeling of anxiety. This would be the most responsible as well as the most dangerous task that had been given me, but I was reasonably confident that I could do it. I had been under shellfire so often that I thought I had nothing more to learn about that; I knew what it was like, very disagreeable, but endurable. And I had been up to the infantry front line, within sight of the enemy, across the battlefield where the dead men were still lying. Yes, I could do it. It would probably be a very difficult day, I should be glad when it was over. But when it was over, I should be able to feel that now I had done everything, there would be no worse experience for me to go through.

I was not going alone. Vernon of B Battery was coming with me. He was the officer from South Africa who had joined the brigade on the same day as myself. I liked him very much; there was no one whom I would have preferred for my companion. We made our plans together on the afternoon of the day before the Attack. Zero Hour was at 4.20, but we had no responsibility for the first wave of the attack, two other officers were going out for that. Our responsibility began at Z + 100 minutes when the second wave was to go through. By that time we were to be at Bank Farm, in our present front line, we were to follow up from there, finding out how far the infantry had gone and the strength of the opposition against them. We were to lay out a telephone line forward from Bank Farm and send all our information there. Another telephone line from Bank Farm to the rear was already in operation, its maintenance was the responsibility of the Royal Engineers, not ours.

'It all seems fairly straightforward,' Vernon said. It was his first time also as Forward Observing Officer on the day of an attack, and we went over our plans again, to make sure that we knew all the times correctly. Then we arranged to meet at two o'clock on the road by our batteries.

It was a dark night, but our eyes soon grew accustomed to the darkness, and it was quiet. This time in the morning was often the quietest part of the day. At first we were on a road, we were to call in and see the Colonel on our way up.

Colonel Richardson and Cherry were asleep, but they woke up and welcomed us in a very friendly manner. The Colonel put on his spectacles and blinked at us amiably from behind them. I think he disliked sending us out into danger as much as he would have disliked going there himself.

'Information is what we want,' he said to us. 'All that you can get: where we are, where the enemy is, any strong points that are still holding out. You supply the information, we do the rest. It's not only our own guns, we can get the heavies behind us to fire at anything that's too big for us.'

He and Cherry were both very encouraging. It was going to be a much better show than last time, they said, all the enemy pill-boxes had been pounded to bits. But I remembered what Jack had said, that anyone could be optimistic if he lived in the kind of place where they were. Then they wished us good luck and we went out into the night again.

Now we had to leave the road, we had to clamber over trenches and shell-holes. This was where the two front lines had been a fortnight earlier. We could only go very slowly, our signallers had more than a mile of heavy telephone wire to carry in addition to all their ordinary equipment, which included two lamps. We had eight signallers, four from each battery, my Bombardier Turner was in charge of the party, and we also had four men from a trench mortar battery who had joined us at Brigade Headquarters. They were to act as runners if we could not get our information back by telephone.

We had decided not to try to reach Bank Farm before Zero Hour. It would have been difficult to find our way there in the darkness and there was no advantage in going so far forward. We would stop at the top of the ridge and wait there until it was light enough to pick out Bank Farm. We should have plenty of time to get there before Z+100.

We stopped in an old German trench, part of their reserve line before the battle started. It was only half past three, we were in good time. Vernon closed his eyes and dozed off, but I felt no desire for sleep. Now that we had started I was no longer aware of anxiety, only of excitement. I was looking forward to the day. The deep trench was full of other soldiers, but I did not know who they were or what they were there for, no one was speaking.

At a little before 4.20 we went outside and climbed half way up the parapet so that we could see. Then there was a roar of guns behind us, we checked that our watches were right, and looked in front to see what was going to happen. All the enemy rockets were going up, and over our heads red points of light sped through the darkness, our own shells rushing to burst on the German lines. We could see the flashes of their explosion, and nearer to us German shells began to fall. But the noise was much less than it had been when I was standing in the middle of the guns.

Daylight slowly came. Now we could see the battlefield. In front of us the ground sloped down very gradually for about half a mile. Then began to rise again, a little more steeply. The Steenbeke was in the bottom, a few stumps of splintered willows marked where the course of the stream had been. That was our front line, or it had been at 4.20. That must be Bank Farm, a little to our right, just across the stream. By this time our infantry ought to be on top of or over the ridge on the other side, but it was not yet light enough to see any movement there. We could see the pill-boxes on the top: Iberian, Delva Farm, Gallipoli. They did not look as though they had been pounded to bits, but perhaps it was all right, it was very hard to see. They were just low blocks of concrete, not more than three or four feet high. Bank Farm was another. There were about a dozen in sight altogether, some ours, some his; or they had been his, they ought to be ours now. There was nothing else to see. Nearer to us some of our wounded were already coming back, their white bandages showed out clearly in the surrounding greyness.

It was time to be off. The enemy was putting down a heavy bombardment in front of us, but most of the shells were falling in the same places, and before leaving the safety of the trench we worked out a zig zag course for ourselves, so as to avoid them. We tacked across the sea of death. In a straight line we had only a thousand yards to go, but it took us nearly an hour. The sun came up above the horizon in front of us as we were going. The long summer day had begun.

Up to this time everything had gone well for us. We had arrived at Bank Farm, we were in good time, our party had suffered no casualties, we had not even been particularly frightened, none of the shells had fallen close to us. Now we were to go up the slope on the other side and find out where our infantry had got to.

But we never went beyond Bank Farm.

I saw one of our machine guns firing from a trench at a short distance on our right. If the attack had been successful there ought to have been no German within range of a machine gun from here by this time. And machine guns were generally fired over open sights. If those gunners could see the enemy then he could see us. Vernon also had seen the machine gun firing and had drawn his own conclusions. 'We'd better find out what's happened before we go any further,' he said.

We separated. There were plenty of people to ask, but no one could tell me much. No one that I saw was doing anything, everyone looked as though he was wondering what to do, except those who had already decided to do nothing. Then I saw Tommy Rust, one of A Battery's officers, and a friend of mine. I knew he had come up the night before, he was acting as liaison officer to the infantry, he would be able to tell me. He was a very smiley person as a rule, but he did not smile now. It had been all right at first, he said; then the infantry had met a counter-attack; and the pill-boxes had shot at them from behind. I understood him to say that some of our men had come back, but he could not stop with me, he was going somewhere with the infantry colonel.

I saw Vernon looking for me and went to where he was. His information was much the same as my own. 'It seems as though they haven't been pounded to bits,' he said. At that moment we saw some men coming down the slope in front of us. They didn't seem to be walking properly, they looked as though they were walking in their sleep. I saw Tommy's Colonel going out to them. 'Come on, lads!' I heard him say. 'I'll take you up there.' They took no notice of him, they just walked past him. He called to some of them by name. 'Come back with me, I'll lead you there myself, don't let the Regiment down.' He was an oldish man, his voice was pleading, not commanding. They went on walking. Some of them stopped when they got to the trench at Bank Farm, others crossed over it and went on up the hill. It was the first time I had seen men who were finished. 'We must tell Brigade what's happened,' I said.

'We can't,' Vernon said, 'there's no line.'

'Is it down?' I asked. I thought he meant it had been cut by shellfire.

'I don't think it's ever been up.'

'What do you mean?'

'I don't think there's ever been a line back from here.'

So there was nothing we could do. The attack had failed, our men were back where they had started. All our guns would be doing no good at all. Adding on a hundred yards to their range every few minutes as though the infantry were close up to the curtain of fire. But the infantry was back here, what was left of them.

We sent back one of our runners, but I did not feel sure that he would ever find his way to Brigade Headquarters. At the best it would take him an hour and he would certainly never return to us. We sent a second one a few minutes later, I made him go a different way.

Then I went to find Bombardier Turner, he might be able to suggest something. 'I'll try a lamp,' he said, when I had explained the situation to him. 'The sun's good,' he said. It was a satisfaction to find someone who knew what he could do and was going to do it, and his voice was the same as on any other day. Within a few minutes he came to tell me that he was getting an answer from the ridge behind us and that we could send messages through to Brigade Headquarters. We sent one immediately. The attack on our front had failed, we said; the infantry was back at Bank Farm; there might still be some parties of our men up on the ridge in front, but the pill-boxes were still held by the enemy.

It was not yet seven o'clock.

All this time we had been under fire. Shells were falling over the whole area, in the valley of the little stream, on the side of the hill where we had come from, up to the crest behind us, which was as far as we could see. But the shellfire was not particularly heavy and Bank Farm was receiving no more than its share of attention. In front of us we could not see so far, the ground rose more steeply, we could not see the top of the ridge, or the pill-boxes, which had been the cause of our failure. But the bottom of the shallow valley, where we were, may have been under enemy observation from somewhere. At any rate the shelling suddenly became worse, I was aware that shells were falling all round us.

'I don't like this, we'd better get down,' Vernon said.

But there was no place to get down in. There were two pill-boxes at Bank Farm, both very strong, but one was the head-quarters of the infantry battalion, the other a dressing station. There was no room for us in either. There was a trench at the side of the pill-boxes, but it was so wide and shallow that it was almost useless for protection. But in one place there was a low wall beside the trench. It was on the wrong side of the trench, the non-German side, so that one was completely exposed on the side from which the shells were coming, but it was better than nothing, and we made our way to it quickly. Half a dozen other artillery officers were already there,

79

sheltering behind it. We joined them, crouching down at the bottom of the shallow trench, with the wall behind us. I was at one end, Vernon was next to me. I did not know where our signallers were, I hoped they had found some sort of shelter, but the shelling was too heavy to go and look for them.

I hoped it would only last for five or ten minutes, concentrated shelling was usually over in a short time. But it went on. Some of the shells fell very close, and they were big ones. I flattened myself against the earth and the wall. The dressing station was about twenty yards from me, on my right, I was the nearest one to it. There was not room inside for all the wounded men who had been brought there. Some had to be left outside, or were taken outside if they were hopeless cases. They were a long time dying. Unconscious they may have been, but they heard the shells coming. Their crying rose to a scream as they heard the sound of one coming, then fell away to a moan after the shell had burst.

I learnt to distinguish the different crying voices. Sometimes one stopped, and did not start again. It was a relief when this happened, the pain of the crying was unendurable. But there were new voices. The crying never stopped, the shelling never stopped.

Then I stopped noticing the crying voices. I was conscious only of my own misery. I lost all count of the shells and all count of time. There was no past to remember or future to think about. Only the present. The present agony of waiting, waiting for the shell that was coming to destroy us, waiting to die. I did not speak to Vernon, Vernon did not speak to me. None of us spoke. I had shut my eyes, I saw nothing. But I could not shut my ears, I heard everything, the screaming of the shells, the screams of pain, the terrifying explosions, the vicious fragments of iron rushing downwards, biting deeply into the earth all round us.

I could not move, I had lost all power over my limbs. My heart throbbed, my face was burning, my throat was parched. I wanted a drink, there was lime juice in my water-bottle on my back, but I could not move my arm to pull it towards me. I could think of nothing but my own suffering. Still the cruel shells screamed in their fiendish joy, still the sun beat down on us.

It stopped. I did not realise that it had stopped, I do not know how long I had been lying there, thinking that it still went on, but I heard a voice speaking and I opened my eyes. A newcomer had joined us, an officer in the Engineers, he was standing by the other end of the trench, furthest away from me. To my surprise I recognised him. It was someone who had been at school with me, five or six years before. I had not liked him. One of the masters had called him Fairy because he was so clumsy and the nickname had stuck. He still looked clumsy. There was a smear of dried blood down one of his cheeks. He kept on touching the wound with his finger and then looking at his finger to see whether the bleeding had stopped.

'Lot of wounded up at the top,' he was saying. 'Any of you fellows coming up with me?'

None of us spoke.

'They're crying,' he said. 'I've heard them.'

Still no one spoke.

'We can get a stretcher,' he said.

One of the others spoke for us all. 'We've got our own job to do,' he said.

He waited for another minute, standing there, fingering the course of the blood down his cheek. None of us moved. 'No one coming?' he said. Then he went away. I did not see where he went to, I never saw him again.

We got out of our hole.

'I feel awful for not going with him,' Vernon said to me some time later.

'It wasn't our job,' I said.

'I know,' he said. 'I feel awful.'

At some later time he tried to go up the hill by himself. If I had known he was going I might have gone with him, he did not tell me until he returned. He had not gone very far, he said; they were sniping. 'I hadn't the guts to go on,' he said. While we were standing talking together the back of his hand was scratched by a thin splinter of shell, he licked the place with his tongue and put on some iodine. 'If it had been a bit bigger,' he said, 'I might have got away.'

We couldn't go back yet, it was only twelve o'clock. But we were doing no good where we were, we could see nothing from Bank Farm, there was no telephone line, we were no longer even in lamp communication with the ridge behind us, Turner said there had been no reply to his signalling for some time past.

We waited. I saw that the other artillery officers were going back. Tommy Rust said there was no possibility of our making another attack that day, there was no one left to make one. If anyone did any attacking it would be the Germans, he said.

'Let's go,' I said to Vernon. 'Let's go back to the ridge, we can speak to Brigade from there.'

He agreed. 'We can always come back here if they want us to,' he said.

I don't think I could have gone back, I had a horror of Bank Farm. It was the most terrifying place I had ever been to, or imagined in a nightmare. I did not mind where we went, so long as we left Bank Farm.

We went back up the hill, not to the place which we had left at dawn, but a little to the left of it. That was where Turner had been signalling to, and we knew there was a line from there back to our batteries. We had to wait for some time when we arrived there, the other artillery officers were there before us, they were all telephoning to their brigades. But at last it was our turn and we got through to Cherry. I was hoping he would say we had been out long enough and tell us to come in. But he didn't. He said we had been quite right to come back on to the ridge, we could see from there, but we must keep a good look out for enemy movement; there was quite a chance of his launching a strong counterattack, we must report at once if we saw anything. And if nothing happened we could come in as soon as it was dark, he said.

Dark! It wouldn't be dark for another seven hours. He might as well have told us to stay there for ever.

We had just finished speaking to him. The telephone was inside a pill-box, the other officers had gone outside, we were looking at each other. There was the sudden scream of a shell, followed by a very loud explosion. Everyone was trying

82

to rush inside through the narrow doorway, there were screams of agony outside. 'Who is it?' we were all asking. It was Gladwin and Dearden, two of those who had been up at Bank Farm with us. Dearden was dead already, Gladwin was brought inside. There was a doctor in the pill-box and he went to where they laid him, but there was nothing he could do for him, he said. He just shook his head when he came back to us.

We went outside. It might be more dangerous out there, but I could not endure the moaning of the dying man, I'd had as much as I could stand for one day. Anyway, we had been told to look out for enemy movement.

We found a place about a hundred yards in front of the pill-box, and our signallers laid out a line to it from the telephone pit. There was a small patch of flat ground on which we could lie down and a shell hole close to it in which we could shelter if we had to. But we did not have to use it, no other shells fell close, the peace and stillness of a summer afternoon seemed to have descended on the battlefield.

There was peace behind the German lines also; I could see no movement anywhere. Down the hill to Bank Farm, up again on the other side. Somme, Gallipoli, Iberian—there they were, low grey slabs of stone in a desert place, like the huts of primitive man. And beyond that ridge there were other ridges, I counted three or four, there was grass on the furthest one. I could see grass and trees and red brick houses, the village of Passchendaele again.

Some way to the right, but almost due east of where we were lying, a grey obelisk stood out on a hillside. That was Zonnebeke church, all that was left of it, the village had gone, only this one wall of the church remained. My eyes followed the line of the railway coming out from Ypres. It crossed the low ground on an embankment, then went into a cutting near the ruins of the church and disappeared from sight.

Once during the afternoon I saw half a dozen Germans coming down the hill past the church. I saw them only for a moment, I called to Vernon, I moved my glasses away from them and when I looked again I could not find them. Neither of us could see them. They had so utterly vanished that I wondered if they had ever been there. The sun beat down on us, there was no shade anywhere on the battlefield, there was no variety of colour, just the hard brown of sun-baked mud.

'I think it's almost harder to bear on a day like this than when it rains,' Vernon said.

I did not want to eat anything, my mouth was too dry and when I took a drink of lime juice out of my water bottle it was warm and bitter to the taste.

We took it in turns to close our eyes for ten minutes.

We stared at Zonnebeke church.

We spoke to Cherry again. As there was no sign of a counterattack developing we thought he might tell us to come in, but he only said 'Keep on watching.'

Another hour passed, but when I looked at my watch it was only twenty minutes. I hoped it might have stopped, but Vernon's agreed with it.

Oh, the misery of this desolate land!

'Did you ever imagine it would be like this?' Vernon asked.

'I've forgotten what I imagined,' I told him.

The sun was hardly moving.

'If we'd come away from Bank Farm sooner we should have been the ones who were standing outside,' Vernon said.

The same thought had occurred to me.

'It fell right in the doorway,' he said.

I had a sudden idea. If I rang up the Major he might suggest to Cherry that we had been out long enough, Cherry would take more notice of him. I succeeded in getting through to him.

'Where are you?' he asked.

I told him.

'Anything happening?' he asked.

'Not now,' I said.

'What sort of a day have you had?' he asked.

'Not very good,' I said nothing more and he rang off, but sometime later Cherry spoke to us. 'Anything happening?' he asked.

We told him that everything seemed quiet.

84

'Well,' he said, 'it's only seven o'clock, but I should think it would be all right for you to come in now.'

We did not delay. Our patient signallers would have stayed up there without protest for the rest of the day, and night as well, but now they moved with alacrity. Bombardier Turner, who was a serious-minded young man, gave me a quick passing smile. It was the first time that day I had seen anyone smile.

We came to the crest, we did not once look back, now we were going down on the other side. We could see where our guns were and the ruins of Ypres in the saucer below us. The rays of the sinking sun gave them a strange beauty. The sun had been with us all day, in our eyes as we were going forward to Bank Farm, in our eyes again now as we came down to the Bellewaardebeke.

'This time last week I was in Piccadilly Circus,' Vernon said. 'You're lucky, you've got your leave still to come, you'll forget all about this when you go home, it will only be a bad dream.'

I suddenly felt an extraordinary affection for Vernon, I wanted to have him always at my side. Together we had been down into the valley of the shadow, together we had climbed a little way out of it, a little way out of the pit. But we had nothing else to say to each other. We parted on the road, in the place where we had met, just eighteen hours earlier. I watched him till he was out of sight, then turned and walked towards my own mess.

Frank and the Major were finishing their dinner when I came into the dug-out. I smiled at them, there was nothing else I could do, I did not want to talk.

'What's it been like?' Frank asked.

'Put some food inside yourself,' the Major said. 'Eat first, talk afterwards, that's the rule.' And he poured out a whisky for me.

Afterwards I did talk. I had never talked so much, words poured out of me. The faces of the men who had been dead for a long time, the demoralised soldiers coming down the hill, and the poor old man of a colonel who had tried to rally them, the intensity of the shellfire, the cries of the dying, the death of the two gunner officers when we came back—it all rushed out of me. And the sun all day, glaring, burning, indifferent. The sun had added to my wretchedness.

'We've all had to go through it,' Frank said when I had finished. The gentleness of his voice surprised me. The Major wanted me to tell him more about Bombardier Turner. 'Was he under fire when he was using his lamp?' he asked. I did not really know, I had not been with him all the time. 'I think we were all of us under fire most of the morning,' I said.

'He did very well,' the Major said. 'His lamp brought us the first information that the attack had failed. If it hadn't been for him we should have gone on firing into the blue till kingdom come. Not just ourselves, but all the other brigades. That's the worst of a creeping barrage. We might as well have been chucking oranges at Fritz for all the harm we were doing him.'

He said he would put him in for a decoration, and some weeks later Bombardier Turner was awarded the Military Medal. But before the award came through he had been badly wounded, one of his legs had to be amputated. I wrote to him in hospital in England to tell him about the award, and he seemed pleased to have been given it. 'You got it for me, sir,' he wrote back. But how could a medal make up for the loss of a leg? He never walked again without crutches, and he was a young man.

'You seem to have done pretty well yourself,' the Major said. But I had not told them about my paralysing fear in the shallow trench, nor anything about Fairy. For a moment I thought of telling them, telling them I had been so frightened that I could not move and that I had been afraid to go up to the top of the hill. But I said nothing more, I had said enough. Now that the first rush of words was over I no longer wanted to talk about what had happened. I wanted to think about it, but I would not talk about it again, neither to my friends, nor in my letters home. Vernon knew, but no one else should ever know the extremity of the fear to which I had been reduced.

But several days later, happening to find myself alone with

Frank I mentioned to him that a sapper officer at Bank Farm had gone up to the crest in front in full view of the enemy in order to bring back some of our wounded, and I asked him whether he thought it was the right thing to do.

'No, most certainly not,' he said. 'It needs at least two men to carry one wounded, and the chances are that they would both be hit before they brought in a single man. What's the good in that? It's crazy to do that sort of thing in the middle of a battle; you've got to wait till it's over.'

Mathematically he was right. Losing two men in an attempt to save one was obviously of no use, but it made no difference to my belief that I had failed, and I should like to have asked Edward what he thought, his answer might have been different, I believed. But I never asked him. What made it harder for me to forget was that I had always thought myself a better person than Fairy in nearly every way.

The Major sent me down to the wagon lines on the morning after the attack, Jack coming up in my place. I was glad to go down. I wanted to be alone for a few days, and it was easier to be alone at the wagon lines, I had a tent to myself. I wanted to try and find out why I had been so afraid, and what I could do to prevent its happening again.

For fear of that sort was horrible, debasing, abject-making. I had never been afraid like that before. I had been rather less afraid than most others, not more afraid. I had felt frightened under fire, but I had remained myself. At Bank Farm I had ceased to be myself, I had become another person, one out of whom all courage had been poured away. It could not be just fear of death, I thought. For I had always known that I might be killed, everyone at the front must know that. I might have been killed on half a dozen previous occasions.

It seemed to me that my fear must have been due to a combination of circumstances. First, there had been the faces of the dead men. I had seen them before, but never so many. One couldn't avoid seeing them, one was given no warning. You took a step forward, and there the body was, lying on its back at the bottom of a shell-hole. My friends did not seem to mind, they were tougher than I was. Vernon said he just felt sorry for them. I did mind, I couldn't help it. I should have to try and make myself more familiar with the sight. Until I had done so, it would continue to make me feel sick. It made no difference whether they were Germans or our own people.

Then there had been the sight of our men coming back down the hill. They looked awful too. They were alive, they were moving, but more like puppets than men. There was no expression on their faces, it was as though they had lost their souls. And in the moment of seeing them I realised that our attack had failed utterly. It had been a worse failure than the first day of the battle, we had not gained a yard on our part of the front.

And then the concentrated bombardment. It had started suddenly, before I was prepared for it. Always before it had been no more than half a dozen shells, it had been all over in a minute or two; or else I had been inside a dug-out. At Bank Farm we had been practically lying in the open, and it had gone on for about a couple of hours. If I had known beforehand that it was going to happen I could have braced myself to bear it. Another time I should know. I should know that one always might come under fire on the day of a battle, out in the open, without a place to run to.

If these were the reasons for my fear it seemed to me that I need not suffer again in the same way. I had been warned now. I should be ready for that kind of fear the next time. It did not matter being afraid of death. Everyone was. Everyone wanted to live, not to die. Death might come, it had been hovering very close to us at Bank Farm. But there was nothing one could do to prevent its coming, or make it less likely. Feeling afraid did not lessen the risk. So what was the use of feeling afraid! All that suffering, and no advantage. The only sensible thing to do under shellfire was to find the best place that was available and stay there. Wait for the shelling to stop. It was simply a matter of endurance, like enduring any other pain.

I felt triumphant, I thought that I had conquered fear. Lying in bed in the morning in the peace of the wagon lines, hearing the sound of gunfire distantly, and nearer at hand the rustling of leaves outside my tent and the stamping of feet of horses,

I thought that I should never feel that terrible fear again and a great weight was lifted from my mind. Life was beautiful. I loved it. I did not want to die, but if death had to come I would not let the fear of it spoil the rest of life beforehand.

I felt so confident that I wanted to return to the line at once, to come under fire and show myself that I was not Bank-Farm afraid. I almost looked forward to the next time that I should have to go out as Forward Observing Officer on the day of a battle. I would do nothing foolish, I would take no unnecessary risks, if or when the shelling started I would take cover at once and remain there till it was over. But I should not suffer as I had suffered that morning at Bank Farm, I had solved the problem of feeling afraid.

I thought I had conquered fear, but of course I was deceiving myself. I never conquered it.

Life went on as before.

The Major told us the war had lasted long enough and he was going to make a separate peace and take no further part in it. Edward could command the battery, he said. Edward would like that, and the experience would be good for him if he wanted to become a Regular after the war.

Edward was not present to hear these remarks. He and Josh were up at the guns by themselves. Jack had gone on leave, Frank and I were at the wagon lines with the Major. I had never heard Edward say that he wanted to be a regular soldier, but the Major said oh, he had often talked about it, and it would suit him very well, the army was just the place for a boy like Edward.

'The trouble about the war,' the Major said, 'is that it stops you doing all the interesting and worthwhile things.'

At that time of year, he said, one ought to be thinking about partridges, and he intended to start thinking about them. He had brought his shot-gun back with him after his last leave, and now he was going to use it. Every day he went out shooting in the fields round our camp. He was happier than I had ever seen him, he was hardly drinking at all. He was particularly pleased because Major Fraser of A Battery was down at his wagon lines also, and the two went out together. Major Fraser was an Old Etonian. 'He's shot all over the place,' the Major said. 'With all the swells. So of course he fancies himself.' What made the Major so pleased was that he was being the more successful of the two.

I thought that Edward and Josh had been left up at the guns for a long time and I suggested to the Major that I should go up there. I couldn't of course take Edward's place, but I could either relieve Josh or stay up there with both of them, thus lightening for each of them the amount of work there was to do.

'What's all the hurry about?' the Major said. 'We'll give ourselves one more day. Or even two. It won't do Josh any harm to stay up there, he's seen much less of the war than the rest of us. And as for Edward, he prefers being up there, he always has preferred it, he's not interested in horses, he can't find anything to do with himself at the wagon lines.'

He was mistaken. The next morning there was a rude and angry letter waiting for him on the breakfast table. It had come down from the guns during the night. Edward had been looking in his diary and had counted the number of days that he had spent in the gun line, and the number the Major had spent there since the beginning of the battle. He was doing three-fifths of the Major's work, he said, and all the captain's; the Major did damn all except enjoy himself when he was at the wagon lines, but he was drawing his major's pay all the time. Edward said with a good deal of rudeness that it had got to stop, there was to be a more equal division in future.

The Major laughed and showed us both the letter. 'Poor old Edward!' he said. 'Something's bitten him. Fancy keeping a diary so as to be able to count how many days you've done in the line. I wonder what's upset him. We shall probably find they've been playing poker with A Battery and have lost money. Ten to one that's what it is. Edward hates losing money, he's a bit close with his money, that's the only thing I have against him.'

He did not hurry. He went out shooting again in the morning, but after lunch he set off with Frank to walk up to

90

the guns, leaving me to follow when the others came down. 'But if they're going into Poperinghe and you would like to go with them,' he said, 'tomorrow morning will be time enough.'

My sympathies were with Edward and Josh. Although he had been very nice to me I thought the Major was slack, and that he had behaved selfishly in staying at the wagon lines so long. But when the other two arrived I found that I was included in their resentment.

'Wagon line hero!' Josh shouted as soon as he saw me.

Edward was so angry that he did not speak to me. He and Josh went into their tent and began changing their clothes at once, I could hear their angry contemptuous voices. They were going into Poperinghe and I had been looking forward to going with them. I had not been there since the day at Bank Farm. I could not afford to go with the Major, he spent too much money there; and Frank did not go at all, he was saving up. But it was very clear they did not desire my company, they would not have accepted it.

'Wagon line hero!' Josh shouted from the tent when he saw me outside. 'If there's one type I can't stand,' he said, 'it's the sort of fellow who tries to shirk out of all the danger.'

I might have looked in my diary, but I knew without looking that my score was bigger than his, and he had not done a Bank-Farm yet. But it was no use trying to argue with them. 'Wagon line hero'—was all Josh would say, and Edward said nothing. They did not reply to my 'Cheerio!' as they were going off. They went in one direction, to Poperinghe; and I went in the other, up to the line.

I felt very disappointed. I did not mind what Josh called me, I was accustomed to his mockery. He was altogether unlike myself, and I was certain that I could never win his good opinion, I did not especially desire it. But Edward I admired more than anyone else in the brigade, and in the last few weeks, since the beginning of the battle, he had become much more friendly. But now I had lost all that I had ever gained with him.

'Well!' said the Major, when I arrived at the battery position. 'How are they? have they got over their childish display of petulance?'

'They called me a wagon line hero,' I said.

'Don't pay any attention to them,' he said. 'Everyone knows that's what Josh would like to be himself, a wagon line hero. He gives himself away by calling you one. But Edward has no right to talk to you in that way. He can say what he likes to me, but I won't have him making offensive remarks to my young officers, I'll give him a good talking-to the next time I see him.'

'Actually, it was only Josh who called me a wagon line hero,' I said. 'Edward wouldn't speak to me.'

'He'll be feeling better in the morning,' the Major said. 'There are some very good qualities in that boy, but he has no control over his temper. That's the only thing I have against him. He's always working himself up into a state about something or other of no importance. I've spoken to him about it, I wanted to help him. But it's no use, Master Edward always knows better than anyone else.'

He had left a hare that he had shot at the wagon lines for their lunch on the following day. He believed in heaping coals of fire, he said; turning the other cheek, all that sort of thing.

'I expect they'll be too proud to eat it,' Frank said. 'They'll probably give it to the servants.'

'Oh, don't you believe it,' the Major replied. 'They may tell us that's what they've done, but Josh is as fond of a good meal as anyone else, and so is Edward. You won't find either of them giving away good food.'

We had a very good dinner ourselves. There was a partridge for each of us, chipped potatoes and bread sauce, and two fresh vegetables. Medley had excelled himself, he enjoyed giving us a good meal as much as we enjoyed eating it. Major Fraser from across the road had been invited to come and share it with us.

Afterwards the two majors talked. They had seen the world, they did not just talk about shells and the bloodiness of war. Listening to them I almost forgot that I was sitting in a dug-out by the Bellewaardebeke, that shells were falling outside, and that to-morrow or the day after I might have to go up to Bank Farm again, or Plum Farm or Apple Villa or

92

some other evil place. I was very happy. It was a great deal more enjoyable to be sitting here where I was welcome, listening to the interesting conversation of the two majors, with Frank putting in an occasional remark, a great deal more enjoyable than I should have found it at Poperinghe with Edward and Josh, listening to their grumbles about the war and all the rest of us.

Major Fraser stayed till after midnight, and the Major went on talking for a long time after he had gone. 'The great thing,' he said, when we were going to bed at last, at some time between one and two o'clock, 'the great thing is to remember that we're civilised human beings. We know this, and we try to keep up a decent way of living. This is where we are more fortunate than people like Edward and Josh, who can't see further than their own noses. I'm sorry for them.'

He was awake and about again soon after seven o'clock, he never seemed to need much sleep. 'Six hours for a man, seven for a woman, eight for a fool,' he was fond of saying. He was still in very good spirits when he came back from visiting the men.

'I've a good mind to stay up here always,' he said. 'Those other two will soon get tired of kicking their heels at the wagon lines, and then they'll come begging us to change places with them.'

'Not Josh,' Frank said, 'he won't come. You'll live to be as old as Methuselah if you have to wait for him to come.'

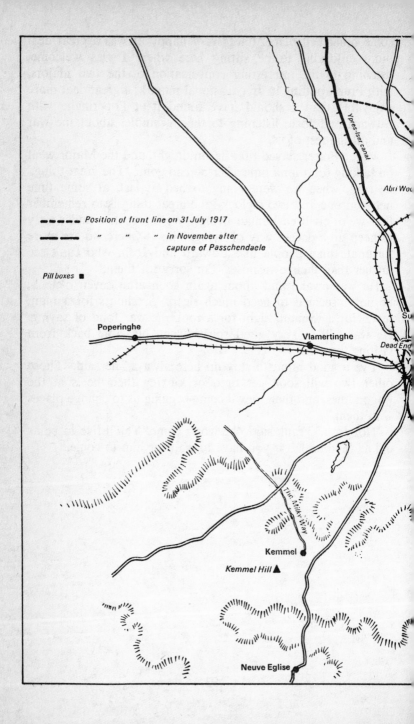

Position of front line on 31 July 1917

" " " in November after
capture of Passchendaele

Pill boxes ■

Poperinghe

Vlamertinghe

Ypres-Iser canal

Abri Wood

Su

Dead End

Y

The Milky Way

Kemmel

Kemmel Hill ▲

Neuve Eglise

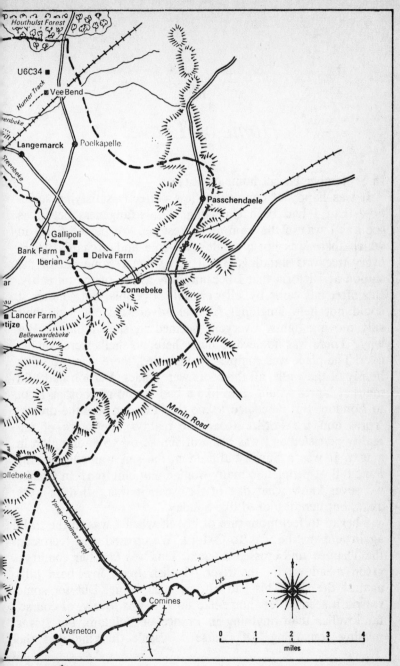

Houthulst Forest

U6C34

Hunter Track

Vee Bend

enbeke

Langemarck   Poelkapelle

Steenbeke

Passchendaele

Gallipoli

Bank Farm   Delva Farm
Iberian

ar

au

Lancer Farm

tijze

Bellewaardebeke

Zonnebeke

Menin Road

ollebeke

Ypres-Comines canal

Lys

Comines

Warneton

0   1   2   3   4
miles

D*

10

Home on Leave

In September I went home on leave.

It was happy of course, but less perfectly satisfying some-how than I had been expecting. The strangeness began as soon as I was in the train at Folkestone. We passed fields in which there was not a single shell-hole and orchards where every tree was standing. But it was when I came out of the station at Victoria that I became fully aware of the unreality. Bus after bus came by, all were full of people, not soldiers. I could not help laughing. All the advertisements with their silly moving lights. Everyone seemed in such a hurry. But why? There was no need to hurry here, no shells were coming over. The place was completely unshelled, there were no holes in any of the walls, all the roofs were intact. Vernon had told me that Ypres would seem like a bad dream as soon as I got to London. But it seemed to me that London was the dream, Ypres and the Potijze Road the reality. The sense of un-reality persisted as I was being driven across to Paddington in a taxi. It was a Sunday afternoon, the sun was shining, the Park full of people. So many women and children! In France we never knew what day of the week it was, all days were alike, but here it looked like Sunday.

I began to feel more sure of myself when I was in the train again and on the way to Oxford. We crossed and recrossed the Thames, and crossed it again. This was familiar country: green meadows by the river, English trees, low bare hills against the sky. This had always been home. But for some reason it seemed less home-like now. It was lovely, of course, far lovelier than anything in France or Belgium, but I was missing something. Of course I wasn't thinking that the

Potijze Road was my home now, that would have been absurd. But it was odd that I should be thinking so much about the others, and odd that I should not be going to see any of them for ten days.

It was wonderful when I arrived at home. Wonderful to feel so much happiness, and to give it, wonderful to be so perfectly loved. But the feeling of strangeness remained. On my subsequent leaves I was more successful, but on my first one I never completely succeeded in adjusting myself to the change. I was happy. I enjoyed the quietness, the luxury of sheets on my bed, the absence of fear. Above all I was happy in the love of my parents, but I had to try and conceal from them that I was missing something, that I could not put the men of C Battery out of my mind.

My parents wanted me to tell them everything about myself, everything that had happened since I went out, but there were some things I could not tell them. I could not make them understand. I could not tell them that I had become a different person myself. They might not have liked my new friends. If they could have understood, they would have liked them, but how could they understand when they had not been out there!

I enjoyed being with my young sister. She laughed with me, she did not ask me questions about the war, there was nothing she wanted to know about it. For her my leave was no more than a brother's home-coming, but for my parents I had returned from the gate of death and was due back there in less than a week's time.

And all the time I was thinking about the others, wondering whose turn it was to go up to the O.P. and what the shelling had been like today.

I took off my uniform and put on my own clothes, thinking that this would help me to remember where I was. But when I was in the town, a soldier, a corporal in the Oxford and Bucks, stopped to ask whether I didn't want to be out there, with all the other lads. I do not remember my reply, but a true answer would have been that I was there, not here in the middle of Oxford.

My parents took us, my sister and myself, to Brighton for

a few days. They thought the sea would help me to forget, but I did not really want to. Juliet, my pretty young cousin, who lived there, would have made a fuss of me, she always wanted to have me with her, and she asked me questions about everything. Was I always in danger? Had I ever been afraid? What was a battle like? Were Belgian girls as pretty as English ones? But she did not really want to know the answers and I did not want to tell her. She was talking to me because I was an officer in uniform, the only one there.

Then we returned to Oxford, and I to the front a few days later on the 8.50 am from Victoria, my parents watching forlornly on the platform until the train was out of sight.

Out at Rest

I found all the others at the wagon lines when I got back to Vlamertinghe. The Brigade had just come out of action.

'Thank God, you've come back on the right day!' Josh said as soon as I walked into the mess. 'I'd have cheerfully murdered you with my own hands if you hadn't.' He was waiting to go on leave himself, and could not go until after my return.

'You're lucky, you've done well for yourself,' Edward said. 'We're going out to Rest tomorrow.'

'We've had a pretty hectic time while you've been away,' Jack said. He told me the names of our casualties.

'We made another attack,' Frank said, 'but we stayed in the same place. How's Oxford?'

The Major wanted to know what shows I had seen in Town. I hadn't seen any. I told them I'd had a marvellous time, I'd enjoyed every minute of it. I did not say I was glad to be back, I did not know whether I was. But at any rate it was a relief to be only one person again, just a part of the B.E.F., no longer a mixture of two quite different people.

Josh rode off the next morning as soon as it was light. The leave train left at ten o'clock, but he had heard that the railway station at Poperinghe was being shelled by a long-range gun, and he wasn't taking any risks, he said. 'You won't find me sitting in a train that may be shelled,' he said, 'not with a leave warrant in my pocket.' He was going to join the train at a place further down the line, he was prepared to ride all the way to Boulogne if necessary.

'What's the betting that we never see him again?' the Major said to the rest of us at breakfast. 'I'll lay anyone odds of five to four against his ever coming back. Who'll take me? Fifty francs to forty against our ever seeing him again in this country.'

Edward took him.

We marched out to Rest after breakfast. We went a long way back, so far that we were almost out of range of the sound of the guns. We were billeted on a farm, we had a comfortable room in the house for the officers' mess, but our tents were in an orchard. By day so much was happening, and there were so many other noises on the farm, that we hardly noticed the sound of gunfire. Only in the early morning, when it was louder, we heard it; and sometimes again at night as we were falling asleep, and the noises of the day had ceased. The War was still there, that distant murmuring of the guns was no more than a threat and a reminder, but we should have to go back there again, we had only escaped for a little.

But for the moment we had escaped.

Football, battery sports, riding—these were our occupations now. I learnt that we had a very good football team, we played matches against the other batteries and one or two other teams that were resting in the same area, and did not lose any of them. I was now as proud of my battery as any of the others, and as sure that there was not a better one in France. None of the officers was nearly good enough to play in the football team, but we all took a keen interest in our matches. Sergeant Appleby, happily recovered from his wound, came into the mess in the evening, and he and the Major discussed the composition of our team before every match. Appleby was a beautiful player, he had played professionally before the war, I had never seen such skill. We could not lose, I thought, when Appleby was playing for us, so calm and confident and always with a smile on his face. Some of our other players were rough, tempers sometimes flared, there were arguments with the referee, but Appleby checked every outburst at once. He was indisputably in command. Even the Major took second place in the battery on the day of the match.

Riding was the Major's chief interest now. He told us on the first evening that he would expect all his officers to come out with him before breakfast every morning. Frank refused. He said that he had to risk his life every day in the line, but he was not going to do so when we were out at rest. He lay in bed jeering at Jack and myself, because he said we hadn't the courage to follow his example. The Major told us he was disappointed in him. The men liked to see their officers riding and jumping, he said; Frank thought it did not matter, but he was quite mistaken. 'I should say it's one of the things that matters most for an officer,' he said. 'Men will always follow an officer who's got the sporting spirit.'

Edward usually came with us, but Jack and I went out every morning, and often we were joined by some of the officers from the other batteries. Frank had been right in what he said about me, at first I should have preferred to stay in bed, I was frightened of following where the Major led us. But my riding improved. In England, in the riding-school, I had learnt how to hold on as well as most of the other cadets, and we had been taught the various tricks—jumping, and vaulting back into the saddle while running along beside our cantering horses. But it was the horses that had the skill.

Now for the first time I began to enjoy riding, and to make my horse go where I wanted her to go. I was not always successful, she was very powerful, sometimes she ran away with me still. But I was growing very fond of her, she was a beautiful light bay, and when officers in other batteries came to praise her good looks or her jumping I felt as proud as though the credit belonged to myself.

At first I fell off nearly every morning, but always after a fall I would find the Major waiting for me, and he would tell me what mistakes I had made. 'You rushed that one,' he usually said. 'You didn't hold her in, you've got to take charge, you know—you're the man.' Sometimes he would say it was her fault, not mine. 'Look at her face when you get up,' he said. 'If she's got a dirty face, then you needn't blame yourself.'

Before our rest came to an end I was hardly falling off at all.

The Major was making a steeplechase course, we all knew

101

there was to be a great race meeting, open to all the brigade, before we went back into the line. The Major himself was a good rider, but not as good as he would like to have been. Major Cecil, our former captain, was a better one. Edward rode with more courage than skill, Josh was too heavy, Jack and I were both too nervous to make good riders.

'You'll enter for the race, of course,' the Major said to me. 'You ought to have a very good chance on that big mare of yours, there's nothing she can't jump.'

I did not want to go in for it, the jumps were frightening, but I seemed to have won the Major's good opinion and did not want to lose it. There were to be half a dozen races altogether, but the Officers' Open Chase was the big event of the day. Everyone from the Colonel downwards would be there to watch, and I dreaded the thought of making a fool of myself in front of the whole brigade. The Major himself was one of the favourites.

Josh had come back just in time for the great day, only a week later than he should have been. He had been ill, he said, but none of us believed him. So the Major had lost his bet with Edward, but for the moment nothing mattered except the race. Jack scratched his entry, he said Dolly had injured her fetlock, but no one else had noticed her limping. I spent a very uncomfortable morning, as nervous as on the evening before a battle. But the Major said a little nervousness beforehand was not a bad thing, it meant that all one's powers were alerted.

Josh was making a book on the race. Frank worked out the odds for him. Sergeant Denmark told me he had put ten francs on me for the honour of the Left Section.

'I didn't think you were so daft,' I said, using his own favourite word.

'You needn't be afraid of anyone on Theodora,' he said.

'She's all right,' I agreed, 'it's the man on her back who's no good.' He told me to hold her in before taking each jump. 'Don't let her rush them,' he said.

The race was a disaster for the battery. The Major came off at the second fence, he said one of the other riders had bored him as they were coming up to it. I went round the first time safely, but then fell off just as I was beginning to think how easy it was and when I was running third or fourth, not far behind the leaders. Edward finished the course, but was unplaced. The race was won by an outsider. Major Cecil, the favourite, finished fourth. Josh cleared five hundred francs, more than a month's pay, he was the only one of us to derive any satisfaction from the race.

It was an unpopular result in the battery, and the Major was in a black mood that night. 'Just like he is after a battle.' Jack said. 'We might as well be up in the line.' He and I had come out to our tent in the orchard because he was making himself so disagreeable in the mess.

But presently Josh came out to us and told us that we could go back. 'He's all right now,' he said.

What had really upset him, Josh said, was the fact that he had made so much money. And he hadn't liked having to pay Edward fifty francs because he had returned from leave. 'He thinks Edward nobbled me,' he said. 'Silly chump! If he had told me beforehand what he was going to do, I might have done something about it.'

But everything was all right now. Josh had said he was going to celebrate, he was going to spend all his winnings on a tip-top dinner for us all in Cassel or somewhere. We would paint the place red, he said. 'That's bucked him up,' Josh said. 'Now he's beginning to see the funny side of this afternoon. It was damned funny.'

I had other lessons to learn besides riding.

Jack asked me one afternoon to ride with him into the little town. He wanted to do some shopping, he said; and he had found a place where there were two very pretty sisters. I was not interested in what he said about pretty sisters, but I knew that I should enjoy his companionship on the ride.

I changed my mind, however, when I saw Suzanne. She was very beautiful. I had not expected anyone so attractive or so young. She looked about sixteen. In England a girl of her age would have been at school still, and as shy as myself; we

103

should have found nothing to say to each other. But Suzanne began talking at once, she talked to me, I did not have to think what to say to her, she spoke in a mixture of French and English which sounded more enchanting than any language I had ever heard; and when she smiled at me I could think of nothing except how to make her smile again. I moved closer to her, I could not take my eyes off her face.

She was talking to me about myself. How cruel it was, she said, that one so young should have to fight. I was a brave English soldier, but all English soldiers were brave. She did not know what would have happened to herself and her family and all the people of France if it had not been for the brave English soldiers.

I asked her to speak more slowly. How I wished that my French was better: It had seemed a waste of time at school to learn French, now I could see the reason for learning it. She laughed at my pronunciation of her language, she spoke with exaggerated slowness, smiling between every word, her eyes shining. I was enraptured by her loveliness. And she was still talking to me about myself, as though I was the only person that mattered to her. We had come back to recover ourselves after the trenches, she said; she could see how much I had suffered, my suffering showed in my eyes; but I was brave, I pretended it was not difficult; she did not know how anyone was able to endure so great hardships and dangers.

Jack meanwhile was talking to the elder sister. She was not at all pretty, I thought; and I wondered that anyone should want to look at another girl when Suzanne was in the same room, but he seemed content. Jack was better at French than I was, he was talking quite easily, but I was not listening to what he said. All my attention was centred on Suzanne. She was talking at her ordinary speed again, and I understood only a few words of what she was saying. But it did not matter. I only wanted to look at her. I smiled at her, pretending that I understood what she was saying. She smiled back at me. There was nothing else in the world that mattered but that she should go on smiling and looking at me.

Before we left I bought an expensive silk handkerchief from her. I did not want it. There was nothing in the little souvenir shop that I did want, a handkerchief would do as well as anything else. I wanted to buy something from her, I thought that our hands might touch when she gave it me.

But a much more wonderful thing happened. She put the handkerchief into an envelope for me, and as she did so a little box slipped down and fell on to the counter between us. I moved to pick it up and put it back in its place, she gave me my envelope at the same moment, and a lock of her hair brushed against my cheek as we moved. It was only for an instant, it was so slight that I might not have known anything had touched me, but it was a lock of a girl's hair. The girl was Suzanne, who was more beautiful than anyone I had ever seen.

I was not conscious of anything else. We left the shop. We were riding back to camp. Jack was talking, but I did not know what he was saying. Suzanne's hair had touched my cheek. The world was more beautiful than I had ever imagined. Nothing like this had ever happened to me before. A bird was singing, but the bird was my own joy. A girl's hair had touched me. My cheek had felt the electric touch. Sing, sing for joy.

'We must go there again,' Jack said, when we had dismounted and our grooms had led the horses away. 'You seemed to be getting on well with Suzanne. There's sometimes an old dragon of a mother in the shop, but we were lucky this afternoon.'

I did go there again, but I went alone and I waited for an evening when all the others were out. Then I took the battery bicycle, I did not want to have my groom with me, no one should know where I was going, and I rode along the dusty paved road to the little town.

I was lucky, or so I thought, for I found Suzanne alone in the shop. This was more than I had dared to hope for, and I had been wondering how to get her to myself. She remembered me and seemed pleased to see me, she smiled again and spoke in her lovely mixture of English and French. She was so beautiful that I would have spent all the money I had in buying bits of lace or postcards or candlesticks that I should have no use for in the line.

But after a few minutes her manner changed. She stopped smiling, she answered my questions monosyllabically, like an English girl, she moved further away from me. She was much cleverer than I was. I did not know what was in her mind, but she knew what was in mine. Girls are quicker than boys, they learn to look after themselves, they are not so defenceless. All my knowledge came out of books, she knew what life was, and how to deal with a situation that was not to her liking.

I realised I was doing badly this time, and I lost my head. I made the mistake that the Major was always warning me against—I rushed my fence and took a bad fall in consequence.

'Mademoiselle,' I said appealingly, 'we are going back to the war.'

I was lying to her, we were not going back, there was no talk of our going back yet, but I wanted to win her compassion, I wanted so desperately to kiss her.

I moved towards her and tried to put my arm round her, but she was much too quick for me, she ran away before I could touch her. There was a door leading out of the shop into the rest of the house, and she ran to it and stood there, holding the handle of the door, ready to open it if I took a step towards her.

And she would have opened it, she would have called her sister or the old mother Jack had told me about. I was utterly defeated. I was terrified of an angry woman. I could endure shellfire, but not the contempt of a girl or the anger of her mother.

But I tried once more. I had heard Jack say it was the easiest thing in the world to kiss a girl. It was what they wanted, he said. They wanted to be kissed even more than we wanted to kiss them. I moved one foot towards her, I so longed to kiss her or at any rate to touch her hand or her hair.

'Mademoiselle,' I said, 'Je suis triste.'

But she made no reply, she only shook her head and put a finger to her lips.

I went out of the shop. I was still hoping she would call me back or at least say good-bye, but she made no sound or movement.

I felt angry and ashamed of myself, not for having tried to kiss her, but for having failed.

I had completely failed. I had got into the habit of rather looking down on Jack. I liked him very much, but I thought I was a better soldier than he was, and therefore a better man. But he could do what I was unable to do, and at that moment there was nothing in the world I so much wanted as to kiss or to have kissed Suzanne.

How I wished I had taken a lesson from Juliet in Brighton!

I had a wretched ride back to camp. Only a few days ago I had been so ecstatically happy, a door had been opened and I had seen a new heaven and a new earth; now it had been slammed in my face and I no longer believed in the beauty on the other side of the door. My pride was bitterly hurt, and I was afraid of being laughed at. For the others would certainly get to know what had happened, Jack was sure to go to the town again and Suzanne or her sister would tell him, and he would tell the others.

Josh was the one whose mockery I particularly dreaded when he got to hear. He was always making fun of my youth and innocence. 'Here comes our cock virgin,' he sometimes said. Once he had introduced me in this way to two stranger officers he had invited into the mess. 'Take a good look at him,' he said, 'he's the only one in France.' And at the thought of the mockery I should have to endure I wished I had never seen Suzanne. She had given me a moment's happiness, but it was not worth the price I should have to pay for it.

But the story never became known. Either Suzanne did not tell, or Jack kept quiet about it, and I was grateful to whoever it was. Gradually the bitterness of my disappointment lessened, and I was glad that I had seen Suzanne. I still remembered my extreme unhappiness at the moment of leaving her, I saw her so clearly standing against the door, unsmiling, ready to open it, with her finger against her lips. But I remembered her beauty also, and the exhilaration of the moment when her hair had touched my cheek. I had been angry with her, I thought she had given me nothing, but I was mistaken—her gift was one that I never lost.

Our Rest went on. We never had such a long one again. And up in the line so did the battle. The September attacks were more successful than the August ones had been.

'They seem to do better without us,' Frank said.

'Someone should tell them so,' said the Major, 'then perhaps they'll leave us here for the duration.'

I applied for four days leave in Paris, and it was granted.

12

Paris

'I only know one reason for going to Paris,' Josh said, 'why do you want to go?'

'I want to see the sights,' I said.

'At your age you ought to know nothing about them,' he mocked.

Two other officers in the brigade went there at the same time, Major Fraser of A Battery and Jamieson, a big Australian in B. Major Fraser was a very good officer and the Colonel's favourite, but he kept aloof from the rest of us. He stayed at the most expensive hotel in Paris, Jamieson and I were content with the second most expensive one. But we all three met together for a drink once a day.

Paris intoxicated me.

It was unlike any place I had seen or thought of. The leaves were beginning to fall in the boulevards, but it was still warm enough to sit outside, drinking coffee or sipping an aperitif, and watching the world go past us. This was a world with which I was altogether unfamiliar, and yet I felt at home there, more at home than in London, in spite of all the blue uniforms of French soldiers. Blue uniforms and well-dressed attractive women, there was so much colour, none of the drabness I had seen in London.

Jamieson helped me to feel at home, he gave me a sense of security in this new world. He was several years older than myself and up to this time I had seen little of him. I knew that Vernon liked him, and he and Edward had the reputation of being the best poker players in the brigade, though they were very unlike, Edward young, impulsive, enthusiastic, Jamieson impassive and unsmiling. Both were equally ruthless, that was the resemblance between them, and they were calm in the moment of danger.

Now I made friends with Jamieson. He spoke in a drawling voice that probably showed where he came from, but he never talked about Australia. Nothing ever surprised him, nothing aroused his enthusiasm, but he missed nothing.

'They're all in the profession,' he said disparagingly, noticing my look of admiration for some women who had just passed us.

I was astonished.

'I thought women of that sort always looked old,' I said.

'Not in a place like this,' he replied. 'They wouldn't get any clients if they did.'

'But they look nice people,' I protested.

'Why shouldn't they be? They're doing a useful job.'

'What happens to them when they do grow old?' I asked.

He shrugged his shoulders. 'Some make good marriages and settle down,' he said. 'Some of them don't.'

I was interested and puzzled. I had never seen prostitutes before, or not knowingly, or only in towns down the line— Havre or Boulogne—where they certainly did look old and were without any physical attraction for me. If all prostitutes were old and ugly, then one could just feel sorry for them, nothing else. But if these women were prostitutes, the matter was not so simple as I had supposed.

Two very attractive women came into our restaurant one evening and sat down at a table near us. One of them was especially beautiful, I had noticed her before and was pleased to see her again and that she should have happened to come so near us. I looked at her as often as I could, trying not to be seen to do so. She was not like Suzanne, she was older, her face lacked Suzanne's gaiety, her eyes did not smile. I did not want to touch her or make her smile at me, my feeling for her was altogether different, I just wanted to look at Helen of Troy, I thought.

'She's one of them,' Jamieson said.

'Oh, she can't be,' I said. I had never seen anyone who looked more queen-like.

110

'I ought to know,' he replied. 'I have the best possible reason for knowing.'

The next morning he told me that Major Fraser had laid a proposition before him. It concerned myself, he said. The Major had a friend in Paris, Jamieson told me; and if I liked, she would provide me with a companion who would be perfectly safe. The Major thought I might not realise how great the risk was; that was why he was making the suggestion; he stressed the fact that I need feel no anxiety whatever with his friend's friend. And the cost would only be two hundred francs.

Only!

Two hundred francs was a lot of money for a junior officer. But I had spent so much already that another two hundred would not have made much difference, and there would be nothing to spend money on when we went back into the line. But I had no desire to accept the offer. To want to kiss Suzanne was one thing. I had seen her, I knew how attractive she was. But to go to bed with a woman I had not seen was a different matter altogether. I never considered the possibility of acceptance.

'Please thank him,' I heard myself saying, 'but I don't think I want to.'

'I didn't think you would,' Jamieson said.

But I did buy some postcards of girls to pin up on the earth wall beside my bed when we went back into the line. I knew my parents would have been distressed to see what I was doing and this made me feel uncomfortable, but the pictures would help me to sleep and that was important.

We left Paris on the evening of the following day. I was not sorry to go, I had had enough of it. Another day or two of such luxurious living and I might not have wanted to return to the hardship and danger of the line.

On our last afternoon we visited Napoleon's tomb. I was impressed by the number of other soldiers there, and by the variety of their uniforms—there seemed to be men from every one of the allied nations. In my new enthusiasm for France I thought it was right that men should have come from every far corner of the earth to pay respect to the greatest of all soldiers. But Jamieson, the Australian, interrupted my thoughts: 'It was a good thing we beat him,' he said, 'they're an unstable lot.'

Major Fraser returned before us. The brigade had gone back into the line, we were all recalled by telegram, but Jamieson and I arranged to miss the afternoon train and hoped that the Major would have done the same. We had some difficulty in finding where the brigade was, but none in explaining about the train, Jamieson was always convincing. The brigade had not gone back to the same part of the line, we were further north, on the left flank of the British Army, the French were next to us, then the Belgians, then the sea. A different part of the line, but the same battle, the same mud, the same prospect of casualties—another attack was to be made in a few days.

The others were all in low spirits when I returned, and the mud at the wagon lines was awful. Frank was depressed because there had been no mail for three days, Jack and Josh because we were returning to the line, to fight more battles. But I sensed that something had happened while I was away to account for the general gloom. No one was in the mood to talk, the Major had gone home on leave, Edward was up with the guns by himself. Josh asked me if I was still what I had been, and I told him of Major Fraser's suggestion, expecting he would call me a damned fool for not accepting. But to my surprise he was indignant with Major Fraser. 'That's not the right way at all,' he said, 'he ought not to have suggested it.'

I was astonished. I suddenly realised that Josh liked me, liked me as I was, in spite of all his mockery. For a moment I thought of telling him about Suzanne, I wanted him to know that I was as much attracted by a pretty girl as anyone else. But I didn't. I wondered, however, what he thought was the right way. I liked Frank's way. He was miserable because there had been no letter for him for three days. I thought I should enjoy having a similar reason for misery.

Back in the Mud

Josh and I rode up to the gun line the next morning. Edward was as taciturn as the others had been. But there were two special officer-tasks for the battery, he told us: a dawn-to-dusk job at the O.P. and a 24-hour liaison duty with the infantry.

'Better toss up,' he said.

'I don't mind doing the O.P.' Josh said, 'If you would prefer the liaison.' I ought to have suspected that he had obtained fuller information, that he already knew the O.P. was nearly three miles behind the line and the infantry battalion head-quarters practically in it. But even if we had tossed and I had won I might have chosen the liaison duty. All the others could kiss girls, I couldn't. I had to show myself that there were some ways in which I was better, that I was less afraid of danger.

I set off with two signallers immediately after lunch. On this occasion and always afterwards when I had to cross over the wastes of death I divided the way into four parts. The guns were in a reserve position at Abri Wood, where they did no firing, and from there to the Steenbeke, a distance of about a thousand yards, it was comparatively simple. We came under fire at once, but no shells fell dangerously close, and there were other soldiers in sight all the time and shelters to run to if necessary. The second stage, from the Steenbeke to the Broenbeke, was worse. It was always difficult getting across the Steenbeke. There were a lot of guns in the shallow valley, the enemy knew this and shelled it by day and by night. One had to wait at the top of the declivity, wait for a lull, and then go quickly. The third stage, after the Broenbeke, was easier in one respect because there was a duckboard track laid over or round the shell-holes. I tried not to look at the dead men. There had been heavy fighting in the last ten days, we had made a considerable advance, but at great cost. The ground was littered with the bodies of the dead, Germans, English, French. 'They're all here,' one of my signallers remarked, 'you can take your choice.' How many others there may have been under the water in the shell-holes I could not tell, but there were very many that I did see. A few were still recognisable in death, they might almost have been sleeping. I was grateful to them for looking alive.

The last stage was the worst of all, though there was less shellfire as one came closer to the line. This was always the part I dreaded. We were in view of the enemy, his eyes were on us. It was quite flat, there was no cover of any kind, there was no one else in sight, there was nothing to see. A few pill-boxes, thousands of shell-holes, full or half full of water. Nothing else close at hand, but in the distance, a mile away, was a dark line between the sky and the bare desert of mud. That was the Houthulst Forest, all of which was still in German hands. That was where the enemy eyes were.

I always had a feeling of being watched, that a German gunner had his gun trained on a certain point of the track and was waiting for me to get there. So strong was the feeling that sometimes I left the comparative security of the duck-boards, where at any rate one was safe from drowning, and walked across the mud.

We came to our journey's end, the headquarters of the infantry battalion holding the line. It was in one of the captured pill-boxes, Louvois Farm. The French had named many of these. The liaison officer's duty was to stay with the infantry, make friends with the officers at H.Q., bring fire to bear on any targets they gave him, and sometimes to investigate a complaint of short shooting. It was good for us, the gunners, to see how much better off we were, and nearly always I got on very well with all the officers I met from the Colonel downwards. There was always a telephone line at H.Q., so that I was in touch with Cherry and could pass on to him any message from the infantry colonel.

My 24-hour tour of duty passed slowly, but without incident;

I was relieved by another officer in the brigade in the early afternoon, and was always much happier going down than I had been coming up. Crossing the Steenbeke I met Major Fraser. The old Etonian was the best-dressed officer in the brigade, perhaps the only one who took any trouble over his appearance, but now he was unshaven and haggard and mud-splashed from head to foot, but he smiled at me wanly. 'I think we've met before,' he said, 'a place called Paris.' He told me he was on his way to a meeting of battery commanders with Colonel Richardson.

Edward also had gone to attend the meeting, and while we were by ourselves Josh told me what had happened while I was in Paris. There had been another flaming row between the Major and Edward. 'No one seems to know what it was about,' Josh said. 'I told them both they were behaving like silly school kids, but I couldn't stop them, and the very next day there was this order about medical students being allowed to go home to finish their training, and Edward at once said he was going. He wishes now that he hadn't, he doesn't want to leave the battery, but he'd be a fool not to go. His brother in the R.F.C. has just been killed, so he thinks he ought to go home for the sake of his parents as much as for himself.'

14

Vee Bend

A few days later we were given our preliminary orders for the attack.

On X-Day we were to establish a new O.P. in a much more advanced position than the one Josh had been to and on the following day, the day before the attack, C and D Batteries were to move from Abri Wood up to the Broenbeke. A and B were not going so far forward, they were going to the Wijden-drift, nearly a mile behind us.

Edward told me to be responsible for the new O.P. I was to get up at half past six and find my way to it. A telephone line had already been laid, Cherry had told him, but there might be a few breaks in it.

I set off immediately after breakfast. My signallers mended forty or fifty breaks, under fire all morning. Then they told me it would be quicker and more satisfactory to lay out a new line instead of patching up the old one. Soon after midday they had completed the task and I was at 'Vee Bend', the new O.P. It was not far from Louvois Farm, where I had gone to do liaison duty, a little further back, but within sight of it, and facing the sinister Houthulst Forest. There was a good pill-box, that was what mattered. I had eight signallers with me, two of my own and two from each of the other batteries. One was wounded before the end of the day.

I found some confusion when I returned. The Colonel had changed his mind. Because of Edward's youth he decided to send B Battery to the Broenbeke and to give us the supposedly easier position further back. Edward was furious. 'I won't have anyone saying I'm too young,' he said to the

116

Colonel, and persuaded him to stick to his original plan. But Frank, in charge of the wagon lines, a long way back and in communication only by mounted orderly, heard of the first alteration but not of the second. Thinking that the guns were to move a comparatively short distance he had sent out all the teams to bring back a big supply of ammunition. This had exhausted the horses and when he heard that the guns, after all, were to make the longer advance, he had ridden up to tell Edward that the horses might not be able to achieve it. He explained that he had acted from the best of motives because he knew how much ammunition the guns would require. Edward was angrier than ever. 'You've no business to think,' he said to Frank, 'you take your orders from me. I promised the Colonel I could get my guns up and now you're letting me down.'

I was sorry for Frank. Jack told me that Edward had been bloody rude to him. But Frank said Edward's anger was justified, although it was not his fault. Getting the guns up to the right place was the only thing that mattered.

However it was all right. Frank came up again very early the next morning with the limbers and firing battery wagons and teams of eight horses instead of six. The mud was appalling. But the horses were rested and whenever we came to a particularly bad place the gunners got down and pulled on the wheels, the horses strained on their traces, and soon after twelve o'clock the guns were in position by the side of the Broenbeke, ready to fire, teams and wagons were on their way back and we had not suffered a single casualty. All the way along we had passed abandoned wagons. Some had been destroyed by shellfire, others had skidded into the swamp at the side of the road and could not be pulled out. I saw some unfortunate mules being shot because they could not be got out.

We had a quick meal and then Edward said he wanted me to take him up to the new O.P. so that he could register the guns. On our way there he told me we were to provide a Forward Observing Officer for the attack on the next morning. He was to be at the O.P. before Zero Hour, and it would have to be myself because I was the only officer who knew where

117

it was. I was fed up. I thought it was time Jack or Josh did something, everything was being put on to me, one of them could have come with us now to find out the way to Vee Bend. Besides, I knew it would be a dangerous job and I had a particular reason for not wanting to go into danger at this time. We were all superstitious and someone had lit three cigarettes with one match a day or two before. He had tried to light four, but the match had burnt his fingers and gone out. My cigarette had been the third. I had told myself that if I could survive three days I should have expiated the bad luck, but tomorrow would only be the third day. Moreover, it would be exactly three years since the death of my brother, and that was the sort of trick fate liked to play, to have two brothers killed on the same day. We got up to Vee Bend during a lull, but the enemy began shelling again at once. I wanted to take cover inside the pill-box, but Edward was in a hurry to do the registration. If we waited it might be too dark to see where our shells were bursting, he said. The registration was done and we started to return along the duckboard track by which we had come up. "Hunter Track" it was called. Almost at once we heard an aeroplane behind us. It was a Boche, he was flying low above the track, firing his machine-gun.

'Oh hell,' said Edward. 'Damn and blast him!'

Edward was frightened. I had never seen him frightened before. I was so surprised that I did not immediately follow his example and drop into one of the shell-holes beside the track. 'Get down, you damned fool!' he said. We lay very still, pressing our faces to the earth. I heard bullets singing through the air and plopping into the mud. The Boche flew out of sight, then turned round and came back again, still firing. 'Where are our bloody airmen?' Edward said. 'Why the hell do they let the Boche have it all his own way?' He supposed they had all gone back to get their tea. But neither of us was hit. For some reason I was not especially frightened, perhaps because I was angry with Edward, angry for putting all the jobs on me, angry because he was going away, it would be like a brother leaving the family.

We returned to the Broenbeke together. There I read very

118

carefully all the orders that concerned myself for the following day, before going back to Abri Wood where, at any rate, I thought, I can be sure of a good night's sleep before I set off. I was frightened now, and very tired.

But I hardly slept at all. Zero Hour was at 5.35. I told the signallers to call me at two o'clock. But I was uneasy, I was afraid of oversleeping, I kept my boots on to prevent myself from being too comfortable. Gas shells were falling outside, they made an altogether different sound from high explosive. What a damned nuisance, I thought, we shall have to wear our masks. That will make us slower and it will be harder to see. It was a relief to hear the signaller outside groping his way in the darkness. 'Five minutes to two, Sir,' he said, raising the gas curtain, 'and there's gas about.' I got up at once and we left within a few minutes. The shellfire had stopped, but there was a strong smell of mustard gas and we had to put on our masks. It was drizzling. I should have to wear my heavy coat and I knew it would make me sweat like a pig and tire me. In front of us as we walked, the sky was red and this helped me to keep direction. It looked as though one of our airmen had found something inflammable behind the fringe of the Houthulst Forest.

Halfway up I was to meet the other F.O.O. Garnett of A Battery was coming with me. A and ourselves were rivals. Each of us thought our own the best battery in the brigade, and we took some satisfaction in disparaging their officers, except Major Fraser whom everyone liked and admired. Garnett, we said, was a medal hunter and not so brave as he pretended to be. He annoyed me as soon as we met. 'Checked all your equipment?' he asked. What the hell had it got to do with him whether I had checked my signallers' equipment? In our battery we knew our signallers could be depended on to check their own. Perhaps he thought that because he was in A he was in charge of the whole party, my signallers as well as his own. Then he said 'You know the way, I'm told. You lead, I'll follow you.' They all talked as though I was the only man in the army who knew the way to Vee Bend. Worse was to come. We started to talk about our job and it was clear to me from what he said that he intended to do all the going out to

119

collect information, I was merely to send back his information. This was ridiculous, it did not require an officer to send back information over the telephone. I had seen nothing in the orders to suggest that he should be the only one to go out. We ought to take it in turns or else go together as Vernon and I had done at Bank Farm. But he said Major Fraser had made it quite clear to him that he alone was responsible for obtaining the information. Obviously, I thought, he wants to get all the credit for whatever we do, I was just to be the telephonist. Well, if he wanted to go out all the time I would let him, I had no wish to go out in front of Vee Bend, I had been there and knew what it was like.

When we came to Vee Bend I was dismayed at first to find the pill-box full of infantrymen who were obviously going to take part in the second wave of the attack. I had to explain that it was an artillery O.P. The Officer in charge offered to take all his men outside. 'Not bloody likely,' I said, 'there's room for us all.' I was certain the place would be heavily shelled as soon as our bombardment began. We waited inside until a few minutes before 5.35, then went out. Garnett said we must be prepared for any eventuality. He spoke to Cherry on the phone, told him we were in readiness and that he was going out in front as soon as it was light enough to see. He told me that the Colonel had said it would be a good show, we had learnt how to overcome the enemy's defensive system.

The barrage opened behind us, the rockets went up in front, the German guns replied. Garnett went off to obtain his information and I waited outside the pill-box.

Some wounded men came past me, the walking wounded. They had nothing to tell. Then a few prisoners. Very few. Then I saw a Staff Officer going up towards the front line, a real Staff Officer with red tabs on his collar. I had never seen a Staff Officer so near the line on the day of a battle. Then Garnett came back. I had not expected to see him so soon, he had taken a telephone out with him and was to relay his information back to me. But his signaller had not taken enough wire, he said. It was strange that he shouldn't have checked it, I thought. He said that first reports were satis-

P. J. Campbell in 1917
before going out to France

At Watou in 1917

The author on Lady

An 18-pounder gun in action

The Cloth Hall, Ypres, taken by the author in 1919

ee Bend where the Observation Post was.
aken by the author in 1919

The March Retreat, 1918. The stores and huts had been set on fire to prevent their falling into German hands

Troops moving up for an attack on the Hindenburg Line, 1918

factory, but enemy shellfire was heavy. I could have told him that it would be. Then he went out again.

I saw the Staff Officer returning. He came across to where I was standing and asked me if our telephone line was working. I told him that it was.

'Then it's the only one that is,' he said.

'We have good signallers, Sir,' I said.

He was not only a brave officer, but a very capable one, and he had found out more about the attack than Garnett had. I listened to the report he was making on the telephone, and it was clear to me that the attack was not going well.

Garnett admitted this when he came back for the second time. The conditions up there were terrible, he said. He had never seen anything like it. The mud and the water in the shell-holes! There were no trenches, there was no front line, he said. The men were just lying in shell-holes—some of them seemed to have stayed in their holes instead of going out to attack.

Not that he had been up to the front himself. He admitted that he hadn't. 'You can't get there,' he said. 'What with the mud and the sniping.' And it was very difficult to find out what was happening, he said, we had gained some ground but probably not very much. We each ate a bully-beef sandwich. Then he went out again.

He went out half a dozen times during the morning. Each time he returned sooner than before and stayed longer inside the pill-box before going out again. I was beginning to like him. I certainly disliked him less than I had at the beginning of the day.

'I'll go out next time,' I said.

He protested. 'I don't see why you should do my job for me,' he said. But there was no conviction in his voice, he was quite willing now to let me go instead. It was quieter, enemy shellfire was only sporadic by this time. If I went out once I should satisfy my conscience, I could find out for myself what was known about the result of our attack, and whether there was anything for the artillery to do. Then perhaps we need neither of us go out again, we could relax.

Taking one signaller with me I set out. There was a pill-box in front of us, about half a mile away. Garnett had not been there, but it was certain to be a headquarters of some kind, I should find someone there who could give me information. That was where I should go. Inside our pill-box I had forgotten my superstitious fears of the previous day, but they returned as soon as I came out and began to move across the dreadful and deserted waste. It was deserted, there was no living creature within sight. Between ourselves and the low concrete rectangular block I was aiming for there was nothing to be seen except mud, shell-holes, and water. We floundered through the mud, slipping, stumbling, trying to avoid the bigger holes and deeper pools, and with every step safety was receding, danger coming closer. All the trees at the edge of the Houthulst Forest had been destroyed, they were no more than gaunt stumps. No enemy could be hiding behind them but, beyond the stumps, the forest was darker, I just saw a dark mass. That was where the Eyes were, the Watching Eyes. All the time we were moving nearer to them, nearer, nearer. But it was the quiet time of day. Some of our own guns behind us were firing, I heard the sound of their shells passing overhead; and a few German shells burst within sight, but none fell near us.

Bending low, to make myself a smaller target, looking down for the best place to fall if I heard a near one coming, I began to hope. We were closer now to the grey block than we had been when we started. I could count on four or five seconds' warning, time enough to fall.

Four or five seconds! I got no warning at all. We were half-way across when it happened. I saw a hole opening between my feet, water and mud leaping away, I heard the scream of the oncoming shell and the blast of its detonation in the same instant. We were blown to the ground, muddy water splashed down on us from every side, but the swamp saved our lives, it smothered the shell's explosion, we were not hit. We got up and staggered on, neither of us speaking. I stopped under the wall of the pill-box and opened my mouth to speak, but no words came out, only meaningless sounds. There was a flask half full of neat whisky in my hip pocket, I took it out and swallowed a mouthful, then passed it to my signaller who did the same. It may have been a chance shell, fired at random, but there were no others and I believe we had been seen by an observer in the dark forest, an observer in communication with a high velocity gun firing a shell that travelled as quickly as sound.

I went round the corner and into the pill-box. My voice was still not wholly under control, but my questions to the officers inside—the headquarters staff of an infantry battalion —were intelligible, as were their answers.

No, they had gained very little ground, and there was no possibility of their making another attack that day.

Yes, they could show me on the map more or less where our line was.

No, there was nothing the artillery could do for them.

Yes, their casualties had been heavy.

One of them offered me a drink, but I knew they would need all that they had. I should be going back when night came, they would have to stay.

We went back as we had come. Nothing happened to us. I had decided not to tell Garnett about our narrow escape from death. Everyone had narrow escapes, no one was really interested in those of another person, we always thought he was exaggerating. Garnett came out to meet us.

'My God!' he said. 'Are you all right?' He had been watching us from the back of the pill-box, he had seen the shell burst, we had been completely enveloped in its black smoke.

'It was like a miracle when you came out of the smoke,' he said. 'I should never have forgiven myself if anything had happened to you.'

He talked as though he had been personally responsible for our near obliteration. I was touched by his solicitude on my behalf. He insisted on my going inside the pill-box and sitting down. He kept on saying how selfishly he had behaved. I couldn't help thinking that his care for me gave him an excuse for staying inside the pill-box himself, but he had suddenly become human, now I could talk to him. I realised that he was not a medal hunter, he was simply a very conscientious soldier without much sense of humour. He admitted that he had been frightened nearly out of his life in the morning, I told him I had been so frightened that I could not speak. We agreed that we could not go out again, that our legs would not take us.

We were to stay out until dusk, but if I had been by myself it would have been dusk at half past four. I wanted to suggest to Garnett that we should go, but we stayed for another hour or longer. We stood outside together, watching the light fade over the dreary wilderness. 'There might be an S.O.S.' Garnett said. 'There often is after an attack, we may be the only people looking out for it.' But darkness came down, no lights went up, the battle was over—for that day.

But even then Garnett was reluctant to leave. 'There ought to be somebody up here by night as well as by day,' he said. 'I've a good mind to ring up Cherry and suggest it, and say that I'll stay here until he sends someone up to relieve me. There's no need for us both to stay, you go without me.'

I said that if the Colonel wanted the O.P. to be manned all night, Cherry would already have arranged for someone to come out. But he did not feel sure of this. 'They're slack, you know,' he said. 'They don't take their responsibilities so seriously as you and I would if we were in their shoes. They really need someone to ginger them up.'

I couldn't bear the thought of his suggesting that another duty should be added to those we already had, and in the end I persuaded him to return with me.

'I'll have a word with Major Fraser when I get back,' he said, 'and see what he thinks.'

We walked back in single file along the duckboard track, stopping when we came to the Broenbeke and separating, I to go to my battery, he to his at the top of the higher ground between the streams.

'I should never have forgiven myself if anything had happened to you,' he said again. 'I shan't forget today.'

I thought it was probable that I should not forget it either, but he meant that he thought I was almost good enough to serve in A Battery.

Edward told me that he did not need me up at the guns, and that I had better go back to Abri Wood. I should find Josh there also, he said; he wanted Josh in the morning, but I could stay there for another day and night. 'You've got some sleep to make up,' he said.

I could hardly get back to Abri Wood, I was nearly finished.

'Come on, old boy,' Josh said, 'there's a tiptop dinner waiting for us.'

For the first time in a week I enjoyed eating. I enjoyed sitting down. I enjoyed feeling safe.

'Now you look more like your mother's son,' Josh said when the meal was over. 'Scrape off some of the dirt, and she might recognise you.'

I fell asleep. Josh said afterwards that he and the servants had carried me to bed and then undressed me. I stayed in bed half the next day.

I was reading "Framley Parsonage" and enjoying it very much. It described such a peaceful existence. The hero put his name to a bill and got into financial trouble, but that could not be so bad, I thought, as being F.O.O. on the day of an attack. Putting your name to a bill—I could only guess what it meant, but I did know what the other was. And one day, please God!, we should return to a similarly peaceful existence, in which we had only bills to worry about.

But we had not yet come to the bottom of the pit, we were still slithering downwards, the battle was still on. I do not know when it began to have a name, "Third Ypres" or "Passchendaele". To all of us it was just *the* battle, the battle which had started on July 31st, was still being fought in the middle of October, and was to continue for another two or three weeks.

With the Major on leave and Edward taking his place in the gun line, and Frank in charge of the wagon lines, there

125

were only the three of us—Jack, Josh and myself—to take the special duties, and every third or fourth day it was my turn to be liaison officer or to go up to the O.P.

The Broenbeke

Once I was liaison officer with a battalion of Grenadier Guards.

Was I a Regular soldier, was the Colonel's first question.

'No Sir,' I said.

Had I been at Eton, his second.

'No, Sir,' again.

He appeared to take no further interest in me as a person, but I was impressed by him and what I saw that night. The discipline of the Guards was very strict and their behaviour even in the line very formal. The attitude of men to their officers and of junior officers to senior ones was always correct. Their conversation was serious, I heard none of the flippancy or cynicism that I was accustomed to in our own mess, and somehow this made the war seem less futile.

I admired the Guards, but did not feel at home in their company.

The Guards Division was relieved during the night that I was up in the line with them. The Grenadier Guards went out, an English county regiment came in, and the difference was perceptible immediately. Now, everyone was talking at once, there was an atmosphere of warm-hearted bustling, lovable inefficiency; packs and gas-masks, revolvers and field glasses were thrown down anywhere. Now we were all amateurs who hated war, but knew that it had to be fought and would go on fighting until it was won.

The Colonel of the incoming battalion was going with his adjutant to visit his outpost line and I offered to go with him. But he shook his head. 'No, Guns! Why should you come?' he said, 'it's not your job, it's ours.' I liked being called

"Guns" by the infantry. There was an implication of mutual trust in the use of the word.

But I was pleased that he had not accepted my offer, I did not want to leave the safety of the pill-box. There were no trenches here, the so-called front line was nothing more than a set of unconnected shell-holes, each manned by a few men, existing somehow where they had been put until relieved after 48 hours. I was much better off than an infantry platoon commander of my rank and he was better off than the men under him.

On another ocasion, Louvois Farm (the infantry battalion headquarters) and Vee Bend (the O.P.) both played a part in the night's adventures. The infantry were not in direct communication with our Brigade Headquarters, they could not themselves ask for artillery help. This was why they needed a liaison officer. But I was told that Vee Bend was now manned by night as well as by day, and therefore messages could be signalled by lamp to Vee Bend and then on by the telephone line we had laid. Soon after dark, however, my signallers came to tell me they were receiving no answer from Vee Bend. I had Shortwood and Foster with me that night. They were the two signallers who had accompanied me on the first time I went out across the waste of death, while we were still at Lancer Farm. They had, as it were, held my hand on that ocasion, had taken me out and brought me safely back, and always afterwards I was pleased when I knew they were coming with me. They were as much a single unit as Gilbert and Sullivan or Huntley and Palmer. One had a villainous face, the other a cherubic one. In fact, both were first-rate signallers and first-rate down-to-earth Yorkshiremen, the kind of men responsible for our eventually winning the war. I don't think either was decorated except in the memory of those who, like myself, had the privilege of serving with them.

Now they came to tell me they were getting no answer to their flash-lamp.

I decided to send both back to Vee Bend, to find out what was the matter. It was dark, but they said they would be able to find the way there but not to return to me unless I guided them by flashing the lamp.

They set off. I gave them three-quarters of an hour. Then I went outside again and, setting the lamp in what I believed was the right direction, I began flashing a succession of dots and dashes as I had arranged with them before they started.

They were away a long time. I began to feel anxious for them. They might have lost the way, they might have been wounded, they might not be able to see my lamp. German shells were falling at no great distance, but I did not feel anxious on my own behalf. I had something to do. That stopped me from thinking about the shells, even from noticing where they were falling. I knew that the lives of my two men might depend on me.

They came at last, suddenly out of the darkness. I had not seen or heard them until they were within a few yards of me. They were as pleased to be back as I was pleased to see them, and I gave each of them a mouthful of whisky from my flask. But their news was bad. There was no one at Vee Bend, they said, the place was deserted. They had reported to our Brigade Headquarters by telephone that we were not in communication, and Brigade had said they would attend to the matter. But I knew that it was another brigade of artillery, not ours, that was responsible for the night O.P. and whether or when Cherry would succeed in getting anyone up there was more than I could guess.

I had to go and tell the infantry colonel that I was not in touch with anyone. If he needed artillery support during the night I should not be able to obtain it for him. He was alarmed, and angry. If I couldn't do anything for them, he said, I might as well not be there. I tried to put the blame on the other brigade, he put it on myself, and I knew that he was justified in doing so—it was an artillery failure, and I was the only artilleryman present.

Luckily it was a quiet night. The infantry had no occasion to ask for artillery support and in the morning, though not until then, I was able to tell the colonel that I was now in touch with the batteries behind us.

The officers of this battalion of the Highland Light Infantry to which I was attached that night were more than

129

usually friendly, and I wanted to regain their good opinion, not only for my own sake, but because it was the chief reason for our existence—to fire at the enemy when the infantry required us to.

I was very proud of being a gunner.

Edward proved a good battery comander while the Major was away. In spite of his youthful appearance the men trusted him. He could do nothing to lessen their danger or discomfort, but he cared, and showed that he cared. The valley of the Broenbeke was shelled day and night, but our good fortune continued. We had fewer casualties than A and B Batteries in the supposedly safer position behind us, and fewer than the other brigades on the Broenbeke. There were guns all way along the road by the side of the stream.

The stream! The road! How misleading words can be! The "stream" was a succession of mud-and-water-filled shell-holes, the "road" a causeway of shell-splintered planks, unfit for wagons of any kind. All our ammunition had to be brought up by pack-horse.

Edward was now my friend as much as any of the others. We shared a tiny pill-box at the top of the rise behind the guns. There were two, the signallers lived in the other, and we still had the good one at Abri Wood. There was no going down to the wagon lines at this time, but we took it in turns to go back to Abri Wood for a night's rest.

Then the Major returned from leave and took his place with the guns. Edward went down to the wagon lines, Frank came up. So for about a week there was an extra subaltern and that meant fewer duties for each of us. The Major immediately found a larger and drier pill-box. 'There wasn't room to swing a cat in Edward's place,' he told one of our visitors, 'if it had been a bit bigger we could have swum in it, the water on the floor was nearly deep enough.' But he praised Edward for standing up to the Colonel and refusing to go to the other position. 'You should always put your guns as low as you can,' he said, 'not on the top of a hill.'

I was told one morning there was a visitor in the mess who was asking for me, so I went down from my tiny box, wondering who it could be. The man was a captain in the R.A.M.C., I recognised him, his home in Oxford was near mine and he explained that his mother and mine had been talking together and had realised we were close to each other. He was medical officer to one of the other brigades by the Broenbeke and he had been told to look me up. I took out my case and offered him a cigarette. That was always the first thing to do.

'No, thank you, I don't smoke,' he said.

Then I offered him a drink—that was the second thing politeness required.

'No, thank you, I don't drink,' he said.

We talked for a few minutes about the Broenbeke, comparing casualties, agreeing that it was a terrible place, but I was not finding him easy to talk to, and presently he got up to go. I tried one more opening, for I thought he might have some advice to give me. 'Read any good books lately?' I asked.

'I don't have time for reading,' he said, 'but I always try to read a few pages of Homer at night before falling asleep.'

Then he left, I watched him walking down the hill and along to his own brigade.

'Who was that joker?' the Major asked, when he had gone.

'His name is Lawrence,' I said, 'and he's a brother of that fellow we were reading about in *The Times* who's always blowing up trains behind the Turkish lines.' Frank and the Major both knew who I was talking about and were impressed in spite of themselves.

We laughed, after he had gone, at the thought of there being anyone at the front who neither smoked nor drank, and read Homer in preference to anything else.

We could laugh, we had to laugh, there was laughter every

day because we were all young and there was no jealousy between us, and because laughter was the only way of survival on the Broenbeke.

Back on the Wijdendrift, A and B were having a worse time than ourselves. Casualties among officers had been particularly heavy. Jamieson had been gassed, Vernon wounded. Major Fraser also was suffering from the gas, he had lost his voice and could only speak in a whisper, he was coughing all the time. He ought to have gone into hospital, but he hung on, he said he would be all right in a day or two. But he had to go in the end, and he never came back to us. He lived for ten years after the war, but never wholly recovered from the gas and died in early middle age.

B Battery was so short of officers that we were ordered to send them one of ours until the arrival of reinforcements. I was dismayed when I heard that one of us was to go. I knew it would have to be Josh or myself, we were the two who had most recently come to the battery.

'Toss for it,' the Major said.

It had never occured to me that I might be sent away from my battery. I would rather have gone up to do an extra liaison, under all the Eyes in the Houthulst Forest. I certainly was not going to volunteer this time, however much Josh might want me to.

But Josh said 'I don't mind going. I don't mind where I go so long as there is a good roof on top of me. I like you all very much, even Frank, although he grouses about his mess bills, but one place is the same as another when you get to my age.'

'It will only be for a week or two,' the Major said.

It was only for one night. The roof was not a good one. A and B Battery officers were sharing a dug-out, and that night a gas shell came through the doorway and exploded inside, and all its occupants were made casualties. One of them died a few days later. The other three were less seriously blistered by the liquid gas, but they were all taken to hospital, and the next news we had of them was that they were on their way to England.

We were all very sorry about Josh, for our own sakes if not for his.

'It's what he's been hoping for ever since he came out,' Frank said.

But Jack was not sure whether mustard gas was what he wanted. 'Some people say it prevents your having children,' he said. 'If you got it badly enough I suppose it might prevent your having anything else.'

'We shall miss him,' Frank said. 'Our whisky bills will be less, but we shall have no more roast chickens, it will be bully beef and maconochie from now on.'

I had never thought I should miss him so much, but the mess suddenly seemed empty without his big presence, his loud voice and his laughter.

The Major was angry. 'A gas shell!' he said. 'One gas shell! I ask you! They've been living there all this time, and they haven't made a place strong enough to keep out a gas shell. Well, they shan't have any more of my officers. They can do what they like with their own, but I won't give them any more of mine to squander. They can ask and go on asking, they can whistle themselves blue in the face, but they won't get any more from me.'

But they did not ask us to send anyone else. A and B were taken out of action, they had hardly any fit officers left. C and D stayed on.

I was less robust than some of the others, more likely to suffer from the cold and getting my clothes wet. I started coughing a lot and talked of going to see our doctor.

'How's your cough?' Jack asked me one evening.

'It's getting better,' I told him.

'Oh, bad luck!' he said sympathetically.

133

I had to do one more liaison duty, had to cross the wastes of death under the Watching Eyes once more.

There was an officer in D Battery called Percy White, brave and very capable. He had risen from the ranks, and been out continuously since Mons. I had heard his major say that he had done more than anyone else to hold the battery together during this difficult time. He came one morning to where I was standing by our guns and told me he had just come back from the worst twenty-four hours he had ever experienced in all his service.

'Talk about shell-fire!' he said. 'Sniping with machine-guns! Bodies! One of the pill-boxes was full of them. Smell of mustard gas all over the place. Mud and shell-holes every-where.' He hoped he would never see the god-forsaken place again.

'Where is this place?' I asked. But I knew what he was going to say before he opened his mouth.

'U Six C Three Four,' he said.

'That's where I've got to go this afternoon,' I told him.

Before setting off I stopped at the bottom of the hill to speak to some of my men. They were far worse off than we were, living and sleeping (if they could sleep!) on the lip of a water-filled shell-hole, permanently wet and with only a few sandbags (if they were lucky!) to protect them from the flying splinters. There had been another infantry attack a day or two previously. It had achieved no more success than the one before, but we had fired hundreds of rounds of ammunition and the empty shell cases were useful for pinning down groundsheets on the least muddy parts of the swamp. Someone had brewed a pot of tea, and everyone within sight now had a mug in his hand. It was difficult to find wood, but Yorkshiremen were better than most at finding things and at improvisation. All the cooks were devoted men, somehow they supplied hot meals.

134

The infantry were in a worse plight than we were. Exposed to the bullet of a sniper whenever they moved, and with fewer hot meals. And still the battle went on. It was the ultimate in suffering. Gethsemane and the Broenbeke!

Sergeant Denmark was there, grousing as usual.

'If only we could feel we were doing some good to somebody,' I said to him.

'Reckon it may have done some to you,' he replied.

There seemed to be almost a note of approval in his voice.

We went on, my two signallers and I.

I was full of fear and foreboding as we left the world of men in the valley and went up the hill into the lonely wilderness, because of what White had told me.

But we were as fortunate as he had been the reverse. An easy journey up, unseen by the Eyes, a quiet night, friendly foot-sloggers when we arrived. It did not even rain, or less heavily than usual, and I managed to avoid seeing the pill-box where all the dead men were. And the next day I walked blithely down the hill, leaving the Houthulst Forest behind me. I never saw it again until the War was over when I went back to see whether it still had the power to inspire terror in me. My father was with me. He only saw a lot of shattered tree trunks and I did not tell him what else had been there once.

It was in early November that we escaped from the Broenbeke, and a day or two later we heard that Passchendaele had at last been captured. By the Canadians.

Passchendaele! There was a green hill far away, I had seen it with my own eyes just before the battle began, when Edward took me with him to the O.P. from the Summer House, in front of the Canal Bank. Far away! Neither of us could have guessed how far away it was on that sunny July day. And there was no city wall unless the pill-boxes were part of it. It had been a green hill when I first saw it, but now of course it was just black mud, like everything else.

The ultimate in suffering! But God had kept his promise

of salvation. Every material thing destroyed, but humankind and humanity had somehow survived. The suffering on the Broenbeke had probably been in vain, but not the suffering in the Garden.

16

Down South

Edward left us, to return to England and become a civilian again, a medical student instead of a soldier. During his last days with the battery he and the Major appeared to be vying with each other to see who could be most complimentary.

'We all owe our lives to him,' Edward said, 'you've only got to look at the other batteries and see what has happened to them. D have lost more than half their strength, A and B about half, but we've not lost more than a quarter of ours. It isn't only that he has a good eye for a gun position and finds a strong pill-box, he also stands up to the generals who want to bugger us about. They get no change out of Major Eric. He knows that keeping down casualties is the most important thing, and if he gets an order which he thinks will put lives at risk unnecessarily he just ignores it, no matter who it's come from.'

And the Major said to the rest of us 'Of course he's got to go, but it's a thousand pities. He's got the making of a really good officer and I would have recommended him for his majority when he'd had a little more experience. I've always known there was something special about him and I've always said so.'

It was a sad day for the battery when Edward went and he himself was the saddest person in it. He had spent a small fortune on cigarettes and beer for the men, and after breakfast on his last day he went out into the lines to say good-bye and shake hands with every man in the battery. I saw tears on his cheek when he came into the mess to say good-bye to us. 'I shall never find a place like this again,' he said, 'it's been like home to me.' Then he rode away to the station with his groom and some time later I saw Edric returning with the two horses. 'He has guts, that boy,' the Major said, 'and that's the only thing which matters when all's said and done.'

Only Frank could see a silver lining. Edward had escaped from the War. This was a miracle, and if one miracle could occur then there might be another and next time it might be he who escaped.

We were given a short rest before returning to the line, but we were not so happy as we had been in September. We were all of us worn out, the Broenbeke seemed to have taken away our power of finding any enjoyment.

Then we were ordered to entrain for an unknown destination, and for a day or two there was the excitement of mystery and playing a guessing game. This did not last. 'You're for Bapaume,' the Railway Transport Officer told us at the station, 'and unless you're quick you may find the Boche gets there before you.'

Strange things had been happening down south, on the Cambrai front, and were still happening. We had read about them in the newspaper. One of our armies had made a surprise attack, using tanks instead of artillery preparation which had the effect of warning the other side. The attack had been very successful, we had broken their line. But then the Germans had made a surprise counter-attack and had broken ours. They had been even more successful, they were still advancing. This was why the RTO said we should have to be quick.

We were quick. Our train averaged nearly twelve miles an hour instead of the usual eight or nine. But no one seemed in a hurry for us when we arrived at our journey's end, and we were kept waiting at the station for several hours. The Major was temporarily in command of the brigade, and he had gone on ahead, taking Frank with him to see the country before dark, and I was left to follow with the battery.

I did not know where to go and had to wait for orders. It was cold waiting. The sun had set, it was nearly dark before we set off. Le Transloy, Rocquigny, Manancourt—those were the names of the villages through which I was to pass. They had a pleasant sound after the harsher Flemish names. But

I had no map, and in the darkness it was not easy to find the way. The roads were deserted, and the villages, though easily recognisable as villages, were without inhabitants. This was part of the territory that had been given up by the Germans at the beginning of the year. They had made a voluntary retirement after blowing up all the houses and cutting down most of the trees.

The night was very cold. I walked most of the way, leading my horse behind me, because it was warmer to walk. The men had been singing at first, but the singing stopped long before we came to the end of our march, and then there was only the sound of the horses' feet and the wagon wheels behind me. I was tired and hungry as well as cold. At last I heard someone coming towards us. It was a guide who had come to lead us to the place where we were to spend the night.

'What sort of a place is it?' I asked.

'Just a field, sir,' he said.

The long wait at the station and the cold march had made me bad tempered, and the thought of camping in an open field added to my irritation. We had been living in huts while we were out at rest, and I hated the cold. But Frank, to whom I started grumbling as soon as I saw him, was unsympathetic. 'Don't you know there's a war on?' he said, and I felt ashamed of my outburst. What sort of a veteran was I if I could not endure a little cold weather! It had been shellfire and mud in Flanders, now it would be the hardship of winter that I should have to learn to bear.

But a hot meal was soon ready for us. The cooks were the most popular men in the battery that night. Then there was a double rum ration. Tents were pitched, my servant had laid everything out for me, I only had to climb inside my sleeping-bag, and then put all the clothes I had on top of it.

In the morning the ground was white with frost, but we had all slept well. The sun came up, and after breakfast I felt myself again, almost ready to enjoy whatever the day might bring. We rode out to look at the battery positions which we were to occupy. We were on that part of the front where the Germans had made their break-through, but their advance had been halted before we arrived. The alarm was over, only a feeling of unease remained.

It seemed strange to be riding on horseback within two or three miles of the enemy. Everything was strange on that bright sunny morning: the hard dry ground, the absence of shell-holes and the sound of gunfire. Every now and then the silence was broken by the sound of a gun firing, but at Ypres the noise had been continuous.

We seemed to have the place to ourselves, our little party, two officers from each battery riding over the white deserted plain. It looked like a Christmas card, but there was no holly.

'We might be on Salisbury Plain,' Frank said, 'playing at being soldiers.'

Our first battery position was on the edge of a wood that was almost undamaged. We stayed there for three days without firing or being fired at. Then we were sent to another position a few miles away where we had some firing to do, and some shells came back at us. But it was very different from the Broenbeke.

'It's going to be rather serious,' Frank said, 'if either side in future can attack the other without warning.'

'It's not cricket,' the Major agreed.

He went with the Colonel and the other battery commanders to a conference of senior officers at which the lessons of the two recent battles were discussed.

'Trench warfare is a thing of the past,' he told us on his return. 'It's back to proper soldiering in future. No more of this mucking about in shell-holes and pill-boxes. The Brass Hats have always said it was wrong, and now Cambrai has proved them right. They say we shall enjoy it much more!'

'What exactly are we going to enjoy?' Jack asked.

'Oh, galloping about in the open, firing over open sights, saving the guns—all that sort of thing. We may all win Victoria Crosses.'

The Major was in his flippant mood, it was impossible to tell what had been said at the conference.

'You can't think how pleased the Staff are,' he said, 'at the idea of fighting properly again.'

'What about the Boche?' Frank asked. 'Has he agreed to the new rules?'

'Oh, I forgot to ask that one. I know there was a lot of talk about attacking.'

'Who's going to attack whom?'

'I think they said it would be Fritz's turn next.'

We were all to go in for winter training, the Major said, and the generals themselves were coming to watch us.

Jack said that he did not like change. 'I don't know the first thing about open warfare,' he said. 'It will be a funny thing if we start wishing ourselves back at Ypres.'

Winter training began at once. The guns had been brought out of action, but we were only a few miles behind the line, in readiness to go back immediately in the event of another attack. The Major was enthusiastic for the first few days. He enjoyed riding about on the downland in the bright winter sunshine with all the battery behind him, giving orders that none of us knew how to execute, and amused at the resulting confusion. 'We shall give the generals a surprise,' he said.

Jack was very worried. 'I haven't a clue as to what I'm supposed to do,' he said to me. 'It was all right up at Ypres, we just sat in a pill-box all day and went up to the O.P. when it was our turn.'

We all agreed that fighting in this part of the world would be very different from what it had been in Flanders and we wondered what 1918 would have in store for us.

'It may be better than 1917,' Frank said. 'At any rate we shan't have that gluey mud.'

'We shall have something else instead,' Jack said. 'It's more likely to be worse.' 'They did things better in the old days,' he went on, 'they used to go into winter quarters and no one had to sleep alone. I haven't seen a woman since September, except some I saw from the train working in the fields.'

'You're lucky,' he said to me, 'you seem able to get along without them.'

I could not get along without them. I wanted Suzanne more than ever and imagined myself with her every night as I was getting into my narrow sleeping-bag. Now she was smiling again, as friendly as she had been at first, talking to me about myself, wanting to console me for the suffering she saw in my eyes. She looked more beautiful than ever. My imagination made me very happy.

17

Year's End

1917 was drawing to its unregretted end. The dry frosty weather had given way to rain and the night bombers were flying over the wagon lines area. Everyone felt in need of jollification, but Christmas gave us very little. Peace and Goodwill were conspicuously absent, as were the shepherds and their flocks. There were a lot of magpies, but no other living creatures in this desolate land from which the Germans had retired after completely destroying it. There was no girl nearer than Amiens, fifteen miles away, Jack told us, and no possibility of getting there. 'It's a bloody awful war,' he said, and everyone agreed with him.

The Major decided to give a party on New Year's Eve, and he invited Major Cecil, Garnett and two or three others. 'We'll show them what C Battery can do,' he said, and he told the servants to polish glasses and brass shell cases for candlesticks. They even contrived to make paper decorations for the drab little hut that was our mess.

The party was a great success, and no one enjoyed it more than the Major. For some days past he had been very depressed, he was missing so many of his friends in the other batteries. But the party made him a different man, tolerant, light-hearted, as eager as a schoolboy for fun and games. The weather had changed again, there had been a fall of snow on the previous day, and when dinner was over he suggested a snowball fight. Soon there were snowballs flying in every direction, most of them aimed at the Major. All the servants joined in the fight and they also combined against him, he was the most popular officer in the battery. But being an artillery major he knew the importance of having a good

143

supply of ammunition and I think he must have made a pile of snowballs before the game started, for he was giving as good as he got.

It was a dangerous game, for the snowfall had not been a heavy one and the snowballs were mixed with bits of chalk and stone. Besides, we had dug narrow trenches outside our huts in which to take refuge when the night flyers came over and we heard bombs dropping. We had not had to use them yet, but now I fell into one when I was running away from somebody. For a moment I thought I had broken my leg, but getting out I found I could walk. Then I realised I had drunk too much champagne, I was not accustomed to drinking. I went into our hut and lay down. I shut my eyes and kept still, hoping the sickness would pass. But it was no good, I should have to go out again and get rid of it. Fortunately I was able to avoid the others. They were making so much noise that it was easy to keep out of their way. I went away from the camp and was very sick. I felt better at once and half thought of going to join in the fun again; but I decided not to. I'd had enough, it was getting late, I did not want to fall into another trench. Next time I might break a leg, and that would be a poor way out.

I did not want any way out, I wanted to stay where I was. For as long as the war lasted this was where I belonged. At first I had just been an individual, now I was part of the battery, the battery was part of the brigade, and the brigade was part of the B.E.F. All my friends were in France, and all the men in France were my friends.

All the men in France! I had no enemies, or only the Staff, and they lived so far away that we did not think of them as part of us. Life was very simple at the front, you just served.

Now I was accepted. Everyone in the battery accepted me. At the beginning I had not been accepted because I knew nothing about war and nothing about life. I knew all about war now, everyone said the Broenbeke was as bad as anything there had ever been. I had not learnt much more about life. Major Fraser had offered me a chance of learning, but I had turned it down and did not regret doing so. Knowledge

144

of the war had come to me simply and naturally, I had not gone out of my way to look for Bank Farm or the Eyes of the Houthulst Forest. I believed knowledge of life would come in the same simple and natural way when I was ready for it. There was a big picture of a naked woman on the wall of the mess, left there by the hut's last occupant. I loved looking at her breasts and beautiful long legs. One day it would not be just a picture I was looking at. She, my girl, would be in bed beside me, I should be kissing her breasts, running my hands along the silkiness of her thighs, finding the wonder between them.

The light touch of Suzanne's hair against my cheek had set my heart on fire. But there was more than that to come, more even than kissing. I had not succeeded in kissing Suzanne, but that was because of the language barrier. A girl wanted to be told that she was beautiful, that you adored her and needed her more than anything else in the world. I could not say any of these things to Suzanne because of my bad French, but I should say them all to my English girl when I found her. Words could be very persuasive. And then the ecstasy of passion! That was what Jack called it, and I knew Frank was looking forward to it as the supreme moment of life.

The ecstasy of passion! It would be as momentous, as unforgettable as coming under fire for the first time. That night at Neuve Église and the nights spent with the working party at Gibraltar Farm had changed me into a different person. There would come another night that would change me again. The first change had been as frightening as it was thrilling, but the second would be altogether wonderful.

I was still thinking about Suzanne's beauty when I heard the voices of the others outside. The snowballing was over, the guests had gone, now Frank and Jack were coming in. We three slept in one part of the hut, the Major had a small room of his own, leading out of ours. They came in, walked unsteadily across the hut, and sat down on my bed.

'Hello!' Frank said. 'Where did you go off to? What have you been doing?'

'Just thinking,' I told him.

'I feel bloody awful,' Jack said, 'it's all this mixing of drinks.

145

I told the Major I wanted to stick to whisky, but he kept filling my glass with bubbly when I wasn't looking.'

'And you kept emptying it,' Frank said.

'Well, you've got to be matey at a party.'

Now the Major had gone into his little room, and we heard him singing in his tuneless voice behind the thin partition.

> 'Old soldiers never die,
> Never die, never die,
> Old soldiers never die,
> They simply fade away.'

'He sounds cheerful,' Frank said.

'Wonder how long it will last,' said Jack.

I wanted to be alone with my thoughts and was not sorry when they got up, went across to their own beds and started to undress. Presently I heard them discussing the war. Jack was saying he could not stick it much longer. Frank told him he would have to. 'We stuck it on the Somme,' he said, 'and we stuck it on the Broenbeke. We can stick it as long as we've got to.'

'But you've got to admit it's a hopeless dawn.'

Then Frank looked at his watch. 'It's long after midnight,' he said. 'Happy New Year to us all!'

'Don't be so bloody sarcastic,' Jack said.

The singing next door had stopped and, one by one, we fell asleep.

The Ebb and Flow of Battle

FOREWORD

After the Russian Revolution in April 1917, the Bolshevik Party, which soon obtained power, decided to make peace with Germany. The Germans, no longer having to fight on two fronts, could, therefore, transfer troops from the east to the west, and this gave them numerical superiority over the Western Allies, Britain and France. Their commanders (Hindenburg and Ludendorff) realised, however, that they must win the war quickly, before the Americans were ready to take part in the fighting. We were warned they were preparing a massive attack on the western front and that it would probably fall on that part of the line held by the British Fifth Army, of which the Army Field Artillery Brigade in which I was serving was a part.

Early in January 1918 I was returning from ten days' leave in England. In France there was snow on the ground and no glass in any of the windows of the train. Perhaps I was lucky to be in a coach, not in one of the trucks marked HOMMES 40 CHEVAUX 8, but the truck might have been less cold. Whenever the train stopped, which was frequently, we got out and ran to warm ourselves but the warmth was soon lost again in our glass-less coach. Some mornings later I woke with a very sore throat, and as it did not get better our doctor sent me into hospital, where after a while my tonsils were cut out.

The snow was still lying and I walked by myself across the open from the operating theatre to my ward.

But this did me no hurt and on 4 March I was discharged fit for duty. I spent that night at the Officers' Club in Peronne and with the help of a lorry found my way the next morning to our battery wagon lines, outside the little broken village of Nurlu, some three miles behind the line.

One

'What kind of a war is it?' was one of the first questions I asked Jack.

'Oh, pretty good,' he replied. 'The guns are five thousand yards from the line, the men spend all their time playing football, you can ride up to the O.P.'

Football at the guns! Horses at the Observation Post! I remembered Ypres last year.

'I don't ride there myself,' he was saying. 'I always feel safer on my own feet. Mind you, there's a lot of breeze,' he added presently.

'What about?' I asked.

'They think Fritz is going to make a big attack, and that it will be on our front.'

'When?'

'Oh, any day now. You've come back just in time for it.'

While I was in hospital I had heard some talk of a forthcoming German attack, but had paid no attention. I supposed that people at the back might always be more nervous than we were. It seemed to me most unlikely that the Germans were going to attack. It might be an agreeable change if they did, we had done all the attacking in 1917. One failure after another. Now the Germans could have their turn.

'It doesn't seem likely,' I said.

'Oh, I don't know about that,' Jack replied. 'And of course we shall get it in the neck if he does come over.'

Jack was always gloomy. He was so pessimistic that he made the rest of us laugh; he cheered us up, we felt certain that nothing would ever be as bad as Jack expected. At any rate there was no sign of an attack at present. Jack himself had said how quiet it was, and I could hear for myself. At Ypres last year we had bombarded the enemy for weeks before our attack, but this morning there was hardly a sound of gunfire, it was more peaceful than anything I had known.

Hardly more than nine months had passed since I joined the battery, a boy almost straight from school, but because the greater part of that time had been spent at Ypres and Passchendaele I already considered myself a veteran. Ypres had been all shells and shell-holes, mud and desolation, but here there was grass, and men played football only three miles from the line.

For the last six weeks I had been away from the battery, first in hospital, then at a convalescent camp. Six weeks was such a long time that I had lost touch with all my friends, and now I felt like a stranger in my own home. No one was expecting me.

Jack had mistaken me for his servant when he saw a figure in the doorway of the hut. 'You can bring me my breakfast now,' he called out. Then he looked up and his smile of welcome convinced me that I was glad to be back. I had been wondering whether I should feel glad to see my friends again or depressed to be at the War again.

'We all thought you were never coming back,' he said.

He told me the battery news while he ate his breakfast. The Major had gone home. 'He fell off his horse in a race and was kicked on the knee,' Jack said. 'There didn't seem much the matter with him, but he went on leave a day or two later, and the next thing we heard was that he was in hospital with a broken knee-cap. What with the war and all the whisky he drank, my own opinion is that he'd had as much as he could stand.'

I was sorry and said so.

'Oh, he was drinking all day and playing hell every night,' Jack said. 'You don't know what he was like at the end.'

I could guess. But he had helped me at the beginning when I felt lonely and lost. Before I came to C Battery I had spent a month in an ammunition column, which must have been one of the worst units in the army. I had been miserable. But C Battery was a different world, and Major Eric, easy-going, ironical, tolerant (when he was sober), and amused by my innocence, had been nice to me and I felt grateful to him, whatever he had been like at the end.

Besides, I disliked changes. Now we should have to adapt ourselves to the ways of some other commander. Major Eric had been very popular with the men. Like themselves he was a Yorkshireman, a Sheffield man, they had known him before they joined up, they thought it right for him to command them. 'He's our mascot, the Major is,' old Driver Oaks had once said to me, 'we don't need no black cat when he's with us.' Now he had gone, and for a moment, in spite of the sunshine outside, I felt a foreboding of misfortune.

'Is Jamieson commanding us then?' I asked.

'For the moment,' Jack said. 'But there's somebody else coming. A fellow called Bingley. He seems to have influential relatives, so the Colonel is keen to have him. But Jamieson is as sick as hell, he thought he was going to command the battery.'

I liked Jamieson. He was a big Australian who had been promoted and come from one of the other batteries in the brigade to be our second-in-command shortly before I went away, but I knew he was not liked by everyone. Frank disliked him, he had been hoping for the promotion himself.

'Where's Frank?' I asked. As senior subaltern in the battery he should have been in charge of the wagon lines, not Jack.

'On leave. And I'm due to go when he comes back. *If* he comes back,' he added gloomily.

'Why shouldn't he come back?'

'I never expect anyone to come back when he goes on leave. Not at the right time anyway. Look at the Major.'

'Is Frank getting married?'

'Not this time, next time he says. It's been next time ever since I knew him. I'm beginning to wonder if he ever will get married.'

But I knew Frank's girl was still at college, she was taking her Finals in the summer.

'He's as sick as hell about Jamieson being promoted before him. He says he was commissioned before Jamieson and has been out here longer.'

Frank as sick as hell about Jamieson, and Jamieson as sick as hell about Bingley. It seemed silly.

Jack agreed that it was. 'Can't think why Frankie wants to be a captain,' he said. 'It's more responsibility. I sometimes think I was better off in the ranks. Officers have a more comfortable time, but you stand a better chance of surviving in the ranks.'

Then he asked me about myself. 'Couldn't you have worked things?' he said.

'Not with tonsils,' I replied.

'I'd have had a damned good try, you look pale enough to have got home.'

'I always look pale,' I said, 'but there wasn't much the matter with me.'

'I'm so bloody healthy,' Jack said. 'That's my trouble.'

When he had finished breakfast we went out into the March sunshine and walked round the horse lines. I thought the men looked pleased to see me back, most of them smiled at me. I was not a Yorkshireman, but they had accepted me and they knew I was proud of belonging to their battery. Young Corporal Albert hoped I was feeling champion again. 'I've had no one to sign my letters, Sir,' he said. He knew I would always put my signature on envelopes addressed to his girl without looking inside. I liked Corporal Albert, he was always ready with a smile or a friendly remark, and I could understand what he said; the voices of some of the older Yorkshiremen were almost unintelligible to me.

Then I spoke to Edric, my groom. 'Lady will be glad you're back,' he said. 'She needs more exercise, she's too fat.' He would call my mare Lady, I wanted to change her name to Peggy, but Edric quietly ignored my wishes. He thought a horse had as much right to her name as a man or woman. Walkenshaw, my servant, had been with me while I was away from the battery. He was glad to be back, I saw him talking to his friends and wondered what he was telling them about our time behind the front.

After lunch we rode up to the gun line.

When the battery was in action it was always split into two parts. There was the gun line, where the guns were, usually about two miles behind the infantry in our front line; and there were the wagon lines, where the limbers for moving the guns were kept, and the ammunition wagons, and all the horses, two or three miles further back, out of range of most enemy guns.

The battery commander, generally a major, lived in the gun line; his second-in-command, a captain, at the wagon lines. The four or five subalterns were sometimes in one place, sometimes in the other. They took it in turns to come down to the wagon lines for a rest. So did the gunners. The drivers were always at the wagon lines with their horses, though they took ammunition up to the guns and drove up with the gun limbers before a move. Every gunner and every driver had his special position and responsibility in the battery, changeable only when casualties made change necessary.

The signallers, an elite in the battery, lived in the gun line. On them depended all our communications. The other specialists, shoeing smiths and veterinary sergeant, battery clerk, stores men lived at the wagon lines. The officers' servants went wherever their officers were. There were cooks in both places.

Our 18-pounder guns only had a range of six thousand yards. We could shell the enemy front line and fire at targets immediately behind it, but could not reach anything further back. More distant targets were engaged by the 60-pounders and six-inch howitzers.

The guns were in a long hollow of the downs, between two ridges. The men were not playing football, but were lying about in the sunshine and looked very content. Jamieson gave me a friendly greeting. He had two officers up with him: Hughes had joined the battery shortly before I went away, but this was the first time I had seen Durham. Hughes had been a Welsh policeman before the War; he had enlisted and risen to the rank of sergeant in France before going home to take a commission. Durham also had been in the ranks and in France before he was commissioned, he was hardly older than myself. I liked the look of him, he had red cheeks and a gay smiling face. I felt sure I should have more in common with him than with Hughes, but I already felt a considerable respect for Hughes.

I went to talk to some of the men in my section. There were six guns in an 18-pounder battery, and I was in command of the Left Section, Numbers 5 and 6 guns.

'You've had a long holiday, Sir,' Sergeant Denmark said in his rough disapproving voice. Once I had been afraid of Denmark, he was so gruff and I thought he hardly troubled to conceal his scorn of my ignorance and immaturity. But by this time I hoped I had risen in his esteem and I had learnt that only his manner was unfriendly. He was without fear, and the best sergeant in the battery, I knew that I could depend on him in any crisis. He never had a great deal to say to me, or to anyone else, and he never brought me letters to sign. So far as I knew he did not write any. But he told me now that he was sweating on a leave, he was high on the list and hoping to go within the next few days. Sergeant Denmark was one of the older men in the battery. Most were in their early or middle twenties; some, like Denmark, were over thirty; a few were forty. These were the battery old men, we had to take care of them.

Jamieson was going up to the O.P. and he took me with him. We rode through Heudecourt, a shattered village on the top of the ridge in front of the gun line, and then past the three other batteries in our brigade, A, B and D. They were all nearer to the line than we were, but two of our guns were still further forward, and some way to our right. They were in charge of another new officer, called Griffith, whom I had not yet seen. 'You'll see him soon enough,' Jamieson said.

A and B were 18-pounders, like ourselves, but D was a Four-Point-Five howitzer battery.

The strength of the brigade was about thirty officers and a thousand other ranks and the same number of horses.

I knew all the thirty and was on terms of personal friendship with all except a few of the most senior ones. But with those in the other batteries there could not be the same intimacy there was in our own. We were like brothers, sleeping side by side, within touching distance, sharing whatever possessions we had and the contents of any parcel that came for us.

We did not ride all the way. We left our horses below the last hill, then walked over the crest and down the other side to the O.P., which was in a railway cutting. From the crest of Chapel Hill there was a wonderful view, back as far as Nurlu, where our wagon lines were, and forward for a long way over

156

enemy-held territory. At Ypres it had been difficult to see anything from our O.P.s; I had never seen a living German soldier, except prisoners. Now I saw some, and it gave me a strange feeling. They were our enemies. They had to try and kill us, and we had to try and kill them, but they looked like ourselves and were doing ordinary things. I saw a party of men digging, and two others came out of a red-cross post, I saw the flag fluttering in the breeze. They were a long way off, nearly two miles from us, but they were Germans, they were our enemies.

No one was trying to kill anyone on this warm sunny afternoon. We could not have fired at the men I saw, they were beyond the range of our guns; but none of our longer-range guns was firing, and the enemy had not fired at us as we came over the crest of Chapel Hill and walked down to the railway line. The front line was as peaceful as Salisbury Plain.

Jamieson told me the names of the places we could see–two villages, some copses, the ruins of a sugar beet factory, ridges and ravines. I asked him what he thought about the likelihood of a great German attack, but he was non-committal. 'He may think it's his last chance of winning before the Yanks are ready,' he said; but that was all he would say. He said nothing about Bingley, and I did not tell him what Jack had told me. Bingley might never come. In war nothing was certain until it happened.

I did not stay up with the guns. Jamieson said there was no room for another officer. Indeed one was enough at present, he said, so Hughes rode back to the wagon lines with me in the evening. We raced each other along the downland way, it was perfect galloping country. 'More like a Sunday School treat than a war,' Hughes said as we were riding into camp.

There was nothing for us to do. I went joy-riding every day, galloping over the empty unspoilt country, sometimes alone, more often with Hughes or Durham, chasing the hares, putting up the partridges. After Ypres it was lovely to be in country like this. At Ypres we could not ride at all because of the mud and the shellholes, and when we went further back the country was cultivated and some of the Flemish farmers tried to stop us riding over their land. Here there were no civilians at all. This part of France had been given up by the

Germans in a voluntary withdrawal after the Battle of the Somme, a year before. They had destroyed the houses and cut down the fruit trees before they went, but the country was unspoilt. There were no civilians for ten miles behind us, and not many soldiers—only the divisions holding the line. This was another reason why I did not believe the enemy was going to attack us. If our generals really thought they were, then the back areas would have been full of our reserves. But we saw no one, we had the place to ourselves.

But there was a great deal of talk about a German attack in our Orders, Jack had not exaggerated.

'Where are all these rear defence lines, green and purple and red?' I asked one day. 'I've seen no sign of them.'

'They only exist on paper,' Frank said.

We both laughed, but I did not think it mattered. Even if there was an attack we should hold the enemy, we should never be driven back as far as Nurlu; or only after a long time. The Scottish Division in front of us was very good, the enemy would not get past.

Ours was an Army Brigade of Field Artillery, we were moved from one division to another, according to where we were needed. We were a composite brigade, C Battery was the only Yorkshire one, the men in the other batteries came from Lancashire, and Colonel Richardson, the brigade commander, himself a Lancashire man, was considered by some to favour the other three. As a loyal member of C Battery, but not a Yorkshireman, I thought I could be an impartial judge and I had never noticed any favouritism, but Frank said we were put in the worst position every time.

Frank had returned from leave, and a day or two later Captain Bingley arrived and took over the command of the battery. He seemed likeable. He was elderly, and old-fashioned in his ideas, but he left us alone. Jamieson said he was no good, but we had known he would say so before he saw him. Jamieson in fact had behaved badly. He came down to the wagon lines and said quite frankly to the rest of us that he had handed over to Bingley without telling him all that he needed to know. 'He can find out the rest for himself if he wants to know,' he said.

And as though it was not enough to have two captains in

our battery who were not on speaking terms, there was also this antipathy between Frank and Jamieson. I hoped that leave in England and the company of the girl he loved would have helped Frank to forget his disappointment over promotion, and that he and Jamieson would now settle down and work together, but he was more bitter than ever. 'If Bingley makes a mess of things,' he said, 'it will be Jamieson's fault. He had no right to clear off to the wagon lines so soon, he ought to have stayed up for a couple of days until Bingley had found his feet and knew what we were doing."

I was not worrying at the thought of a German attack, but I did worry about these dissensions in the battery. I loved the battery and had once thought it was the best in France, but it did not seem so good now. I heard less laughter and singing as I walked about the lines and there was more bad temper. It would be strange, I thought, if we could survive Passchendaele and all our casualties and then go to pieces at a time when there was no fighting at all. Even Jack commented on the state of affairs. 'If they go on in this way,' he said, 'I shall wish the Major back.'

He was going on leave, now that Frank had returned, but he seemed more than usually depressed.

'I shan't get very far,' he said. 'They'll cancel all leave and recall everyone as soon as the German Offensive starts."

'Cheer up!' I said, pouring him another whisky. 'You'll miss the first day anyway, and that will be the worst.' I was mocking him, I did not believe these stories of a German Offensive, but his mind was still running on it.

'You know,' he said, 'I always wonder when I go on leave who I shall find here when I get back.'

'We'll take care of ourselves,' I said. 'Don't worry.'

Durham also went on leave. Leave warrants were coming round more quickly than ever before, at the present rate I should be due for another myself by the end of the month. Now there were only four subalterns left, Frank, Hughes, and myself with Bingley in the gun line, and Griffith at the forward section, leaving Jamieson by himself at the wagon lines.

Life was as easy and as comfortable in the gun line as it had been at the wagon lines, and there was not much more to do. I liked Bingley as a man, but as a battery commander he did not inspire confidence. He fussed about trivialities, but appeared to be unaware of what mattered most in a battery, or any other unit—the spirit of comradeship. Frank said he would be all right when he had settled down, and anyway he was better than Jamieson. But even Frank could see the absurdity of some of his behaviour. He was taking the talk of a great German attack very seriously and every night he slept with a loaded revolver by his side.

'Got to be careful if you go into his dug-out before he's properly awake,' Hughes said. 'He may think you're a Fritz.'

'You've nothing to worry about,' Frank told him. 'He won't shoot you, it's to shoot himself, he's terrified of being taken prisoner.'

He was absurd. How could the enemy break through and overrun us before we knew what was happening?

He was one-quarter Irish, he told us; and four-quarters aristocratic birth, his conversation implied. But none of us was interested in hearing about his cousins. He accepted me because I happened to have been at school with a young nephew of his, but Hughes had not been at any school, not what Bingley called a school, and was not accepted by him. Hearing that my father was an Ulsterman, though it was Southern Ireland that he knew, Bingley said we would have a party on the evening of March 17th, to celebrate Saint Patrick's Day, and he invited Major Villiers of A Battery and one of his subalterns.

The weather was perfect. Bingley had been sitting in the sunshine for most of the day in a green canvas chair that he had brought with him from England, with his eyes half closed, listening to the cries of the men who were playing football at the upper end of the valley. 'This is the life,' he said. 'There's nothing like this in England now, England's a depressing place in war-time."

But his anxiety returned after dinner when the night's orders were brought in. There was more in them about the great German attack, it was expected tomorrow, an under-officer had been taken prisoner and had given information that all the storm-troops were now in readiness behind the line. Bingley followed me outside when I was going to bed. 'We've got to be on the *qui vive* all the time,' he said. 'I've

160

told Hughes to go up to the crest in front before dawn, and I want you to see that he goes.'

I was dismayed at being told to spy on one of my friends, and though Bingley had only been with us for a week that should have been time enough for him to learn that Hughes was completely reliable.

'These ranker officers are all the same,' Bingley was saying. 'Some of them are good up to a point, but you can't depend on them.'

Hughes went up to the crest in the morning. Went and came back again. There was no attack. 'Quiet as a nun's wedding night,' he said at breakfast in answer to our question. There was another alarm the next night. This time it was our aeroplanes, which had seen all the roads behind his line packed with German transport moving up. I was going to believe in the Great Attack when it happened.

Then the weather broke. Thirty-six hours of drizzling rain frayed all our tempers, we always felt irritated when every dug-out became full of wet coats and muddy boots. But after tea the rain stopped and we had an enjoyable argumentative evening. I was late going to my little shelter in the bank, each of us had our own, and I sat there for some time longer, reading and writing up my diary. Writing up my diary and bringing it up to date always gave me a sense of fulfilment, a feeling that now I was ready for whatever was going to happen next.

Two

I seemed to have hardly fallen asleep when I heard someone speaking my name. It was Thirsk, the signaller sergeant. He had raised the gas-curtain over the entrance to my shelter and was shining his torch in my direction.

'Captain's orders, Sir,' he said. 'He wants you to go up to the top of the hill.'

'Now?' I asked irritably. 'In the middle of the night?'

'Yes, Sir. It's four o'clock, Sir. To keep a good look out and send back information.'

Oh, blast the Captain, I thought, blast his nervousness. Well, I reflected it would be light in an hour or two, then I would come back and finish my sleep, I could stay in bed all morning if I liked.

Sergeant Thirsk had gone away. Dressing took some time, for I was in pyjamas, I always undressed completely when the war was quiet.

Sergeant Thirsk came back. 'Sir, he wants you to go quickly,' he said in his soft and unhurried voice. Thirsk was one of the best non-commissioned-officers in the battery, and one of the nicest men. I had never heard him raise his voice or speak angrily, but his signallers were so well trained and so devoted to him that they knew what to do before they were told.

'Any noise outside?' I asked him.

'No, Sir. Only mist.'

At last I was dressed. I put on my soft hat. No need to wear a steel helmet in a war like this. Two signallers were waiting for me outside, and we were about to set off when for the first time I became aware of the sound of gunfire up the line. That was nothing unusual in the hour before dawn, but

162

this morning it seemed heavier than usual. Telling the signallers to wait I went back to my shelter, changed the soft hat for a helmet, and pulled my gas mask round to the alert position in front. Now I was ready for anything.

We began walking up the hill. Thirsk had been right about the fog, it was very thick. But there was a telephone line running along the ground up to our forward section, and I held this in my hand to guide me. Every minute I was expecting the noise in front to die away, this was the usual procedure, but instead of becoming less it seemed to intensify, and now it was not all in front, some shells were passing overhead and falling behind us, and one or two burst at no great distance from ourselves. I began to feel uneasy. We had reached the top of the hill by this time, but the fog was thicker than ever and though day was breaking I could not see more than five yards in front of me.

Then we came to a break in the telephone wire, it had been cut by one of the shells, and because of the fog we could not find the other end. The line had also been broken behind us, I was no longer in communication with anyone, I was stuck at the top of the hill, unable to see more than five yards in any direction. The fog was cold as well as wet, and it was shutting out something else besides the view, it was preventing my finding out what was happening. I felt alone and lost. I certainly should lose my way if I went on, but I could not go back until I had obtained some information. All three of us searched the ground for the other end of the wire, but without success.

The fury of the guns had increased. Now there was gas as well as high explosive. I could not see where any of the shells were bursting, but I could hear the gas shells, they made a different sound when they burst, and I could smell the sickly mustard gas mixing with the clammy smell of the fog.

Something *was* happening up in front and I did not know what it was. I began to feel afraid. It was not the ordinary fear of shells. That was nothing, that stopped as soon as the shelling stopped. This was a new fear and it was not going to stop, it lasted for more than four months, it was the fear of the unknown. A line of infantry came out of the fog, brushing past us on their way up to the line, each man touching the

163

man in front, so as not to lose him. I hoped that one of their officers might have something to tell me, but they knew nothing. They had been in reserve, they had been ordered up—that was all they could tell me. The gas became worse, we had to put on our masks, now it was impossible even to try to look for the other end of the wire. I kept on taking off my mask to smell whether the air was clear, and putting it on again. Sometimes the fog seemed to clear a little then it came down again as thick as before.

In one of these clearer intervals, clear of fog and gas, my signallers found the other end of the wire, and now the line had been mended behind us also, we were in communication with the battery again. I spoke to Bingley, I had no information to give him and he had none for me, but he told me to go on to the forward section, where Griffith was. My signallers told me that Sergeant Thirsk had been badly wounded while out mending the line between ourselves and the guns. I was sorry about this. Thirsk wounded and Denmark at home on leave, they were two of the pillars of the battery, our loss of them was certain, nothing else was certain yet.

I found Griffith eating his breakfast. He was a little Welshman, rather unattractive in appearance, and we had not found any qualities in him to make up for this. Jamieson had sent him up to the forward section to get rid of him, and Bingley had left him there. But he did not appear to mind, and on this worrying morning I was impressed by his unconcern.

'What's happening?' I asked.

He looked at me solemnly while he went on munching. 'Truth to tell,' he said at last, 'I don't know.' He had opened fire with his two guns when the bombardment started, but as nothing seemed to be happening he had stopped. They had suffered no casualties. 'You can't see a thing outside,' he said, as though not knowing that I had been out in the fog for five hours. Hearing that I'd had no breakfast he offered to get me some, but I was not hungry, I ate a slice of bread and marmalade while we were talking and drank some tea.

It was half past nine. I went outside by myself and wondered what I ought to do. It was quieter now, the gunfire on both sides had almost stopped. I heard some machine-gun fire, but not close at hand. Whatever it was that had been

164

happening up in the line seemed to be over now. It was reasonable to suppose that the attack, if there had been an attack, had been repulsed. There might be another, later in the day, but for the moment the situation was under control. I began to think I had been unnecessarily alarmed.

At that moment some figures came running towards me out of the fog. They were on top of me almost before I had seen them. Germans? Of course not. What an absurd idea! But why were they running?

'Jerry's through,' one of them said. He was bewildered, frightened, out of breath from running.

'What's happened?' I asked.

'Jerry's through,' he said again. 'He's in Epehy, we've got no officers left.'

The fog had already swallowed the other men with him, and in a moment he also had disappeared.

I went very quickly back to my signallers and spoke to Frank on the telephone. He put me through to Cherry, the adjutant, at Brigade Headquarters, and I told him what the man had said to me, but he did not accept the truth of the story, it was in contradiction to all the rest of his information, he said. Everyone liked Cherry, but he was too optimistic, he always believed good reports and disbelieved bad ones. So now when he told me that the enemy attack on our front had been repulsed, I did not know whether this was a fact or if it was only what he wanted to believe. Epehy was about a mile in front of where I was and part of our main line of defence. 'These men that you saw,' Cherry said, 'I expect a shell had burst in the middle of their trench and they panicked,' but he told me to keep a sharp look-out, and to let him know at once if I saw anything of the enemy.

I went back to my place. No other figures came running out of the fog. The fog itself disappeared, and the hills and valleys lay bathed in bright sunshine for the rest of the day, the bare sides of Chapel Hill on my left and in front of me, another railway line below me, coming up from behind and running east towards the enemy, and Epehy out of sight, just over the crest on my immediate front. 'Keep a sharp look-out,' Cherry had said. I looked and looked, but there was nothing to see. No German soldiers, no British ones, only the sunlight on the bare hillsides. Was there a battle being fought? I could see nothing of it. Everything looked the same as on any other day.

The hours crawled by. Sometimes I was alone, sometimes Griffith came out to talk to me, or I went to talk to him in his little shelter. He was not a lively companion, but I was glad not to be alone on a day like this. Frank rang up from the battery, 'Keep a sharp look-out on the railway line,' he said, 'there's a report that the enemy is advancing along it." I ran out to my place and searched the line through my glasses. I could see nothing, there was no one there, no one on the part of the line that I could see, only the lengthening shadows creeping across the track.

'I can't see anyone,' I said to Frank.

'No, the report's been denied now,' he said.

At dusk I returned to the battery, and as soon as it was dark the two forward guns were brought back to the main position, it was too risky to leave them for another night. I was hoping to find that I should laugh again when I was in the company of the others, but Hughes was away, he had been sent up as liaison officer at Infantry Battalion Head-quarters, and Frank was as worried as I was. Bingley was in a terrible state, he told me. 'I've had to hold his hand all day,' he said.

Only Griffith was in the mood for talking that night. 'Well, I was ready for that,' he said when we had finished dinner. He was always ready for his meals and usually said so. He made a few trite remarks, but none of us were paying any attention to him, and presently I saw that he was writing in his diary.

'I see that it's the first day of spring,' he remarked, 'and in some ways it has been a real spring-like day, hasn't it?'

'Oh, for God's sake, stop talking,' Bingley said.

I went to bed, but tired though I was I could not sleep. Cherry's last report on the situation was that on our front we had not lost a yard of our battle position, only some unimportant outposts. But on our right the situation was obscure, he said; and that amounted to admitting we had been driven back. Frank said that so far as he could gather we had no reserves and that if the Boche attacked again in the morning in the same strength we should not be able to hold him. This

166

was the fear which was keeping me awake; if he attacked again in the morning!

I tried to persuade myself that he must be too tired to do so, remembering how exhausted we had always been at Ypres on the night after one of our attacks. I fell into a troubled sleep at last, but was woken before daylight, woken by the bombardment of German guns, there was nothing tired about them, they sounded terrifyingly fresh. Again there was thick fog, again there was no news. Bingley did not send any of us up to the top of the hill, he seemed incapable of any action. 'O my God!' he said as he came into the mess, 'I can't stand another day like yesterday.'

The fog rolled away and the bad news began to come in. At first it was all from the right. Even Cherry was depressed. He said it was difficult to sort out the conflicting reports but there was no doubt that the enemy had penetrated our battle line at some points.

'O my God!' said Bingley.

Then we heard that one of the divisions on our right had lost the whole of its battle line.

'O my God!' said Bingley.

Then it was Roisel, the enemy was in Roisel.

'O my God!' said Bingley. 'It will be another Sedan.'

I went to sit beside Frank, who had the map in front of him. He pointed to Roisel, due south of us, five miles away. It meant the enemy was half way to Peronne already, and that we were in some danger of having our retreat cut off.

'We ought to be doing something,' Frank said. 'Why aren't we firing?'

One reason was that we did not know the position of the enemy or where our own men were, all the telephone lines in front were broken. Hughes could have told us what the position was, he ought to have returned by this time, he would know where the enemy was, but nothing had been heard of him since the previous night.

'At any rate we could fire on our old S.O.S. lines,' Frank said. Every gun had a line on which it was to open fire in the event of enemy attack. But Bingley said we must conserve our ammunition, we should need it later on.

Cherry rang up again. This time he had information about

167

our own front: Chapel Hill had been lost, Chapel Hill, our battle line, our main line of defence.

Still Bingley did nothing. 'We must wait for the Colonel's orders,' he said, 'he will tell us what to do.'' It was a great mistake, he said, to act on one's own initiative, one always found out afterwards that one had done the worst possible thing.

He could not sit still. He kept on getting up and going outside and walking to the end of the line of guns. Then he would come back into the mess and sit down for two or three minutes before going off again. Shells were falling outside, but he was not afraid of shellfire, it was responsibility that he feared, or losing his guns, or being taken prisoner.

'We ought to be doing something,' Frank said again, while Bingley was outside. 'It's absurd to talk about conserving ammunition, we can get more.'

He tried to get through to Brigade Headquarters on his own authority, but there was no answer, they were on the move. The other batteries were already moving back, they had been in front of us, on the far side of the village of Heudecourt, now they were moving into the valley behind us, where we were to join them later in the day.

'I've a good mind to go out myself and see if I can find out what's happening,' Frank said. He was continually taking off his spectacles and polishing the glass with his handkerchief, then rubbing his eyes with his knuckles before he put them back. I could see he was very worried.

But Bingley said there was no need for him to go, and anyway he could not spare him at present. 'We must wait for the Colonel's orders,' he said. The important thing now was to be ready to move back when the order came, it might come at any moment, and we should be in a regular pickle if we were all over the place when it did come, we could do all the firing we wanted after we had moved back.

At three o'clock Hughes returned in a very bad temper. 'Bloody Brigade forgot all about me,' he said. 'Never sent anyone to relieve me, I might have been a bloody stiff by this time for all they care.'

His bad temper was not on his own account, it was because he was desperately worried.

168

'Talk about stiffs!' he said. 'Never seen so many in all my born days.'

'Ours or theirs?' I asked, but I knew what his answer would be before he spoke.

'Ours, every man jack of them, Jocks and South Africans. Jerry brought up his trench mortars in the fog and smashed our trenches to bloody bits.'

'What's happening now?' Frank asked.

'God knows! They were expecting Jerry where I was in ten minutes. They told me to clear out. "Give me a rifle and I'll stay," I said. But they said it wasn't my job to stay and be killed with them.'

'How long ago was that?' Frank asked.

Hughes looked at his watch. 'Half an hour,' he said. 'Jerry will be there now.'

'O my God!' said Bingley. He tried to ring through to Brigade, but there was still no answer.

Then he went outside again and this time Frank followed him. Presently Frank returned by himself. 'I hope you don't mind," he said to me, 'but I've asked Bingley and he's told me to send you up to the top of the hill. I would have gone myself, but you see what he's like, I have to hold his hand all the time. You'll have to lay out a line as you go. Be quick, and for Christ's sake try to find out what's happening.'

I did not mind going. It was really a relief to have something definite to do, for the first time that day. I set off at once, with two signallers, unrolling the wire as we went. It was fairly quiet, there was some firing in front, not a great deal. Again the sun was shining out of a cloudless sky. If there is anything to see, I thought, I shall see it today. But I knew that things had a way of happening out of sight.

I looked at my watch, it was half past three. We came up to the crest and went on a little way, passing the village of Heudecourt on our left. We went about a thousand yards from the battery, I could not go any further, there was not enough telephone wire. Anyway, there was a good view from here. I could not see into the bottom of the hill below me, that was dead ground from where we were, but I could see all the far side up to the crest of Chapel Hill.

I lay down on the ground and got out my field glasses, I

169

put them up to my eyes, resting on my elbows. And immediately I saw them. Germans. Thousands of them. Pouring down the side of Chapel Hill. It was the chance of a lifetime. Never before had I seen Germans to shoot at.

'BATTERY ACTION!' I yelled to the signaller behind me.

I pulled out my map and opened it and quickly began to work out the range and angle of fire. Quick, quick! The Germans were coming down the hill in waves and in short rushes. They ran for about a hundred yards, then dropped down for a minute or two, then came on again. My excitement made me slow. Frank will work it out for me, I thought, if I tell him exactly where they are. He was very quick and accurate at map work. I told my signaller to ask him to come to the telephone quickly, but before he could do so there was a message from Bingley: 'Captain says we can't fire,' my signaller said, 'Guns are all packed up ready to move.'

I rushed to the telephone myself. 'THE BOCHE WILL BE HERE IN TEN MINUTES,' I screamed. I was going to add 'unless we stop him,' but as I paused for breath I heard the calm voice of Signaller Burton at the other end repeating my message to Bingley, who must have been standing near the telephone pit. 'Mr Campbell says the Boche will be here in ten minutes, Sir,' I heard him say. He made it sound as though we had invited them to tea and they had rung up to say they would be a few minutes late.

Bingley himself came running to the telephone. 'What's this,' what's this?' he said. 'Germans here in ten minutes! What do you mean, ten minutes? You must be mistaken. We've had no orders, the Colonel would have told me. What do you mean?'

I made a great effort to control myself. It was stupid of me to have exaggerated, the top of Chapel Hill was three thousand yards away, I did not know how long it would take the enemy to come. But in one respect the situation was even more serious than I had at first supposed, my first thought had been that these Germans were attacking our front line, now I realised that our line was somewhere below me, in the ground that I could not see, these Germans coming down the

170

hill were to make the next attack and O God! there might be
no one left to resist them.

'There are waves of Germans coming down Chapel Hill,' I
said, speaking as calmly as I could. 'We must fire at them.'

'They must be our own men,' he said.

'They're Germans, I can see the shape of their helmets and
the colour of their uniforms.'

He did not know what to do. 'The guns are all packed up,'
he said. 'I'm expecting the Colonel's order to move back any
minute.'

'We must fire,' I said, 'no one else is firing at them.'

'That shows they are our own people.'

'They're Germans, no one else is firing because there's no
one left.'

'Are you sure they're Germans?'

'Absolutely certain,' I said.

'Well, you can have two guns,' he said at last. 'But you
must be careful with the ammunition.'

Careful with ammunition! For weeks past we had been firing hundreds of rounds every night, without knowing whether
we were inflicting a single casualty. Now in broad daylight
when I had the whole German Army to shoot at he told me
to be careful of ammunition.

I gave my orders to the signaller and waited to see where
my ranging shells burst. I had done my calculations very
badly, the first two shells fell so far to the right that I almost
missed them. I corrected the line. But the next pair burst too
high, harmlessly up in the sky. Shrapnel was the right weapon
to use against enemy troops in the open, but the shells should
burst fifteen feet above them, not a hundred. I corrected the
fuse. I had to make three or four corrections before the shells
were bursting at the right height, and by the time I had done
so the first waves of enemy were out of sight, safely in the
dead ground below me. But there were more to come.

All this time we had been under fire ourselves. We might
have been seen by an enemy observer, but Heudecourt and
the whole of the top of the hill was being shelled, we were not
a particular target. A few of the shells fell close to us, one
showered earth and chalk on to the map on the ground beside
me. I put my arms round my face to protect it, but took no

171

other notice, I was too excited, I kept my eyes on the opposite hillside, waiting for the Germans to appear.

Then I saw them get up and begin to run down the hill. 'FIRE,' I shouted over my shoulder. Ah! that was better, I could see some of the enemy ducking their heads as they heard my shells coming towards them.

'FIVE ROUNDS RAPID!' I shouted.

But there was no report behind me, no shells passed above our heads. What had happened, what had gone wrong? The enemy had escaped me again.

'Captain says we must go in now,' my signaller said. 'Order's come, and we're to go back. He's told guns to stop firing.'

I rushed to the telephone again and asked to speak to Bingley, but he had gone. I tried to speak to Frank, but he was not there. 'Is Mr Hughes there?' I asked. 'No, Sir, he's gone back.'

There was nobody. I gave up. My signallers were looking at me questioningly.

'What are we to do, Sir?'

'We've got to go back,' I said.

We walked down the hill without speaking, the signallers rolling the wire up again as we walked. I was bitterly disappointed with myself. I could pretend that it was all Bingley's fault, but in my heart I knew that I had failed, I was the only person who had *seen* the enemy. If Frank had been in my place he would have ordered the guns to go on firing, whatever Bingley said. So would Hughes. If Bingley had tried to stop them they would have insisted on speaking to Colonel Richardson. That was what I should have done. Asked to be put through to the Colonel. But I had not thought of it. Now it was too late. The chance of a lifetime, and I had thrown it away.

Some weeks later I was awarded the Military Cross. The citation read: He directed the fire of his battery from a most forward position, inflicting heavy casualties on the advancing enemy, exposing himself to great danger and supplying much valuable information throughout.

172

I was distressed when I read it. It was not true that I had inflicted heavy casualties on the enemy.

Jamieson must have recommended me, he was the only person I had told. Happening to be alone with him a few nights later I told him about the Germans I had seen, and how I had tried to stop their advance, but Bingley would not let me fire. I put all the blame on Bingley when telling the story, but I did not pretend that I had been successful.

I wanted to win the Military Cross, and sometimes as I was falling asleep I had imagined myself doing some brave action. But to win it for something I had not done was distressing, and at first I felt unhappy whenever I caught sight of the purple and white ribbon on my tunic. What would my friends in the battery think if they knew what had really happened! Better to have no medal than to lose their respect. But they said they were pleased and they seemed to think it was all right, my having the medal. If they thought so, then it was all right for me, and I soon became proud of the ribbon. By the time the War came to an end I no longer even felt regret at my failure to kill Germans on Chapel Hill.

Three

Two guns had already left by the time I got back to the battery in the valley and two others were on the point of leaving, but the last two were still in position under the bank, there was no reason why I should not have gone on firing with four guns, or even with all six, for another ten minutes at least. Two wagon loads of ammunition were being taken back with the guns, and Bingley told me to go with them and then to return with the empty wagons for another load. I did not see Frank or any of the others.

We were only going back a thousand yards, into the next downland hollow. We had to go up our valley for a few hundred yards, then turn right, cross over the ridge, and go down into the next valley. The three other batteries in the brigade, A B and D, were there already. There was a horse for me and I rode quickly after the little column, which had just left.

I was still feeling very unhappy because of my failure on the hill. I did not speak to anyone and was not clearly conscious of anything that was happening round me. The wagons were unloaded and in a few minutes I was on my way back with them to the old position. There should have been two limbers as well, for the last two guns, but I had not seen them, I only had the two empty wagons with me, perhaps someone had told me not to wait for them, they would be following. I was riding in front at ordinary walking speed, there was no hurry. I did notice a line of men coming towards me down the side of the hill, they were on my right, they would not actually pass me. I did wonder who they were and what they were doing, but it was not unusual to see a small party of infantry returning from the line.

I was still thinking about the enemy I had seen on Chapel

Hill, not so much about them, I was not wondering where they were now, I was wondering what I ought to have done. But my thoughts were suddenly diverted. I heard a roar of aeroplanes in front, and looking up I saw them coming over the ridge, very low, hardly above tree-top level. Maltese crosses on the underside of their wings! Good God, they were Germans! I had never seen so many. Stop and hope they would not see us? or gallop on? One was coming straight towards us.

'GALLOP,' I shouted over my shoulder.

We flew across the downland, crouching low over our horses. I heard the stuttering of a machine-gun. But in a second or two they were past us, and I could hear my two teams galloping behind me. Over the ridge, down into the hollow, along the bottom, still at the gallop. Then we drew up. One horse slightly wounded in the neck. Good God, what an escape!

Shells had begun to fall round us as we were galloping, we had escaped them also. Everyone on the old position was talking at the same time, everyone was marvelling at his own escape and at ours. I saw another line of men coming down the hill towards us. They would come past us, straight through our position. I went to tell Bingley that I was back. He was not worried about the enemy aeroplanes or the shells, he seemed calmer now than he had been all day. But before I could speak to him an officer came out from the moving line of men and went up to him. 'You'd better clear out,' I heard him say. 'The Boche is in Heudecourt, he'll be here in a few minutes, we were the last to leave.'

For once Bingley made up his mind quickly. There were still two guns on the position, and there were the two wagons with their teams which I had just brought up. In a moment the wagon bodies were unhooked, and their limbers hooked up to the last two guns. In a moment they were galloping up the valley, along the way I had just come. Everything else was abandoned: two wagon bodies, nearly a thousand rounds of ammunition which I might have used against Chapel Hill, maps, orders, telephone wire, stores, everything left behind. I hadn't got a horse, it wasn't my own horse I had been riding, none of us had a horse, we were running straight up the hill, that was the shortest way into the next valley. Bingley and myself, the sergeant-major, gunners and signallers. Once I heard myself laughing as we pounded up the hill, it seemed so funny. We were under machine-gun fire, I heard the bullets as we came to the top of the hill, and shells were still falling round us, but the guns were safely over the hill, I could see them in front of us, galloping still.

We could stop running when we were over the crest and going down into the next valley. Edric saw me walking and came to meet me with my horse. But I was puzzled, I was trying to work something out and could not get the answer right. If the Boche was already in Heudecourt, had been there for a quarter of an hour or more, if these lines of retreating infantry were the last men to leave, then why were we here? We had come back a mere thousand yards. If the Boche was already in the valley we had just left, how long would it be before he came to this next one? Had something gone wrong?

I could not think clearly. Too many things had been happening too close together. Possibly I was dreaming, all these events had the absurdity of a dream. I decided to go and find Frank, he would probably have an explanation. But as I was going towards him I heard a curious noise. An explosion of some kind, but not a shell bursting.

'They're blowing up their guns,' someone said.

'Who are blowing up their guns?'

'A and B, they've got no teams up.'

The lines of infantry were passing through us again.

'Time you got out,' an infantryman said. 'No one between us and him.'

I heard two more of the same curious explosions, some little distance away. All the four batteries of our brigade were in line in the valley, A, B, C, D, in that order, A on the right. The curious noises had come from the right.

So it was real, I was not dreaming, A and B were abandoning their guns, and the Boche would be here in a few more minutes. We had six teams up. Six teams and six guns, one for each. They were not the gun teams, but they would do. Everything else would have to be left behind.

'Be quick there,' Frank was shouting.

One of the guns was stuck, it had fallen into a deep shell-

176

hole, the horses could not pull it out. 'We shall have to leave it,' I said. Bombardier Frith dismounted and got into the hole, he put his great shoulders to the wheel of the gun and heaved. The wheel moved a little, but then slipped back. He tried again. The other guns were already on the move.

'We must leave it,' I said again. If the other batteries were leaving all their six guns, we could leave one. Bombardier Frith did not speak, his face never moved, he heaved on the wheel with all the great strength of a Yorkshire miner, it was moving, two or three gunners were helping him now, but it was Frith who held the wheel, Frith never let go till the gun was out of the hole. We were the last to leave. Everything else was left behind in the valley, another thousand rounds of ammunition, two or three wagons, all our mess stores, the gramophone and our records, all our personal kit—there were our neatly-rolled valises, lying together where the mess cart had put them down, now the empty mess cart would be half way back to Nurlu, there had been nothing else to carry our valises, and I should have only the clothes I was wearing.

I was riding at the rear of the column, Frank was up at the front with Bingley, I had not seen either Hughes or Griffith since coming down from the hill. We were under machine-gun fire again, but not aimed, there were no enemy in sight. But if they were in the first valley by this time, we might at any moment see them on the crest above us, and then we should come under aimed fire.

For a few hundred yards we were going along the valley, parallel to the line of the enemy's advance, then we turned sharply right, away from him, along the track leading to Nurlu, where our wagon lines had been. It was as we were turning, as the front of our little column was beginning to climb the hill that I had a sudden impulse to go back, I was going back to get the rug out of my valise.

Without a word to anyone I turned round and galloped back along the way we had just come, along the deserted valley, past the ill-fated gun position, back to the pile of neatly-rolled valises lying on the ground where the mess cart had dumped them.

Two men were there. Germans? No, English officers. One was sitting in Bingley's green canvas chair, the other was unrolling one of the valises, my valise. Where on earth had they come from?

'Time you got out,' I shouted. 'The Boche will be here in a few minutes.'

'We're waiting for him,' said the man in the green canvas chair.

I saw they were both padres. 'Most of our men who are left have been taken prisoner,' said the man in the chair, 'our place is with them.' The other man was taking the rug out of my valise.

'I want that,' I said, 'it's what I've come back for.'

'Oh, it's yours, is it?' he said. 'Sorry.'

'Take anything else you like,' I said. But I was pulling things out of the valise, wondering what else I could take. Quick, quick! Any minute now!

The man in the chair had come over to me, he gave me a sheet of paper, torn out of his note book, on which he had written his name and address. 'Write to my wife,' he said.

I took the paper, I shook hands with them both, I grabbed my big writing case, it contained my 1917 diary, the book I was reading, and a letter from a girl. Then back on to my horse, and I was galloping along the valley again, I had been a bit longer than I had intended because of talking to the two chaplains, but I should catch up with the others, probably before they had even noticed my absence.

But at the same corner, at the very place where I had turned back before, I nearly rode into three other men. Scottish machine-gunners. One of them was wounded, the other two were wheeling him along on a bicycle. They had got him down the hill, but it was proving more difficult to push him up on the other side. I dismounted again before I had thought what I was doing. 'We can put him on my horse,' I said. Between us we lifted the wounded man into the saddle. This was another delay, I reflected, the rest of the battery was already over the top of the hill and out of sight; but galloping, I should soon catch them up when the friends of the wounded man had taken him again at the top, it would be easy for them to wheel him on the level.

I was leading my horse, the two men with the bicycle were behind me, but when I looked round at the top of the hill they were not there. Somehow they had got in front of me, they were quite a long way off, they were riding away on the bicycle. I shouted. But they did not hear me, or may not have wanted to, and the sound of my own voice made me realise how alone I was. Alone with a wounded soldier in the middle of a battle! The cyclists were out of sight now. There was no human being in sight. The rest of the battery and the retreating infantry had crossed the plateau and were now hidden from me in lower ground. Somewhere behind us were the Germans. I turned round to look, but they had not yet come over the crest behind me. Our army on one side, the Germans on the other, and between the two myself and my horse and a wounded Scottish machine-gunner on her back.

The battlefield was as silent as it was deserted. The aeroplanes had gone, the shellfire had ceased. The calm evening sunshine lay over the downland, the shadows were beginning to lengthen. It was beautiful. The battlefield was beautiful. I could not see into the hollow where our guns had been, I could only see some of the abandoned guns on the other side of the track. They looked out of place, incongruous with the peaceful scene, one or two were pointing up to the sky at a grotesque angle. But there was nothing else to mar the quiet dignity of the downs, there was nothing else to see, only some deserted guns and a wounded man on a horse.

Well, I had got myself into a proper mess. But there was no way out of it now, I should have to look after my wounded man until I could hand him over to the care of someone more fitted than myself. Fortunately I knew the position of a Field Ambulance on this side of Nurlu. But it would take a full half hour to get there, it would be nearly dark, how on earth could I find the battery in the dark! I knew it was retreating through Nurlu, everything had to go through Nurlu, but I had no idea of its destination on the other side. And what should I say to Frank and Bingley when I did find them! It was a serious matter to go off without orders in the middle of a battle. I did not really think Bingley would want to court-martial me, but I knew that my behaviour could be described as desertion in the face of the enemy.

The man's wound was worse than I had at first supposed. He was in pain, I was afraid of his falling off, I could not have

179

lifted him back by myself. I had to support him in the saddle as well as leading my horse. I put the rug round my shoulders and gave him the writing case to carry, so as to have both hands free. He dropped it on the way, I never saw it again. But I still had the rug.

The sun was only a little way above the horizon, a great red ball in front of me as I walked up the last hill and came to the Field Ambulance. A doctor, a captain in the RAMC, was on the point of driving away in a car. I explained to him what had happened and waited for him to free me of my responsibility. But he said he could not take my soldier, all their wounded had been evacuated, the last ambulance had left.

'You must take him,' I said. 'I can't leave him for the Boche, and I can't go on leading him all over France, I've got to find my battery.'

The doctor looked at me, he looked at the wounded Scotsman, who had taken no part in our conversation, he and I had hardly exchanged a word on our way.

'All right,' he said. 'I'll take him.' He called to someone behind him. Two men came out of a hut, they lifted the man down and carried him away on a stretcher.

At last I was free. Now I must get to the other side of Nurlu as quickly as possible, that was where I must begin looking for the battery. The enemy was shelling Nurlu, there was a cross-roads in the middle of the village, everything had to pass it, guns, wagons, lorries, everything, and the enemy's fire was directed at the cross-roads. Big stuff. It sounded like eight-inch, one shell every two or three minutes. The wagons waited on the road at a safe distance, waited for a shell to burst, then galloped past the danger spot at a mad speed, half a dozen at a time. One too many went. I heard the scream of an approaching shell, followed by a tremendous explosion, and a great cloud of black smoke rose into the air.

I saw what had happened as soon as I turned the corner, dead men and horses lay sprawled across the road. One man was still alive, I saw him struggling to get up, and while I looked I saw another man come out and raise the wounded man in his arms and move him a little, out of the way of other galloping wagons.

It might be one of our wagons that had been hit, I thought,

180

between us we might be able to hoist another wounded man on to my horse. I rode quickly up to the cross-roads. 'Anything I can do to help?' I asked.

But one look at the face of the wounded man was enough to show me there was nothing I could do, nor anyone else. The man who was holding the dying soldier looked up at me, I saw his black regimental badge, it was another padre. He was kneeling in the most dangerous place in Nurlu, at that moment there may have been no more dangerous place on the whole of the Western Front. I should have to change my opinion of padres, I thought. We did not have one in our brigade, only a doctor, but I had come across several, always behind the line, they had not been impressive. Now it seemed there was another kind of padre.

'Are you a doctor?' he asked. He was kneeling on the road, holding the dying man in his arms, looking up at me.

I shook my head.

'Then go away,' he said. 'In God's name, go quickly.'

But I turned round for a last look as I was riding away. I saw the dead men and the horses lying across the road, no wagons were coming by, another shell was due, I heard it coming, I saw the padre bend low over the man he was holding, but the shell burst a little way off, smoke and brick dust filled the air, but this time it was only a house that had been hit. That was my last sight of Nurlu.

I looked everywhere for the battery. I stood at the side of the road, looking at every gun or wagon that came past me, hoping to see a familiar face. Then leaving the road I went to every place I could see where there were horses, and at one of these I found our wagon lines. Jamieson was there, he had moved back during the afternoon, he told me. He also was looking for the guns; but less zealously, I thought, than I had been. He told me to stay with him and I was glad to do so. It was not my right place, but at any rate I was no longer lost. To my surprise I saw Hughes and Griffith there. I did not ask them how they had become separated from Bingley and Frank, and they asked me no questions. A meal was ready, we sat down on the ground, but before we had begun to eat there was an order for us to move immediately.

Putting some biscuits into my pocket I got back on to my

horse, and as I did so I felt that all my strength had gone. Excitement and a sense of responsibility had kept me going through the last four or five hours, from the moment that I had begun walking up the hill towards Heudecourt; now suddenly, as darkness fell, I knew that I was finished, I could do no more.

And as my strength had gone, so had my courage, and instead of wanting to be up in the front of the battle I was eager to go back, to get as far away as possible from the enemy, to go more quickly, not to be held up on the road, the road was packed with other transport, we were stuck, we should never get away. I did not know where we were going, but it seemed only too probable that the enemy would get there first.

Now for the first time a realisation of the magnitude of our defeat came over me and overcame me. This was the most catastrophic defeat that Britain had ever suffered, and it seemed to me that I was partly responsible for the disaster. I could have stopped the enemy on Chapel Hill, I ought to have done so. We had left two thousand rounds of ammunition behind us, if I had kept my head we could have fired them all, we might have killed two thousand Germans. That was my job—to kill Germans, not to go galloping about with a rug or taking a wounded Scottish machine-gunner on my horse.

To left and right of us the blackness of the night sky was lit up with explosions. Petrol stores and ammunition dumps were being blown up, to prevent their falling into the hands of the enemy. Huts were blazing all round us. At one stage of our march I found Corporal Albert riding at my side. 'Some of the lads is saying, Sir, that we're luring Jerry on,' he said to me. 'What do you think, Sir?'

I could see his white anxious unhappy face by the light of the burning huts. He was frightened, he needed re-assurance, he wanted help from me, to be told that it was all right, but I could not help him, I was as unhappy as he was, and more despondent.

'I don't know,' I said. 'I don't know what to think.'

We stopped at last. I did not know where we were. We did not seem to be anywhere. But there were no Germans. It was very cold. Ropes were put up between the wagons, the horses were tied to them, horses and men were given something to eat. 'The servants have got some grub for us,' Hughes said. I followed him into a hut of some kind, there was a roof over our heads and candles were burning, it was a relief to get out of the cold night. Somebody was saying something about eggs. 'At least three hundred,' I heard Hughes say. 'Poor devil had to pack up a second time and leave everything.' That was why we were eating buttered eggs, I supposed; but I hardly knew what I was eating, I was so tired.

I fell asleep lying on the floor. Once I woke up and heard Frank swearing. So he had succeeded in finding us, though we had failed to find him. I heard him saying that none of the men with the guns had any food at all. That was why he was swearing. He would have liked to swear at Jamieson, whose responsibility it was to feed the gun line, but not being able to swear at him he cursed the luckless Griffith instead. Everyone in a bad temper always swore at Griffith. I heard the two of them riding away into the darkness of the night. I felt mean to go on sleeping and lying in the warmth of the hut, but only a direct order could have made me move.

I awoke again an hour or two later, before daybreak. It was the German guns again that woke me, but this time they were more distant, we had retreated a long way. At once I remembered everything, my failure and bitter discouragement. But soon the others began stirring, and I felt better when we began to talk. I was able to enjoy my breakfast eggs. But most of the men had been out in the open all night, some without blankets had had to walk about all the time because they were too cold to lie down.

Bingley and Frank and Griffith arrived with the six guns, and they were given their eggs. 'Hello!' Frank said crossly when he saw me, 'what happened to you? Where did you go off to?' But he was not interested in my answer, it was easy to be evasive. Bingley never noticed I was there, he probably had not noticed my absence either.

Then Colonel Richardson, the Brigade Commander, came with all his Headquarters Staff, and there were eggs for them too. The Colonel said we had nothing to reproach ourselves for, we had fought magnificently, the courage of the whole of the Fifth Army had been beyond praise, we had been outnumbered, five or six to one, but everywhere we had put up the most determined resistance, and the Boche casualties had been simply enormous. I did not believe all that he was saying, but perhaps it had not been such a terrible defeat as I had at first thought.

Cherry said we had nothing to worry about. The French were marching to our assistance at full speed. Two Army Corps, a hundred thousand men at least. We had only to hold on for one more day. I did not believe him either, but perhaps somebody some day would come up from behind to help us.

The Colonel and Cherry rode away. Bingley also went away. He was on the verge of collapse and the Colonel sent him back to get some sleep. Frank went with him. Jamieson stayed up with the guns. It was a relief to have him in command. He was imperturbable, he behaved as though nothing out of the ordinary had happened. Hughes, the Welsh policeman, was equally calm. 'Jerry's turn today,' he said, 'our turn again tomorrow.'

Four

The Retreat went on.

We stayed where we were, in the Frenchman's hut, eating more of his eggs, until afternoon. From a high bank behind the guns I saw an enemy battery driving along the road out of Nurlu, the road where we had been the night before. I hated them. They looked so arrogant, so sure of themselves. Nobody was firing at them, there was nothing we could do, they were far beyond the range of our guns. I watched them driving along the road, then coming down the side of the hill, over the green turf of the downs. I saw them halt, the guns were drawn up in position for firing and the horses taken back over the hill. It was effortlessly done, no one making any attempt to stop them, I might have been watching a ceremonial parade.

This may have been the battery which fired at us during the afternoon. The shells did us no harm. Most of the men were asleep in the sunshine, making up the sleep they had lost. They woke up, looked at the shell bursts, which were a little way from us, and went to sleep again.

And sometime after this we received the order to retreat again. We came to the little town of Combles. There was nothing left of it. Now we were out of the unspoilt country and coming into the devastated area, the old Somme battle-field of 1916. Villages were mounds of rubble, woods were splintered stumps, there were tumbledown trenches on both sides of the road and coils of rusted wire.

We passed through Combles and climbed the hill on the other side. There we stopped. The guns were drawn up in line, ready to open fire if we had to. We went to look for sleeping places for ourselves in the old trenches.

185

'If we had some rum,' Hughes said, 'we could put it in our tea, if we had any tea.' Presently there was rum and tea for everyone. And a hot meal.

'I was ready for that,' Griffith said.

My own spirits began to rise, we seemed less on our own, there was a battery of 60-pounder guns close to us. I went with Jamieson to talk to some of their officers.

'We shall have to use the *Daily Mail* War Map if we have to fire,' their battery commander told us. 'It's the only one we've got. Our thoughtful Staff has omitted to supply us with maps of the back area.'

'They know the British never retreat,' Jamieson said.

He and I shared a little shelter leading out from one of the old trenches. Though it was less cold there than at ground level I should have been cold with only my one rug, but Jamieson shared his blankets with me, and it was while we were lying side by side in our narrow cell that I told him about the Germans I had seen on Chapel Hill.

Again we were wakened early, this time not by German guns, but by an orderly from Brigade Headquarters with our orders for the day. Sitting up in the trench I read them over Jamieson's shoulder. O God! We were to send out an officer at once with a gun and a hundred rounds of ammunition. To engage the enemy over open sights, to inflict casualties and hold up his advance. It was my turn, Hughes had gone out by himself during the previous afternoon and Griffith had been taken by Frank in the night. But this was something far worse, it was a suicide job, it was asking to be killed.

'Shall I go?' I said. I wanted to be able to pretend that I had volunteered.

Jamieson did not answer at once, and I was aware of a faint spark of hope, for I could see from his face that he agreed with me that it was suicidal, and he was asking himself which of us would be the least loss to the battery. My hope increased, for if I was right I guessed what his answer would be.

'No, I'll send Griffith,' he said.

It was unfair, Griffith was given all the rotten jobs, but I could not have offered again, and I could not help admiring Griffith as he rode away with his gun. He seemed utterly un-

186

concerned, he was only worrying about his breakfast, which there had been no time for.

'They'll give him breakfast in heaven,' Hughes remarked, as we watched them going down the hill.

None of us thought we should ever see him again, or his gun or any of the men with him. For engaging the enemy over open sights meant that he could see you as easily as you could see him, and Griffith and his men would be overwhelmed as soon as they appeared over the skyline, they might be surrounded by enemy infantry at once, they would certainly come under very heavy fire.

Soon we were on the move again ourselves, the retreat was continuing. First I saw our infantry, what was left of them, wearily climbing the hill towards us, and then the enemy coming down the opposite slope into Combles. If that was the way Griffith had gone he might already have been taken prisoner.

Jamieson and Hughes had already left with the guns, I had not yet started, some of our wagons had gone to fill up with ammunition and Jamieson had told me to await their return. They had returned and I was about to set off with them when I saw Hughes galloping towards me.

'Got to go and find Griffith,' he shouted as soon as he was within hearing.

'But he knows he's got to come back on his own,' I said. 'He knows that no one's going out for him. I saw the orders.'

Hughes had seen them too. I tried to persuade him not to go, I thought he was certain to be captured or killed. I pointed to the enemy on the opposite slope.

'Got to obey orders,' he said crossly. He added that it was not Jamieson's fault, it was some crazy idea of Brigade's.

'Where is Jerry?' he said, and I showed him again the enemy I had seen.

'I'll see if I can keep out of their way,' he said, and he turned half right and galloped down the hill.

I was very distressed. Even if he succeeded in avoiding the enemy he did not know where Griffith had gone, he might be anywhere; how could Hughes find him? Griffith might be no great loss, though he had some good men with him, but to lose Hughes as well would be a disaster.

They all returned safely. During the afternoon we found them waiting for us at a cross-roads. Hughes laughed when I asked him what had happened. 'Don't think he gave Jerry much of a headache, between you and me,' he said. Griffith had not gone very far, he had not engaged the enemy over open sights. He had taken his gun behind a hill and had then opened fire without having any idea whether he was hurting the enemy. Before they had fired a dozen rounds the breech jammed, and while Sergeant Tommy Doff was trying to repair it Griffith sat on the ground and began to eat the breakfast he had brought with him. That was where Hughes had found him.

'Can you beat it!' he said. 'Sitting on his arse, eating his grub, and old Jerry on both sides of him.'

I wondered how any of them had escaped, but Hughes said he knew the country well, having fought in those parts in 1916.

All day we were retreating. Guillemont, Trones Wood and Delville Wood, Bernafay Wood, Montauban, Carnoy, Maricourt. Names I had heard for the first time while I was still a boy at school. On this one day we crossed from one side to the other of the old Somme battlefield, giving up in one day what had taken us four months to win.

At Maricourt we turned south, leaving the upland plateau on which we had been since our retreat started, and descending steeply into the valley of the River Somme. There, at a place called Suzanne, and a little before dusk, we stopped. Bingley and Frank were waiting for us at Suzanne. I was hoping that Jamieson would have remained in command for some time longer, but Bingley was a conscientious person and he said he was himself again now, leaving us to wonder what that meant. Whatever it might mean, Bingley was in command of us again now, and Jamieson went back to the wagon lines, which were a little way in the rear.

Unlike the other villages neither Maricourt nor Suzanne was completely destroyed. They had been behind our line when the Battle of the Somme started in 1916. Every house was damaged, but walls were still standing. The battery had halted a little way out of Suzanne, and we found a small deserted army hut in which we could eat and sleep. Orders for the next day arrived as we were finishing our meal. Again we were to send out an officer, but this time he was not to take a gun with him. This time it was a much simpler affair, he was to take two signallers with him, find out where the enemy was, and send back information.

Bingley told me to start at half past four, so as to be up on the hill above the river before daylight.

Five

The signaller on duty called me, lighting the candle at my side, saying that my signallers were waiting for me. I had only taken off my tunic, and puttees and boots, and within a few minutes I was ready to go.

We set off in the darkness, walking up hill, away from the river valley, back towards Maricourt and the high ground we had come from on the previous day. It was not a particularly difficult job that I had been given: to find out where the enemy was and send back information. Any infantry officer would have something to tell me about the situation so far as his battalion was concerned, I intended to speak to two or three if I could, then make my own report from what they told me, and send it back to Cherry at Brigade Headquarters. I should have to send one of my signallers, we had no telephone line. But from my point of view this was not something to be regretted. With only two signallers to send back, I should have to return with the third report myself, which might well be the end of my job. By then probably we should be in retreat again.

But though there was no reason to suppose that my task would be unduly difficult, I was feeling very depressed as we started off. Tiredness and the continuous anxiety of the last few days had undermined my confidence and strength. I was afraid, I felt alone, none of the others in the hut had woken when I went out, I should have felt less discouraged if one of them had been awake and had wished me luck before I started. And as for the battle, it seemed as though we should go on retreating for ever, I could see no end to it.

It was not difficult to find the way, there was a track leading in the right direction and enough light to follow it. But no one else was about. We met nobody on our way, the night was quiet, hardly a gun firing. We came to a wood and walked along beside it. Track and wood ended when we came to a road running left and right of us. I could tell we were at the edge of a cliff, the river Somme was below us. Here I would wait until daylight.

I had not long to wait. The valley was hidden in fog, almost up to the level of my eyes, but even as I watched the sun began to break through and the mist to dissolve. The river was two hundred feet below me, an almost sheer drop, and the spectacular sight took my breath away. All the upland country was the same, there was no variety in it, but here was a broad and beautiful valley, the river flowing through lakes and lonely marshland. My first thought was that this was a line we could hold, the enemy could never get across if the cliff was held by a few resolute men; but as soon as I looked at the map I saw that he would not have to get across, the river was flowing east and west, he would come over the uplands, he could turn this position with no difficulty at all.

I stood at the side of the road, in an old trench, looking down into the valley below me. The war seemed to have stopped. The guns were silent, we were alone, there was neither friend nor foe in sight, only the grey ruin of a church by the river, lit by the morning sun, like an old ruined abbey in the middle of a deserted land.

Then to my dismay I saw Major John coming up the hill behind me. He was the commander of our D Battery, the man most disliked and most feared in the whole brigade. Without fear himself he expected others to be equally unafraid; he despised you if you showed fear, and I had been feeling afraid ever since I woke up. I knew he would expect me to go with him on some crazy enterprise, he was always doing crazy things. Though he had often been wounded, he seemed to bear a charmed life.

At Heudecourt, for instance, on the night of the disaster, when A and B Batteries blew up their guns, he had gone forward alone to find out where the enemy was, ordering his battery to stay where they were until he returned. Frank had been telling us about him. 'He thought we had lost the war,' Frank said, 'and his idea was to wait for the Boche and then open fire at point-blank range until they were themselves all killed.'

Of course his battery had not stayed. The infantry had told us that the Boche would be here in a few minutes, what was the point of waiting to be taken prisoner? They had retreated with us, never expecting to see their commander again. But somehow he had escaped capture, and had gone berserk, Frank said, when he returned and found his battery was not there.

This was the man who was now coming up the hill behind me. There was just a chance that he might not know me and might go on by himself; he had never spoken to me, he talked with generals, not with insignificant people like myself. But it was a vain hope, Major John knew everyone.

'What's happening here?' he asked in his unpleasant voice. He had a habit of ending his sentences with a short disagreeable laugh, you could not tell if he meant what he said or if he was mocking you. I told him nothing was happening at present and that I had seen no sign of the enemy. For a minute or two he stood beside me, looking through his field glasses at the country in front of us. I looked through mine, hoping to give an impression that I was doing a useful job.

'No, there's nothing for us to do here,' he said. 'We'll go on to Maricourt and find out what's happening there.'

It was as I had feared. *We'll* go, he had said; go out looking for trouble!

But an extraordinary thing happened. As I walked beside him I no longer felt afraid. I was walking normally, erect, not bending down so as to be nearer the ground. He talked, I listened. He talked to me as an equal, not as a senior officer to a very junior one, not as a high-up Indian Civil Servant, which was what I knew he had been before the War, but as one soldier to another. He talked about the battle we were fighting. He admitted that there had been a moment when he thought that everything was lost. 'No plan of retreat, no reserves, what generalship!' he said.

We ourselves enjoyed criticising the Staff and Higher Command, and it was a satisfaction to hear a senior officer like Major John doing the same thing. His subalterns said that divisional generals came to ask his advice, and they had heard him say to one of them, 'You don't want the War to end because you will go down in rank when it's over, but I shall go up,' referring to his position in India.

We came to Maricourt, which was on the high plateau, a little way back from the river valley. There was an old trench at the edge of the village in which half a dozen infantrymen were standing. They called out to us to get down. Major John looked at them, but did not answer.

'Get down!' they said again. 'You're under observation.'

'I think you're mistaken,' he said.

He deliberately stepped across the trench and stood on a little mound of earth on the German side. He raised himself to his full height and stood there while I might have counted twenty.

'You can see for yourselves,' he said, 'that there are no Germans within a thousand yards of us.'

I did not know what he was going to do next, he was no longer taking any notice of me, and it seemed the right moment to eat one of the sandwiches that my servant had made for me the night before. I offered one to him when he rejoined me.

'I don't see why I should deprive you of your breakfast,' he said. He had brought nothing for himself, and it was in keeping with his character that he should come out to see for himself, and alone, instead of sending one of his officers as Bingley had sent me.

I said I had more than enough for myself. He looked at my packet of sandwiches. 'They look very appetising,' he said. How anyone could use such a word to describe one of Walkenshaw's sandwiches, I did not know. My servant had many good qualities, but sandwich making was not one of them. He cut two thick slices of bread, smeared them with butter, and put a slab of bully beef between them. But Major John was as indifferent to food as he was to danger, he ate only because he was hungry, and he was hungry now.

We were sitting on the top of the trench with our legs dangling inside, opposite each other, and he was talking now about other wars and other generals, Napoleon, Clive, Marlborough. I was able to comment on what he was saying because of my own interest in history, but he may have been talking to himself more than to me. Refusing my offer of another sandwich he got up to go. I wanted to go with him, I would have followed wherever he led me, but he told me that my place was in Maricourt, I was to stay there as long as I could and supply Headquarters with accurate information.

My courage remained high for an hour or more after he had left me. He had not only restored my confidence in myself, he had made me believe that the war was not lost. The Germans had missed their chance, he said; they had not destroyed us, they would find it difficult to move their guns across the devastated area, we should have to go on retreating for another day or two, but our reserves would have time to come up and then the enemy would be stopped.

He had given me back my courage, I no longer wanted to get away from Maricourt. But then a disconcerting thing happened. I was standing in the trench, looking out in front of me, resting my elbows on the parapet, exposing myself more than was necessary in order to see. A foot or two above my head there was an old strand of yellow telephone wire, sagging between two posts. Suddenly the wire snapped, one of the ends fell on to my steel helmet with a little tinny sound, and in the same instant I heard the crack of a rifle in front of me.

The sniper had missed. But the realisation that he had seen me and that his aim had been so nearly accurate was very frightening and I felt my confidence slipping away again. I moved to another part of the trench and now I was very careful when I looked over the edge.

It was the first sign of enemy activity that I had seen, but shells soon began falling on Maricourt, and a little later on my right I saw our outposts falling back. On other days this had been the prelude to the enemy's advance, we had seen our men coming back and then the enemy coming forward, and I assumed that this was about to happen now and that Maricourt would be abandoned. It was time for me to think about my own retreat. I had already sent one of my signallers back, now I sent the other with a written message to Headquarters about the men I had seen coming back.

I stayed in the trench a little longer, waiting for Germans to appear, but now I wanted an excuse to return and I found one when the infantry in my trench got up and started to go back. They told me they had been ordered to retreat, that the enemy was already in one part of Maricourt. I ought to have obtained confirmation of what they said, but it was what I had been expecting and I went to Brigade Headquarters and told Cherry that the Germans were in Maricourt. This was incorrect. Cherry was better informed than myself, because Major John had only just left him and he had found out far more than I had. The Germans had not yet attacked Maricourt, there was no present intention of abandoning it.

Cherry took me outside and from where we stood we could see German shells falling on the village, there was a pall of dark smoke over the houses. That showed it was still in our hands, and I felt ashamed of my inaccurate report. If I had not been so frightened by that sniper's bullet I should have used my eyes and seen for myself that we were still holding Maricourt.

Since it had not fallen my place was there, and I suggested that I should go back. But Colonel Richardson was considerate to his junior officers, and he probably realised that I could take no more for the present. He sent me back to the battery, where I found the others on the point of sitting down to a lunch of hot maconachie stew, and after that and a much stronger drink of whisky than I was in the habit of taking I felt restored. I would not have minded going back to Maricourt, but Bingley had no orders for me.

I was not the only person who had had a bad morning, Hughes told me—Bingley had lost his chocolate. I heard about it from himself during the afternoon. It had been stolen out of his saddle-bag, he always kept it there, for use in an emergency, everyone knew that he kept chocolate there, he had done so in every battery in which he had served, and this was the first time it had ever been taken. Of course he knew what men were, he said, they did take things, but not from their own officers; that was the point; he would not have minded if it had been men from another battery, but no one else could have taken it, he wasn't worrying about the loss of the chocolate, it was the fact that these Territorials had such a poor sense of loyalty that they would steal even from their own officers. That was the mark of a second-rate battery, he said.

He had a bad afternoon as well. The sun had gone behind clouds, it looked as though it might rain, and Bingley had lost his mackintosh. It had been left behind at Heudecourt with all the rest of our kit. But getting wet, Bingley told us, always brought on his rheumatism, and if he got an attack of rheumatism he was no more use than a sucked orange, he said. He went outside, looking anxiously up at the dark clouds, and I heard him asking an infantry officer who went by if he happened to have such a thing as a spare mackintosh. He rang up Cherry, telling him of his predicament, and either he or the Colonel found something for him.

I had time to write a short letter to my parents, the first I had written since the battle started, and I gave it to a dispatch rider who was passing by on a motor bicycle. But he lost it or forgot about it, or he may himself have become a casualty. The letter never arrived, and my parents not hearing from me for so long thought I was killed or a prisoner. Frank was reading *The Times* and the first account of the battle that we had seen, the others were sleeping. I heard Frank's short bitter laugh, not a cheerful sound at any time. 'We have fought the enemy to a standstill,' he quoted, 'and I think you'll be glad to know that we're all in our usual high spirits.'

Dusk was descending before we received the order to retreat again, the guns had stayed in the same position for twenty-four hours. Maricourt had not yet fallen, it was still being shelled. I could see the pall of smoke over the village as we moved out on to the road. Major John's battery was still firing when we went past them, he never left any of his ammunition, he always found some enemy to shoot at. I saw him standing behind one of his guns as we went by and he saw me and gave me one of his grim smiles. The look on his face made me think that he knew about my fear after he left me and how I had taken back inaccurate information, and I was disappointed at the thought of having lost his good opinion, which I believed I had won in the morning. But I could not help it, it was impossible to live up to his standards; and even he, I thought, might have been shaken by that sniper's bullet. I could hear the tinny sound on my helmet still.

For hour after hour we marched through the night or were halted on the road, waiting for orders. At first we were in the valley; there was a smell of marsh and mist and I could see the dim shapes of trees by the river. Then we began to climb. Road and hill seemed to go on for ever. At first I heard singing and laughter, but as hour followed hour the men became silent and then there was nothing to hear but the sound of horses' feet on the road, the straining of harness, and the jolting and creaking of wheels.

The night was bitterly cold. I was so cold that I could not ride my horse. I dismounted and walked along the road, leading her behind me. For much of the way Frank was walking at my side. We hardly talked, but there was companionship even in silence.

'Shall we ever get there?' I asked once.

'We shall get somewhere,' he said.

There were French civilians in one of the villages we passed through. We had crossed over the area of devastation, now we were on the other side, in country that had never yet been fought over. Like ourselves, the inhabitants were in retreat. We saw them bringing out their possessions and loading them up on to carts, as much as they would hold, or there was time for.

'Here we are!' I heard someone say at last. The guns and wagons had pulled off the road into a field. Edric came and led my horse away, but I remained standing where I was. I was too tired to move.

'This is the stuff for the troops,' Hughes said, bringing me a mug of tea well laced with rum. I followed him in the darkness along a railway track until we came to a little hut, like a plate-layers', beside the line. Inside the hut there were three beds made of wire netting, with railway carriage cushions for mattresses. Griffith was already asleep on one of them, Hughes and I lay down on the others.

I did not wake up until eleven o'clock. The door of the hut was open, the sun was shining, Hughes was not there. 'Where's Mr Hughes?' I asked Walkenshaw when he brought in my tea. 'Gone out two hours ago,' he said. He told me that the Captain had sent a message for me to go, but Hughes being nearest to the door had woken up when the signaller came in, and he said he would go in my place. 'He said you were pretty near whacked,' Walkenshaw said.

It was a blow to my pride to hear him talking about me in this way, but our servants always discussed us of course. When Hughes returned he did not tell me that he had gone out instead of me and when I thanked him, he said it was nothing, he wasn't tired, he said, he'd had a slack time the day before, I would have done the same for him, he said.

The Retreat went on.

During the night we had retreated nearly to the river Ancre, which flows into the Somme a few miles above Amiens. Bingley sent me to reconnoitre the river crossings, to find out whether the bridges were strong enough to take our guns and whether the Germans were already across the river. I saw an infantry captain by himself among the trees in the valley and decided to ask him for information. We talked for a few minutes, he had not a great deal to tell me, but he said he thought the enemy would not reach the river for at least another half hour.

What a strange war it had become, I was thinking. Here was I sent out to find where the enemy was and no one seemed to know, and here was this infantry officer, alone and distraught-looking, appearing hardly to know where he was or what he was doing. We were in no obvious danger, there was no sound of gun or rifle fire, but in half an hour or less the wood might be full of Germans. There were no trenches or shell-holes, we were beside a clear running stream, with tall poplars above our heads and spring flowers at our feet.

'It's a funny war,' I said. I thought he would know what I meant.

But he did not know. He looked at me, he saw my artillery badges, he was on foot, I was riding; he may have been the only survivor from his company. 'It may be for you,' he said, and the sound of his voice still hurts after more than fifty years, I hated his thinking that it had all been easy for us.

The battery was already across the river when I returned, Bingley had found a better place. He had just made the discovery that his revolver was lost, and he was nearly frantic. Now he would not be able to shoot himself if the enemy broke through. It was his servant's fault, he said; he always put the revolver at his side, within easy reach, when he went to sleep; but this morning his servant had moved it when he

198

brought in his cup of tea, and then in the hurry of getting off it had been left behind.

The loss of his revolver upset Bingley more than anything else that happened during the Retreat. He was not afraid of death, but he was afraid of being taken prisoner and he had made up his mind to shoot himself if the enemy broke through. Now there seemed a greater danger of this than before, we were in open country, it was just the place for a German cavalry attack.

He frightened us all with his nervousness, he kept on looking over his shoulder in the direction from which the Uhlans might be expected to appear. But it was all right. Sergeant Appleby, the captain of our football team and the most popular NCO in the battery, found a revolver and presented it to the grateful Bingley.

'You've saved my life,' he said to the smiling Appleby. This incident wiped out the memory of his lost chocolate on the previous day, and now Bingley had nothing but praise for our battery. 'You've only to look at Sergeant Appleby,' he said, 'to know that he's worth his weight in gold, and when you have good N.C.O.s you have a good battery.

He consulted Hughes, who as an ex-policemen, he thought, might know the best way of holding a revolver if you had to use it against yourself. But Hughes was no help to him. 'Can't say I've ever tried,' he said.

Revolvers were not the only things being found on this strange day. Army canteens and French estaminets were being abandoned, we all had full pockets, and bottles of wine fitted comfortably into the baskets meant for shells in the gun limbers. I myself had a bottle of red wine in each pocket of my British Warm overcoat. Cherry had given them to me, he had come out of the estaminet in which Brigade Headquarters had spent the night with his arms full of bottles. 'Pity to leave this good stuff for the Boche,' he said.

We were not the only people in retreat, all the villagers were on the move. I noticed one family with a dilapidated wagon piled high with furniture, an old woman was pushing a hand-cart and a little girl driving a black cow. Somehow the cow escaped, the girl ran after it, but was unable to recapture it, but it was easy for me on my horse to catch it and bring it back to her. She smiled at me. 'Merci, monsieur,' she said.

It was pleasurable at such a time to receive the smile of a nine-year-old child, but I was distressed by the plight of these refugees. I felt we had failed them. They were depending on us to keep the enemy away from their homes, but the enemy was coming. Retreating was a part of our job, but it was not theirs, they were losing nearly all that they had, the whole course of their lives was in danger. They were old people, old people and children, they were without the strong middle-aged group of their families, they seemed to have lost hope of better things. I saw an old man and his wife walking along a road under fire. A shell burst on their left, then one on the right, but they took no notice, they just walked on, looking neither to right nor left.

The Retreat went on.

But on this day we did not go back so far as on other days. In the evening we came to a village called Lavieville. Not one of the houses had yet been damaged by shellfire, but not one was inhabited, all the people had left. We chose a house for ourselves at the edge of the village, there was a long garden at the back and through a gate in the wall there was a way on to the road where our guns were.

The house had already been ransacked, the floors in every room were covered with old clothes and rubbish. Other soldiers had probably visited the house before we arrived. But it was a roof over our heads, it provided us with beds and with some of the other comforts of ordinary life, chairs, and a table to eat at. Bingley said he had forgotten what it was like to eat in a civilised manner.

Tired though we all were we did not immediately go to bed after dinner. There was the wine to drink. We sat up talking, the events of the last few days and nights were beginning to take shape in our minds, we saw them in order, no longer like the disconnected sequences of a dream. The wine gave us encouragement and new hope.

The next morning there was no order to retreat. During the afternoon Australian soldiers came up from behind, they went along the road past our guns, up towards the line. This was the first time I had seen Australians, they were unlike any of our own divisions, and on this first occasion I was not attracted by them. They were noisy and swaggering, they did not march along the road, they just walked, they seemed to be without any kind of discipline. But they looked very different from the exhausted infantry in front of us, the men we had seen coming back day after day. Towards evening they came back once more. At dusk I saw them coming over the skyline, they came through our guns as more than once they had done before. But this time the enemy was not following, they were coming back because they had been relieved, the line was holding, the Australians were there.

I stayed by the guns. I could hardly believe it was over. Only a week had passed since the battle started, but it seemed a lifetime ago and that we should go on retreating for ever. I stayed by the guns until it was too dark to see, I was still expecting to see a line of retiring infantry coming back in front. But no one came, there were only the ordinary sounds of war in front, the Retreat was over.

Now I could go. I walked through the narrow garden and into the house where the others already were. How ordinary everything had become again! Frank was writing to his girl, Bingley sitting quietly in a chair, he was not pacing up and down the room, he had not lost anything, and Griffith was waiting impatiently for the servants to bring in dinner. Only Hughes looked up when I came out of the darkness into the candle-lit room. 'We were just coming to look for you,' he said. 'Thought you might have forgotten the time.'

Six

The Retreat was over, but the memory of defeat remained and we waited anxiously for the beginning of the second round, knowing that one victory would not be enough for the enemy, he had to destroy us if he was to win the war.

All through the months that followed we were waiting. Every night, as I got into my sleeping bag, I was aware that I might be wakened in the morning by a fierce bombardment, the preliminary to the next German attack, and that would mean it was about to start again: another retreat, more danger and anxiety, utter weariness again. The Australians were fresh, their morale was high, but the finest soldiers in the world could not stand up to an attack in such overwhelming strength as that which had fallen on us on March 21st.

Bingley was wounded on the second morning after our arrival in Lavieville. Like many other things during his brief time with us it need not have happened. He was standing on the road by the guns, talking to Major Villiers of A, whose battery was now back in action at our side. The enemy was shelling the road, Villiers got down into one of the slit trenches we had dug the day before, and he advised Bingley to join him. But Bingley was not afraid of shells, and he remained standing there, talking and smoking his pipe. A shell burst a few yards from him, and he was seriously wounded.

He was carried into the house and our Scottish doctor at once came up from Brigade Headquarters. He was in a good deal of pain, but the doctor said he would be all right, so there was no need for us to feel distressed on his account. Even now he was fussing about a triviality. This time it was his pipe, he had dropped it when he was hit, they had carried him away without it. It must be on the road still, and it was a very special

202

pipe, a birthday present from some aristocratic friend.

Hughes told him not to worry, if it was there we would find it and send it after him to the Casualty Clearing Station. But he had no intention of going to look for it. 'What a hope the man's got!' he said after he had been taken away. 'Jerry's been shelling the place all morning; does he really think anyone's going to look for his blasted pipe? Lady What's-a-name can buy him another.'

Bingley had been with us for 17 days. It seemed like 17 months. And in that time the morale of the battery had sunk to a lower level than ever before, far lower than after months of fighting and heavy casualties at Ypres. Yet he was a likeable man. It was his misfortune, and ours, that he was in command of a battery at a time of crisis.

Griffith also was wounded, a few days later. I was up at the O.P. when it happened, but the others told me that he was in too much of a hurry for his breakfast. They were all by the guns, the enemy was shelling the edge of the village, the others decided to wait until he stopped, but Griffith went on and was hit before he got to the house. We were fortunate in our casualties at this time. The rest of us were all of one kind, but Bingley and Griffith were different and would always have stuck out.

Jamieson came up from the wagon lines to take command, and at once we all relaxed. He gave orders when they were necessary, we could see they were necessary, there was no fuss, no fault-finding, and decisions once made were adhered to. Jamieson was reserved, even rather unfriendly, seldom joining in conversation with the rest of us, but we had confidence in him. We knew that he knew what to do.

But within a few days there were greater changes, affecting the whole brigade. Captain Jamieson was promoted to the rank of major, he left us and went to command B Battery in place of Major Cecil who was demoted and brought down to the rank of captain. This was because he had blown up his guns at the beginning of the Retreat, without justification it was considered, and not very effectively. Everyone knew it was Major John's doing, he was the real commander of our brigade, not the well-meaning Colonel Richardson. Major John disliked and despised Cecil. He told the Colonel that he would not serve in a brigade in which *that man* held the same rank as himself, and the Colonel gave in to him.

Major Villiers of A Battery had lost his guns at the same time, he had been the first to give the order for destruction, Cecil had merely followed his example, and John would have liked to treat Villiers in the same way. But his rank was substantive, he could not be brought down without a court martial; besides, he was the brother of an earl, and even Major John could not succeed in forcing the Colonel to abandon an earl's brother.

Captain Cecil came back to us, as our second-in-command, a position he had held once before. None of us especially liked him, but we were sorry for him and felt he had been unfairly treated. We got a new battery commander at the same time. Major Poland, who had been John's second-in-command, was himself a Yorkshireman and ought to have got on well in our battery, but he was tolerated rather than liked. He was friendly to everyone in fair weather, but apt to become morose at other times, and there was a streak of meanness in him. He drank a lot of whisky when someone else was paying for it. 'I'm a proper Yorkshireman,' he was fond of saying. "Take owt, pay for nowt! that's my motto.' The difference between himself and the other Yorkshiremen in the battery was that they only pretended to be mean.

But after Bingley we were not particular about our battery commander.

A few days later I was sent up to the O.P. on a 24-hour duty. I felt ill at ease when I was told to go, I had a presentiment of evil. There was nothing to account for my feeling, the O.P. was not in a particularly dangerous place, I had been there before, and except on the day when Bingley was wounded, we had not been shelled much, it had been quiet since the end of our retreat.

But though there was no reason for my foreboding the feeling was very strong, and after leaving the battery in the late afternoon I turned round for a last look before we went over the crest, wondering if I should ever see the place again. This was a sop to superstition in which I often indulged, hoping that it might somehow increase my chance of a safe return.

Our walk up to the O.P. was so uneventful, however, that I

began to forget my fears, and the officer in B Battery whom I relieved told me that it had been as peaceful for the whole of his time. Visibility was poor, it had been misty all day, and now at six o'clock from the O.P. trench at the top of the hill I could hardly see down to the railway embankment, half a mile away, which was our front line. Beyond the railway was the river, the Ancre; beyond the river, the wooded marsh. It was the place where Bingley had sent me to reconnoitre the river crossing, the place where I had spoken to the infantry captain.

On a clear day you could see all the high ground on the other side, on the left you could almost see the little town of Albert, up the river and now in German hands. Almost but not quite, the town itself was hidden by a curve of the bare hill on which the O.P. was situated, but on my first visit I had seen the roof of the church over the hill and the diving madonna. She was one of the sights of the war zone. She had been hit by German shells before the battle of the Somme started, so that with the infant Jesus in her arms she looked about to plunge into the street below. There was a superstition that we should lose the war if she fell and the Engineers had propped her up in this diving position. But now she had fallen, our own big guns had brought her down after the enemy's capture of Albert.

Twenty-four hours was a long time, and we made a bad start. My signallers had brought up a dud telephone. They were a very inexperienced pair, a boy who had joined us shortly before the Retreat, and an elderly man who had come only since it ended. They should not have been sent out together, but because of casualties we were short of signallers. I should have to send one of them back to the battery for another telephone. But the boy said he could not find the way in the dark and the man said he was afraid of going by himself. He was in a pitiable state, literally shaking with fear; it was his first visit to an O.P. and he had never been under fire. I felt exasperated with him, we were in no danger at all, we might have been sitting on the grass in England. 'Stop being such a bloody funk,' I wanted to say to him, but I remembered in time that it was less than a year since I had been new to the War, and I had been afraid before there was anything to fear. I sent them both back, and they were better when they returned, the older man had stopped shaking, they had achieved something, they had achieved it on their own, and this had given them confidence.

The night passed very slowly. The mist turned to drizzling rain, my signallers were dozing in the shallow trench, but I walked up and down all night, counting the hours by the number of cigarettes I smoked and allowing myself a mouthful of rum every hour. It kept me warm, I was getting very wet.

Daylight made a reluctant appearance, but I continued to walk up and down. The rain had stopped, but it was too misty for me to see, or to be seen from the enemy O.P.s on the other hillside. Shortly before seven o'clock, however, the mist thinned out and I got down into the trench. Now I could see down to the railway embankment and the trees in the valley, and dimly the shape of the high ground across the river.

I was standing there, looking down at the valley, but not consciously seeing anything, not consciously thinking at all, when suddenly every nerve in my body was alerted by the opening roar of bombardment across the river. My presentiment had been right, the attack was coming. A moment ago there had been utter silence, all the valley at peace, now every gun on the other side was firing and I saw bursting shells wherever I looked.

For the moment we were in no danger. The shells were falling in front of us, astride the railway embankment, our front line, or passing overhead on their way to the batteries and our reserves. None fell near us, our telephone line was not broken yet, I was able to speak to Cherry at Brigade Headquarters, to watch what was happening, to look out for any movement in the valley. For half an hour I was watching, watching and waiting. Then I heard a different sound, the sound of a shell coming close, and I crouched down in the trench.

I have called it a trench, but in fact it was nothing more than a hole in the ground. A trench with its depth and narrow opening would have afforded us protection from anything but a direct hit; but this hole was less than two feet deep and wide at the top. Any shell falling within fifty yards might have killed us all and during the next hour and a half at least

206

a dozen burst very close. Now that danger had come my signallers behaved admirably. The young one brought out his rations and began to eat, the older one sat quite still beside me. He probably thought it was like this every morning at the O.P. No wonder he had been scared. He was frightened of course, but no more so than myself. Indeed in his relief at finding that he could endure, that he did not have to scream or feel he was going mad he may have been less afraid than I was. At any rate he was all right and he continued to be all right for the rest of his time in the battery.

I was very afraid, knowing how great our danger was. I was expecting death, and the expectation paralysed my mind. My eyes were open, my hearing was very acute, I heard each shell coming towards us and could tell where it was likely to burst from the sound it made.

My senses were alert, but I could not think or speak, I did not reply to the signaller at my side. I just waited for death, pressing myself more closely to the earth whenever I heard a near shell on its way. Then I felt the ground shake, heard the iron splinters whizz past us, smelled the fumes of the explosion, saw the dark smoke drifting overhead.

I watched a family of frogs as I waited. They had appeared from somewhere, the noise was frightening them and they were trying to get out of the hole. Again and again they jumped, they very nearly succeeded, but always fell back again when nearly at the top. I could have told them they were safer where they were, and I wondered whether to put them back if they did succeed.

Then the sound changed again. I became aware that shells were no longer falling round us. This was the critical time: now the enemy was attacking and therefore his guns could not shell the area over which his infantry was expected to advance. I stood up and looked down into the valley. At first I saw no one, there was no movement on the railway embankment nor in the wooded valley. But before there was time to think out what this might mean I saw men getting up on the railway line. They were Australians, not Germans. They did not appear to be in trouble, they were not being fired at, none of them fell, but I saw them come down from the embankment and start to climb the hill towards me. Still I could see

207

no enemy. But the Australians were coming up the hill. This was what we had seen day after day during the Retreat, our men coming back, then the enemy following, and I had no doubt that it was about to happen again. I sent my signallers back with written messages, first one, then the other, the telephone line had been broken long since, but I waited where I was for the Australians.

They were a long time coming. They came up the hill very slowly. They were not firing, or being fired at, I could see no Germans, but the view on my left was blocked by the curve of the hill, I could only see directly in front. At last the men drew level with me and I asked the nearest of them what was happening.

'The bastards on our left let the bastards in,' he said.

'We got a lot of the bastards,' another man added.

An officer told me that the battalion on their left had been driven back, and that they themselves in consequence had been ordered to fall back to the crest of the hill behind me. It was time for me to go, I went back to Brigade Headquarters, which was nearer to the line than the batteries were, I gave Cherry a gloomy report on the situation. None of the Australians had seemed despondent, but they did not know what it was going to be like, they had not experienced a retreat, I thought my pessimism was justified.

But once again Cherry was better informed than I was, this time not because of Major John, but because he was in touch with the Headquarters of the Australian Infantry Battalion, which was in the same hillside. He said the situation was well in hand, that our battalion had repulsed the attack on its front, and though it had fallen back now it was about to take part in a counter-attack.

I did not believe him, I thought that as usual he was making the news seem better than it was. But the Australians did counter-attack, they regained nearly all the lost ground, our battalion returned to the railway line. Cherry wanted me to go back to the O.P., but I could not yet return to that hole of fear, my mind had not recovered. I went instead to another hilltop looking down on the railway embankment and wooded marsh, but without such an extensive view across the valley. Major John sent one of his officers to the original O.P. during the afternoon, but his signaller was killed there, so I thought my unwillingness to return had been justified.

Nothing else happened that day.

The German attack had failed. It was not a major attack, as I had at first supposed, only a minor one, but it had failed. The enemy had gained nothing, we were still in the same position, the Australians had shown that their confidence in themselves was justified, and we began to share it.

A few days later we were taken out of the line, into a reserve position. We were relieved by an Australian battery, and Major Poland sent me up to the O.P. with their commander to show him where it was. We walked up there together, and because I liked him and wanted to make a good impression I was pleased at being able to answer all his questions. I could tell him the names of all the places behind the enemy line and show him where they were on the map. I also told him about our very unpleasant time there, the hole had been made a little deeper now, but he agreed with me that more work should be done on it.

The rest of the battery had already gone when we returned. I was to complete the relief, there were certain things that had to be explained to the Australians, a few stores to hand over. They were critical of what we had done, but every battery on taking over a position always criticised the work of their predecessors, it was part of the routine. When this was finished I went into the mess to wait for Edric, who was coming up with our horses. It was their mess now, ours no longer. We had moved out of Lavieville, the village had become too dangerous. We had brought the guns a few hundred yards back, they were under a bank in which we had dug shelters for ourselves. The mess was the largest and most comfortable of these.

Three or four of the Australian officers were in the mess and I listened to their conversation. They were talking about the German attack in the North, in Flanders. On the same day that he had attacked us in the river valley the enemy had made a major attack up there and already it had met with great success. The Australians had just come from Flanders, from the very place where the new attack was being made.

'Fritz waited till he knew we were out of the way,' one of them said.

'These Britishers are no good,' said another.

'Shut up!' said the Captain who had been at the O.P. with me.

'Well, look where they've run to! We should never have run like that.'

'You don't know what you're talking about,' said the Captain. 'We've never had to face an attack like one of these.'

But the other insisted that the English had no fighting spirit.

I was so angry at what they were saying that I got up, intending to walk out of the dug-out, but I was faint from lack of food, I had eaten nothing all day except a slice of bread and marmalade, I staggered and had to sit down again. At once their attitude changed, and my own opinion of Australians changed for ever in the same moment. The Captain told his servant to make tea straight away, and the man who had said that Britishers ran away got up and opened a bottle of red wine, and we all drank together.

'That's only our way of talking,' he said. 'We talk big, but you mustn't pay any attention to what we say.'

I learnt not to. It's what people are that matters, what they do, not what they say. During the weeks that followed I often heard the Australians talking big, but I no longer minded. They were magnificent soldiers, and when I was in need they never failed to help me.

I enjoyed my tea and was feeling a new man by the time Edric came for me. I did not join the rest of the battery that night, I was to stay with a single gun a short way in front of the others. Vernon of B Battery had one of his guns in the same place. We spent the night together in a wayside shrine by the road. Vernon was a friend of mine; I was always pleased when chance brought us together. I had friends in all the other batteries, but there had been no opportunity of talking to any of them since the beginning of the Retreat. Now I could talk to Vernon, he told me all his battery news and I told him ours as we lay side by side on the narrow tiled floor of the shrine. Our conversation was entirely about the war, about the events of the last two or three weeks and the other officers in the brigade. If there had been less to say on that subject we might have talked on another, but we could have talked all night without wearying each other, it was talking about the War that helped us to endure it.

'We mustn't forget to thank Mary,' Vernon said in the morning. 'She couldn't have protected us from shells, but she's done what she could, she's kept us warm during the night.' We had both slept well. It was a strange place in which to wake: the painted stars on the domed ceiling of the shrine over our heads, the blue-mantled madonna looking down on us from her niche in the wall, outside the distant muttering of the guns and the deserted country road between two villages.

Later in the day we rejoined our batteries. They were almost out of·range of gunfire, but we were in readiness to return at an hour's notice if there was another attack. Our tents were by the side of a wood, there were bluebells in it and enormous cowslips in the meadows. I had never seen France looking so beautiful. I had never looked at Spring until now, I had always taken it for granted. This year it might have come too late for me to see it, and I might not see another. I looked at the young leaves on the trees, I had not known that anything could be so lovely.

It was while we were resting by the bluebell wood that the men who had been on leave during the Retreat came back to us, Jack and Durham, Sergeant Denmark and more than twenty others. They made us up to strength again. They came marching into camp one afternoon, looking rather sheepish, like boys who had been playing truant and did not know what kind of reception they would be given. We cheered when we saw them and their faces broke into smiles.

'We thought we should be sent to another unit,' Jack said, when we were having tea in the mess, 'we thought you would all be dead, or prisoners anyway.'

We told them everything that had happened, we were all talking at the same time, and at the end Jack told us what he had been doing. 'It was a rotten leave,' he said. 'I was thinking about you all the time. I went out with a girl once or twice, but it was no good, I couldn't do a thing. You can't

211

even get any kick out of kissing a girl when you're thinking that all your friends have gone west.'

He said he had felt miserable all the time, and not only because girls had been unsatisfying. 'You can't talk to people at home,' he said. 'They haven't a clue what it means, even the best of them, and some of them think of it as a kind of entertainment.' Someone, he told us, had suggested going up to Beachy Head for a picnic, so as to hear the guns. 'I said I'd heard them,' Jack said. And someone else had asked whether he had ever taken part in a battle. 'They don't call this sort of thing a battle,' he said. 'They think you have to be drawn up in squares, facing each other.'

'I'm sorry I missed it,' Durham said, as we were undressing that night. 'It must have been rather fun.'

'It wasn't,' I told him. 'It wasn't funny at all.' But now that it was over I was glad myself not to have missed it.

We were still in the same place when the Commander-in-Chief issued his famous Backs-to-the-Wall Order of the Day, which, it has sometimes been claimed, had such a stirring effect on us. We read it. 'Many of us are now tired,' Frank quoted. 'Has he only just found that out?' I never saw any of our men reading it, but they may have done so, for Sergeant Denmark said we seemed to have got ourselves into a proper mess while he was away. 'It's about time we chucked up the sponge,' he told me.

He was always grumbling, nothing was any bloody good in his opinion. But I knew he would be the last to give in, he would go on fighting and enduring to the end, and I always felt a braver man when I was with him.

We did not go back to Lavieville when our short rest came to an end. We were attached to a different Australian division, we were sent a few miles south of where we had been before. Now we were between the rivers, the Somme in front of us, the Ancre at our back.

Another great attack was expected, it might come any day now. We were digging hard. The guns were out in the open, near the top of the hill above the Ancre. We were living in two copses growing out of little round hollows, into the sides of which we could dig. Hughes and I were making a shelter, four feet wide, long enough to lie down in, as deep as we

212

could dig it. Hughes was as good with a spade as he was with most other things. 'Tisn't exactly comfortable,' he said, 'some people might prefer Buckingham Palace, but we want less roof space.'

Any day now the attack was expected, the great German offensive which was to complete what they had begun, to drive us into the sea, to cut between ourselves and the French Armies. So when very early one morning we were awakened by a great enemy bombardment I never doubted that the day had come. Shells were falling all round us, gas and high explosive. We lay very still in our hole, we had put our boots on and were ready to rush out to the guns when the SOS rockets went up, the signal that the enemy was attacking and for us to open fire.

But the rockets did not go up, and gradually the bombardment died down. On our front only a small attack had been made, and had been easily repulsed. Across the river Somme, however, on our right, the attack had been much heavier, we learnt, and Villers Bretonneux at the highest point of the plateau above the river had been lost. This was a disaster. From the village you could look down on the spire of Amiens Cathedral, only nine miles away. We should have to retreat again, Amiens could never be held with the enemy in Villers Bretonneux, and many of our positions between the rivers were now under observation.

But that night it was recaptured. The Australians made a night attack, one force going round the village on the north side and another on the south. They met in the middle, then turned back and overran the enemy positions inside, killing or capturing every German there. They had done it again, the Australians had done it again, for the second time they had completely defeated a German attack.

We were all jubilant. Cherry and Colonel Richardson talked as though the War was as good as won, disregarding the huge advance which the enemy had made in Flanders and the fact that the major attack on our front had not yet been made.

'We've only got to kill another million Boches,' the Colonel said. 'Then we shall all be able to go home.'

I thought I had killed one on my last visit to the OP, and

Durham caught some ammunition wagons that had come up too near the line before it was dark. He said he got in among them with three or four salvoes.

We were jubilant about Villers Bretonneux, but there was no other reason for rejoicing. Another great attack was certain to be made, and even the Australians would be driven back by the hordes of the enemy. There was nothing to look forward to, all leave had been cancelled, there was no chance of our going out of the line for a rest, there was not even a town within reach where we could go for a dinner or to laugh at one of the divisional entertainments; and winter, which might put an end to the fighting for a while, was still months away.

'I suppose it will be another Hundred Years War,' Jack said.

Seven

April was passing into May. Riding down to the wagon lines one afternoon I saw swallows circling above the river, and the beech leaves fully out over my head were rustling in the light wind as I dried myself after my bath. I had got rid of the lice on my body, but what about those on my clothes?

All through May we were waiting for the Germans to come. The Australians were not passively waiting, they ruled over no-man's-land by night, they harassed the enemy by raiding his trenches. Fritz was going to get the surprise of his life when he came, they said.

We had to leave our copses in the little rounded hollows above the river, they attracted too much attention from the enemy. We had just begun dinner one evening, we had finished the soup and were waiting for the servants to bring in the main course when a heavy bombardment began. I hoped it would be nothing serious, a few salvoes, a dozen shells altogether. Then we could go on with our dinner, I was hungry. But as soon as it became clear that the shelling was not going to stop, I moved to the back of the dug-out, with my back to the wall of chalk, and went on writing the letter I had started before dinner.

The men were in one of the copses, the officers and our servants and the signallers in the other. The men had one good dug-out in their copse, we had one in ours, all the servants and signallers were inside it now with ourselves, about a dozen of us, all crowded together, no one talking, or in such subdued voices that only the man next to the speaker could hear what he said. Most of us would have been killed or seriously wounded if one of the shells had hit the roof, but we were probably safe from anything except a direct hit.

It was disagreeable. Shells were coming over at the rate of two or three to the minute, we were shaken by the concussion, we could hear trees and branches falling, but I was not particularly frightened. It was when one was alone that shellfire was so frightening, or when one was under fire in the open. Now we were all together, there was nothing that had to be done until the shellfire was over, and the back of the dug-out was the safest place. I went on writing.

But Durham was standing in the entrance, rather foolishly because there he was more likely to be hit by a flying splinter. He was watching the shell-bursts and telling us where each one was. 'That was a better one,' he would say, meaning a nearer one; and then as though giving orders to the German gunners, 'Five minutes more right.' I could see that Major Poland sitting at the table was growing restless. He had been inside a dug-out when it was hit some months before, and his wounds had recovered more quickly than his nerves.

A shell burst very close. The earth shook, bits of chalk off the wall fell on my writing pad, the wood was full of smoke and the smell of cordite. There was silence. Then we all heard Durham's drawling voice stating the obvious. 'That one was not very far away,' he said.

'If you have nothing more sensible to say, keep your bloody mouth shut,' said Poland angrily.

Durham and I grinned at each other when he wasn't looking.

It stopped at last. I was suddenly conscious of the silence, there was no shell on its way through the air. I looked at my watch, it had lasted eighty minutes. We all began talking at the same time, waiting where we were for another minute in case he was playing us a dirty trick. Then we ran across to the other copse to see how the men were. One man had been wounded, not very seriously.

But our dinner had gone. So had the cook-house.

As soon as it was light the next morning Major Poland took me with him to look for another battery position. He had had enough of those copses to last him a million years, he said, and he blamed himself for choosing a place marked on all their maps, of course they could not resist shooting at it. He decided to leave two guns where they were, the men must dig deep slit trenches beside them, but he found a place for the other four behind a bank half way down the hill. It was annoying when we had put so much effort into our digging in the copses, now we should have to begin all over again; but Poland's decision was a wise one, and we were not so heavily shelled under the bank.

After a quick breakfast I went up to the O.P. and spent the rest of the day there. In retrospect I seem to have spent most of the long summer at that O.P. on the high ground between the rivers, looking down on the Somme. It was the loneliness of the OP that made the days there seem so long, the loneliness and the width of the view. It was in a short piece of trench high above the village of Sailly-le-Sec, and you could see all the world—the Somme, a long straight silver line in the middle of the picture, villages and church spires among the trees in the valley; and then mile after mile of rising upland, more villages, and trees on the skyline, marking the long straight Roman Road, the road from Villers Bretonneux to Peronne and St Quentin, places utterly remote, so far were they now behind the German line.

At first the country looked undamaged. Until a few weeks ago it had been far behind our line and never fought over. Now we were beginning to destroy it, we and the enemy between us, shelling the villages, cratering the fields, killing the trees; but the concentration of guns was not nearly so great as at Ypres in 1917, and even by the end of the summer, even in the front line area, villages from a distance still looked almost untouched and there were far more living trees than dead ones.

At first there was a lot of activity behind the German lines —men digging or walking about, lorries and wagons on the roads, horses in their wagon line area, even the smoke of a distant train. Few of these targets were within range of our field guns, occasionally I saw a party of men to shoot at, more often I had to ring up Cherry at Brigade Headquarters and ask him to ask for the use of some longer-range guns. Nothing ever happened, none of my distant targets was disturbed. The fact was there were very few heavy guns in action on our part of the front, some had been lost in the March Retreat, and the fear of losing others in the next attack kept them well back, field guns were expendable, bigger guns were not. This was another reason why the country looked unspoiled, our small guns could be very effective against infantry in the open, but they did little damage to anything else.

Eventually I stopped reporting what I saw, and after the first few weeks there was less to report. All that vast expanse of country in front of me, and no living creature to be seen on it!

But there were aeroplane fights to watch, particularly in the late afternoon. That was the time for the dog fights. I was watching half a dozen of our machines one evening returning from a sortie over enemy territory. They were crossing the line when suddenly I heard fierce bursts of machine-gun fire and German triplanes swooped down on them out of the clouds. I had not seen the triplanes until the firing began, neither had they. It was all over in a moment, two of our machines were on fire, a third was fluttering down to the ground, like a leaf in autumn, the enemy was away again.

Three out of six! I felt sick with anger and frustration, I would rather have endured a period of heavy shell-fire in my trench than be the witness of such a tragedy. Two spirals of black smoke against the evening sky, and the other machine still falling, so slowly, that it seemed it would never reach the ground. It fell beside the river, in no-man's-land, less than a mile from where I was watching. There it lay. It looked un-damaged. Surely it would rise again, like a bird after alighting. But it lay still, between the armies. No one got out, no one went towards it, only the river moved, flowing serenely by.

But an hour or two later I saw a huge explosion far behind the enemy line, ten miles away. A great column of smoke rose hundreds of feet into the air, and I counted twenty smaller explosions. That was some consolation for the lost aeroplanes, but on every subsequent visit to the O.P. I was reminded of the unhappiness of that evening by the sight of the aeroplane, still lying where it had fallen, the fluttering leaf that had reached the ground.

All through those long summer days in that long summer I stood in the little trench above the river, gazing and gazing through my glasses at the enemy-held country until my eyes

218

ached and I could look no more. I learnt the names of every wood and all the villages, I knew the contour of the hills and the shape of the lakes in the valley. To see so much and to see nothing! We might have been the only men left alive, my two signallers and I. And yet I knew there were thousands of hidden men in front of me. Australians on our side of the line, the enemy on his. But no one moved, everyone was waiting for the safety of darkness.

Once or twice I left the safety of the trench and went out alone, down the hill towards Sailly-le-Sec. The ground fell away steeply below the O.P., but then rose again, so that one was swallowed up within a few minutes of leaving the trench. I told myself that I might obtain some useful information, there might be a company or battalion headquarters in one of the gullies, but in fact I wanted companionship, to hear another voice. But I saw no one, and it was frightening. I was afraid of losing my way, of not being able to find the O.P. again, I might take a wrong turning and wander into the German lines. There was a story of an Australian barber who had ridden up on a bicycle from the transport lines, he wanted to see the place where his friends were, but he went too far, he rode into the enemy.

I stopped going out on these adventures. I talked to my own signallers instead, I read my book. I reckoned I could read a book in a day at the O.P., the kind of book I took with me, I did not feel able to read any other sort.

At last it was time to return to the battery. One was supposed to stay up at the O.P. until it was too dark to see, but I came away at dusk, or even a little sooner if the enemy was not shelling the top of the ridge behind us. Choosing a quiet moment one got out of the trench and walked quickly up the hill. The first half mile in the evening, the last half mile in the morning, that was the dangerous part, one was under observation, and a party of three men might be worth shooting at. Once or twice I thought we were chased with shells. But over the skyline one relaxed. Now there was the evening meal to look forward to, hearing what sort of a day the others had had, and telling them about my own.

A long day at the O.P. but then, if one was lucky, two or three days and nights at the wagon lines.

Edric would come for me with our horses in the late afternoon, and then there was the enjoyment of the long ride
back, cantering at first until we were out of the danger zone,
more slowly when we were across the river and marsh. Edric
would ride beside me as we walked up the hill on the other
side, telling me the news of the wagon lines—the night
bombers had been over, the Australians had been pinching
horses from some of the other batteries, we should have to
watch out for Lady with so many horse thieves about, and
there was a craze for playing Housey-Housey, some of the
men played every fine afternoon; he explained the game to me.

The wagon lines were a long way back. Across the Ancre,
up the hill, over the Albert-Amiens road, and then the wood
was in sight, the tops of the trees showing above the skyline.
The horse lines and the men's bivouacs were under a bank
below the wood, our tents at the wood's edge. It was a delightful change to be there: to undress and sleep on a camp
bed, to be wakened in the morning not by shellfire but by the
trumpeter blowing reveille, to bath, and then to spend most
of the day doing what one liked.

There was some work for us to do at the wagon lines, but
not a great deal. I went out riding, chiefly for pleasure, also
to learn my way about the country, such knowledge might be
useful one day; and as mess secretary it was my job to buy
whatever luxuries I could find, eggs, a chicken, lettuce. The
French farmers would sell us anything they had, and there
were army canteens in the back areas.

I also drew money from the Field Cashier, for ourselves
and to pay the men. Paying was not difficult for me. The
others sometimes got into a muddle when they were paying,
they might be a hundred francs out at the end of the afternoon; but Bombardier Ewell, the battery clerk, and I were
both confident that the amounts would balance when I was
paying. I was quick at mental arithmetic, there were plenty
of things the others could do better than myself, I knew little
about horses, I was no good at roofing a dug-out or repairing
a gun, but I could add up correctly.

I enjoyed paying because it brought me into contact with
all the men at the wagon lines, there were always some
gunners among them as well as the drivers, they took it in

turns to come down, as we ourselves did. I found it difficult to talk to some of the men, difficult even to understand what they said. My upbringing had been different from theirs, I shared the War with them, but little else at that time. But I wanted to make them aware of my friendship for them, and smiling as I paid them was a way of showing my feeling.

In the evening I talked to Captain Cecil. I had been expecting to feel some embarrassment in his company; he had been a major, now he was only a captain, we had called him Sir, but one did not sir a captain; I thought it would be difficult to be natural with him. But he showed an unexpected dignity, accepting the situation and making no attempt to assert authority over us when we came down to the wagon lines for a rest. I had liked him before, and I liked him again now.

He was bitter about Major John, who was responsible for his degradation. He said that John had given the Colonel an untrue account of what happened that night at Heudecourt, and that the Colonel had allowed him no chance of replying to his accusations. I could well believe that Major John's personal dislike of Cecil had influenced what he said, but not that he had invented a story in order to discredit him. Cecil believed the worst of Major John, but I knew that I admired him more than anyone else in the brigade.

We sat up late into the night, talking not only about the War and other officers in the brigade, but about life in England, the life that some day we might go back to. Cecil was nearly ten years older than I was, already a partner in his father's firm, and married on his last leave—he told me he was hoping to become a father before the end of the year. But he treated me as an equal and I was pleased. Talking to him at the wagon lines, sometimes for an hour or two I almost forgot the great German attack we were waiting for.

The wood closed round us as we talked, and the stars came nearer.

May was passing into June. The young corn behind the guns was several inches high, and the sun rose so early that however early I got up I never arrived at the O.P. before daylight, there was always that last half mile to walk down the hill under observation.

The enemy made his great attack, the third he had made since March. But it was not on our part of the front, it was made on the French front between Rheims and Soissons, against the French and four unfortunate British divisions, which had been sent to a supposedly quiet part of the line after suffering very severe casualties in the earlier attacks.

I was sorry for the French, they were being driven back as we had been, Paris was in danger for a while, but I was thankful that we had escaped for the present. It was only a respite. Everyone believed that the attack on the French was only a diversion, to draw our reserves away from the vital front, the enemy knew that he must defeat the British before he could win the war. But for a few weeks at any rate we should be left alone, he could not mount another attack without a pause.

Major John was killed. The camouflage over one of his guns was set alight by the heat of its own firing, and there was a lot of ammunition by the side of the gun. He ordered everyone else to leave the position, but he stayed, fighting the fire single-handed until the ammunition blew up.

He ought to have known this would happen, his own subalterns could have told him. And what would the loss of a gun have mattered, or all the ammunition in the brigade! Guns and ammunition could be replaced, Major John never was.

But D Battery, his battery, was a howitzer battery, most of his service had been in 18-pounder batteries, he had only been with D for a few months, since recovering from his last wound, he did not realise that howitzer ammunition was more likely to blow up, he had not deliberately thrown away his life.

Nearly everyone, now that he was dead, began to speak well of him and to tell stories of his courage. Even the Australians admired him. They said they did not want to go about in his company, he was too much of a glory-boy for their liking. They all knew him by sight, everyone knew him because he went everywhere, he was always going up to the front line, to see for himself, to find out what he wanted to know. His officers said that he was often out all night, he liked to see the sun rise over the enemy lines, they said, he had told them that it filled him with exhilaration.

They said he was mad, everyone agreed that he was mad, but everyone was proud of having known him, we boasted about him, he became a legendary figure. Only Captain Cecil remained of the same opinion as before. Others could say what they liked, he said, but he wasn't going to pretend that he had admired Major John or was sorry he was dead.

I had met him on my way up to the O.P. one morning, not long before his death. He had not spoken to me, but he had acknowledged my salute with a tight smile in which there was no unfriendly look. He was not a glory-boy, he did not love danger or glory, he despised both. But he had set himself a standard and he had to live up to it. He could not accept anything that fell below it, never for himself, hardly for anyone else. He was the greatest soldier I was ever to serve with.

Colonel Richardson was now free to do as he liked. He had told Cecil that he could feel no confidence in him as a battery commander, but he put him in command of our battery now, Poland went back to command D, the battery from which he had come, and Frank became a captain and our second-in-command.

The rest of us were not altogether pleased with these changes. We had liked Captain Cecil well enough, but we wondered how we should get on with Major Cecil. He cared too much about his own comfort, he was a selfish man, and there was no room for selfishness in a small dug-out. After himself he seemed to care more for his dog than for anyone else. She was a black-and-white setter, far too big an animal for the gun line, she was always in the way. Everyone in the battery was waiting for the day when she would get in the way of a shell, but Betty, like her master, knew how to look after herself.

The long summer passed slowly. Days in the gun line, followed by days at the wagon lines. Away from the smell of the dead mule and the smell of gas-drenched grass, away from the Seven Sisters, seven trees (only six now) by our two forward guns, away from shells and the ceaseless rumble of gun-fire—down to the silences of the wood and the clean smell of midsummer. But even at the wagon lines we had bombing raids, twice a night sometimes when the moon was shining, one of my drivers was killed; and the weight of summer had taken the place of the lightness of spring.

We also lost a number of horses and in the last year of the war it was almost as difficult to get good remounts, as replacement horses were called, as to get good men. Sometimes we had to accept mules, which could survive in worse conditions than horses and on less food. But in C Battery we were fortunate or favoured and to the end of the war we remained nearly one hundred per cent horse-drawn. The drivers of course loved their horses, but every man in the battery was proud of their good looks. Our horses made us believe in ourselves, gave us confidence that we were a good battery.

There were two great beautiful cart horses, Billy and Prince, the one a chestnut, the other black, that went every afternoon with a G.S. Wagon (general service) to draw our rations for the next day from the nearest dump. Prince was killed in one of the night bombing raids on the wagon lines and we all felt poorer.

For a while I was on less friendly terms with Frank than I had been before. He was happier than I had ever known him, but he seemed to have gone over to the other side now that he was a captain, Cecil's side against ours. A captain's pay was considerably better than a lieutenant's, he could afford marriage now. But besides this, a captain's job was the safest in a battery of Field Artillery, he had a better chance now of surviving.

'I don't intend to take any more risks than I can help,' he said to me one evening. 'I consider that I've done my share of fighting, I've had nearly three years of it.'

How could any of us believe we had done our share until the War was over! I at any rate had done so little as yet.

'You'll have done your share too,' he said, 'by the end of this year.'

I thought I should probably be killed before the end of the year. I had not thought so at first, but now I was losing confidence in my chance of survival. One had a lot of lucky escapes, but there came a day when one's guardian angel was not looking, his back was turned, and in that moment it happened. My luck could not last for ever, I'd had my share of lucky escapes, even in the last few weeks there had been two —the sniper's bullet at Maricourt, the near misses in the shallow O.P., the hole of fear, on the hillside above the river.

Up to the guns again. Back to the Seven Sisters (only five now) and the untended green cornfields, back to the noise and dirt and discomfort, to the sickly smell of the gas-drenched grass in the valley, and the smell of the dead mule —it was a guide on a dark night between our main position and the two forward guns.

We were making a mine dug-out at the forward section, each of us spent a night up there in turn. I liked to work with the men when it was my turn. Every one of them knew more than myself about the construction of a mine dug-out, I was the most unskilled labourer. They took no notice of me, they talked as though I was not there, but I was one of them, I knew they trusted me.

How airless it was in the deep mine dug-out! The candles flickered and then went out. When this happened the man nearest to the top of the steps lifted the gas curtain and looked out, shouting down to the rest of us whether it was night or morning. If it was morning we came up, yawning, smelling the freshness of the day outside. Even the gas-soaked cornfields were fresher in the dawn than the air at the bottom of the dug-out. Then sleep.

June was passing into July. The dry fields were splashed with scarlet poppies.

June was the first month in which the enemy had made no major attack. Why was he waiting?

The Australians were preparing an attack of their own. They were going to show the enemy that they also had the power to dictate events. It was not to be a major attack. Not yet. The village of Hamel, between the Somme and Villers Bretonneux, was the objective. The village was on a ridge that looked down on the Australian positions, it hampered their movements, it would certainly make a general advance

225

more difficult if at some later time that was decided on. Hamel and the Vaire Wood ridge were to be captured. An American battalion was to take part in the attack. On the Fourth of July, American Independence Day. It would almost be the first time that American soldiers had been in action, it would be the first time ever that they had fought side by side with ourselves.

Our brigade was ordered to move forward into the valley of the Somme. We moved by night. The guns were to be silent until the morning of the attack, we were so close to the front line that we could not even walk about on the position by day, we were under observation from Vaire Wood. The guns were in front of a bank, they were covered with branches of trees to make them look like part of the brushwood. We used fresh branches every night, bad camouflage was worse than none at all, it showed you were trying to hide something.

We worked through the short summer nights, digging shelters, putting away and concealing the ammunition which had come up, covering our tracks with grass. After the night's work we slept. Though we were so close to the line it was one of the quietest places I ever was in. The little village of Vaux nearly hidden in trees was in front of us, on our right two hundred yards away the road leading to the village, and on the other side of the road the marsh began, river and lakes and marsh, together they formed the valley, and somewhere in the valley was our front line, somewhere his. Our position was hardly shelled at all. Sometimes in the afternoon it was so quiet that you expected to hear Vaux church bell ringing, or the clock striking the hour.

'Come for a bathe in the lake,' Durham said when I woke up one afternoon. I refused, it seemed madness to bathe so close to the enemy. But he would not let me alone.

'You said you were longing for a bathe.'

'You said how hot and sticky you felt.'

'You can't let B Battery think they're better than we are, they've been bathing.'

'Anything
B can do
C can do
Better,' he sang at me.

226

He made me go with him. We had to crawl through the long grass down to the road, but we were safe when we got there, the tall trees in the valley hid us from the enemy's view. We walked down to the lake, we looked for and found a place where the water was deep at the edge and there were no reeds; we undressed, we dived into the clear cool water.

'Don't splash so much,' I said. 'They'll hear us.'

He turned over on to his back and kicked his legs in the air. We dived again and again, we swam out towards the middle of the lake, the water was all a-glitter in the bright sunshine. Afterwards we sat on the bank, dangling our legs in the water, feeling the warmth on our naked bodies, hearing the water's lap against the reeds and the gentle breeze at the top of the poplars and silver willows.

We went there each afternoon. I almost forgot that I was a soldier, I became a boy again. We were out of uniform, for the moment we had no responsibilities, we need not even think about the war until nightfall. The fact that we were close to the enemy even added to our enjoyment, we were like boys from school who have deliberately broken bounds and are half hoping to hear a master's voice for the excitement of having to escape from him.

We had our excitement one afternoon, for while we were dressing a German gun opened fire on the valley. We were in no real danger, we were not in the line of the shells, we were completely hidden from sight by the tall trees on the other side of the lake. A lot of the shells fell into water, bursting on percussion and sending great spouts of water twenty or thirty feet into the air. We laughed, it was a spectacular display.

'Very poor shooting!' Durham said. 'No points at all!'

The war was like a game to him, a game not to be enjoyed, but to be won. He was always giving points to our side: for bathing in the face of the enemy, 3 points; for watching his shells burst in the water and do no harm to anyone, 3 more. He never allowed the enemy any points at all. Nothing could destroy his gaiety, he was the only one of us who never became depressed. His slow deliberate voice, his laughter, his healthy good-looking face—he was worth a lot of points to our battery.

We were malicious enough to enjoy our bathes even more because of Major Cecil's discomfiture. He wanted to come with us, but had not the courage to do so. Instead, he walked back more than a mile and bathed in the River Ancre, and the long double walk in the heat of the day, or as he said, the presence of mustard gas in the water gave him a bad headache and he could not eat his dinner. We still had the natural cruelty of boys.

Zero Hour was at ten minutes past three on the day of the attack. All the guns in the valley opened fire, all the guns on the high plateau behind us, this time it was our bombardment, not his. It was too dark to see anything, but some time later I climbed to the top of the terraced banks behind our guns and looked across the valley to the rising ground on the other side. Through the smoke and semi-darkness I saw a line of tanks ascending the hill, and infantry following. I could see the red flashes of our own shells bursting along the ridge beyond the tanks, beyond the village of Hamel, which seemed already to have been captured. I saw no Germans.

You don't see very much of a battle when you are taking part in it. In March I had seen lines of German infantry coming downhill at a run, now I saw tanks going up a hill and our men walking quite slowly behind them. That was all I saw of two battles. It's much better on TV or at the cinema, the battles there look far more realistic.

Only a few shells came back at us. All the signs were that the attack was succeeding. Later in the morning Cherry gave us the official report: All objectives captured and 1,500 prisoners, our casualties not heavy. Some Australians passing by on the road gave us more details of the victory, the Yanks had fought very well, they said, they were fine soldiers, but a bit rough.

That evening we were taken out of the line, we were to march through the night to St Sauveur, nearly twenty miles from Vaux, in the valley of the Somme, but on the other side, the safe side, of Amiens. But that was to be only a temporary stopping place.

It looked like Rest, Cherry said; and not before it was time. We had been in the line for months and months and months. This was the best time of year for going out to rest,

I was thinking, as we marched through the warm summer night; long days, and the cleanness of the country away from the smells and the sultry heat in the battle zone. We were tired, but rest would restore us, make us ourselves again, a happy battery, working together. We might even go back as far as the sea, it was not a great distance from St Sauveur. The thought of bathing in the sea went to my head. The Somme lake had been enjoyable, but the Sea!

In the morning, after daylight, we saw Hughes coming to meet us. He had been sent on ahead to arrange about billets in St Sauveur, we were nearly there now. It was clear that he had heard news.

'Is it the sea?' we called out to him. 'Where are we going?' 'Y-prez,' he said, 'bloody Y-prez.'

Eight

So Flanders was our destination.

Jack said it was like going home. The Somme gave him the creeps, he said, he could see a picture of his corpse lying out on one of those ruddy bare hillsides; Ypres was at any rate a more cosy place to be killed in.

The rest of us laughed at the thought of Jack seeing a picture of his own corpse. 'Well, it's going to be our turn one of these days, whether we like it or not,' he said. He might feel pleased at going back to Flanders, but the rest of us were not; and when the train was carrying us along by the sea, so near to England, so infinitely far away, it was almost more than I could bear, and I saw some of the men turning their faces away.

My own depression had been gradually lifting. Peaceful days and nights at the wagon lines, bathing in the lake, the Australian successes, even the mere passing of time all these were helping me to forget the nightmares of March and April, I was more relaxed, less nervous about the morrow as I was falling asleep, able to make plans about the next day. And the year was half over. If we could hold out until it ended, then the Americans would be ready and the tide would begin to turn.

But all my depression came back when we arrived in Flanders.

We learnt at once that the next German attack was now expected up here. Not on the Somme. That was why we had been brought up. The battery was in action in what had been wagon line country in 1917, there were deserted camps all round us. But as a result of the enemy advance in April it was now in the fighting area, all the surrounding country was

230

dominated by Kemmel Hill, which the Germans had captured. There was no getting away from Kemmel Hill, wherever we went we could see it. And it could see us. I had never disliked a hill so much, it looked so menacing. It was Kemmel that first brought back my depression.

Two guns were in front of the others, a forward section again. They were behind the Scherpenberg, another wooded hill, like Kemmel but not so high, and not dominating the enemy positions as Kemmel dominated ours. The guns were side by side on the concrete floor of an old stable, part of one of the derelict camps. There was a tin roof overhead and a strip of camouflage netting along the open side, which had to be taken down when the guns fired. But no firing was done by day, the position was too close to the line, about a mile away.

There was no protection by the guns, but a house some fifty yards away had been converted into dug-outs. There were three of them, all strong. The dug-outs were all right, it was the thought of having to leave them and run across to the guns under fire when the attack came—that was the frightening thought. I was in charge of the forward section.

It was a sinister place. Jack said that the Somme gave him the creeps, this lonely derelict country behind the Scherpenberg had the same effect upon me. Once it had been attractive country, the Scherpenberg had been a pretty hill. Now it was a waste land, rough grass, a few forlorn huts, shell-holes; all the trees on the hill, which was just inside our line, were fleshless skeletons.

Since no firing was done by day I did not have to stay at the forward section. I spent the night there, returning to the main position in time for lunch and going up again in the evening. 'The attack is expected tomorrow,' I was told one day as soon as I rejoined the others. Major Cecil described the situation to me. The line was not being held in strength, he said, a withdrawal was intended; my two guns were to be sacrificed, I was to go on firing them for as long as possible, then to blow them up, no attempt would be made to save them, it would be impossible to get teams up during an attack.

This was even worse than I had feared. I had not expected

to be left on my own responsibility, to have to make all the decisions myself, including the hardest one—the right moment for blowing up the guns.

'It looks as though you will be on your own from the moment the show starts,' Major Cecil said.

I spent the afternoon reading all the orders. There seemed no doubt about the attack; prisoners had given the date, our airmen had reported the arrival of trains at all the railheads and seen the roads behind the line packed with men and transport moving up. It was a repetition of what we had been told on the eve of March 21st, I had made fun of it then, but it had been true.

I read with especial care the orders that concerned myself and my forward guns: . . . to go on firing for as long as possible . . . open sights . . . inflicting heavy casualties . . . holding up the enemy advance . . . then destroying the guns . . . ensuring their complete destruction . . . afterwards rejoining the rest of the battery.

Rejoining the rest of the battery! What a hope! We should all be killed before we got away. If we carried out those orders!

I should have felt less discouraged if we had still been behind the Australians, but the English division holding the line on our front seemed to consist only of young soldiers straight from home with no battle experience. How could they stand up to an attack like that of March 21st! Would they run away? Or would they wait to be taken prisoner? I might see them coming back over the skyline, or I might see no one at all until I saw the enemy.

And another thing. It would have been less difficult for me if the men up with the forward guns had been from my own Left Section; if Sergeant Denmark had been with me, he would have done what I told him to do, and I would have done what he told me to do, I had complete confidence in him. But they were not my own men, and Sergeant Tweedie was not reliable. On the surface he was more respectful than Denmark, but when we were in a tight corner he might be the first to disappear.

I went up earlier than usual. Jack wished me luck as I was leaving. I knew I should need it. I sent for Sergeant Tweedie as soon as I arrived at the forward position and told him about the expected attack and what was required of us. He showed no concern whatever.

'Then we've got to be ready to blow up the guns, Sir,' he said, and he fetched two shells, unscrewing their cases. I watched him carefully. I had a vague idea as to what had to be done, but blowing up guns was not one of the things we had been taught at cadet school. He made sure that the caseless shells fitted easily, point inwards, into the mouth of the guns, then took them out again and put them on one side.

'Then you put another shell in the breech in the ordinary way, Sir, and fire.'

It sounded very simple.

'You need a longish bit of wire to tie to the trigger, Sir, and it's best to get round a corner before you pull.'

He went away to find some wire. He might be all right in the morning, I thought, no one could have set about the preparations in a more matter-of-fact way. The barrels of the guns would be completely destroyed by the explosion of the two shells inside. Major Cecil was said not to have destroyed his guns effectively on the first day of our retreat, that was the basis of the charge against him, the reason for his demotion.

Tweedie came back with the wire and hung the pieces over a nail on one of the stable beams.

'I'll see the lads know where they are,' he said. 'Will that be all, Sir?'

I gave him the details for our nightly harassing fire. It would be especially important tonight, for the enemy would be moving up to his assault line in the darkness, and short sudden bursts of fire might inflict a lot of casualties on him.

Then Tweedie went back to the dug-outs, but I remained standing by the guns. The light was beginning to fade, but I could still see all the ground in front rising to the Scherpenberg, and we had taken down the camouflage netting at the side of the stable in preparation for our night firing.

I could make some of my decisions now, I thought, while it was light enough to see. The enemy bombardment would probably start at about four o'clock, before daylight, the sun rose at five. It was certain to be very heavy, and nothing

233

would be gained by bringing the men outside in the dark. But as soon as it was light we ought to come out. But we should have no protection inside the stable, we shouldn't last long here under heavy shellfire. It might be better to stay inside the dugouts until the shellfire was less heavy, the enemy would have to stop shelling the forward area as soon as his infantry began to advance, that would be the time when we could inflict most casualties.

Yes, that would be best. Wait inside under cover until the shellfire became less. That would tell us he was coming. Then we would rush out and wait until we saw him. The more I thought about it, the clearer it was to me that our job was to fire at him at short range. Other batteries could fire at him in his front line before he attacked, but ours were the only guns in a position to fire at him over open sights as he was attacking, as he came down the side of the Scherpenberg.

But how long could we go on for? I had never fired over open sights, I did not know of anyone who had, not at short range. It was little more than a thousand yards to the crest of the hill, we should come under rifle and machine-gun fire almost immediately. We should get cover from sight, perhaps even from bullets, behind the gun-shields, but anyone walking about inside the stable or carrying ammunition to the guns would be seen and shot at. And if our own infantry were falling back in front of the enemy we should have to wait until they were out of danger, probably it would be too risky to fire at a range of less than a thousand yards, but we could fire as the enemy was coming over the crest, and go on firing. The crest was the place. I would get both guns laid on to it as soon as we came out in the morning.

But I should have to watch the enemy's advance, see how far he was getting. With all these huts about, he might work his way round behind us and then rush the stable. I put up my field glasses for a last look at the country in front, I looked at the crest, moving my eyes along it, wondering where he was most likely to appear first, then at the deserted broken huts, finally choosing one of them, half way up to the crest. When I saw an enemy there or at any point in line with it, then I would give the order to blow up.

Some of the men with me were very good, young Gunner

234

Dee was first-rate. Whatever he might be doing he always had a cigarette between his lips and a mocking remark ready to come out of them, usually at the expense of one of us or a senior N.C.O., but spoken so quietly and with such a friendly smile that even Major Cecil did not take offence. Dee would be all right, smoking and mocking as he fired his gun, he was a first-rate gunner too, but some of the others were new men and Sergeant Tweedie was unlikely to set a good example. I could imagine him coming to me, I could hear him saying Better go, Sir, while we can. . . . We can get new guns, Sir, we can't get new men. . . . Probably he would bring me the bits of wire ostentatiously—If we wait too long, Sir, there won't be time.

It was nearly dark now, too dark to see. I went back to my dug-out, the smallest of the three, there was just room in it for my wire-netting bed and an empty ammunition box which served as a table.

Presently I heard our ammunition wagons on the road and we all went outside to unload them and carry the shells into the stable. I enjoyed talking to the drivers, but when they had gone back, when the last sound of horses and wagon wheels had died away I felt we had been deserted, they were returning to the safety of the wagon lines, we were waiting for the enemy to come, day would break as usual for them. But for us?

Three or four times more we went outside for the night firing. The last burst of fire was finished soon after two o'clock. Two hours to wait! This would be the hardest time. The men's dug-outs were very close to my own, I could hear their voices, but only an occasional word of what they were saying. They were playing cards, I heard a lot of laughter. I wanted to go and be with them, generally when I was alone on a job I would spend a part of the night at any rate in their company. They would move up when I went in, making room for me to sit down among them, but then go on with whatever they were doing, as though I was not there.

But tonight I thought it would be a mistake to go to them. It might make it harder for me in the morning, harder to get their obedience when I ordered them out, ordered them to go on firing. If I had been on equal terms with them an hour or

235

two before, they might not appreciate the difference when I had to be an officer again. I had never ordered men to risk their lives in this way, and go on risking them. Young Dee would carry out his orders, and perhaps the others would follow his example, they all liked him. I had a sudden idea, I would recommend him for the Military Medal if we both survived the attack, he certainly deserved one.

Three o'clock. I was trying to read my book, but I did not take in what I was reading. Instead of words on the page, I saw Germans, Germans coming over the crest, lines of Germans advancing down the hill, single Germans crouching behind the derelict huts. The card players were still at their game. Once, in a silence, I heard Dee's voice and then general laughter. Who was he mocking or mimicking now, I wondered. Myself perhaps, they must all have noticed my nervousness when we went outside for the night firing, for each time I had made sure that the two caseless shells and the bits of wire were still in their right places.

Half past three. I thought of writing a letter to my parents to thank them for the happy life they had given me. But it was too late now, there was no one to whom I could give my letter, it would never be delivered. Anyway, I could not have written, I was listening all the time for the first sound of the German guns, the opening of the bombardment. I should not have known what I was writing. Better to do nothing. Just keep still.

Four o'clock. The card-playing had stopped, there was no sound from the other dug-outs, they had all fallen asleep. It would not matter, the bombardment would waken them.

A quarter past. I had taken my watch out of my pocket and put it on the table in front of me. The candle, stuck into an empty bottle, had nearly burnt down, I lit another and put it on top of the old one, watching the shadows flicker on the sandbagged walls as I did so.

Half past four. Any moment now. All my senses were alert. I looked at the map again, making some notes on it about enemy trench mortar positions that had been reported. This was something to do, it helped to pass the time away. Silence still outside. He was late. It must be getting lighter, but the gas blanket was drawn so closely across the entrance that no light could come through. I felt tired, it had suddenly come over me.

Five o'clock. Hope began to rise. I could see the minute hand of my watch moving.

Five minutes past.

Ten past.

I waited, holding my breath, for the minute hand to reach the quarter. Then I got up, drew aside the blanket, and went out. The sun was up, it was over the crest, above the place where I had expected to see Germans by this time. And a lark was singing above the waste fields. Even the sad flat Flanders landscape looked beautiful in the light of a new day. A safe day. There would be no attack now. It must have been postponed for some reason. Tomorrow instead, probably. But a day was a long time. Twenty-four hours. Fourteen hundred and forty minutes.

I went back into the dug-out, blew out the candle, and fell asleep without undressing.

Nine

The German attack was never made.

It had been intended, it was not a hoax. At the time we did not know why it had been postponed, we knew nothing of Ludendorff's difficulties, nor did we want to know the reason; it was enough for us that it had been put off and that there was no immediate talk of its being put on again. We did not know that the tide was turning, had already turned in fact. Neither did Ludendorff.

We did not stay in Flanders. We were sent back to the Somme country as soon as it became apparent that the German attack was off. Again we were hoping for a fortnight's rest before returning to the line. 'Then we'll get you off on leave,' Cherry said to me encouragingly, I was next but one on the list. Again we were disappointed. We learnt as soon as we were out of the train that it was Villers Bretonneux again for us, the little town on the high ground above the river. And at once. We had at least been given one day's rest at St Sauveur on the way up, now we were to begin our march back to the line that very night.

The Battery was in a bad state. Our casualties had been very slight in Flanders, they had not been heavy at any time during the summer, far less than at Ypres the year before, but I had never heard so much grumbling. Chiefly it was the result of war weariness, the War had lasted so long, it would go on for ever and ever, there had been no leave since the beginning of the Retreat, there was nothing to look forward to.

But Major Cecil was responsible for some of the discontent. He was an unpopular battery commander. He had a sarcastic tongue, he wanted everything to be done in his way, he made no effort to cultivate a friendly relationship with the men under his command, the affection of his dog seemed to be enough for him.

'When's the Major coming back?' was a question I had often been asked during the summer. When they spoke of the Major the men meant Major Eric, who had gone home with a broken knee-cap at the beginning of the year. He had been as popular in the battery as Cecil was unpopular. He had been far more abusive than Cecil ever was, I had often heard him blasting someone or other, but the men had not minded. 'The Major, he plays hell with us when he's in a bad temper,' his servant, Hewlett, said to me once, 'but no one minds what he says, he wouldn't hurt a fly.'

Major Eric was a Sheffield man, a lot of the battery had known him before the War, they knew his family, they considered it right that he should command them, it was almost a feudal relationship; and in return the Major talked to them about their homes, he understood them, they knew that he took a personal interest in them.

But Major Cecil was without the gift of making himself liked. He was almost equally unpopular with the officers. I had a row with him on the morning of our return to the Somme. It had begun to rain while we were detraining, everyone was wet and in a bad temper, we marched a mile or two, then halted in a wet field, where we were to stay until nightfall. There was a house for us in the village and I went there, hoping to find a fire where I could dry my clothes. Major Cecil was there already. He told me his servant had been put on to some job, getting firewood or peeling potatoes, but he had taken him off it. 'His job is to look after me,' he said. 'Someone else can peel the potatoes.'

I was mess secretary, that was why he told me. I said that all the servants ought to take their share of whatever had to be done, it would not be fair if one of them did nothing.

'Fair or unfair, those are my orders,' he said. 'Tell Bombardier Medley that it's not to happen again.'

'You can damned well tell him yourself,' I said.

He told me I was getting too big for my boots, and I slammed out of the house, out into the rain again, back to the wet horse lines in the wet field, where the men were putting up their wet bivvies. They were all bad-tempered, and I agreed with them that it was a bloody awful war.

For the rest of the day I kept out of Cecil's way. After dinner he rode on ahead. 'To make sure of a good night's rest,' I said to the others, but I knew that in fact he was going to a conference of battery commanders with the Colonel. But he would be able to go to bed when it was over, none of the rest of us had any sleep that night. Frank to my annoyance took his side in the argument about the servants. Now that he was a senior officer himself he said their servants had more to do, and that Medley ought to have made a different arrangement. But Jack and Durham agreed with me, Hughes was on a course, he had been away from the battery during most of our time in Flanders.

'Don't worry,' said Jack sympathetically. 'It doesn't matter and there's nothing you can do about it.'

'Yes there is,' I told him. 'I can apply for a transfer to the R.A.F. or the Heavies.'

'No you can't,' said Durham. 'You've got to stay here, we need you.'

I was taken aback. It was as unexpected as it was comforting to be told that I was needed. I knew that I should not really choose to leave the battery.

We began our march at eleven o'clock that night. Some of the men were drunk when it was time to start, they had been to the estaminets in the village and they were not accustomed to wine. I was dismayed, it was further proof that the battery I loved was going downhill. Sergeant Denmark was completely sober, but he was in one of his bolshevik moods when I commented about our bad start and the fact that one of the other sergeants had obviously drunk too much.

'The officers have their good time when they get the chance,' he said. 'I reckon we have a right to do the same.'

I might have replied that we did not get drunk when there was a job to be done, but I remembered that we had dined in a restaurant on the previous evening before our train left, and that he had probably heard our loud voices when we returned to the station.

The men soon marched themselves sober. Long before daybreak I heard their cheerful ribald comments going up and down the line of our marching column. It was seven o'clock before we reached our destination and we were still on the near side of Amiens. It had kept fine during the night, but the rain soon started again. There was a lot to be done, we all got wet through once more. At lunch time Major Cecil told me that Medley needed keeping up to the mark, the servants had a soft job, he said, and if they didn't watch out he would return the whole lot to duty, there were plenty of other men who would be glad to take their places.

I did not tell Bombardier Medley about these threats, but he knew that Cecil had been finding fault again and he told me that he wanted to return to duty. 'I've had about as much as I can stand,' he said. 'If he thinks we've got cushy jobs, let him try and get someone else. We all want to go back. All except Richards, he can do the whole flicking lot by himself and find out what it's like."

Richards was Cecil's own servant, a decent young man, but in danger of being spoiled by Cecil's treatment of him. I calmed Medley down. We could not possibly do without him, he was not only a good cook, but a brave man who made sure that we got our meals whatever the Boche was doing.

I got two or three hours sleep during the afternoon, but we were to march again as soon as it was dark. The guns were to be taken away for calibration, Durham was going with them, the rest of the battery was to continue its march up to the line, through Amiens, I was to go on ahead with half a dozen guides, leaving one at each of the last turnings. We had got to arrive in our wagon line area before dawn, Cecil said. What was all the hurry about, why all this night marching?

I set off with my guides before the rest of the battery. We made quite a cavalcade, for there was a similar party from each of the other batteries and Major Villiers, the brigade second-in-command, was leading us. It was not yet midnight when we came to the outskirts of Amiens. Hardly anyone was left in the big town, the enemy was only nine miles away, the place was within gun-fire range. Not a great deal of damage had been done yet, in the darkness none was visible, but this added to the unnaturalness of our ride through the town. This great city and no one living in it! Once or twice a figure scurried across the road in front of us, and I saw an old woman behind a wall of sandbags. All was in darkness. I was aware of big houses and walled gardens, or broad streets and tram lines, boarded-up shops, the dark mass of the cathedral. It might have been a plague town, from which all the inhabitants had fled.

At last we came out on the other side. The noises of war were louder now and the sky in front of us was lit up by the flashes of guns. Still we rode on. We had turned away from the river valley, we were going uphill, I could see banks by the side of the road and little woods; it was the old familiar upland country, but now we were on the south of the Somme, we had been on the north side before we went up to Flanders.

I was riding beside Vernon, my friend in B Battery. I had not seen him for two or three weeks, the other batteries had not been near us in Flanders. He told me that he had applied for three months special leave to South Africa, where his home was now, he had not seen his parents for three years. I said I hoped he would get it, but I was almost selfish enough to hope that he would not. Three months was a long time, he would be away for nearly six altogether, I could not envisage a time so far ahead, I might never see him again, I hated the thought of losing another friend.

'I shall come back of course,' he said.

I knew he would. Some people seized with both hands any opportunity of escaping from the War, but not Vernon, I knew that he meant what he said. But I might not be here when he came back. I wanted to tell him about my row with Major Cecil and that I was thinking of applying for a transfer. He also had suffered from Cecil and I knew he would be sympathetic but would advise me to stay where I was, which was the advice I wanted. But after passing through Amiens I was too tired to talk, it was our third night without sleep. We spoke less and less, we were falling asleep.

'Look out!' he suddenly cried, bumping his horse against mine and catching hold of my shoulder. 'You were nearly off that time,' he said.

I tried to wake myself up, but the desire for sleep was almost irresistible.

'You drowse for ten minutes,' he said. 'I'll see you don't fall off. Then you can watch for me.'

So we went on. It was the darkest hour before the dawn.

At last we stopped. We had left the road, we were on a grassy track, I could see a big wood in front of us. We tied up our horses and lay down on the grass.

I was awakened by a shout: 'The batteries are here,' and looking down the track I saw them coming towards us. Day was breaking, I was shivering with cold, Vernon led his battery into one part of the wood, I guided ours to another. I saw the tired faces of the men as they dismounted, hardly anyone spoke, even during the Retreat we had not been more exhausted. The wagons were parked, horse lines put up, everyone working mechanically. Walkenshaw brought me a cup of very strong tea and showed me where he had unrolled my valise on the ground. I was asleep in a few minutes.

I woke up once and heard the voice of Hughes. So he had come back from his course. 'Hello!' he said, seeing my eyes open. His cheerful smiling face was wet with sweat. 'Coo!' he said. 'Known it colder than this in December.'' But I could not wake up, or say how pleased I was to see him. When I woke again it was the middle of the afternoon. My head ached, the wood was full of horses and shouting men. And smells and flies, there were flies buzzing everywhere.

'No one is to go out of the wood by day.' Major Cecil said when we were all together at tea. The servants had done a good job, they had put up the mess and all our little tents.

Why ever not, we all wanted to know.

We were going to attack, and the Boche was not to find out that a lot of fresh troops had come into the area. The guns were not to go up until the night before the attack, or to fire at all before zero hour. It was hoped that we should take him by surprise.

So that was the reason for all our night marching, and why the guns had been taken away for calibration. The normal thing to do was to check their accuracy by observed firing whenever we went to a new position, but on this occasion we were not to give our position away until the battle started.

'What about the horses?' Frank asked. 'Are they to stay inside the wood all day?'

243

There was no water in the wood. The horses would have to go all the way to Boves, more than a mile away, three times a day. It was absurd to suppose that Boche aeroplanes would never see them, it was absurd to think we could deceive the Boche, he always knew what we were going to do, he would be ready for us. But it was rather exciting, after he had been attacking us for so long. Even an unsuccessful attack of ours might be less disagreeable than a successful attack of his.

My head was still aching the next day. In the afternoon I rode up to the line with Jack to see the position we were going to occupy. It was behind Villers Bretonneux, only a thousand yards from the enemy, but we rode all the way because it was raining and there was no visibility. The afternoon was quiet, there were not many shell-holes on the position, we agreed that the place might have been worse. There was also a shallow trench close behind, Hughes was going up with a working party that night to make it deeper and dig some shelters.

We were both soaked when we got back to the wood. It had been fine when we set off and because it was so hot we had not taken our coats. Then the storm broke. There was so much water in my boots when I took them off that I could pour it out. With any luck, I thought, I'll get pneumonia or rheumatic fever. That would do as well as applying for a transfer.

By this time I was beginning to enjoy my row with Major Cecil, I had not spoken to him since our arrival in Boves Wood, but one of the others told him about my headache and to my disappointment he was considerate. 'You've had a harder time than anyone else lately,' he said to me, 'I shall leave you behind at the wagon lines when the guns go up.'

I should have preferred to go up with the guns, I felt part of the battery when I was there, but only a supernumerary at the wagon lines; but I was not feeling well, I wanted to sleep and go on sleeping, and there was more time for sleep at the wagon lines. But there was so much noise in the wood. It was full of horses and men, full of Canadians, who were going to make the attack on our front. Wherever you went there was a latrine and the wood was deep in horse dung, the place was a paradise for flies, in the August heat and the mud after the rain.

In the morning, however, I felt better. The guns were going up that night, the attack was to take place the next morning. Orders had been received that we were to be ready to travel light, everything inessential was to be left behind, to be dumped in the rear if necessary. The others were all wondering what they should take and what they should leave behind, but not being concerned in this, since I was remaining at the wagon lines, I rode off after breakfast to draw money from the Field Cashier and look for canteens.

I enjoyed my ride, I always enjoyed seeing and learning my way about in new country. It was a satisfaction to feel well again and to escape even for a few hours from the smells in the wood. I went alone. I saw Edric coming to meet me on my return. There was a particular smile on his face, not his ordinary smile of welcome, it meant that he had news.

"Major's come back," he said.

"What major?" I asked, but of course I knew who he meant. Major Eric. I was amazed. The news was rippling over the wood, three other men told me before I reached the mess.

There he was. Sitting the wrong way round on his chair, resting his arms on the back of it, his cap on the back of his head, the buttons of his tunic undone, a glass on the table beside him; it was as though he had never gone away. He smiled at the look of astonishment on my face. Everyone was laughing. Even Major Cecil seemed pleased to see him, they were old friends. But what was going to happen now? We could not have two majors in one battery. Would Cecil become a captain again, and Frank a lieutenant? We had always said to one another that if he ever came back he would turn up in this way without any warning, but we had not expected that he would come back.

'You can't get rid of a bad penny,' he said.

He was enjoying our surprise and our pleasure in seeing him. But why hadn't he come back before, a broken knee cap need not have kept him in England for six months. He knew all about us. Who had told him? No one had written to him, so far as I knew, he himself never wrote a letter. But he knew all the places where we had been and who had been killed and who wounded, he even knew about Bingley's revolver.

'Nice chap, but out of his element,' he said. 'Like a fish out of water.'

He did most of the talking at lunch. He told us he had read *The Times* from cover to cover during the March Retreat.

'I was expecting to see some familiar names in the list of Victoria Cross winners,' he said.

'What a hope you had!' said Frank. 'It was terrible. We did everything that we should not have done and nothing that we should have done. We ran away more than once. The other batteries were worse, that's all we can boast about."

I felt rather sorry for Cecil at this reference to the other batteries, but he said nothing, and Major Eric went on, 'Sergeant Denmark was the man in my mind, I knew no Fritz could frighten him, I imagined him firing his gun at point-blank range.'

'He was on leave,' I said.

'So he has just told me.'

He knew all about us, but he told us nothing about himself, where he had been, what he had been doing, why he had come back at last. Frank told us, Jack and myself, later in the day that he knew all about it. His woman had left him, he said, she had taken up with another man. That was why he had come back.

'How do you know all this?' Jack asked.

'Everyone in Yorkshire knows about her, she's notorious,' Frank said. 'And the sooner Eric stops running after her, the better for him. I know he's got a lot of money, but not enough for the like of her.'

Frank enjoyed having a story to tell, but he may have been right. I thought the Major seemed different after his return. He was quieter, he drank as much as before, but he was less hospitable, he was not always inviting other officers into our mess. Not many of his friends in the brigade were left, and he did not appear to want to make new ones. He enjoyed talking to the men as much as before, at any rate to the old Yorkshire ones, they made less than half the battery now. He preferred their company to ours, none of us could come as close to him as they did.

They were delighted at his return. 'Now our luck will change, Sir, you just see,' old Driver Oaks said to me, and he added, 'the Major, he buggers us about, but we'd rather be buggered about by him than by any of the others."

The guns went up to the line that night. Major Cecil went with them. Major Eric stayed behind at the wagon lines with Frank and myself. 'You don't swop horses in mid-stream,' he said.

We were about to attack. It was our turn now.

Ten

Up at the guns Zero Hour was at twenty minutes past four, down at the wagon lines I was wakened by the bombardment. I got up and looked out of my tent, it was quite dark in the wood and there was a thick mist. What was happening up there! But it was easy to imagine the scene, I had been there so often—all the German rockets, calling for help, their guns replying, the fountains of earth leaping up where each shell burst; and the thunder of our own guns, it was almost impossible to hear yourself speak on the morning of a battle. We were probably having a bad time, I thought, being so close to the line. I tried to distinguish the sound of enemy shells bursting from the cannonade of our own guns, but Boves Wood was a long way back, and at a distance it was all one noise, a sullen ceaseless reverberation. The drums of death.

For once I was not directly concerned, I was in safety at the wagon lines, I could go back to sleep for another hour. The morning mist was cold, and it was a physical pleasure to feel the warmth of my sleeping bag when I got back inside it.

When I woke again the noise had almost stopped and this was surprising, battles lasted for more than an hour or two, whether we won or lost. The silence was rather disconcerting, I could interpret noises, but silence, even this comparative silence, was a new feature in a battle. There was no news yet. The wagon lines were to move at nine o'clock, unless the order was cancelled before that time.

Taking the horses down to water in the river at Boves I felt a proper wagon-line hero, it was the first time I had not been with the guns on the day of a battle. From Boves I could see the enemy observation balloons against the sky, looking no further away than usual. If the attack had been successful they would have been forced to go further back. We hated these sausage balloons, they could watch everything we were doing.

But no cancellation order was received and we got away from the wood at the right time. It was much emptier now, the Canadians had gone up the night before, they were attacking on the right, the Australians in the centre, and British troops on the left, across the Somme. The roads were blocked, at first we moved very slowly, but there was no enemy shellfire. That was a good sign. Then we saw prisoners coming back, a lot of them. Another good sign. But still there were those damned balloons watching us. They must be able to see all the wagons and lorries on the road. Why weren't we being shelled! What was the matter with his guns!

Then an extraordinary idea occurred to me. Could they be our balloons, not his! Could the attack have been so successful that our balloons were already up there, where his had been only yesterday?

I was riding at the rear of our column, now I went quickly up to the front to tell Frank and the Major about my extraordinary idea. They nodded their heads in agreement. Frank was looking very pleased.

'If everything's gone according to plan,' the Major said, 'we shan't know what to do.' He told me to ride on ahead to the guns and to find out whether it was all right for the rest of the battery to come up. I galloped away. It was unbelievable, nothing like this had ever happened before.

I saw Hughes and Durham standing by the guns and I shouted to them, 'What's happened? Who's winning?'

'We are,' said Durham. 'Forty-love.'

'Jerry's on his way back to Berlin,' Hughes said.

Jack had seen me coming and now he joined us. Even he was smiling. 'I can't make head or tail of it,' he said.

I sent Edric back with a message for the Major, telling him it was all right to come on. Then I got off my horse and listened to what they had to tell me. They all talked at the same time.

'Fairly caught him napping this time,' said Hughes.

'It was bad to begin with,' said Jack.

'Oh, it was nothing. Half a dozen pip-squeaks!' said Durham.

'Well, we had three or four men hit.'

'Could hardly see the tanks because of the fog.'

'You ought to have seen the cavalry going past.'

'Cavalry?' I said in amazement. 'Cavalry?'

'You know,' Durham said impatiently. 'Soldiers on horseback.'

Cavalry coming up from the seaside, where they had been living for years, and going into action! I could not take in such an extraordinary feature of a battle.

They told me they had seen a lot of prisoners and that Major Cecil had invited some of the officers into the mess and given them a drink. One of them spoke good English and he admitted that the attack had taken them completely by surprise.

'But he was still confident of a German victory,' Jack said.

Durham made a contemptuous noise. 'He'll change his mind,' he said, 'when he sees how full the cage is.'

Hughes was rather indignant at Cecil's hospitality. 'Wonder how many of our poor fellows were given a drink in March,' he said. But the others had enjoyed seeing and hearing the German officers.

'What's going to happen now?' I asked. We had been expecting to go forward if the attack was successful, that was why the teams and wagons had been ordered to come up. But they did not know, they only knew that there were no Boche within miles, the guns had stopped firing hours ago because there was no enemy within range.

'It's a shame that we're missing all the fun,' Durham said.

'He'll counter-attack,' said Jack, 'he'll get it all back. Like he did at Cambrai last year.'

We were not sent forward, we stayed in corps reserve in case of a counter-attack. We moved two or three miles during the afternoon, but to a flank, southwards, away from Villers Bretonneux. In the evening I took the horses to water in the little river Luce, we crossed no-man's-land, we went inside what had been enemy land in the morning. His front-line trench was full of bodies, all Germans, they were the first dead Germans I had seen for a long time, I had never seen so many in one place. The sight of them gave me no elation, as once it would have done. Satisfaction yes, we had won a great and totally unexpected victory; but elation no. In March our front-line trench must have looked like that, full of brave Jocks and South Africans.

It was a beautiful summer evening, and the little river Luce was beautiful. It was like a little river in England and the flowers growing at the water's edge, where my horses were drinking, were English flowers. The water was so clean, the field in front of me looked utterly peaceful, but only fifty yards away there was that trench, full of dead Germans, we should see them again on our way back, the grey faces, the poor twisted bodies. They had been bayoneted by the Canadians in the morning, you can't take prisoners in a front-line trench in an attack. Wives, mothers, sweethearts, would not know yet, they would still be writing letters, but the letters would never be read. It might have been us.

I was glad that we were staying behind, but all the others said they were disappointed we had not followed up with the infantry. 'Might have found some of the things we lost in March,' Hughes said, and Frank said they gave army brigades all the dirty work to do, but left them out when it was easy. 'We've got to take the smooth with the rough,' the Major said.

It had already been arranged that he was to stay in command of our battery, Cecil had gone to A Battery in place of Major Villiers, who was unwell and about to go home. When he was leaving us we began to like Cecil again, we parted on the best of terms. I supposed I should never have anything more to do with him, but I was mistaken.

We were still in corps reserve the next morning, no counter-attack had been made. Some of us rode out to look at the scene of the fighting. Except in their front-line trenches there were not many German dead, our advance had been so rapid that most of the enemy had been surrounded and taken prisoner. And we did not see many of our own dead, but in one place there were twenty of our cavalry, men and horses lying where they had fallen, as some German machine-gunner perhaps had got on to them while they were galloping over the field.

There was a captured battery position, and half a dozen artillerymen were lying round one of the guns. Had they, I wondered, been firing over open sights at the Canadians or the cavalry as they came on! Should we have died as bravely that morning? It might have been us, on the stable floor behind the Scherpenberg. How could I feel elation!

We went into their dug-outs, they were strong and more comfortable than ours. Their guns were well concealed. In their officers' mess an unfinished meal, unwashed cups and plates were still on the table. Someone must have rushed in as they were eating, calling out 'The Tommies are here!' I did not know what they called us, we called them Jerry or Fritz or the Boche. *Time you got out, the Boche will be here in a few minutes.*

Their home was very like one of ours, maps and pictures stuck on the walls, shelves cut out of the earth, a sheaf of orders on a hook, newspapers on the table, a half-written letter, a pair of spectacles. I looked at their books, but I could not tell whether they were like ours, whether they were novels or not. Their pictures were certainly different. There was one of a German U-Boat arriving at Constantinople, I could tell it was Constantinople because of the domes and minarets, and sailors from the other ships in the harbour, waving at the submarine, were all wearing red fezzes. Fancy wanting to pin up a patriotic propaganda picture! We only had girls on the walls of our dug-outs, girls in underwear or in nothing at all. Jack had La Vie Parisienne sent to him and he allowed us to cut out what we liked.

He had come up beside me while I was looking at the picture. 'Not much of a thrill there,' he said.

The Major said they were nearer to their homes than we were and were given more leave. 'And you don't need picture thrills,' he said, 'when you can have the real thing.'

As I stood there, in the German officers' mess, looking at their pictures and their books and the little personal possessions that had meant so much to them, as ours meant to us, suddenly I was aware of a great weight being lifted from me. It was over, the nightmare was over, the nightmare that had begun in the spring and lasted all through the long midsummer months. I had woken up from my evil dream. It had

252

begun that morning in the fog. The smell of the wet fog came back to me, fog mixed with gas, I heard the menace of the German guns again, I saw the line of infantrymen on their way up, coming out of the fog, disappearing into it again almost at once. That had been the beginning of it, this was the end.

Not the end of fear or of danger, only the end of a nightmare. Tomorrow or the day after we should go back into the line, I might be killed, but I had always known this might happen and had accepted it, as any soldier must. What I had not known until it happened was the fear of defeat, of disgrace, of running away, of failure. That was worse than the fear of death, that was what had unnerved me.

Now in the German officers' dug-out, with the others round me, talking to one another and to me, comparing the way in which they did things with our way, as I stood there, taking part in their conversation, I knew that it was over. Whatever happened in the future I should never suffer the same fear again, I could feel that the weight had been lifted, I wanted to sing.

But my headaches came back. I thought I had left them in Boves Wood, but they returned. I wanted to sleep. We were still in corps reserve, there had been no counter-attack, but we moved back to Villers Bretonneux, our tents were in a corn field at the edge of the village, we stayed there for two days. I have no memory of them, I was asleep. I may have got up for meals and eaten them with the others, but I went back to sleep afterwards; I may have been woken by the German bombers, it was good bombing weather, moonlit nights, no wind, but I went to sleep again as soon as they had dropped their bombs; the others may have come into the tent where I was lying, I may have heard their voices, but they left me alone.

But at the end Durham came in and shook me gently. 'You'll have to wake up soon,' he said, 'we've got to move.'

'When?' I asked him.

'Tonight. You don't want to be left in corps reserve by yourself, do you?'

'No,' I said. 'I shall be ready.'

I asked him where we were going, but he did not know. 'Somewhere across the river,' he said. I knew that our attack had been less successful on the north side of the Somme. On our front the Canadians and Australians had gained all their objectives, it was the greatest victory we had ever won, but across the river we had not done so well, that was where the next battle would be.

We set off at dusk. It was goodbye to Villers Bretonneux, we never went there again. For myself it was goodbye to Amiens and the Somme and the Ancre also, to the lakes and wooded villages, to the high plateau between the rivers, and all the places where we had dug and laughed and been afraid during the summer.

We marched along the Roman road, the road to St Quentin, westwards, away from the War at first. The bombers were out again, and our road running straight, between dark woods, showed up like a silver ribbon in the moonlight. I knew another way, I had ridden all over this country in the summer, I told the Major we could leave the main road and go down into the valley, where we should be in shadow, I knew the way, we could cross the river by the same bridge, and from there it was easy.

So for a while I rode at the head of the column instead of in my usual place in the rear with the Left Section. It was just a week since we had been marching in the opposite direction, tired, dispirited, as men without hope. Now I was happy. My leave had been put off again, Frank had been given a compassionate leave because his brother had been killed, and I should have to wait at any rate until he came back; but I was happy. We were on our way to more fighting, and fighting meant wounds or death for some of us, it would be one battle after another, as it always had been; but I was happy. There was a sound of summer nights in the tops of the tall trees along the river valley. All was well.

'I told you our luck would change, Sir, when the Major came back,' Corporal Albert said to me after I had returned to my ordinary place. All the battery seemed to think that our great victory on August 8th had been won because the Major had come back to us on August 7th. He knew what the men were saying and accepted the position they gave

254

him, but he had a way of making himself liked. 'Lucky, you knew that other road,' he said to me. 'I didn't fancy being stuck up there when those fellows were laying their eggs. Felt too damned conspicuous.'

It was four o'clock when we arrived at our destination, and still dark, but daylight had come before we went to our tents at the edge of a sweet-smelling clover field. Hughes woke me some hours later. He said he had found a pool in the little river near by, the Hallue, where we could swim one or two strokes. 'Anyway, it'll be cool,' he said, 'it's mighty hot here.

The water was very cold, for alder branches arched across the stream, shutting out the warmth of the sun, leaving only darting spots of light on its surface. Afterwards we lay naked in the hot sunshine.

'Feel the better for that,' Hughes said. 'Nothing like cold water for helping us keep our feelings under control.'

Hughes, the Welsh ex-policeman was a strong fine-looking man and at that moment, I thought, he would certainly have been an object of interest to the village girls we had seen on our way to the stream. But his girl was in Cardiff.

The clover field was only a pause on the way. Tomorrow we were to be off again, going forward this time, back into the battle area. In the evening Bombardier Ewell, the battery clerk, came into the mess tent with our orders from Brigade Headquarters. I saw a pink leave warrant among the other papers. Who was the lucky man, I wondered.

'A leave is no good to you, is it?' said the Major, looking in my direction. 'You haven't got a girl crying her eyes out for you.'

It appeared that an unexpected leave warrant had been allotted to the brigade, and the Colonel said that I might have it if Major Eric could spare two of his officers at the same time.

'Can we spare him?' the Major said. 'I don't think we can. What do you say, Ewell?'

Bombardier Ewell put on the polite smile that he reserved for an officer's pleasantry. He knew as well as I did that the Major would have spared every man in the battery to go on leave, or kept only one for himself to talk to. Ewell asked where I wanted to go, he had to fill in my destination on the railway warrant.

I could hardly believe it was real. The others were returning to the line, but I was going on leave tomorrow. England, I should see England again.

Eleven

There were two bad moments on every leave. There was the saying goodbye at home when it was over, and there was the moment of return to the battery when you looked to see, or waited to be told, if anyone was not there.

It took me a long time to find the battery on my return. I was travelling for four days in France, going backwards and forwards, from one place to another. No one seemed to know where the brigade was. That was one of the disadvantages of a small unit like an Army Field Artillery Brigade. We had stayed with the Australians for a long time, but as a rule we were attached to a different division two or three times every month, we were changed so often that sometimes we did not ourselves know what division we were with. We grumbled, we called ourselves Nobody's Children, but in fact we enjoyed our independence, we were less staff-ridden than divisional brigades.

I found the battery at last. We were out at rest, in a part of France I had never been to before, on the edge of the coal-mining country, we could see slag heaps in the distance. The others were having lunch when I arrived, but only the Major and Durham and a young officer called Allison, who had joined us during the summer. Where were the others? I knew Frank would not be there, he was getting married, he was certain to have applied for an extension of leave. But Hughes and Jack?

'It's all right,' Durham said. 'Jack's gone to Boulogne to buy a case of champagne for the mess, we thought we deserved one.'

'Where's Hughes?'

'He's all right too. A nice blighty, he'll be in England by this time.'

257

It was what everyone wanted, a wound that would take you home and keep you there for some months, so I felt pleased on his account, but I knew we should miss him. Someone had said, 'He isn't our sort,' when he first came to the battery. He wasn't, in the usual sense of the expression, but he was the sort we needed and I had often wished I was more like him.

The Major said his wound was a bad one. 'I thought at first he wasn't going to make it,' he said. 'I don't mind telling you we had a pretty sticky time while you were away.' Casualties had been heavier than at any time since the Retreat.

We stayed out at rest for most of September, but I was not altogether sorry when the time came for us to go back into the line. It had been very pleasant, we had enjoyed the summer sunshine, and having nothing to do, and sleeping all through the night; but we seemed to irritate one another more than when we were in the line. 'This sort of life's so unreal,' Jack said. 'The sooner we go back the sooner we shall settle down.'

We went back. On this occasion the change from peace to war was as sudden as it was complete. One evening we were so far from the War that we could not always hear it; the next, we were in the line and being bombed. It was nearly two months since I had been under fire, I had forgotten how very disagreeable it was, but the sound of falling bombs in the darkness close by was a wonderful aid to memory.

We were back in the Somme country. We were in fact only a few miles from Heudecourt, where our retreat had begun in March. All the territory lost in the spring had been regained in the last few weeks, and now we were back where we had started. The battery had detrained at Peronne in the afternoon, we had immediately marched up to the line and here we were, in the dark, in a maze of trenches and barbed wire, bombs dropping, and the teams and gun limbers still on the position.

'Home, sweet home!' said the Major, and he began humming unmelodiously 'Be it ever so humble,

There's no place like home.'

Humble it certainly was: an old tumbledown trench sys-

258

tem, with some poky and uncomfortable shelters dug into the sides. But we were fortunate, none of us nor any of the horses were hurt by the bombs.

We were going to attack the Hindenburg Line, the name of the immensely strong defence system which the enemy had constructed at the time of an earlier retreat. We had attacked it the year before without any success. Now we were going to try again, but no one seemed to think we should do any better this time. Even the Australians said that we should find we were banging our heads against a stone wall.

We had taken over from an Australian battery, one of their officers had waited to hand over the position to us, and when our teams were safely away and the bombers had returned to their own homes he came into the mess, there was hardly room for four of us in the little excavation, and drank a bottle of whisky with the Major. Up to now, he said, everything had gone like clockwork, but the Hindenburg Line—well, he hoped his battery would not have to take part in the attack.

The Major said it was a bit late in the year to be attacking.

The Australian replied that he supposed the Staff had been waiting for the weather to break.

'I suppose Fritz knows all about it,' the Major said. 'We shan't surprise him this time.'

'He couldn't help knowing,' said the Aussie. 'We've been shouting it out.'

It was a discouraging start, and the next morning we were awakened before it was light by an S.O.S. alarm, and at once all the guns in the area began firing.

'It's only breeze,' the Major said. 'Someone's got a fit of the jumps. Fritz isn't going to attack us, he's sitting pretty, waiting for us to come over and be killed.'

The noise soon died down and as soon as it was light the Major said he was going to find out where we were. He took me with him.

'Christ! what a place!' he said when we saw it for the first time. Old trenches, barbed wire, shell-holes. There was nothing else to see in any direction, wherever we looked there were old trenches and barbed wire and shell-holes.

We walked for about half a mile, jumping over the trenches,

finding a way through the barbed wire, until we came to a trench full of Americans.

'Hello!' said the Major to them.

'Hello you!' they replied.

It was a surprise to learn that an American division, not an Australian one, was holding the line in front of us and that they had never been in action before. 'No wonder they had the jumps,' the Major said, as we were walking back. 'I should have had them myself if I'd known,' and he added that he could not see a new division with no battle experience cutting the Hindenburg Line into little bits.

But Cherry and the Colonel said we should find they were all right on the day, other American divisions had been fighting magnificently on the French front, and these fellows were longing to show us what they could do. Cherry said he knew we had already tried to break the Hindenburg Line and had not succeeded, but this time it would be altogether different, the old Boche was on the run, he had been in retreat ever since the beginning of August, he couldn't put the brake on now, all we had to do was to go on attacking, first in one place, then in another, that was the strategy now, we should go on driving him back until he reached his own country. It would be peace before Christmas, he said.

I had been studying the map of the country in front of us. The St Quentin Canal was part of the Hindenburg Line system, a wide stretch of water between steep banks. On our front, however, in front of the Americans, the canal went underground through a very long tunnel. This was where the Americans were to attack, and at first sight it looked easier to break through here then to cross the canal. But the enemy had made his preparations to meet the danger. The map showed one trench after another, and so many rolls of wire that it appeared impossible for any infantry to get through.

I had my first sight of the Hindenburg Line on the following day when I spent twenty-four hours at the O.P. It was a long walk up there, the O.P. was not directly in front of our battery position, but some little way to the south, on a ridge overlooking the canal itself, not the tunnel. I found my way there by following the telephone line, but it had not been used since our brigade took over, and the enemy knowing about our forthcoming attack had been shelling the whole area, the line was broken in so many places that it would have been quicker to lay out a new one. Shellfire was still heavy, we often had to crouch on the ground, and as fast as we mended the line in one place it was broken in another, the line was still dead behind us when at last we reached the O.P., and in spite of all that my signallers could do it remained dead, I was never in communication with Brigade all the time I was there. I might as well have stayed at the battery for all the use I was.

But I saw the Hindenburg Line. I could see where the tunnel was, and where the canal came out of the tunnel by the village of Bellicourt, I could see the deep chasm of the canal between its steep banks, and the German trenches, white scars against the hillside. It was a very strong position. But most of all, it was the wire in front of the trenches that was disconcerting, there was so much and wire was so hard to destroy. It was our job to destroy it, the field gunners'. We had to cut it up using shells that burst on percussion without making much of a hole, heavier guns could have destroyed the wire more effectively, but if they made big craters in the ground, then it was difficult for the infantry to advance. We had already begun our shooting, it was to go on for forty-eight hours.

I could see the strength of the position, it was enough to daunt anyone. How could any troops cross that canal under heavy fire and scale the bank on the other side! An English division on our right was to make the attack opposite the canal, but it looked an impossible task. And how could the Americans get through that wire! They were to make the first advance at Zero Hour, the Australians following behind were then to go through them and make the second, but they would all be held up by the wire, it looked undamaged.

I could also see unspoiled country beyond the Hindenburg Line, undulating hills, villages, little woods, villages fit to live in, trees that bore leaves, a hillside without shell-holes. It was like a Promised Land. But it had not been promised to us, it would be ours only if we succeeded in storming the canal and capturing the trenches on the other side of the wire. If! Cherry had said we should succeed, but it was easy for an

261

adjutant, planning battles but taking no part in them himself, it was easy for him to be optimistic. I hardly dared even to hope.

Yet I longed to walk on those green hills, hills on which no British soldier had ever set foot, to ride through those unspoiled villages, to hear the rain falling on leaves on living trees. It was an ache to be looking at those villages on the hill—Joncourt, Beaurevoir, Villers Outreaux. They looked so near, they were so far away. The Hindenburg Line stretched between us and them.

There was nothing for me to do except look at the country. Early the next morning I saw a German cart being driven along the road behind the canal, close up to the line, I could have shot at it if I had been in communication with the battery. The man was driving furiously, he knew his danger, he must have been delayed in some way and daylight had caught him, now he was galloping back towards safety, whipping up his horse. I was probably the only Englishman who saw him, and I could do nothing. But after one moment's regret at my impotence I felt sorry for him, I hoped he would escape, I was glad when he reached a bend in the road and was hidden from sight.

Then the rain began and the mist came down, and all the green unspoiled country was obliterated, only the white scars of the trenches remained, and the lines of wire, and the deep gash which was the canal.

At midday I was relieved by an officer in one of the other batteries and I started on my way back through the rain.

Almost at once I had a curious encounter. I met a man unlike anyone I had ever seen before in or near the line. He was old, forty at least, and was wearing a long and shabby mackintosh that reached almost to the ground. But it was his head-dress that gave him such a peculiar look. He was wearing a steel helmet, like anyone else, but he had covered it with an old woollen scarf, the ends of which were tied under his chin to protect his face from the rain.

I guessed that he must be a newspaper correspondent. I had never seen one before, but had formed a picture in my mind of what they probably looked like, and here was the picture come to life in front of me. They were not supposed

262

to go off by themselves or to come so close to the line, but this old fellow had evidently escaped from his guards.

I felt sorry for him. He was too old to be out in the rain, and I thought he had the bewildered look that I had sometimes seen on the face of my father when he did not know where he was. I wanted to be nice to him. What they liked, I knew, war correspondents, was to be treated as equals by fighting men, so I talked to him as I would have talked to one of my friends, telling him about my 24 unrewarding hours at the O.P. and the unspoiled country I had seen across the canal. He asked my name and battery and about the part we were expecting to play in the forthcoming attack. I answered all his questions. Afterwards I wondered if I ought to have been so communicative in conversation with a man who was not a soldier; but I liked his face, as much of it as I could see between the flaps of his scarf, I was sure he was trustworthy. I even called him Sir once or twice, out of respect for his age and because of his resemblance to my father.

But I could not stay talking all day, I knew there was a job for me to do when I got back to the battery. So I told him I must go, and he said that he must also. To write up his dispatch, I supposed. I nearly asked him what his paper was, for I thought it would be amusing to get hold of a copy if I could and read about his meeting with a gay intrepid young observing officer—newspaper correspondents always wrote in that style. But I did not ask. If he had wanted me to know he would have told me. I felt of course the more experienced of the pair of us. He could not know anything about the real war, whereas by this time I thought I knew everything there was to be known about it.

I watched him till he was out of sight. I thought he might not realise how close he was to the German line, a wrong turning might lead him into it. So I watched, ready to run after him if he made a step in the wrong direction. Then I hurried on.

Jack was the senior subaltern in the gun line, but he was no good at working out a barrage table, lines of fire and ranges for our guns on the morning of an attack. That had always been Frank's task, but now that he had been promoted and was generally at the wagon lines it had become my re-

263

sponsibility. It needed complete concentration and great accuracy, but it was the kind of work I could do.

I was supremely confident of my ability to do it and of being able to explain to the Numbers One of each gun exactly what they must do.

It took me a long time. Getting up once, to stretch my legs, and looking outside I saw to my surprise that the Major now had been caught by my war correspondent. The Major was inclined to be intolerant and I was afraid he was probably being rude to the old gentleman. But he was following him about and seemed to be on his best behaviour.

'Who was that old fellow?' I asked when at last he came in for tea.

'Major-General Budworth, C.R.A. Fourth Army,' was the reply.

'Well, I'm damned!' I exclaimed.

'He told me he had met you,' the Major went on. 'He was quite complimentary, he said you were the kind of young officer the artillery would need after the war and hoped you were going to stay on in the army.'

I could not help feeling pleased. For once in my life I had made a good impression on a general, the highest-ranking general I had ever seen in the line.

At dusk we moved about a mile forward to our battle position, where Colonel Richardson and Cherry came to see us and to wish us luck for the next day. The news from all fronts was simply stupendous, Cherry said—the Bulgarians asking for peace, the Turks driven out of Palestine, the whole of the Western Front on the move. And tomorrow we should join in, it was going to be the biggest battle of the war and the greatest victory, he said; the Sammies were as good as the Aussies, together they would be irresistible, the Boche simply hadn't a chance.

'We shall go through them,' the Colonel said, 'like a knife through butter. We shall be eating our Christmas dinner in Berlin."

They convinced me. I had seen with my own eyes that our task looked impossible, but their enthusiasm was so great that I was persuaded. That night I believed that we were about to enter the Promised Land I had seen from the O.P., I should walk on those green hills where trees lived and villages were unspoiled. We were all equally confident, even Jack said there was just a chance of things going right.

But the morning was cold and unpromising when we went outside. Zero hour was at ten minutes to six. We opened fire, there was a great crash of artillery. Daylight came, but the fog was so thick that we could hardly see from one gun to the next. Someone said it was not natural fog, but an artificial one caused by our own smoke shells to help the infantry cross the canal and get through the wire. No one knew for certain. No one knew anything. In any case we didn't want a fog back here, we had to make an advance, how could we advance through this! Perhaps the wind had changed and was blowing the smoke back on ourselves.

'It doesn't smell like a victory,' Jack said.

But Frank found his way up with the gun limbers and first line wagons, we were to begin our advance at Z plus two hundred and forty.

'What's the news?' he asked.

Still there wasn't any. We had not seen any prisoners. Perhaps they had gone by in the fog without our seeing them.

We pulled the guns out. We began to advance. Along the Black Road. It was called a road, but the trenches had hardly been filled in and there were shell-holes everywhere. We advanced about half a mile. The fog was clearing, we could see other guns and wagons in front of us. They were not moving very fast. In fact they were not moving at all, we could not go on.

By this time we could see for four or five hundred yards, up to a crest in front. There were wagons and guns all the way up to the crest, but nothing was going over. Everyone knew what that meant, the enemy was still holding the Hindenburg Line, he would see us if we went over the crest.

Just then a gun began firing at us. There was only one gun and it wasn't a big one. But this was further proof that our attack had failed, a gun of this size only had a range of seven or eight thousand yards, indeed from the sound of the shells this one seemed only half that distance away. The place it was firing from ought to have been captured some hours ago.

Being under fire when mounted was always disagreeable,

the drivers could not get down, so we also stayed up. I bent low over my horse's head whenever I heard a shell coming. Frank trotted past me with a worried look on his face, it was his first time under fire since his wedding day.

'If that Jerry could shoot straight he'd wipe out the whole bloody lot of us,' one of my drivers remarked.

We waited there for what seemed a long time. Then the Major said we were doing no bloody good where we were and he wasn't going to stay on this bloody track a minute longer, not for anybody. He ordered the guns to take up a firing position on the right hand side of the road, and when this had been done he sent Frank back with all the teams and wagons. 'Go back about half a mile,' I heard him say. There was still a possibility that we might have to advance later in the day.

All the other guns on the road seemed to have come to a similar decision, and soon the road was empty. We ate our lunch in a trench. Only cold bully. The Major washed his down with a good deal of whisky, he was working himself up into a battle temper.

Then we saw an orderly galloping along the track, up from the wagon lines—Frank had been wounded, he said. Jack was our senior subaltern, but he was out in front, the Major had sent him to find out what was happening. So he told me to go and take charge of the wagon lines. 'Don't go a bloody yard back,' he said.

But the place was impossible, I found. It was being shelled with gas as well as high explosive, three drivers had already been hit besides Frank, and some horses killed. I galloped up to the gun position again and told the Major we should have no horses left to make an advance unless he allowed me to take them further back.

'It's always the same,' he said irritably. 'Put a man in charge of the wagon lines, and he's never happy till he's taken them back to the sea.' But in the end with a bad grace he agreed to let me take them half a mile further back.

So I was by myself on the night after our great attack. It was cold and the rain had begun, summer had gone, winter had come in a day. I was sleeping in the open, but I hardly slept at all. I was kept awake by German shells as well as the cold, and by the restlessness of the horses in the lines. They were tethered close, so that they could not kick one another, but the noise of the shells was frightening them. I was afraid they might break free or that a shell might burst in the middle of them, and the Major would certainly say it was my fault.

But I could have endured it all, loneliness and cold, shells and responsibility, I should not have minded anything if we had succeeded. It was the failure of all our hopes, that was what I could not bear. The Promised Land! We were practically in the same place where we had started. The Hindenburg Line was impregnable, we should never get through.

In the morning Cherry was still saying it was all right. He said that the Forty-Sixth Division had got across the canal on our right, he admitted that the Americans had been held up by the wire and had suffered very heavily, but they were sorting themselves out now, he said. I did not believe anything he said, I'd had enough of Cherry's optimism.

Twelve

October

Three mornings later, on October 2nd, we were ordered to go into action at Etricourt. 'Etricourt!' we said to one another. 'Etricourt!' Something very extraordinary must have happened. Etricourt was more than a mile across the Hindenburg Line. But there had been rumours of success the day before.

The guns had been brought back on the day after the attack to the position from which we had started. Now, at midday, we set off again. Along the same Black Road, in the same weather, a lifeless colourless day, there was no gleam in the sky.

I felt like a man in a dream.

Here was the place where the German gun had shelled us, no gun was firing now. There was the crest in front of us. We were moving steadily towards it, the road was not blocked. The head of our column was nearly there. Now the leading gun was actually going over. We were all going over. And as we came over we could see the Hindenburg Line, we were coming up to the Hindenburg Line. No one was shooting at us! Now we were going through the wire, a road had been made through the wire. Was I really awake!

Here was his front line trench, it was full of dead Germans. Now I could see the tunnel exit. And the canal, the water in a cutting below us, the steep banks. We were across, we were coming into the Promised Land.

The village of Bellicourt, where the canal came out of the tunnel, was still being shelled, not heavily, but with a sulky persistence, and a cloud of dirty-coloured smoke hung over the shattered village. But we were turning to the right, we could avoid going through the villlage. Now we were marching parallel to the canal, but we could no longer see it, the cutting was too deep.

Was it real, or was I in a dream?

I was by myself at the rear of the column, I had no one to talk to. I thought of riding forward to where Durham was. If I could hear him saying, 'Pretty good, isn't it? One in the eye for the old Boche!' then I should know that it was real. But I seemed to be under a spell and without the power to leave my place, I could only ride along where I was.

I could see the Major up in front leading us, now he was turning left, away from the canal, towards the enemy again, into the unspoiled country that I had seen from the O.P., where the villages were fit to live in and the trees bore leaves. I had a sudden idea—I would come back here tomorrow. Durham would come with me; together in full daylight, not in the misty light of an October afternoon, together we would look at all this wonder. I had seen nothing like this on any other battlefield. Today it had been impossible to take it in, and we had never stopped moving. But tomorrow it would be different, we could look as long as we wanted. And at the thought of seeing the place again I began to believe that it was real, this wonder of great victory had been achieved.

But I never saw the Hindenburg Line again.

We came to Etricourt, a hamlet only, there was a belt of trees on one side. The head of the column halted a little further on. The guns were unhooked and drawn up in line, ammunition was unloaded, the teams and wagons were sent back. I was still feeling dazed.

The servants were pitching a tent under a bank. 'What's that for?' I asked Walkenshaw. 'Major's orders,' he replied. A tent in the line! It was absurd. We were not being shelled at the moment, but two German sausage balloons had been watching us. They had seen us coming in, we should be shelled soon; there was no need to sleep in a tent, with a German trench at no great distance.

But the Major said we had finished with trenches. 'It's all over, bar the shouting,' he said. 'It's come sooner than anyone could have expected. We may have heard our last shell, we shall soon forget the sound they used to make.'

So that was the way our crossing the Hindenburg Line had affected him!

Orders for the next day arrived while we were having dinner. The enemy was holding the Beaurevoir Line and we were to attack it in the morning. We were attached to the 20th Australian Battalion, and were to lay out a telephone line to their Headquarters in Estrées and then provide a liaison officer in the morning. Whose turn was it, I wondered; we had all been doing so much in the last few days. I didn't want to go. It was the hardest job in the world, laying out a line in the dark over unknown country. 'You'd better do it,' the Major said to me. Oh, damn! I got out my map and started to look for Estrées.

'I'm beginning to feel sorry for Fritz,' the Major said. 'He's put up a damned good show. I mean to say, he's had most of the world against him, and it's taken us all this time. But he's down for the count now.'

I was planning out my route. Estrées was a biggish village, only just inside our line, so far as I could make out. The Order did not give the map reference of Battalion H.Q., it merely said in Estrées, I should have to find the place when I got there. The distance was about three thousand yards. We should need a lot of wire and it was heavy stuff to carry, I should have to take four signallers with me instead of the usual two. How long would it take? I might lose my way in the dark, we might have to mend breaks if there was enemy shellfire, then I should have to find the position of H.Q. in the village. Zero Hour was at five minutes past six, I must give myself plenty of time. 'Call me at one o'clock,' I said to the signaller on duty.

'It's been a hard slog,' the Major was saying, 'but it will be downhill now for the rest of the way. We shan't stop till we come to the Rhine.'

I wished he would stop talking, I had a lot to do. Anyway, he was talking nonsense. It was absurd to suppose the war was over just because we had captured the Hindenburg Line.

I wanted to find the best way on the map and then to memorise it. There was a track marked going past the bank

270

beside our tent, it started off in the right direction. The track bent left after a few hundred yards, towards a small wood. Should I be able to see the trees in the dark? The contours showed one would be going slightly uphill. Then the track forked, I must take the right-hand one. It led to a deep sunken lane, and the lane went all the way to Estrées, crossing a single-track railway.

'You've got nothing to worry about,' the Major told me reassuringly. 'You probably won't hear a single shell. Fritz has no guns left, we've captured them all.'

Track, six hundred yards, wood, half-right, sunken lane, railway line.

'We shall be glad not to have missed this,' the Major said. 'We're making history.'

I lay down to get some sleep. I fell asleep while the others were still talking, but woke before midnight. There was quite a heavy bombardment going on, up in the line. No German guns left! What rubbish he talked! These were German guns, and so far as I could tell the noise was coming from Estrées. I hoped it was disturbing the Major's rest, but he seemed to be breathing peacefully, I was the only one awake. Track, six hundred yards, wood, half-right, sunken lane, railway line. There was no doubt the noise was coming from Estrées, it sounded like big stuff.

It was almost a relief to hear the signaller outside. He was coming to call me. 'Nearly one o'clock, Sir,' he said. 'The signallers are waiting for you, they've got the wire.'

The darkness outside was absolute. I could see the faces of my signallers, hardly anything else. I could not even see the track where we were standing. If there was one, I lost it at once.

I set off in what I hoped was the right direction, wondering if I could keep straight, repeating the words I had memorised: six hundred yards, wood, half-right, sunken lane. At once the darkness swallowed us.

We had to go very slowly because of the weight of wire my signallers were carrying. Once or twice they called out that they could not see me, and I had to stop and let them catch up. I dared not look behind in case I lost my direction. We seemed to be going uphill. That was right, but I saw no wood.

271

The night was very still. I could feel a gentle breath of air on my face, and there was the sound of the shells in front. Nothing else moved or gave a sign of life. We met no one. I looked up at the sky. Not even a star to help me. But I thought it looked lighter already, low down above the enemy lines. He must know we were going to attack again in the morning, and this was why he was shelling our front-line area. The shellfire made it easy to keep straight, and we were still far enough from Estrées, where the shells were falling, to be in no real danger. By the time we were nearer to them I hoped we should be in the sunken lane and that its steep sides would protect us from flying bits.

How peaceful it was, under the wide sky! I was walking on those green hills that I had seen from the O.P. The unspoiled country! I was perhaps the first English soldier who had walked on them.

Once I should have been frightened of getting lost or arriving late at Battalion H.Q. Now everything seemed easy, the night was friendly and on my side. I was rather enjoying myself; but we ought to be nearing the sunken lane. I counted a hundred double paces, then stopped and peered ahead. My God! here it was! We had come straight to it, even in daylight I could not have found a more direct way.

It was very dark in the lane. There were trees at the top of the bank, arching across, shutting out the sky, but we came to a bridge, and that must be over the railway line, I knew. A little further on I clambered up the bank and in the red glare of the bursting shells I could see the roofs of houses, we were not more than a quarter of a mile from Estrées.

I did not intend to go any further at present. We were in very good time, and it would be madness in this shellfire to go wandering through the village looking for Battalion H.Q. Sooner or later someone was sure to come along the lane. So I told the signallers to stop and we sat down under the bank. I gave each of them a cigarette and for the first time we relaxed.

Almost at once I heard footsteps. Someone was coming along behind us. I got up and stood in the middle of the lane, waiting for whoever it was to appear. Two men came out of the darkness. They were Australians, in the 20th Battalion, they told me. It certainly was my lucky night, they were going straight to Battalion H.Q., to the very place where I had to report.

We set off with them. But though they slackened their pace a little, they were still going too fast for my signallers. I told them to stay where they were, I went on alone with the two Australians. The lane led into a trench, we went along the trench, which brought us to a dug-out at the edge of the village. This was the place, they said. They went inside, they had brought some orders for their commanding officer, I went back for my signallers, to bring them the rest of the way and finish the laying of our line.

I was feeling very pleased. It had been a difficult job, but now all my difficulties were over. We had laid our line and found the Australian H.Q., and were in communication with our own Brigade at the other end, and it was only three o'clock.

The rest would be easy.

All I had to do now was to report my arrival to the Australian battalion commander, telling him about our line and that I was to act as his liaison officer. I should have to stay with him until dusk, sending back information about the attack, shooting on any targets he might give me; but liaison work was straightforward, I always enjoyed spending a night or a day with the infantry, they were always so friendly and so appreciative of any help the artillery could give, the Australians in spite of their rough speech were no exception.

Drawing aside the gas curtain I went down some steps into the candle-lit dug-out and saluted the Colonel, who was sitting with his adjutant at a table, reading some orders, those probably which the two men had brought him, and I was aware of three or four other officers sitting or lying in the darkness at the back. I told the Colonel who I was and that I had a telephone line outside in working order. He was less welcoming than I had expected. He did not acknowledge my salute or speak to me, he hardly looked up, he went on talking in a low voice to his adjutant. I remained standing in the doorway, waiting for someone to ask me to sit down.

Presently he looked up again and this time he did speak.

'You'll find there's more room outside,' he said. 'If I want you, I'll send for you.'

It was like a smack in the face. I was expecting him to say we had done well to get our line up so quickly. I went back into the trench, it was shallow and dirty, I did not mind the dirt; being told I was not wanted was what I minded.

The village was still under heavy shellfire, but we were not in much danger. There was gas mixed with the high explosive, several times during the remainder of the night we had to put on gas masks. And several times also our line was broken and my signallers went out to repair it. We never had to tell our signallers to go out, they went before one knew the line was broken. I was confident of being able to tell the disagreeable Colonel that our line was in working order if he did want us in the morning.

I talked to a Roman Catholic padre, an elderly man and in appearance more like one of his men than like an officer. I wondered if there had been no room for him in the dug-out either. But clearly he did not want to be with the officers, he wanted to be with his men, they were going over the top in the morning, some of them would not be here at night, they needed the comfort he could give them. I watched him going from one little shelter to another, speaking so quietly that I could not hear what he said. I wanted to listen, but it was not my religion; I thought he might resent my presence.

The night passed very slowly. The shellfire went on, we were continually putting on our gas masks and taking them off again. There was a lot of coming and going past us in the trench. Then the Australian soldiers came out of their little holes and moved away, up the trench. I looked at my watch, it was a quarter to six, Zero Hour was at five past. I did not see the padre again and supposed he had gone up with his men. His religion was not my religion, his words would not have helped me, but his courage did. He was the first chaplain I had come across who chose to live with the men, not with the officers.

At five minutes past six all the guns behind us opened fire with a great roar. We waited, waited for the first reports to come back. They were not good when they came—the tanks had not arrived, the wire was uncut, the attack had been held up, losses had been severe. Presently I heard someone calling for the artillery officer and I was told that the Colonel wanted to speak to me. He was looking more disagreeable than ever when I went down to the dug-out again. None of the wire had been cut, he said; why didn't we ever do the job we were supposed to do?

'We only came up after dark last night, Sir,' I said. I knew there had been nothing about wire cutting in our orders, we could not have cut it in the dark.

'Always the same excuse,' he said. 'I don't know what the artillery can do,' he went on, 'they can't cut wire.'

'They can shoot us in the back,' I heard one of the others saying, 'they're very good at that.'

It was a common taunt, but I had never heard of the confirmation of any alleged case of short shooting by the field artillery, and the infantry knew as little about our difficulties as we knew about theirs.

I asked the Colonel to show me the position of the wire on his map, and then I went outside and spoke to Cherry at Brigade Headquarters. The attack had been held up, I told him, the wire had not been cut, and they were saying we ought to have done it.

'Why don't they tell us beforehand what they want?' he said.

I told him where the wire was, and he promised to put all our batteries on to it.

An hour or so later a second attack was launched and it was successful. Messages were brought back from inside the German trenches. Whether the wire had been cut by our shooting or by the tanks, which had arrived in time for the second attack, I never knew; it was more likely to have been the tanks. But anyway the news was better, most of our objectives seemed to have been captured; but there had been a lot of casualties.

For the moment there was nothing else for me to do. I ate one of my slices of bread, but I was not feeling hungry. Then one of the signallers told me he was not feeling well, and the next moment he was very sick in the trench. It was the gas, he said, gasping for breath, a gas shell had burst very close to him while he was out repairing the line. I sent him back to the battery, it was quieter now, the enemy shellfire had almost ceased, we could manage without him.

Then another was sick and I sent him back also. The other two said they were all right, but they were looking green. I spoke to the Major on the telephone, told him about the sick men, and asked him to send me two fresh signallers. The other two hardly lasted until they came. All my signallers casualties! I could not understand it, the gas had been no worse than usual, there was always a smell of gas in the line, we knew when to put on our masks and when it was slight enough to be ignored, we could not be wearing our masks all the time. Besides, I had not see any of the Australians being sick.

Twelve o'clock! Six hours to wait until I was relieved! I was feeling very sleepy, I could hardly keep my eyes open, one night only without sleep should not have made me so tired. I tried to rub the sleepiness out of my eyes, but this seemed to irritate them. Well, I would give in to it, there was nothing for me to do, one of the fresh signallers could come and find me if I was wanted. I went away by myself and lay down under a hedge, where men would not be walking over me all the time, and tried to go to sleep.

But I could not sleep. My eyes had been uncomfortable when I kept them open, now they were still uncomfortable when I shut them. And my head had started to ache. I was all right, there was nothing the matter with me, it was just tiredness, and perhaps also a feeling of disappointment because at the end nothing had gone right. I thought I had done so well, it was one of the best things I had ever done, in future perhaps I need not feel such an impostor when my eye was caught by the purple and white ribbon on my tunic.

Yes, it was disappointing, but there was nothing the matter with me, nothing the matter, nothing. . . . But even as I was trying to reassure myself I knew that something was the matter. It was that bloody gas, I also had been affected by it. There must have been a pocket of the stuff lying at the bottom of the trench, some of the liquid had probably splashed against the side, we had touched it and then eaten our food, I had rubbed my eyes with my fingers. I tried walking about, my eyes were painful now, but I hoped the pain would go if I was doing something. Another four hours to wait before my relief came. I must stick it out, I would not go to the unfriendly colonel and ask him to let me leave early.

But the pain grew worse. I had a terrible fear that I was losing my eyesight, not only were my eyes painful, but I could not see clearly when I tried to open them, my vision was blurred, the trench was dancing from side to side.

Two hours still, I couldn't bear it, I should have to go to him.

Feeling my way along the trench, stumbling down the steps, I went into the dug-out again and spoke to the Colonel.

'Something has happened to my eyes,' I said, 'I can't see, but I think I can wait until my relief comes if you want me, Sir.'

'Of course you must go back to your battery at once,' he said with surprising gentleness. 'I'll send one of my men with you.'

I told him this would be unnecessary.

'How will you find the way if you can't see?' he asked. I said I should follow our telephone line, holding it in my hand.

I backed to the entrance. 'You and your guns did a good job this morning,' he said as I was going out. Then I thought I heard him say, 'I ought to have seen myself that it was not cut.' The last words were not addressed to me, they may not even have been spoken, but in that moment and for the first time I was in communication with the man I have called the unfriendly colonel. I knew from others that about a dozen of his men had been killed on the uncut wire.

I set off. It was not very difficult, the line had been unrolled along the middle of the sunken lane, I was not afraid of walking into a tree or falling into a hole. I walked slowly, as slowly as we had come up during the night. My eyes were very painful and the thought that I might never see again with them was utterly depressing. Any kind of wound would have been better than this.

When I came out of the lane and was walking in the open country there was a sudden and terrifying explosion in front of me. The shock forced my eyes open. A six-inch howitzer, hardly ten yards away, had just fired at the enemy. It had not been there in the night. The gunners must have seen me, but they could not have known that I had not seen them. They looked unnaturally tall, they were dancing across the ground instead of walking, the sky was full of spots, all the trees were waving, the trees I had looked for in the night.

I went on. Now I was afraid that the shock of the gun's firing might have made me drop the line I was holding and I might have picked up the wrong one. I might now be walking in the wrong direction, not towards my own battery. In my misery I nearly stopped walking, I wanted to sit down and cry.

But I heard Durham's voice in front of me, he had come to look for me. He asked no questions, he saw that I did not want to talk, he took my arm and led me for the last few hundred yards, he helped me into a tent. 'Lie down,' he said, 'I'll take your clothes off.' He put me into my sleeping bag. 'I'll get you some tea,' he said. 'The doctor's coming round, the Major has rung up to tell him about you.'

It was wonderful to lie still, in darkness.

Our doctor came. He was a friendly young Scotsman. He gently rubbed some ointment on my eyes, which soothed them, easing the pain. 'What about it?' he said. 'Shall I send you to hospital?'

'Am I going blind?' I asked him.

'No,' he said. 'You'll be as right as rain in a few days, there's no damage done, but I'll send you to hospital if you like.'

But there was no need for that if I wasn't going blind. I only wanted to be left alone now, not to have to talk. 'I shall be all right in the morning,' I said.

I thought I should be, but I had a most unpleasant night, I hardly slept at all. There were guns all round us, firing all through the night, and every time that one fired the shell seemed to pass through my head. I was unhappy as well as in pain, the day that had begun so well had ended disastrously. All my signallers were casualties, they had all gone away. We were unlikely to get them back; they would be sent to another battery, as happened when a man was wounded. Sometimes when an officer was wounded. I wouldn't risk it, I would stay where I was, I did not want to go among strangers.

The doctor came again in the morning. 'What about it?' he said. But I told him I should be all right in a day or two. I only wanted to be left alone, and in darkness. But I could not be left where I was, for the battery was under orders to move forward again. 'I can send you to Headquarters' Wagon Lines,' he said. They were still on the other side of the canal and likely to stay there for a few days.

I was taken back in the mess-cart, and for two days I lay in semi-darkness, hardly talking, hardly eating. On the morning of the third day I was able to open my eyes and read some of the letters that had come for me, but I soon closed them again. I was content to lie there, hardly aware of anything that was happening round me. We moved once at least, I was carried in the mess-cart again.

Walkenshaw looked after me, and though I was among strangers at Headquarters' Wagon Lines I received great kindness. I did not know that men could be so gentle to other men. They told me the news—we had captured the rest of the Beaurevoir Line, and C Battery, my battery, had been bombed, a bomb had fallen on top of the mess, the Major had been wounded, the others had escaped by a miracle.

I hardly took in what they said. For the moment it was not my battery, I did not belong anywhere.

Slowly my eyes improved, but then I began coughing. The doctor said I had got some of the stuff inside me. But I should be all right, he said, I had been lucky, some people took months to recover from the effects of mustard gas.

Then Jack came to see me and he told me about the bomb. It had fallen in the mouth of their tent, the canvas had been cut to ribbons, but the tent had been dug down a foot or two and none of them had been hurt except the Major.

'We knew there was a Boche up,' Jack said. 'We had all heard the three whistles, but the Major said it was one of our own planes and he wouldn't put the candle out. "Put that bloody light out" everyone outside was shouting, and the Major was shouting back, "It's one of our own bloody planes".'

'I suppose he was telling you that Fritz had no planes left,' I said.

'Something of that kind,' Jack said. 'But what really

279

annoyed him was their thinking he couldn't tell the difference
between one of theirs and one of ours. Then there was this
god-almighty crash, and that did put the light out.'

'Do you think he could have seen the light?' I asked.

'No,' Jack said. 'It was just a bit of bad luck. All our tents
were showing up in the moonlight, he couldn't have failed to
see them. I suppose you could say it was good luck really, we
might all have been killed. The Major was cursing like hell in
the darkness, I thought it was just bad temper, but when
someone struck a match and we'd got a light again we found
he'd been hit behind the ear.'

I was very sorry. We had had a lot of battery commanders,
and the Major with all his faults was the man for us. We
trusted him and he trusted us, and the thought of having to
serve under a different commander again was very depressing.
I might have given the doctor a different answer if I had
known that this was going to happen.

'He'll never come back,' I said, and Jack agreed.

'You were pretty slow, weren't you?' he went on. 'All the
signallers went to hospital, why didn't you?'

'I might have got down to the Base,' I said, 'but I wasn't
bad enough to get home.'

'I would have been,' he said. 'I wouldn't have been able to
see a thing until I saw England. By this time you could have
been there and had a pretty nurse holding your hand.'

'They're not all pretty,' I said, irrelevantly.

'They're all the right sex, anyway.

Perhaps I had made a mistake. It would have been nice to
be at home and to have finished with all this, at any rate for
a few months. Now I should have to go back and start again,
it was always an effort starting, going up to the line, knowing
one would come under fire. It would be harder than usual
after the gas and the days spent lying in bed so far behind the
line. But it was too late now, I had made my decision, regrets
were unavailing.

'How's the War going?' I asked.

'I suppose you might say it was going pretty well,' he
replied. 'Mind you, it isn't over yet, we've got the hell of a
long way to go still, but it's beginning to look as though we
should win in the end.'

He told me they had all found souvenirs in the attack on the Beaurevoir Line. Durham had found a pickelhaube helmet and was going to take it home on his next leave.

'But I haven't much use for souvenirs,' he said. 'It's getting yourself home, that's what matters.'

Thirteen

October

It was the middle of October before I went back to the battery. The guns had come out of action for a day or two, everyone was at the wagon lines, I found two new senior officers in the mess in place of the Major and Frank. Major Ricky was a newcomer, I had never seen him before, but Captain Garnett had formerly been a subaltern in A Battery. Now he had been promoted and had come to us as our second-in-command. I knew him quite well. I had begun by disliking him, then I had learnt to like him, now I found him dislikeable again.

'Hullo!' he said as soon as he saw me. 'You all right again? Fit for full duty?'

Now I had not fully recovered and the doctor had told me that I was to do very little at first, but I had not intended to tell anyone what he said. I had intended to do as much as I felt able to, I knew that none of the others would think I was shirking if I did less than my share, they would all be willing to take some of my duties for me. But if Garnett wanted formality he should have it, I would do nothing at all. His voice sounded as though he considered I ought not to be sitting in the mess at that moment, I ought to be out in the horse lines, making up for all the time I had missed. So I told him no, I was not all right again, the doctor had said I was to do light duty only.

'Oh!' he said. He looked as though he was expecting me to bring out a medical certificate in confirmation.

He may have disbelieved me, or he may have thought he should ask the doctor for corroboration of my story, but later in the day he apologised for speaking in that way. He had not

282

realised, he said, how bad I had been; nor that I had returned to the battery at my own request.

It no longer seemed like C Battery with these newcomers in the mess, giving us orders, changing our established ways. I had been looking forward to coming home, but this was not like home, I was feeling a stranger, I got up and went outside, glad to talk to my men. They had not changed, and it seemed to me that they disliked the new faces as much as I did.

Corporal Albert came up to me with his friendly welcoming smile and asked if I was all right again.

'Yes,' I said, 'more or less. But I think I was very slow not to wangle a blighty.'

'I expect it was because you didn't want to leave the battery, Sir,' he said.

He was the first and only person who understood and did not think me stupid for refusing the opportunity of going into hospital. He was perhaps the only man in the battery whose patriotism was still as bright as on the day he joined up in 1914. He was not one of our best N.C.O.s, he did not make men do what they were unwilling to do, he believed their excuses, but for himself he had one simple principle, to serve the battery and all who were in it to the very best of his ability. Of all the officers and men in our battery, I think he was the one for whom I felt the greatest personal affection.

'We should have been sorry if you hadn't come back to us,' he said. 'We don't want to lose any more of our old officers.'

We did lose Jack. He went home on leave a few days later, and before going he took me on one side to say, 'Don't expect me back in a hurry. I've had a buzzing in my ear ever since that bomb, and I'm going to see what I can do about it. A noise of this sort ought to be worth three months at least, and six if I'm lucky.'

He never came back. I had a letter from him some time later, asking me to arrange for his kit to be sent back to England. He had not realised, he said, how bad his ears were; both the drums were ruptured.

Now Durham and myself were the only two of the old officers left.

The guns went back into action, but I did not go with

them, I stayed at the wagon lines. The enemy was holding a line west of Le Cateau, fifteen miles beyond the tunnel and the canal. We had won a great success, but everyone agreed that there was still a lot more fighting to be done. There were French civilians in some of the villages behind us. They had spent four years under German occupation, now we had liberated them; but liberation sometimes meant they had to leave their homes, they were in the danger zone until we drove the enemy back further.

My eyes were still bothering me and I had a troublesome cough. Garnett now was encouraging me to be lazy, he was solicitous on my behalf. 'You ought not to be out here in the rain with that cough,' he said. 'I'll take the horses down to water.' It rained nearly every day.

I could not help liking Garnett, but I was almost the only person in the battery who did. Newcomers to our battery usually began by thinking it was a bad one because it was not so smart as some others. All the older men were Territorials, they thought for themselves, they had not been trained to instant obedience, our senior N.C.O.s were in the habit of expressing their opinions. Major Eric had always listened to what they had to say and had sometimes taken their advice, but Captain Garnett threatened to put my Sergeant Denmark under arrest when he started to argue with him.

'The man was insubordinate,' he said, when I protested afterwards. 'He needs a sharp lesson.'

'Have you noticed his D.C.M.?' I asked.

'Of course I have, but it isn't always the best men who get the medals.'

Garnett and I each had one, so we could agree about this, but I had more to say. 'He got it before I came out,' I said, 'but from what I've been told it might have been a V.C. He's the bravest man in the battery, and now that Major Jack is dead I would rather have Denmark with me in a tight corner than anyone else in the brigade. For my part,' I added, 'I always take his advice.'

Garnett thought it was wrong for an officer ever to take a sergeant's advice, or even to listen to it, but he knew that I knew more about the men in C Battery than he did, and he was beginning to respect some of my opinions.

'Well, I'll remember what you've said about the fellow,' he conceded. 'But he's a difficult man, he's asking for trouble. The fact is that the discipline of the whole battery has been allowed to get slack and now needs tightening up.'

I then went to tell Sergeant Denmark that Captain Garnett had a lot of good qualities of which he was not aware.

'I'm certainly not aware of them,' Denmark said.

I told him Garnett was a very brave man with a very high sense of duty. 'He's got an unfortunate way of talking,' I said. 'That's all.'

'He'll get a bullet in the back one of these days,' Denmark said, 'unless he learns to talk civil.'

He was so angry that I was alarmed. 'Don't be a fool,' I said. 'You would never do anything so daft.'

'I didn't say I would,' was his answer.

I was very upset. Garnett was even more unpopular than I had supposed, it seemed as though he might do as much harm to the battery as Bingley had in the spring. I tried to go about with him as much as possible when he was walking in the horse lines, hoping that my presence might sometimes prevent his speaking to the men in the way they so much disliked.

I had told Denmark that Garnett was a very brave man, and he had been, at Ypres in the previous year. He had seemed not to know what fear was, but he knew now. Once he had appeared to be indifferent to shellfire, now he jumped at the sound of a pip-squeak a quarter of a mile away.

Then one night in our tent before going to sleep he told me about a girl he had met in England during the summer, he had fallen in love with her, she was everything that was wonderful; and though he was altogether undeserving of such good fortune, he said, yet for some miraculous reason she loved him and they were going to get married.

So that was why he jumped at the sound of a pip-squeak in the next field. He admitted it, he was ashamed of his cowardice, he said; but if I only knew what it was like to be in love with a girl of that sort, I should understand.

I was the first person in the brigade he had told about her, he said. He would have liked to talk about her all night. She had every virtue. She could ride better than he could and

285

was as good at games. 'I've always had a pretty good opinion of myself,' he said, 'but she's made me realise how little right I have to.' She was a vicar's daughter and was as good as she was beautiful. He had given up swearing because she did not like it. 'She gave me the hell of a blasting once,' he said, 'because I let out an oath when we were playing golf. She'll have me teaching in her Sunday School before I know where I am.'

'I expect she's a very gentle person,' I said. It had suddenly occurred to me that I might be able to make use of her, I might be able to persuade him that she would not like his talking to the men in the way that he did.

'Oh, no,' he said. 'She puts me in my place all right. She's only a girl, nearly ten years younger than I am, but she stands no nonsense from me.'

I hoped she had a sense of humour as well as every other good quality. I thought she would need it.

He woke me up one night to listen to some bombs. The bombers came over on most fine nights, and the wagon line area also was shelled by a long-range gun. Personally I found bombing easier to endure, an aeroplane carried a limited number of bombs and had to go back when they were all dropped, but a gun might go on firing all night.

Garnett disliked both equally. He had got out of bed and was standing in the doorway of our tent, telling me where he thought each bomb had fallen. 'We must dig our tent further down,' he said, 'I don't fancy being killed when the war has got to this stage.' With a little encouragement from myself he would have gone outside to look for a spade and started digging at once.

We were on the move again. Le Cateau had been captured, it was the biggest town I had seen in the middle of the fighting area and almost undamaged. The wide tree-lined streets, the squares and big houses, the names of faubourgs and hotels all combined to give an air of unreality to what we were doing. It was natural to fight among trenches and shell-holes, but altogether wrong in the middle of a town like this. It might have been our own home. I saw a dozen engines outside the railway station, looking all ready to set off with their trains behind them, and the big church with its tall spire looked ready for a congregation to come and worship. But there were dead Germans still lying in the streets.

There was a huge mound of coal near the station, but no food for us in any of the shops. There was no supplementary food to be found anywhere, we had left the canteens far behind us, we had to live on our rations. I spent a lot of my time riding round the country, trying to buy whisky for the mess, chocolate and cigarettes for the men, but I obtained very little of anything.

I was happy. I was feeling well again at last, we were winning the war, Garnett was beginning to find good in us and Major Ricky was a good battery commander, he gave his orders quietly and was steadier than the Major had been. And I had been up to the line and under fire again, I had done my first duty since returning, it was neither easy nor safe, but it had been successfully carried out and I had felt no more frightened than usual, the gassing and the night at Estrées had not made it harder for me.

Then suddenly, in a moment, all my happiness vanished. Durham came riding down from the guns one afternoon, and he said he had come to congratulate me. I looked at him uneasily, for Durham had a sense of humour that I did not always appreciate, he might be going to say that I had been chosen to go out as Forward Observing Officer with the infantry in our next attack or was to go on a gas course.

'Oh, haven't you heard?' he said. 'You've been promoted and are going to A Battery as their captain.'

I did not believe him, I thought it was part of a silly joke.

'Of course I'm being serious,' he said. 'It was in Orders this morning, we thought you would know all about it.'

I did not want to be a captain, the thought of leaving C Battery was utterly hateful, I had not a single friend in A Battery now except Major Cecil, and I knew he was disliked by everyone there, he was even more unpopular in A than he had been with us when he was our battery commander in the summer.

'I shan't go,' I said. 'They can't make me.'

'Of course you will go,' said Garnett, who was sitting in the mess with us. 'A soldier has got to obey orders.'

I went away by myself and sat down in our tent. I felt more wretched than ever before. It seemed to me that I had been happier during the last year than at any other time in my life because I had been given a man's work to do, and in the end I had learnt how to do it. C Battery had shown me how to, I loved the men who had helped me, they had given me confidence in myself, and now I was to leave them and go among strangers. I had chosen to stay instead of going into hospital when I was gassed because C Battery was my home, I could not be happy anywhere else until the War was over.

But besides this, I did not want to be a captain, I was not ready for promotion. I knew that I was a reasonably good subaltern by this time, I could do O.P. work and liaison duty as well as anyone else, I could read a map and work out the targets for our guns. But the captain's job in a battery was altogether different, he was responsible for the horses and for supplies, and for all the men down at the wagon lines, he had to move and feed the battery. If he made a mistake, if he chose a bad position for his wagon lines, it was not only his own life he put at risk but those of the hundred men under him. I dreaded the responsibility.

I sat for so long in the tent that the light had begun to fade before I moved. The afternoon was over, Durham had ridden back to the guns, I had let him go away without speaking to him again, he had probably thought that the news he brought would be pleasing to me. Garnett was alone in the mess when I went back. He talked to me as usual that evening, but I was not listening to what he said.

I should have to go. It was no good trying to escape. For a moment I had thought of making use of my eyes, they were still causing me some discomfort, I could pretend they were worse than they were, I might go to the doctor and say I wanted him to send me into hospital after all. But I should have felt ashamed of doing that, what would Corporal Albert think of me! No, I should have to go. My only hope lay in persuading Major Cecil that he had made a bad choice. If I told him that I knew nothing about horses he might decide

288

that someone else in the brigade would make a better captain for him.

I rode up to see him immediately after breakfast the next morning, but I stopped at C Battery gun line on my way. I wanted to talk to Major Ricky and I was hoping to see Sergeant Denmark also. He was the first person I saw, he came slowly towards me when he saw me.

'I hear you're leaving us, Sir,' he said.

I got off my horse so that I could talk to him more easily. 'I haven't decided yet,' I said. 'You haven't got to accept promotion.'

'If you don't, it will never be offered you again,' he said.

'I shouldn't mind, I don't want it.'

'A soldier's got to do what he's told.'

It was what Garnett had said. In some ways, not in all, they were very like each other, Garnett and Sergeant Denmark. That might be why they did not get on.

'You don't,' I said.

'What's that got to do with it?' His voice was so gruff that I thought I had annoyed him, but there was no unfriendliness in his face when I looked up.

'I don't know how to be a captain,' I said. 'I'm not good enough.'

'Who says so! You've managed all right so far, you can manage the next step too.'

'It will be so different.'

'Nothing stays the same.'

'I want it to.'

'You don't, you want to do what's right, and the right thing for you now is to be captain of A Battery.'

'All my friends are here, I don't want to leave them.'

He shrugged his shoulders. With him it was his way of indicating that his next remark would be his final one, he would have nothing further to say.

'If we've come out here to please ourselves,' he said, 'it's the first I've heard about it.'

If he thought I ought to go there was no longer any doubt in my mind, only the unhappiness remained. I rode away without looking for anyone else, I did not speak to Major Ricky, I went on to A Battery.

I felt awkward and ill at ease when I saw Major Cecil, but I told him as simply as I could that I did not think I was capable of doing a captain's job and that I was afraid I should let him down.

'That will be my funeral,' he said.

'I've not had enough experience,' I said.

'That's what the Colonel thinks, he said you were too young, but I've never thought much of his opinion. I want you because you do things, you don't just sit about.'

It would have been unfair, I thought, to say that I did not want to come to his battery, that I wanted to stay with my own; but I would say something about the horses, he was much more interested in horses than he was in guns, if I could make him think that his beloved horses would suffer under my care, then he might decide to choose someone else. It was my last hope.

'I know nothing about horses,' I said.

'I know enough for us both,' he replied.

It was very quiet in his tent. The War had become quiet, I heard the echoes of a single gun rolling along the horizon.

'All right,' I said. 'I'll do my best.'

'You'll make mistakes,' he said, 'everyone does, but I don't think either of us will regret our decisions.'

I asked for one more day, I wanted to be a subaltern in C Battery for one more day, but that evening I told Walkenshaw to sew an additional star on each of my shoulder straps and when I dressed the next morning I was a captain. The change was so great that I hardly recognised myself when I looked at my pocket shaving mirror. Walkenshaw and Edric were both coming with me, I had left the decision to them, they were both Yorkshiremen, I knew it would be hard for them to leave their friends and go among strangers. I thought that Edric looked very wistful when I gave him the choice, but with hardly a moment's hesitation he had answered, 'I'll come with you, Sir.' I was grateful to them both, now I should have two friends in A Battery.

After breakfast I went to say goodbye to my own men, all of those who were down at the wagon line. 'All the lads is sorry you are going,' Corporal Albert said, and in that moment I knew how little I had done for any of them. I might have done so much, I had done so little. But it was too late now, it was goodbye for ever.

I did not say goodbye to the men in the gun line, the men in my own Left Section and the signallers who had so often been out with me, I would see them on another day, I could not face them now, it was Sergeant Denmark I did not want to see, I did not want him to see me crying. I rode straight to A Battery wagon lines.

The Battery Sergeant-Major was waiting for me. He called the whole camp to attention as I arrived. Then he took me round the lines while the drivers were grooming their horses, calling out the senior N.C.O. as we came to each sub-section and telling me his name. All the men looked at me as I passed by. I was supposed to be inspecting them, but they were inspecting me. It was far worse than being under shell-fire.

Sooner than I had expected I began to feel at home in my new battery and to find the work less strange. Before starting there I had thought how pleased I should be if Major Cecil realised I was no good and sent me back to C Battery, but as soon as I had started I knew that this would be a most unsatisfactory solution. I was the youngest captain in the brigade and younger than any of my own subalterns, the Colonel evidently thought I was too young for responsibility, but I wanted to show him he was mistaken. I did not really like Major Cecil, but he had said that he believed in me, it would be very damaging to my confidence if he was proved wrong and the Colonel right.

Fortunately I was given a few quiet days in which to settle down. The enemy had been driven back several miles to the east of Le Cateau, but for the moment he was holding a line there, we made no attack, the batteries remained in the same position, I had a little time in which to get to know my N.C.O.s and some of the men and to learn what a captain had to do.

I worked hard, harder than ever before, now that there was no one to give me orders. I found work to do, I never stopped,

I had no time for reading. When I had finished today's work I began to think about tomorrow's. I was afraid of being caught unprepared. Sooner or later it was bound to happen, I was certain to be confronted with an unexpected situation, but by thinking beforehand of all that might happen I hoped to lessen the risk or at any rate the consequences of a mistake.

I saw Major Cecil every day. Sometimes he came down to the wagon lines to see how we were getting on, sometimes I rode up to the guns to find out what the news was and when the next attack was expected. He was often critical of what I had done or left undone, but his criticism was intended to be and was helpful. I liked him better than I ever had before, I even persuaded the subalterns, each of whom came down to the wagon lines in turn for a day or two, that his decisions were not invariably wrong. Finding myself in a position of authority I also found understanding of those who had been there longer than myself.

I saw a good deal of Garnett, although his wagon lines were still in the same place and I had moved mine forward, to the other side of Le Cateau. I often rode across to C Battery in the afternoon, partly for the pleasure of seeing some of my friends again, but also because it was a help to talk with another captain. We had the same problems, I liked knowing what he was going to do, and each of us could advise the other because we knew more about his battery than about our own.

I was already feeling affection for my new battery, and finding that they did some things better in A. And Garnett was finding good qualities in C, though to annoy me he would not say so. He said he had smartened them up a bit. 'The trouble is,' he went on, 'I shan't have time to make them into a decent battery, it will be all over before Christmas.'

I made a bet of fifty francs with him that it would not be. I expected to win my bet, but if I lost, fifty francs would be a small price to pay for peace.

Another great attack was to be launched within the next few days. 'Along the entire front,' Cecil had told me. I was familiar with attacks at the gun line, now I was going to find out what happened at the wagon lines when an attack was made. And

I should be alone, all the responsibility would be mine.

'One great push, and over he goes,' Garnett said optimistically.

But I was uneasy. It was when someone pushed someone else that the unexpected was likely to happen.

Fourteen

November

The attack was coming off tomorrow, the Fourth of November.
I had made my plans, I had tried to think of everything. I
had ridden up to the gun line and listened to all Major Cecil's
advice, together we had discussed every possibility. No definite time had been stated for the guns to advance, it was to
depend on the local situation. 'We probably shan't move all
day,' Cecil said. And Garnett and I had told each other what
we proposed doing.

He had ridden over to see me during the afternoon, and
this had saved me the trouble of going to his wagon lines to
see him. Each of us thought that the other might have remembered something which he had forgotten. He stayed to
have tea with me. Then, just as he was about to return, an
enemy gun began shelling the valley that lay between his
wagon lines and mine. If he went by the quickest way he
would have to pass through the area that was being shelled,
but the alternative route was two or three miles further. He
stood outside the tent, looking irresolutely in the direction
where the shells were falling, trying to decide which way to
go.

'The trouble is,' he said, 'that I've still got a lot to do, but
it seems absurd to take an unnecessary risk now.' He could
not make up his mind.

'Look!' I said, 'I'd like to come with you if you don't
mind, I've still got some questions to ask you. Let's go the
shortest way, he'll probably have stopped shelling before we
get there, and he's just as likely to switch his gun on to the
other road.'

I thought he would like my company and there was not
much danger, only a few shells were coming over, if we rode

294

fast when we came to the valley we might get across the danger area in between one shell and the next. In fact the shelling had stopped. I rode all the way with him to his wagon lines, then turned round and came back to my own. Garnett was more worried about shells now than I was, but I was more worried about tomorrow's attack.

'You've got nothing to worry about,' he said. 'Battles take charge of themselves, they always do. We may think we are in control, but it's quite a mistake. Nothing ever goes according to plan, that's the one thing you can be absolutely sure of.'

I had turned round and was riding away when he called after me, 'You might as well hand over that fifty francs now.'

I laughed. Christmas would soon be here, I said. I was not worrying about my fifty francs, but it was disturbing to think that nothing might go according to plan.

Well, I had done everything I could, better to try and put the whole thing out of my head now. I would have an early night and read in bed before going to sleep. That would take my mind off the attack. Sufficient unto the day!

Zero Hour was at 6.15. The noise woke me, of course, and I knew it was time to get up. The guns were close to the line, my wagon lines two or three miles further back, I was moving them up at nine o'clock.

We set off. I was moving my entire wagon lines, but we were only going half way up. If the attack had been unsuccessful there would be a considerable risk in having horses so near to the line, but if the guns were to make an advance then it would save time if the teams and limbers were already half way up. When we arrived at the place I had chosen I gave orders for the teams to be unhooked but harness to be kept on in readiness. Then leaving the Sergeant-Major in charge I rode on by myself to the gun line to find out what was happening. I might have to ride back at once and bring up the gun limbers for an advance, or leave my wagon lines where they were until further orders were received, or if it was obvious that the attack had failed I should take them all back to the place we had come from. These were the three possibilities—go forward, go back, or stay where we were.

I found there was no news. This was what I had expected, there seldom was any news at first on the morning of a battle. One had to wait for news to come back. Our guns were no longer firing and the enemy reply had been very slight, we had suffered no casualties. But no one could tell us where the enemy was. Cherry said there were conflicting reports. There was no sound of firing in front, nothing to suggest that the enemy might still be close at hand. But if he had been driven back, why weren't we following him? Cherry said he had destroyed the bridges, our infantry were unable to cross the river. It sounded to me like a failure.

The morning passed. After all the excitement of our preparations it was an anti-climax. I had been half expecting to lead the battery forward into enemy territory, liberating the inhabitants, marching through another town like Le Cateau. It was certain to be an eventful day, I had thought, for we had come into a different part of France, we had left the open country behind us, now we were approaching forest land, and there were orchards all round us. We were hemmed in by trees, we could see for a few hundred yards in every direction, but no further, it was impossible even to guess what might be happening on the other side of the leafy fringe in front of us.

The morning had passed, the afternoon was passing, the short November day was slipping away, no Orders had come, there was no news. We sat on the grass behind the guns, chucking stones at a tin because we had nothing better to do.

'Well, we shan't move now,' said Major Cecil at last. 'I said we should probably stay in the same place all day. If I were you,' he said to me, 'I should take your wagon lines back to the old place, it's a better one than where they are now.'

I agreed. I sent my orderly back with a message for the Sergeant-Major, telling him to take them back. But I stayed at the gun line. I would wait for another hour, until it was dark. Orders were bound to come some time, then at any rate I should know what had happened.

They came ten minutes later. The guns were to move forward at once. To the other side of Fontaine-au-Bois, an ad-

296

vance of more than five miles in a straight line. Five miles in the dark over unknown wooded country! And full wagon loads of ammunition.

'Get them up as quickly as you can,' Major Cecil said. 'I'm going on at once, I'll leave guides for you.'

I galloped away, dreading that I might find the Sergeant-Major had already moved. I was in time. But the horses had not been watered or fed and they had this long march in front of them, the Sergeant-Major did not think they could do it without food; and the men would need something before they set off.

I trusted the Sergeant-Major. His judgement on anything to do with horses was better than mine. But I was angry with myself for not having ordered an earlier time to water and feed. Now it would be dark before we were ready to start. Walkenshaw came to ask if I would like my own dinner, but I was too impatient to eat, I could only fuss about in the lines, urging everyone to be quick.

It was after six o'clock before the guns were limbered up and ready to begin their advance. The night was very dark and the road was blocked. All the other batteries, those in other brigades as well as our own, were in front of me. When one wagon was halted, all the others behind had to halt, we were held up every few minutes. It was so dark that I could not see more than a yard or two, I could not see that the wagon in front of me had halted until I bumped into it, and then I could hear all my own guns and wagons bumping into one another. This always made drivers bad-tempered, I could hear them cursing in the darkness. I was in a bad temper too, I wanted someone to swear at, I swore at the guide that Major Cecil had left me, he confessed at once that he did not know the way; it all looked different in the dark, he said.

Then I swore at a driver in some other unit. His wagon had fallen into a shell-hole in the middle of the road, he could not get it out, we could not go past until he had. I cursed him fiercely, abusing him in terms I had never used before. I knew I was being unfair, it was not his fault that his wagon had upset in the darkness, he was only a young soldier, he could not answer me back, and I could tell that my abuse was hurting. But I was on trial, on trial as a captain, and I felt that everything was working against me. Eventually he was able to pull a little to one side and we could pass him.

I knew the map co-ordinates of the place I was to go to, but that was all. Somewhere I had to turn left, but in the darkness it was very difficult to see turnings. One might go past a turning without noticing it or, worse still, one might turn where there was no turning and end up in an orchard or a garden, unable to go on or to turn round.

We were in the village of Fontaine-au-Bois, a long straggling place, all the houses were a little way back from the road, I could only see their dark shapes. All were in utter darkness, there was nothing to show whether any living person was inside them. There were dead German soldiers lying on the road. The trees made it darker still, there were so many, there seemed to be an orchard by every house. Fontaine was probably a well-to-do suburb of Landrecies, that would account for the number of trees. The bodies of the German soldiers had been dragged to the side of the road, but in the darkness it was difficult to avoid them.

I was bitterly disappointed with myself. We should be hours late, all the other batteries would be up before us, Cecil would ask me if I had made a mistake in the day, I hated his sarcasm. And we might be on the wrong road, I might have missed the turning, we might land ourselves in Landrecies. If once you got on to the wrong road in the dark with teams and wagons behind you it was almost impossible to get back on to the right one. This was the first difficult job that I had been given to do as a captain, and I was making a mess of it.

There was less transport on the road now, there was nothing immediately in front of me, but I had to go slowly because of the darkness and because I was peering to my left all the time, hoping to see an unmistakable turning. Suddenly out of the darkness in front I heard the most astonishing, the most unexpected, sound I ever heard at the War—the laughter of girls. And in the next moment out of the enveloping night half a dozen young girls came walking along the road. They jumped out of our way when they saw me, I saw one girl deliberately tread on the body of one of the Germans.

We went past them. It was all over in a few seconds, they had come out of the night, they had gone back into it. I

298

heard nothing but the jolting of the guns and wagons behind me, the tread of horses' feet on the cobbled road. But they had been there, I had not imagined them, I had heard their young voices and seen light-coloured dresses under their dark coats. Girls in the middle of the War! On such a night, in such a place! Anxious and dispirited though I was, yet their extraordinary appearance, as it seemed, made me less unhappy. There still were girls in the world, life was not all fighting and marching, one day it would have a different and a nobler purpose. Their presence on the road was less extraordinary than I supposed, afterwards we met other French people, it had not occurred to me that they would have run away into the forest when the fighting started and were now returning to their homes.

I found the turning. We still had some way to go, but it was easier now, I knew I was on the right road and the darkness seemed less intense. The great forest was on our left, not far away, I could see its dark mass, darker than the sky above. I had to turn left again, into a narrower road, but this turning was easier to find because it was not so dark.

I found the place, I was about to turn, but there was a mounted man in the middle of the road, blocking the entrance. I recognised him, he was a bombardier in C Battery, a man I knew well.

'Excuse me, Sir,' he said. 'Captain Garnett said I was not to let anyone come along here until his wagons returned, he said the road was too narrow.'

So Garnett had got up already and was now returning. I asked how long his wagons would be, but the bombardier did not know. They might be an hour, I thought. I wasn't going to wait out here for an hour when I was so late already. Garnett ought to wait for me since his guns were up already.

'Captain Garnett can go to hell,' I said, and pushing past the bombardier I told my leading gun to follow me into the lane.

Almost at once I heard Garnett coming. We could have waited, we should not have been delayed for more than ten minutes, but it was too late now. I heard Garnett long before I could see him. He could hear us coming along the road and he began cursing us without knowing or caring who we were.

He was hoping to make us turn back, but there was no possibility of our doing so when once we had come into the lane. We might be able to squeeze past one another. If not, I did not know what would happen, we might both be stuck there for the rest of the night.

Garnett had ridden on in front of his wagons, he was obviously in a very bad temper, he started to shout at me. What the bloody hell did I mean by disregarding his orders, who the blazes did I think I was. He told me what he thought of me, he was very abusive. I felt my own temper flaring up, I was about to swear back at him. But what was the use! His voice was louder than mine and he had a far greater vocabulary of abuse. Besides, I was in the wrong, I ought to have waited, and I was too tired to start a slanging match with him in front of both our batteries. But I was very distressed, it meant the end of our friendship, and it was hard that on this night I should lose one of my few remaining friends on top of everything else.

There was room to pass, we all got by, we did not even scrape one another's wheels. There were good drivers in both our batteries. I was riding on, Garnett had gone away. Then I heard someone cantering up behind me. It was Garnett. O God, I thought, he's going to say something else! I couldn't take any more.

'I say,' he said, when he was riding beside me, 'I am sorry! I've been in a foul temper all night, I didn't mean any of the things I said, it's unpardonable to speak like that to a friend, but try to forget if you can.'

He turned round and had ridden away before I could say that it was all right. I wished that I had said I was sorry to the young driver whose wagon had upset.

We were nearly there now. Major Cecil came out to meet us. 'Whatever happened to you?' he said. 'I thought you were never coming, the other batteries have been up for hours.'

Well, we were up now. Guns and ammunition; and there had been no firing to do, so my lateness did not matter. Our return journey was easier, two and a half hours instead of six. But on the way I made up my mind that whatever the risk I was going to keep my wagon lines closer to the guns

300

in future. I would go out in the morning as soon as it was light and find a place for them east of Fontaine-au-Bois.

I was cold and very hungry when we got back, but Walkenshaw had a meal ready for me, and afterwards I fell asleep immediately. But only for a few hours. I was up at seven o'clock and out with the Sergeant-Major, looking for a place to move to.

We found the perfect place, a big farm, with a stream and empty barns and stables. All the farm stock had been commandeered by the enemy, not only was there accommodation for the men, but we could put most of the horses under cover.

We moved immediately after breakfast, before anyone else could usurp our place. But the rain had already begun, we were wet through when we arrived at the farm. It was the first time we had occupied a place in which the owners were living, and I went into the kitchen to warm myself and dry my wet clothes.

War was strange, I reflected. Once I had thought that all battles were the same, but this year they had all been different, and the one we were fighting now was the strangest of all, not like a battle at all. Here was I drying myself by a kitchen stove while the woman the house belonged to was preparing dinner for her family, and a boy of nine or ten stood watching me from the doorway. Yesterday or the day before there had been German soldiers in his home, now he had British ones to look at. He and his family had probably run away into the forest when our attack started, like the girls I had seen the night before, and stayed there until it was safe to return. It was as though they had been playing a game of hide-and-seek, the sort of game I had played myself at the same age as this boy. But this was not a game, it was war, he or his mother might have been killed by one of our shells. All his life he would remember the day when he was caught up in the war, he might remember the wet English officer, the first he had seen, drying his clothes in his mother's kitchen.

Walkenshaw came to tell me that my lunch was ready, he had taken it into one of the other rooms in the farm. Hot stew. There was hot stew for everyone, and everyone was eating under cover, out of the rain. I was hoping that we might be left alone for the rest of the day, but before I had finished eating, an orderly came down from the guns with an urgent message from Major Cecil. Another advance. Gun limbers and first-line wagons immediately.

So out into the rain again. It took us only an hour to reach the guns, but longer to pull them out of the orchard. The heavy rain had made the ground so soft that the wheels sank in, we needed teams of ten horses instead of six and could only move one gun at a time. We had to unhook the two leading pairs of one gun team and put them in front of another team, then when that gun was out on the road, eight horses were brought back to pull the next one out.

But the task was accomplished and there was no difficulty on the road, though we had to go a long way round because the enemy had blown up a cross-roads. He had also blown up the bridge over the Sambre canal, but the Engineers had constructed another and we came into the town of Landrecies as darkness was falling. Through the town, and then for about a mile on the other side. This time there was no difficulty in finding the way and the guns were in position before seven o'clock.

Major Cecil said he had done some hard thinking while he was waiting for us. It was going to be moving warfare for the next few days, he said, and the guns would not be able to keep up unless the limbers and first-line wagons stayed with them; they would be under his direct command.

The idea of keeping horses at the gun line was hard to accept for a moment, but he said it would be quite safe, they had not been shelled all day, the other batteries were doing the same. I was to stay with the rest of the wagon lines, and he suggested that I should move each day to the place where the guns had been on the previous day.

'You'll have nothing to do,' he said, 'except to see that we're supplied with food and ammunition.' But he was going to keep all the best horses, I should have to make do with the others.

We returned to the farm at Fontaine-au-Bois, but the limbers and first-line wagons were to go up again with the Sergeant-Major as soon as it was light, I should follow later. The rain had never stopped, but I was no longer feeling discouraged. Everything had gone well today, I had become a

302

different person. Now for the first time since coming to A Battery I felt sure of myself, I was not afraid of some unexpected occurrence, I would wait until it happened and then deal with the matter as best I could.

I had not long to wait. On the very next morning I learnt that no rations had come up during the night. A wagon had gone to draw them in the ordinary way and simply had not returned. Cecil had said that the only thing I had to do now was to feed them, and it looked as though I should fail on the first day. I knew I should be held responsible, feeding the battery was the captain's job and no excuse for failure was ever accepted, but I was not greatly worrying.

The wagon eventually arrived, and I sent up the day's rations immediately. The midday meal would be late, no other harm had been done. I then rode up myself to find out where the guns were going to. They had already moved, three miles further on. I followed them. 'I wonder you dare show your face,' Cecil said, when he saw me. I told him I had come to have lunch with them. 'Well, you've got some cheek,' he said, 'you eat all our rations at the wagon lines and then expect to share the little we've got left.' He told the servants to give me very small helpings.

Afterwards I rode back to meet my wagon lines, which were coming up from Fontaine, I had told the subaltern who was there to move after the midday meal. I would meet them, I said, by the bridge before Landrecies. The rain had never stopped, I never saw Landrecies in the dry, it looked a depressing place. But what was not depressing was the sight of a field outside the town full of captured guns. There were so many that it really seemed possible now that the enemy had none left on our part of the front. At the gun line they were beginning to say they had forgotten when they last heard the sound of a German shell.

This went on for some days longer. So did the rain. I almost lived in the saddle. Immediately after breakfast I rode up to the gun line to learn what the news was and where they were going that day. Then I had to find the easiest way to bring my wagon lines up. The shortest way was not always the best, low-lying places by the rivers were sometimes under water after so much rain, it was better to go an extra mile, or up an extra hill, than run the risk of being stuck in flood water. I had to go along every road myself to make sure it had not been mined, and that the bridges were all right. I knew that my horses were being used to the limit of their strength and that unless I spared them every unnecessary effort they might not be able to go on.

Sometimes we seemed to be the only soldiers left in the war. Where all the others were I did not know, I never saw them. Sometimes we were the first to be seen by the liberated French people. In the courtyard of one farm where we stopped for a few hours an elderly man came up to me and seized my hand. I thought he would never let me go, words poured out of him and tears down his weather-beaten face. I was on my horse, he was standing beside me, looking up at me with an emotion which at first I hardly understood. I did not know what he was saying, I wanted to say something to him, but I knew no French, I had not troubled to learn it at school. How could I have foreseen the day when an old Frenchman would be thanking me for saving his country!

He stopped at last, he let go of my hand, but he was still looking up at me, he was waiting for me to say something in reply. What could I say! 'Vive La France!' I said, lightly touching his bare head with my fingers, 'Vive La France!' In the end I was nearly as moved as he was.

In another farm I asked for permission to put our horses in the empty barns. 'Permission?' said the woman in amazement. 'You ask for permission?' They would have allowed us to do whatever we wanted, they would have given us everything they had. They were disappointed that I would not sleep in their own bedroom, they cleaned the outhouses where our men were. They were not fit for English soldiers, they said.

There was no time to think about the war, I had too much to do. But sometimes I wondered if it might be coming to an end. Strange things were certainly happening. We met returning prisoners-of-war on the road one day. Italians, they told us they were. Their clothes were in rags, they were cold and hungry. Our drivers stopped on the road and gave them some of their own rations, they could always understand the people of another country.

304

The war had become hushed, it was unlike anything I had known before. Or anyone else. But there was no news about it, we did not see any newspapers, they could not keep up with us. More serious was the fact that our mail often failed to come up.

It might be coming to an end, but no one could be sure. It had happened before that one side or the other had retreated a long way, and had then stopped retreating, and the fighting had begun again, shells and the noise of battle, and casualties, everything as before. This would probably happen again, I thought; it was the most likely thing.

The rain went on. I seemed to have been riding to and fro across France for a lifetime, but in fact it was less than a week since the battle had begun.

Fifteen

November 10-11

Then one morning I was awakened early, before it was light, by someone calling my name, but I had been so deeply asleep that I could not answer at once. It was not only because of my deep sleep that I could not answer, I did not know where I was, nothing looked familiar. Then I remembered. Of course! We were sleeping in houses now, not tents, I was in an upstairs room, I remembered the noise my boots had made coming up the stairs the night before. The man who had called my name was down below.

He called again. 'Hello!' I managed to answer. Then I heard someone coming slowly up the stairs. 'I'm here,' I called out, and he came into the room. It was an orderly with a message from Major Cecil, I was to go up to the gun line at once. I asked the man if he knew why I was wanted, but he could not tell me.

In five minutes I was ready to go. Walkenshaw brought in his usual mug of morning tea, hot strong and sweet, leaves floating on the surface, as I was wrapping my puttees round my legs. 'You've been quick,' I said. 'How did you boil the water?' All the world had been asleep a few minutes before. He only replied with a grin and I guessed that Madame had provided the boiling water. If the French people as well as our servants were going to look after us in future, it would be a more comfortable war.

I found Edric waiting with our horses outside the house, and we set off, trotting along the road up to the guns. The sun was just rising. The rain had stopped at last and the sun had come back. No wonder I felt happy! It had taken me a minute or two to realise the cause of my happiness, but it was the sun of course. I saw its reflection in the puddles on the road, and there were flashes of light, now green, now red, from raindrops in the hedge as we passed by. It was the first time we had seen the sun since our attack started; only a week ago, but so much had happened.

I broke into a canter, because of the beauty of the morning, not because I thought there was any need to hurry. I could not believe there was any urgent reason for my early-morning summons, war had not begun again, there was no sound of battle in front. I was not even listening for the sound of a shell or the sudden stabbing burst of machine-gun fire. How quickly it had changed! A week ago I should certainly have been listening, we were always listening, always ready to jump off our horses or dive into the nearest hole. Now I could be thinking only of the loveliness of the morning as I rode up towards the line.

How beautiful the trees were! Autumn was just as beautiful as spring. Last spring there had been all that anxiety, every morning we had been expecting the enemy to make his next attack. Now there was nothing to dread, nothing even to think about at the moment. I was out riding in the country on this perfect morning and I was twenty years old. Only another month of being twenty, I must make the most of it.

How beautiful the country was! As beautiful as England! This might have been a southern county of England, woods and low hills and a stream in the valley below. It was like places in England that I knew, but more exciting because it was unknown country, every bend in the road showed me a view I had never seen before.

In England I should not have been riding a horse. Soldiers could ride for pleasure, but an ordinary person had to be rich to ride in England. I leaned forward and stroked the neck of my mare. I was very fond of her, and proud of her good looks, I enjoyed being the envy of other officers in the brigade.

No one else was about, Edric and I had the beauty of the morning to ourselves. I slowed down and waited for him to catch me up. We walked side by side. 'This sort of war's all right,' I said, and I remarked on the prettiness of the country. 'Like England,' I said.

But Edric did not think much of it. 'Give me Ilkley Moor,' he said.

'Is it true, Sir,' he asked presently, 'that Jerry has sent envoys to ask for peace?'

I had heard the rumour. For two or three days past the air had been thick with rumours, they came up from the rear with the ration cart.

'I never believe these rumours,' I said. 'Then I'm not disappointed when they turn out to be false.'

But Edric thought there might be something in this one. 'It sounds to me as though Jerry has stopped fighting,' he said, 'and if once he stops he may find it difficult to start again.'

Then he began telling me what he wanted to do when he got back to Civvy Street. He was going back to the Railway on which he had served for a few years before joining up, now he would be a cleaner, he said, then a fireman, and at last if all went well a fully-trained driver.

I should have expected him to do something with horses, for he knew a lot about them and was a good groom. But he said there would not be any horses left in the country in ten years' time. He had evidently been thinking about his future, but I had not begun to think about mine.

We came down to the rushing stream. All the rivers were in flood and flowing fast. We stopped for a moment on the bridge to watch the swirling eddies, running water had a fascination for me. Then up again steeply on the other side, and the guns were on the road at the top.

Everyone at the gun line had gone back to sleep, and Major Cecil had forgotten why he had sent for me. Slowly he yawned himself awake. Then he told me that he thought the time had come to join up the two parts of the battery. He said he was expecting orders to move the guns forward again before midday, but if I brought my wagon lines up as soon as the men had finished breakfast I might catch up with them before they moved.

I was pleased at the idea, it really would make my work easier if we were all together and I should enjoy having the company of the others, for I had generally been alone during the last few days. I rode back at once, quickly gave the necessary orders, and we were ready to move in good time.

But we were too late, the guns had already gone forward. Not so far as usual, however, only two miles, to a position on the other side of the main road from Avesnes to Maubeuge, and Cecil had left a message telling me to follow them.

It was not a long march, but it was a difficult one. The road on which we were had been blown up on both sides of us, we had to go off the road and along an unmetalled lane, over some soft fields, across another stream and then up on to the main road. It was the kind of march I had been trying to avoid all these days and I was afraid that some of my horses might fail me. But it was all right, they pulled better than I had expected, and all the men were in good spirits, either as a result of the change in the weather or because of the rumour that German envoys had come to ask for peace.

I thought our difficulties were over when we got on to the main road, but there was still one more, or one more anxiety. We had to march along the road for half a mile or so before turning east, and at the point where we turned I saw some sappers digging by the side of the road. They were looking for a mine, they told me. A mine had been reported by some French civilians, they thought one was there, and if it was it might go off at any moment.

The civilians were right. Later in the day I saw the mine, it had been found and defused, but I had a few uneasy minutes as we went by. Half a mile further along the road I caught up with the rest of the battery. They were in a first-rate place, there was sufficient accommodation for all of us, the horses under cover and the men in barns. Cecil said he supposed we should be going on again, by tomorrow morning at the latest. But even one night's rest in a place like this would do us all a world of good.

Cherry came to see us in the afternoon and he thought we might have more than one night. We were in front of all the other batteries, he said, and in front of most of the infantry too. 'You've moved fast,' he said, 'but the Boche has moved faster still, he's winning the race, he's back at the Belgian border already.'

'What's going to happen then?' Cecil asked.

'It's all over,' Cherry told us. 'Fritz has had enough, he's legging it for all he's worth back to his own country, we shall follow at our own speed, a triumphal march to the Rhine.'

The trouble with Cherry, as always, was that you did not know how much to believe of what he said; how much might be fact, known to him because as adjutant he saw all the information from Divisional and Corps Headquarters, how much was fancy, the result of his incurable optimism. It might well be true that the enemy was already back at the Belgian border, only five or six miles away, but had he any reason for saying he was legging it back to his own country, how could he know what was in the mind of the German commanders.

They lived in a world of make-believe at our Brigade Headquarters. If they wanted to believe something they stated it as a fact, it had always been like this, they were never abashed when the truth turned out to be altogether different.

In the morning Major Cecil rode off to Headquarters to find out whether or when we were to advance. 'Have everything ready for a move,' he said to me, 'but don't harness up.' Some time later I saw him returning, riding fast, and carrying something in his hand. He waved it at me, whatever it was that he was carrying, when he saw me.

'Read that,' he said, when he came to where I was standing.

It was an envelope, an ordinary envelope, addressed in Cherry's handwriting to the O.C. A Battery. It was only orders for the day, but when I opened the envelope I saw there was only a single sheet inside, instead of the usual sheaf of papers. I opened it and read:

'Hostilities will cease from 11.00 hours today, November 11th.'

'What does it mean?' I asked him.

'The War's over,' he said.

'Do you believe it's true?'

He said there was no doubt about it. The Germans had surrendered, the official news had come through while he was at Headquarters, he had only waited for his copy of the order, and had then galloped back to show it to us.

I looked at my watch. It was ten o'clock already, there was no possibility now of any of us being killed.

'We'll fire a salvo of blank at the right time,' Cecil said, and he rode away to give the order and tell everyone what had happened.

I felt excited, and happy, but in an uncertain subdued way. I did not want to shout or to drink; there was nothing to drink, anyway. I wanted to be with my friends, but none of those of my own age was left in the brigade. Durham had gone home on leave before the attack started, Vernon was in South Africa. There had not been time yet to become intimate with any of the other officers in A Battery or with any of the new ones who had come to the brigade in the last few months. I felt alone, I walked about in the lines but without going anywhere.

At a few minutes before eleven o'clock we all went to where the guns were, drawn up in line behind a hedge. The gunners were in their places, the rest of us standing about, singly or in little groups, behind them. Major Cecil was standing on the left of the line, by Number One gun, he was holding the big battery watch in his left hand and a whistle in the other. He's trying to make it seem like Zero Hour, I said to myself, but he can't, it's not real.

I heard him blow the whistle and all the guns fired. They fired again. Three times altogether. This was the first time I had heard our guns firing blank ammunition. It was not the proper sound, there was no report, as there would have been with live shells. The noise was no more than a bang, and puffs of white smoke hung over the muzzles of the guns and drifted slowly away. Some of the men started to cheer, but their voices sounded as unnatural as the noise of the guns, and they soon stopped. There was Silence. It had come to stay.

We drifted towards the mess.

'O God! what a war!' Cecil said 'Nothing to drink but lime juice. What a peace!'

The other batteries were in the same condition, there was not a drop of whisky in all the brigade.

'What on earth are we going to do with ourselves now?' someone said.

'Work, for a change,' Major Cecil told him.

'They won't pay us for doing nothing.'

'I know,' another suggested, 'they'll use us to tidy up the battlefield.'

In the afternoon I went for a ride with Cecil and we visited some of the other batteries. Everyone was excited, everyone was talking about the wonderful thing that had happened, but there was an air of constraint, everyone was talking loudly, but no one had anything to say. I gave Garnett the fifty francs I owed him, he did not want to take it, he said it had not been a fair bet, it had been obvious all along that I should lose.

Even Cherry was less cheerful than he had been on the previous day. The idea of a triumphal march to the Rhine was off, he said, so far as we were concerned, only the divisional artillery was going. 'They don't want the army brigades,' he said, 'now the fighting is over.'

The Colonel was planning a great re-union of the brigade for next spring. 'A real slap-up affair,' he said. 'Wives and sweethearts as well. In Bolton or Blackburn. For everyone who's ever served in the brigade, we'll do the thing in style.'

The Colonel was a wealthy man and I knew that he would spare no expense to ensure the success of his party, but what was the use of a slap-up affair some time next year! A slap-up affair now, that was what we needed, and what chance was there of our having any affair at all in this lonely corner of North-Eastern France! Besides, Bolton or Blackburn, he had said. That was where the Colonel himself and most of the men in the brigade came from, but I could not think our Yorkshiremen in C Battery would thank him or take the trouble to go, Sergeant Denmark would not be there.

That night we played cards, vingt et un. It was the first time I had ever thought of such an occupation, always before there had been a more worth-while way of passing an evening, but someone suggested it, and there was nothing else to do, we were in need of some excitement. But the excitement was not genuine, it was no more genuine than the sound of the guns had been in the morning.

We continued playing until midnight. Then the others went off, they were sleeping in another house, Cecil and I were left alone. We went outside to relieve ourselves. The sky was full of stars, there was no wind.

'Perfect night for bombing!' Cecil said.

'Do you think it's real?' I asked.

'Listen!' he said.

312

I could hear some of our horses on the other side of the farm, but no other sound. There had never been a night like this. We could hear the silence, it was a little frightening, we had forgotten what silence was.

We stood there for a minute or two without speaking, then went back into the house and into the room where we were sleeping. Slowly we began to undress. We could take all our clothes off tonight, it would be pyjama warfare for all the rest of time.

'It's been a bit flat,' Cecil said. 'I don't know what I was expecting, but certainly not this.'

We got into our beds, but left our candles burning beside us. Cecil began telling me about his plans. He said there was an empty chateau half a mile along the road, no one was living in it. 'We'll go and have a look at the place in the morning,' he said, 'and if it's as good as they say, arm-chairs and chandeliers and four-poster beds, we'll move in.'

I hope he would not want to move. We had everything we needed here.

'I was having a look at the country when we were out this afternoon,' he went on. 'We'll put up some jumps, we'll be able to make a first-rate steeplechase course.'

I was not such an enthusiastic rider as he was, but I agreed that it was a good idea, there had been no steeplechasing in the brigade since the beginning of the year.

'And we must see about a football pitch for the men,' he said, 'they've had no football for donkeys' years.'

He lit another of his Turkish cigarettes and offered one to me, but I had been smoking all evening. 'I'm even running out of these things,' he said. 'I must get my wife to send me out some more. And we ought to see about getting some Gold Flake for the men. Cigarettes for the men and whisky for ourselves, these are really the two most urgent things.'

I promised to ride into Avesnes the next day to see whether any canteens had come up, but I was not very hopeful. Everything was scarce, we had not seen an egg for weeks past.

'You know, it's not going to be all that easy,' he said presently. 'We may be stuck here for months with nothing to do. Football's all very well, but we shall have to think up other ways of keeping the men out of trouble.'

313

This was a new idea to me. Keeping them out of the way of shells, that had been our business in the past, it had not occurred to me that we should merely change one responsibility for another.

'Battery sports,' Cecil said. 'Mounted and unmounted, tent-pegging, competitions for the best turned-out team, and the best driving. We're lucky to have our horses, there's a lot you can do with horses, we may even be able to think of something to do with the guns.'

For some minutes we were both silent. I wasn't ready for sleep yet, but I thought we had said enough about immediate plans. I realised with some surprise that Cecil would be a better battery commander in peace time than he had been in war.

'You know,' he said, 'I rather envy you going up to Oxford.'

Oxford? I wasn't going up to Oxford. To go back to school after all this!

'I never did a stroke when I was up,' he said, 'but you may want to.'

It might be a good idea to go up for a term or two, it would give me time to think what I wanted to do.

'I had a wonderful time there, the best time of my life. There's so much to do, polo, point-to-points, clubs, commem balls.'

These were not the things I should want to do if I did go up to Oxford. Anyway, I couldn't afford them, I wasn't a rich man's son.

'Oxford's just the place for you,' he went on. 'You're cut out for Oxford, it will suit you down to the ground.'

I did not think it would. I could not imagine myself going back to text books and working for exams. The army had suited me. I had enjoyed being one of a team, I should feel lonely at Oxford on my own.

'You weren't cut out for this sort of thing,' he said.

I felt a little annoyed. It seemed to me I had been all right at this sort of thing. I thought I had done as well at war as I was ever likely to do at peace. 'I don't think any of us were cut out for it,' I said. 'It didn't come naturally to any of us.'

He agreed that we had all found it hard at first, but some

314

were more out of their depth than others. 'I can't read a book,' he said, 'but you're always reading. You feel at home with books.'

I didn't. I had felt at home in C Battery, now I was beginning to feel at home in A. I was at home when I was with people I liked, books were only a substitute.

'You will have forgotten all about this after a term or two at Oxford,' he said. 'You'll have forgotten there ever were places called Heudecourt and Villers Bretonneux.'

How could I forget! They were the real places, Oxford was the dream one.

'But we may not forget,' he said, a minute or two later. 'There have been good times mixed up with the bad ones. We may want to talk about them if we ever see one another again.'

If we ever see one another! Of course we should see one another, you did not give up your friends just because a war had come to an end.

I wanted to stop talking now and to be alone with my thoughts, he had given me a lot to think about, Oxford and after-Oxford and seeing my friends. I waited for a pause, then blew out my candle.

'Good night,' I said.

'Whisky and cigarettes then, those will be your priorities,' he said.

They certainly were not. But I would go into Avesnes, I should enjoy being by myself, I should have some time for thinking. One of my priorities in the morning would be to write home to my parents, to tell them I was still alive. I knew how anxious they had been ever since I came out, but I had not felt able to write at once, I had not known what to say. It had never been difficult to write to them before, except when there was no time, but today it would have been.

I had not begun to think about it until now, but the prospect of after-Oxford disconcerted me. I did not know what I wanted to do, I had no ideas. I had learnt how to do this job and could have gone on doing it indefinitely, war had been easy, once you got into the way of it. But the thought of having to make another fresh start, of going out into an unfriendly world. . . . The world was unfriendly, it did not care

315

what happened to you. That would be the difference I should find in after-Oxford. Here, everyone was on the same side as yourself, wherever you went, unless you went a long way back, you could be sure of receiving help when you needed it. But there, it would be a case of everyone for himself.

'I suppose you might say that we have been the lucky ones,' Cecil said.

I thought he was asleep. I pretended that I was, I did not answer him, I was trying to get some of my ideas sorted out, I was afraid he might begin talking about whisky and cigarettes again.

Perhaps it would turn out all right. I would go up to Oxford for a year or so anyway. That would give me time to adjust myself to the new way of living. I should miss all this friendship, but I should enjoy reading again, and History was about people.

It would be all right. Life was less difficult than you expected it to be. The War itself had seemed very difficult in anticipation and I had been very afraid. Not only of danger, but of failing. That first morning when I heard the guns. The noise had been utterly terrifying, though I was in no danger at all, the guns and the shells were miles away.

The sound of gunfire! Heard for the first time on a spring morning, and for the last on a November afternoon. I should never hear it again, there would never be another war like this one. The Last War in History! Well, even if I achieved nothing else in life I had done something, I need not feel my life had been altogether wasted, I had played my part.

The lucky ones, Cecil said we were. I found myself thinking about the others. Now we should become aware of their loss, we had hardly done so until now, we had still been with them, in the same country, close to them, close to death ourselves. But soon we should have to go away and leave them, we should be going home, they would stay behind, their home was in the lonely desolation of the battlefield. Thirty miles of lonely desolation! From Villers Bretonneux to the Hindenburg Line.

But it had not seemed lonely on the day I was there, I had not felt alone in the middle of the desolation, though darkness was beginning to fall. No one else was there, only the driver of the lorry which was carrying me across, and we had not spoken to each other. *They* were everywhere. If I had been able to see and hear them I could not have been more conscious of their presence.

No, they would not be lonely, there were too many of them. I saw that bare country before me, saw it again in the darkness of the room where we were lying, the miles and miles of torn earth, the barbed wire, the litter, the dead trees. But the country would come back to life, the grass would grow again, the wild flowers return, and trees where now there were only splintered skeleton stumps.

They would lie still and at peace, below the singing larks, beside the serenely flowing rivers. They could not feel lonely, they would have one another. And they would have us also, though we were going home and leaving them behind. We belonged to them, and they would be a part of us for ever. Part of us for ever, nothing could separate us.

'Yes, we've been the lucky ones,' I said to Cecil.

But he was asleep.

HAMISH HAMILTON PAPERBACKS

'Among the most collectable of paperback imprints . . .'
Christopher Hudson, *The Standard*

All books in the Hamish Hamilton Paperback Series are available at
your local bookshop or can be ordered by post. A full list of titles and an
order form can be found at the end of this book.

LORD RANDOLPH CHURCHILL

Robert Rhodes James

Lord Randolph Churchill was at once a dazzling and pathetic figure whose mercurial character greatly enlivened the political scene of the 1880s, yet brought about his own downfall. In this outstanding biography Robert Rhodes James brings to life not only the man but also the colourful politics of the period.

'It is a splendid work and will, I am sure, meet with lasting success.' Sir Winston Churchill

'The book is very good indeed in giving the picture of the man. Lord Randolph Churchill returns to life with all his charm, wit, and irresponsibility.' A. J. P. Taylor, *Observer*

BISMARCK
THE MAN AND THE STATESMAN

A. J. P. Taylor

In this outstanding biography, A. J. P. Taylor discusses not only Bismarck's political ideas and achievements but also his strange complicated character. It is a fascinating essay on the psychology as well as the political understanding of a man who remains to this day a subject of controversy.

'Rich, learned, profound and yet highly readable . . . Mr Taylor has written many good books. This is the best.' Hugh Trevor-Roper, *Sunday Times*

TWO FLAMBOYANT FATHERS

Nicolette Devas

'A marvellous account of growing up in the artistic Bohemia of the 1920s with friends and mentors including the still-roaring Augustus John and the young Dylan Thomas, who was to marry her sister Caitlin. Candid, touching and engrossing: one of the finest autobiographies of our time.' – Philip Oakes

THE SECRET ORCHARD OF ROGER ACKERLEY

Diana Petre

A letter opened on his death revealed that Roger Ackerley had had a mistress for many years and that she had borne him three daughters. Diana Petre's memoir describes her father's 'secret orchard', the secretive and isolated world in which she grew up, and attempts to solve the mysteries that surrounded her beautiful and fascinating mother, Muriel Perry.

'Mrs Petre has unfolded her story with skill and candour, and entirely without self-pity. In short, this is a very exceptional and indeed moving book.' John Morris, *Sunday Times*

HUGH WALPOLE

Rupert Hart-Davis

'Rupert Hart-Davis's book is a remarkable feat of understanding and restraint. . . . He shows us the man himself, and the spectacle is delightful.' Edwin Muir

'Fully to appreciate how remarkable an achievement is Mr Hart-Davis's biography of Hugh Walpole, it is necessary to read the book. No summarised comment can convey the complexity of the task accomplished or the narrative skill, restraint and self-effacement with which it has been carried through.' Michael Sadleir

'The most entertaining book about a writer of our time.' Terence de Vere White, *Irish Times*

THE LIFE OF ARTHUR RANSOME

Hugh Brogan

For a man who longed for a quiet existence, Arthur Ransome had an extraordinarily adventurous life comprising two stormy marriages, a melodramatic libel suit, and a ringside view of the Russian Revolution. In this absorbing book, Hugh Brogan writes with sympathy and affection of the author of some of the best loved books for children.

'The wonder is, from Mr Brogan's enthralling account, that Ransome ever got down to writing *Swallows and Amazons* at all.' A. N. Wilson, *Sunday Telegraph*

MARY BERENSON:
A Self Portrait from Her Letters and Diaries

eds. Barbara Strachey & Jayne Samuels

This superbly edited book of extracts from Mary Berenson's letters and diaries provides an absorbing picture of her extraordinary complex relationship with Bernard Berenson, and of their life and work together in Italy.

'Mary . . . writes with a startling, unsettling, often hilarious candour which makes it hard to put the book down.' – Hilary Spurling, *Observer*

A DURABLE FIRE:
The Letters of Duff and Diana Cooper, 1913–1950

ed. Artemis Cooper

For long periods before and after their marriage in 1919 Duff and Diana Cooper were apart, but they wrote to each other constantly, witty, gossipy letters that have been admirably edited by their granddaughter to form this delightful collection.

'It is rare to find a correspondence duo in which both sides are of equivalent verve and strength . . . a unique, inside account of a charmed circle whose members governed England between the wars.' – Anthony Curtis, *Financial Times*

MEMOIRS OF AN AESTHETE

Harold Acton

In this outstanding memoir, deservedly regarded as a classic, Harold
Acton writes a witty and vivid account of the first thirty-five years of his
life from his boyhood among the international colony of dilettanti in
Florence before the First World War, to his maturity when he discovered
his spiritual home in Peking before the old Chinese culture was
destroyed by Chairman Mao.

'He is a connoisseur of language. . . . His prose scintillates. It reminds
one of Beerbohm and Waugh.' Patrick Skene Catling

'A truly magical memoir.' Linda O'Callaghan, *Sunday Telegraph*

NANCY MITFORD
A Memoir

Harold Acton

Nancy Mitford never completed an autobiography. Fortunately she was
a voluminous letter writer and had a genius for friendship and laughter.
In this delightful memoir, Sir Harold Acton has been able to show us,
largely in her own words, almost every aspect of her personality, and her
immense courage during the years of her final painful illness.

'Sir Harold Acton has memorialised a very gifted writer, and a unique
personality, with affection, skill and truth.' Anthony Powell, *Daily
Telegraph*

'The main lesson I derived from Sir Harold's stylish and loving evocation
of Nancy Mitford's personality, is that she gave just as much pleasure to
her circle of friends and relations as she gave to her readers.' Antonia
Fraser, *Evening Standard*

Available in Hamish Hamilton Paperbacks

NANCY MITFORD	Harold Acton	£5.95 ☐
MEMOIRS OF AN AESTHETE	Harold Acton	£5.95 ☐
JOHN MASEFIELD	Constance Babington Smith	£4.95 ☐
MISSION WITH MOUNTBATTEN	Alan Campbell-Johnson	£5.95 ☐
A CACK-HANDED WAR*	Edward Blishen	£3.95 ☐
UNCOMMON ENTRANCE*	Edward Blishen	£3.95 ☐
THE DREAM KING	Wilfrid Blunt	£4.95 ☐
THE LIFE OF ARTHUR RANSOME	Hugh Brogan	£4.95 ☐
DIAGHILEV	Richard Buckle	£6.95 ☐
IN THE CANNON'S MOUTH*	P. J. Campbell	£6.95 ☐
AUTOBIOGRAPHY	Neville Cardus	£4.95 ☐
AUTOBIOGRAPHY	G. K. Chesterton	£5.95 ☐
ANOTHER PART OF THE WOOD	Kenneth Clark	£4.95 ☐
A DURABLE FIRE	ed. Artemis Cooper	£4.95 ☐
TWO FLAMBOYANT FATHERS	Nicolette Devas	£4.95 ☐
THE DIARY OF AN ART DEALER	René Gimpel	£6.95 ☐
PETER HALL'S DIARIES	ed. John Goodwin	£5.95 ☐
HUGH WALPOLE	Rupert Hart-Davis	£6.95 ☐
GOD'S APOLOGY*	Richard Ingrams	£4.95 ☐
HANDEL	Jonathan Keates	£6.95 ☐
ASQUITH	Stephen Koss	£4.95 ☐
THE LIFE OF RAYMOND CHANDLER	Frank MacShane	£5.95 ☐
VOLTAIRE IN LOVE	Nancy Mitford	£4.95 ☐
A LIFE OF CONTRASTS	Diana Mosley	£5.95 ☐
A LATE BEGINNER	Priscilla Napier	£4.95 ☐
BEYOND FRONTIERS		
	Jasper Parrott with Vladimir Ashkenazy	£4.95 ☐
MRS PAT	Margot Peters	£5.95 ☐
THE SECRET ORCHARD OF ROGER ACKERLEY	Diana Petre	£4.95 ☐
ALBERT, PRINCE CONSORT	Robert Rhodes James	£4.95 ☐
LORD RANDOLPH CHURCHILL	Robert Rhodes James	£6.95 ☐
MARY BERENSON	eds. Barbara Strachey and Jayne Samuels	£4.95 ☐
BISMARCK	A. J. P. Taylor	£5.95 ☐
THE YEARS WITH ROSS*	James Thurber	£4.95 ☐

| THE DRAGON EMPRESS | Marina Warner | £4.95 ☐ |
| QUEEN VICTORIA | Cecil Woodham-Smith | £5.95 ☐ |

All titles 198 × 126mm, and all contain 8 pages of black and white illustrations except for those marked*.

All books in the Hamish Hamilton Paperback Series are available at your local bookshop, or can be ordered direct from Media Services. Just tick the titles you want on the previous page and fill in the form below.

Name_____

Address_____

_____

Write to Media Services, PO Box 151, Camberley, Surrey GU15 3BE.

Please enclose cheque or postal order made out to Media Services for the cover price plus postage:

UK: 55p for the first book, 24p for each additional book to a maximum of £1.75.

OVERSEAS: £1.05 for the first book, 35p for each additional book to a maximum of £2.80.

Hamish Hamilton Ltd reserve the right to show new retail prices on covers which may differ from those previously advertised in the text or elsewhere, and to increase postal rates in accordance with the PO.